SUPPLY
OF
HEROES

BOOKS BY JAMES CARROLL

FICTION

Madonna Red
Mortal Friends
Fault Lines
Family Trade
Prince of Peace
Supply of Heroes
Firebird
Memorial Bridge
The City Below
Secret Father
Warburg in Rome
The Cloister

NONFICTION

An American Requiem
Constantine's Sword
Toward a New Catholic Church
Crusade
House of War
Practicing Catholic
Jerusalem, Jerusalem
Christ Actually
The Truth at the Heart of the Lie

SUPPLY
OF
HEROES

a novel

JAMES
CARROLL

**BLACK
STONE**
PUBLISHING

Copyright © 1986 by James Carroll
Published in 2022 by Blackstone Publishing
Cover design by Gunjan Ahlawat

The characters and events in this book are fictitious.
Any similarity to real persons, living or dead, is coincidental
and not intended by the author.

Printed in the United States of America

ISBN 979-8-200-89399-7
Fiction / Historical / World War I

Version 1

CIP data for this book is available
from the Library of Congress

Blackstone Publishing
31 Mistletoe Rd.
Ashland, OR 97520

www.BlackstonePublishing.com

For my mother and for Jenny

INTRODUCTION

Ireland's modern war against England began on an Easter weekend, and, eighty-two years later, it ended on an Easter weekend. The Irish are a pilgrim people, and the progress of that resolution ran from 1916 to 1998, from the Republican insurrection on Easter Monday to the Good Friday Agreement establishing peace among Belfast, Dublin, and London; between Unionists and Republicans; Protestants and Catholics.

That the death and resurrection of Jesus Christ are the brackets within which this history unfolded has profound resonance. A theology that gives primacy to sacrifice, even martyrdom, was embodied in the embrace by all sides of redemptive violence. But the willingness to die for a cause bled into readiness to kill for it. Enemies abounded in Ireland, and so did heroes, but sorting out one from the other depended on myth, denial, and a habit of misremembering. Alas, across most of a century, the self-destroying island was shrouded in green fog, an air of asphyxiation. This novel tells one of the island's stories, or two of them—or three. Such pluralism is what Ireland has learned.

An Irish-American raised to the music of IRA rebel songs,

I learned from my mother that her uncle Jim had died back home in Tipperary in 1916—the mythic year. He died, she said, fighting the British in the great insurrection, the Rising. When I later went to Ireland myself, I sought out the old, abandoned cemetery where my mother's uncle was buried, but what I found shocked me. The weathered grave marker confirmed that he'd died in 1916, but not as an anti-London rebel. The tombstone identified him as a British soldier who'd been killed in France, perhaps at that year's savage Battle of the Somme when, only two months after the Rising, legions of "Micks" were killed. And that simply, in a flash, I was brought into the complex middle-ground of authentic Irish experience—a complicated landscape in which I've built my life.

Supply of Heroes unfolds across that terrain, where either-or absolutism yields to both-and complexity. In this novel—a war story, a detective story, a love story—enemies are not what they seem, and neither are heroes. That is why the narrative centers on an Anglo-Irish family whose place in-between the extremes was laid waste by both sides as the Troubles exploded, as if that hyphen were a sacrilege. The Catholic rebel who intrudes on that forbidden middle space finds his loyalty not so much divided as redefined—redefined by love.

In 1916, while hundreds of Irish Catholics rose up against the British in the doomed Easter rebellion, tens of thousands of Irish Catholics were in France, wearing the British khaki, and many of them, like my great-uncle, died. In the green fog, their stories were lost. This novel aims to bring them back from the dead. I wrote it as a haunted young man, and I am still haunted.

That middle ground where I've made my life is full of ghosts.

Redemptive violence? No. Romantic sacrifice? No. In No Man's Land, where every war draws to a close, the "terrible beauty" of which Yeats wrote is more terrible than beautiful.

My great-uncle's fate opened my eyes. After that, I moved the emphasis of remembrance from the much mythologized glories of the Easter Rising to the brutal actualities of World War I—actualities mostly lost to Irish Catholic memory. November poppies are rarely seen on Dublin lapels.

The current of mayhem that began flowing out of the River Somme—forever marked by the million casualties of that 1916 battle—ran on through the rest of the century, with one horror building on another. That horror is my subject.

In the decades since I first published *Supply of Heroes*, a tremendous hope was lifted up not only by Irish peace-making, but by the non-violent end of the Cold War. But as I write today, the current of a brutal new war is rushing through Europe again, this time out of Vladimir Putin's Russia. Therefore, the dark themes of my novel, alas—we humans being what we are—still apply. But so must its hope, for we humans also refuse to let hope go.

I take this opportunity to lift up the memory of an exemplar of that hope—the great Irish peacemaker John Hume. He defended the hope for a better Ireland across his entire life, and in doing so he made the great peace possible. His slogan was "a new Ireland," and he created it. *Supply of Heroes* was part of what led to my being introduced to John Hume, and to my being invited, astoundingly, to call him friend. For me, that alone is enough to justify the pages in this book.

I want to acknowledge certain debts I owe to those who helped me with this work. Among the literary sources from which I drew information and inspiration, three were especially useful: Paul Fussell's *The Great War and Modern Memory*, John Keegan's *The Face of Battle*, and William Irwin Thompson's *The Imagination of an Insurrection: Dublin, 1916*. I am grateful to these authors.

With large-hearted energy and good cheer, my manager Daniel Sladek ushered this book back into print by introducing me to the fine people at Blackstone Publishing, to whom I offer, along with Daniel, a special word of thanks. I am proud to be on the Blackstone list.

When *Supply of Heroes* first appeared, I dedicated it to my mother, Mary Carroll, whose story started mine; and to Jenny Marshall Carroll, my daughter who, while I was writing this book, came into the precious life I share with her mother, my dear wife, the writer Alexandra Marshall. Jenny died shortly after being born, but she has been an unforgotten presence to our whole family all these years. With unfaded love and gratitude, I renew the original dedication for this edition—"For my mother and for Jenny."

Boston, 2022

1

Even before their last kiss something, not time or place or that vicious circumstance, divided them. Each had firmly in mind an idea of how such farewells as this were to be enacted. Their ideas of the scene were similar; by the late spring of the war's first year everyone in London knew how young wives saw husbands to the War Train at Victoria, with what stoic cheer, but also what lapses of heavy, pointed silence. Despite its horrors up to then, the war had yet to really show itself, and so it was still a chivalric moment, full of association. The unselfish sacrifice of an entire nation was implicit in the welling eyes of those women, and its disciplined restraint in the fact that tears never overspilled those ruby cheeks in the public setting of a crowded, bustling, noisy train platform. This was courage and resolve; even nobility. These were people for whom such notions still carried resonance. Farewell was the first and sweetest act of war, the only one the women were admitted to until the soldier's eventual return, when they nursed him or buried him. But even that prospect, now, while terrible, had its loveliness. In prospect, death lacks loveliness utterly except in war.

An observer would have seen the young woman and man as

types of a species—British bluebloods, him in his mustache, Sam Browne, jodhpurs, and polished boots, fresh-stitched captains' diamonds on his sleeves, her in the flat-hipped practical dress, plumpness nowhere, not of Victoria but of Victoria's grand-daughters—but an observer could not possibly have read their silence. For an unbearably short time he had been with her and their two young children at her parents' house in Chelsea. It was the leave to which he was entitled, having, with his men, just completed training, having been promoted unexpectedly from first lieutenant to captain, and his regiment having been ordered at last to France. And at the end of those precious, fleeting four days, he and this woman, whom he loved more than he loved, even, his children or his father or the memory of his mother or his native land or God, had quarreled bitterly.

She looked up at him. "I'm sorry, Douglas."

He shook his head. "It was my fault, darling. It was my fault." And he meant it. True, one would think a man going off to war had the right to know that his wife and children were where they belonged, where he wanted them, where she'd always promised they would be. But he saw grief in her eyes and he knew it had nothing to do with him. Her father was dead exactly a month now, having gone down on the *Lusitania*, sunk May 7. Douglas knew that the bottom of her world had fallen out from under her, and he knew how afraid she was for her mother. But when she told him that she and the children were going to stay permanently in London instead of going home, he reacted with a fierce, disapproving imperiousness that was not uncommon among men like him but which, between them, was unprecedented and therefore frightening to both. His anger had made him crudely insensitive and he had accused her of using her father's death as a pretext for leaving Cragside. Only after he'd seen the fury of her denial had he known it was true.

He took her into his arms and felt her settle against him. At last the rigid tension that had so threatened their parting melted, drained away. He touched her hair with his lips, inhaling the fragrance that was at once familiar and always new. The fragrance of his wife's hair never failed to stir Douglas, to draw him to her, to surface his longing. She possessed him totally, not as a mere owner possesses, but as a demon does. And this feeling of having been willingly bewitched, of having had the field of all his senses occupied by this woman *as* woman, brought with it, as always, the wonder that she should be his. He had been braced to say a steely good-bye in which neither would admit to feeling much of anything. Instead emotion swelled his chest. If he'd tried to speak, it would have choked him. He closed his arms around her and pressed her until he could feel, even through that clothing, her breasts against him. The old fear of losing her stalked across his mind; now he saw it was that that made him hate the thought of her in London. He closed his eyes to see her again as he had in the beginning and, remarkably, even in that chaos of setting and feeling, the door on his cherished memory opened.

———

The scent of lime combined with the sound of countless bees humming as they worked the flowers of the arching fruit trees that lined the pathway from the great house down to Coole Lake. He had slipped out of the crowded drawing room, throwing off the stifling pall of his seniors' arcane chatter. The midsummer eve had cast its spell over the lush estate—Coole Park was a softer place than Cragside, though as beautiful—but there was a spell too in the high-toned melancholy to which Douglas had surrendered. He was twenty-one years old, only recently come down from Balliol, and he was quite naturally afraid that the self-anointed seers of Oxford would prove right about his life in Ireland. He hadn't struck an attitude of his own as yet and hung suspended between his mates' contempt for the island, born palpably of ignorance and English bias, and his father's worship of it, born partly of wounds suffered years before and partly of a fierce commitment to the work of his land, work he expected his son to join him in. It had never occurred to Douglas not to come home; that was because his father's will in this, as in all things still, was the only will. Not that his father didn't know that Douglas would have to be wooed back from the last enchantments of Eton and Balliol, but that in his opinion, between the appeal of the English mode of Britishness and the Irish mode of Britishness there was simply no contest, hadn't been since the Normans made Celts of themselves. His bright young son would see that clearly quite soon enough. Nevertheless, Douglas's father was making sure to remind Douglas of all that Ireland still offered their kind, and not the least of that was the swirling life of intellect and art that had for its center, in the summer at least, Coole Park. It was an estate only fifteen miles east of the coast and Cragside. But Douglas's hesitance revealed, and even his father knew it, that by the beginning of the twentieth century what had been true for the poor for generations was becoming true as well for the rich; the reasons to leave Ireland were obvious. What one wanted was reason to stay. Hence the invitation to accompany his parents on this social weekend, the first time he'd been so invited as an adult.

The British aristocracy did nothing so well as their holidays in the country and the Irish Ascendancy had its cherished version. Mostly the gentlefolks of both islands spent their weekends shooting, hunting, and drinking, but in this green corner of their class the bluebloods took their cues from one of history's great bluestockings. Lady Augusta Gregory reinvented the meaning of such gatherings.

Douglas's parents knew he was far from bookish, but they nevertheless expected to impress him with Lady Gregory's menagerie. Even at Oxford they had spoken of that confluence of talent. Shaw had made a large mark already. Yeats was noticed and Synge commented upon. Eventually it would be said that Ireland was producing genius as no place had since fourteenth-century Florence, and indeed, just then in 1906, Lady Gregory's circle was as illustrious as it would ever be again. On that weekend several of the famous *artistes* were there, together with various Sligo and Galway gentry and a friend or two from London. But the verve of all that splendid conversation—the plethora of *mots!*—only made Douglas feel plodding and young and quite as provincial as his Oxford friends assured him he was. And so he'd slipped away as chairs were being rearranged for the reading of Lady Gregory's new play about Irish traitors in the time of Queen Elizabeth. Instead of to literary revival, he'd given himself to the scent of lime, the humming of bees, and the simple pleasure of walking alone from the great house to the lake.

And then he saw her. She was sitting by the lake alone, watching the sun begin to fall in the western sky toward the blue Connemara hills. He thought at once, Here is an Irish beauty, here is where their legend comes from. She seemed part of the scene, curled over her knee, head resting on her arm just the way the curling hills beyond rested on the valley. For the first time since his return Douglas laid aside his impulse to compare with England. What were the languid girls in punts to this? It wouldn't last, he knew, but this first sight of her—the essence of its power that she had not seen him—was incomparable. As with the scent of lime and the sound of the nectaring bees, he saw her simple elegance with an unprecedented acuteness.

He startled her when he approached, and when she stood he forgot to speak. She was tall and dark. She had perfectly cut features, strong brown eyes, black hair that she began at once to collect and tie behind her head, all the while staring back at him. She wore a pale yellow dress that covered her to her ankles, but her feet were bare, and the sleeves of the dress were pushed up past her elbows. He was aware at once of her sexuality, not for any reason she gave him, save her refusal to lower her eyes. Douglas looked again at her feet, and the nakedness of her ankles was fatal to him. He looked once more into her face and saw that, despite her womanliness, she was younger than he was.

When her ribbon was tied, she lowered her arms as she waited for him to speak.

He said, posing as an Oxford rake posing as a Gaelic bard haunting Coole, "I've always hoped to come upon a beautiful Irish lass on the shore of an exquisite lake at twilight."

"Have you now?" she asked, and he was shocked to hear even in three words the distinctive Catholic brogue. A peasant girl? But her bearing, her dress, her direct manner, her clear self-possession made that impossible. Was she the daughter of Catholic gentry or a rich Galway merchant? He'd thought her parents were weekend guests, like his, but was she a secretary of some kind? He was mystified. And then he saw that she wanted him to be, and that if he was playing, she was.

He took a step toward her. "And the legends say that twilight is the moment to ask her for her secret."

Suddenly the Irish lass burst out laughing. "Why her secret, of course, is that she comes from London!"

———

Soldiers swirled around them. A shrill whistle sounded. Pamela pulled back to put her mouth at his ear. "Your father has Jane, darling. He doesn't need me."

Douglas nodded, though his thought was that her mother had Edward, who was a curate at a church in Knightsbridge. Mrs. Wells was one of those rare mothers in England whose son was not in the army, but she had a dead husband. "The important thing is you," he said. "I want you to be where you . . ." He veered. Instead of saying ". . . belong," he said, ". . . want to be."

She kissed him. "Thank you."

The train whistle blew again.

Douglas looked at his wristwatch. An innovation, wristwatches were unknown until the war, and then, once issued to officers, they were ubiquitous. Other ranks got safety razors.

The War Train was due to leave in eleven minutes.

The press of Tommies quickened. They were carrying duffel kits on their shoulders and many balanced tied cake boxes their mothers had just given them. A newspaper story had run early in the war about a mother carrying a plum cake to her departing son, who wept when he received it, and since then it was all mothers knew to do. The sight of a soldier carrying a beribboned cake box anywhere in London now meant he had been dispatched.

Pamela said, "What I really want is that you stay." She put her face against his shoulder. "Not just to have you, but to have you safe. I'm afraid."

"Don't be, darling," Douglas said automatically.

After a moment, she asked, "Why is their hair shorn like that?" Pamela, still with her face against his shoulder, was looking sidelong at the hustling soldiers. Their hair was trimmed to the skin above their ears.

"Lice," Douglas said, but he thought it an odd question for someone who'd just shuddered with fear.

"I read they cut it short like that in case of head wounds, for ease in treating them."

Douglas stroked her cheek. "That's another reason not to be afraid. They haven't cut my hair, have they? I won't be hit."

She looked up at him. She knew as well as he did that junior officers were more likely than anyone to be killed. The original British Expeditionary Force had been liquidated the previous autumn at Ypres, where they'd barely stopped the Germans from outflanking the Allied line along the sea. In the six months since then, the Germans and the British had been attacking each other without effect along the brutal western trench line in Picardy and Flanders. A massive British force of eight hundred battalions of a thousand men each was in France by now, almost all recent volunteers like Douglas. Yet even this force had been matched by the Germans. The war had settled into stalemate, and though each side harbored the dream of breakthrough, the damage they inflicted on each other had been in no case decisive. They waged war, as some were describing it already, by attrition. Even on days when no assaults worth reporting occurred, an average of seven thousand British men and officers were wounded and killed. Subalterns, lieutenants, and captains, whistles blowing, led their platoons and companies out of the trenches, and that was why a higher percentage of their ranks fell than any other.

Pamela stared into her husband's eyes, plying her fingers in the fringe of hair above his ears. "I couldn't stand it if something happened to you."

"It's how I feel about you." Douglas paused, considered whether to go on, then did. "It seems to me you're the one who will be in danger. That's why I wanted you in Ireland, not for my father's sake. For yours. He would take care of you and of Timmy and Anne."

"But we're not in danger, darling. You are."

Douglas nodded. "I should say good-bye to them."

He turned. Standing in the arched entranceway leading from

the waiting room a few dozen yards away was the nanny. He waved at her. She turned and disappeared into the waiting room.

Pamela said something, but in the din he did not hear her. He leaned forward and cocked his ear. "Shall I get you a pillow?" She smiled, though obviously with great effort, and indicated a nearby cart that was piled high with blankets and pillows covered in starched linen. An attendant stood by.

Douglas laughed. "He hasn't sold many, has he? English officers can hardly go to war with their heads upon pillows, can they? What would the men think?"

Just then two officers stopped at the cart, one a major, the other a captain. The major took a blanket and a pillow and strode away, leaving the captain, with *his* pillow, to pay. It took a moment for him to find the coins. When he turned the major was already headed down the platform toward the first-class cars in which the officers rode. Hard as it was to imagine, this train was no mere London-Paris express. It went from Victoria three times a week with only the army for its passengers and the war itself for its destination. The journey would take not weeks or days, but only hours. The Front in France was closer to London than was Liverpool or York or Exeter, even if what went on there seemed as far removed as combat with the Boers or the dervishes had. Now, those had been proper wars. Wars belonged in places like the Transvaal or Sudan, not across the Pas-de-Calais.

"Tyrrell!" The captain with the pillow stopped short in front of Douglas and Pamela, and only then did they recognize him. It was Peter Towne, whom Douglas had befriended when they read law together at Lincoln's Inn. They'd played cricket on the same team and they'd had adjoining chambers in their last year. Douglas had gone to London the year after he'd met Pamela at Coole Park. He might have studied law at Trinity in Dublin but for his longing to be near her. He had had the greatest successes of his life: prompt admittance to the bar, to her family's affection, and to her heart. Towne had been at their wedding six years before, but they hadn't seen him since.

"Good Lord!" he said. "And Pamela! How are you?" He kissed her cheek, then he and Douglas shook hands vigorously.

"And what's this, Peter?" Douglas indicated the pillow. "Your battle shield?"

Towne blushed. "Oh, Christ, Tyrrell, my C.O. had to have one. What could I do?" His eyes fell on the regimental badge on the breast pocket of Douglas's tunic. "What's that?" He touched the badge with his stick. In Douglas's regiment officers disdained the stick as an affectation.

"The Connaught Rangers, Peter."

"Good God, Douglas! Connaught? A Paddy regiment?"

Douglas and Pamela exchanged a glance. Both were aware of the whiskey pouring off Towne's breath.

He laughed. "But of course you're Irish." He smiled at Pamela. "One forgets."

She smiled back at him. "No, one doesn't." Pamela may have been English, like Towne, but she wanted it clear whose side she was on even in this petty fencing. She remembered how Douglas's Lincoln's Inn friends never let up on him and it embarrassed her, as if they were like that because they were English and not because they were men. It was with their "good-natured" leg-pulling that men made their points and, if you asked her, how they kept each other small.

"You should be with us, Tyrrell." He punched Douglas's shoulder, ignoring Pamela's implied disapproval. Towne still plowed through every thicket of personal awkwardness like a flogged animal. "We have an entire Inns of Court battalion. Fourteenth London. Regular Army. You qualify. I could get you in. Matter of fact, our old pupil master, Engleman, is the colonel."

"No thanks, Peter. Fourth Connaught for me. It's my home outfit. I returned to Ireland, you know."

"I didn't know. Good God, why?" Towne turned to Pamela. "He didn't drag you along, did he? Poor Pamela." He put his arm around her. "I warned you. You should have married me." Not even Towne would have been so forward without being a little drunk.

Pamela slid gracefully, playfully, away from him to go to Douglas.

"I'm serious, Tyrrell. Inns of Court. They're all our friends. Men from our time, just before and since. And it's a *London* regiment, my friend."

"Hence the pillow?"

"Damn your blasted cheek!" Towne threw the pillow at Douglas. It hit him and Pamela together, and fell to the ground.

Douglas picked it up and handed it to him. "Mind your cushion, Captain." He smiled. "Where are you off to?"

Towne's eyes flicked at Pamela. One saw him reading in his mind the stenciled sign they all were trained to carry there now, Careful What You Say. The Hun Has Listening Apparatus and Can Hear You. He looked down the platform, along the length of the train. His C.O. was gone in the throng of khaki.

"Béthune," Towne answered quietly, but the name of the town told Douglas nothing. Béthune was the main railway juncture behind the British sector, and it served as a staging area. From Béthune units fanned out along the Front fifty miles to the north and south, to the sea and to Albert, near the River Somme.

"My regiment's due at Saint-Omer," Douglas said. All he knew about his destination was that it was near the border with Belgium.

Towne looked at him sharply. "Saint Homer's the jump-off for Wipers." He looked briefly at Pamela.

At that point in the war no Englishmen could speak the name of Ypres—or the slang version of it—without a shudder because of what its defense in November had cost the BEF. But the BEF, even decimated, had held, and now Ypres was a symbol of the Allied resistance. It would never be abandoned, but it would never be securely held either, because the Germans occupied the surrounding hills. Since autumn the steady "wastage" had continued. There were constant rumors that the next German offensive was about to come, but there were also rumors to the contrary. If the Germans ever took Ypres, they would be able to close off the British ports at Dunkirk and Calais and to sweep across Picardy toward Paris, forcing an Allied retreat all along the Front.

"What do you hear about it?" Pamela asked. She tightened her grip on Douglas's arm.

Towne shook his head, suddenly sober. "Holding steady. I shouldn't worry. We have Fritz outnumbered three-to-two all along the Front. He has his hands full with the Russians. We won't see the big show this summer. We'll be tending fence, won't we, Douglas?"

Douglas nodded. "It's what I've told her."

"And now you Harps are here, Fritz wouldn't dare move." Towne flicked Tyrrell's regimental insignia. "What's that fellow's name, Coochee something, the Irish warrior?"

"Cuchulain."

Towne nodded and put his hand out. "Welcome to the fray, old man."

Douglas shook his hand.

Towne turned to Pamela, as if to kiss her once more, but her expression stopped him. She did not release her grip on her husband's arm. Towne touched the visor of his cap, raised his eyebrows, and went away whistling "It's a Long Way to Tipperary."

When Towne was gone Pamela turned to Douglas and asked fiercely, "What will it be like? What have they told you?"

Douglas shook his head. "They don't tell you that. How can they?"

Pamela looked back toward Towne, but he had disappeared into the crowd. She said with a large sigh, "I hate it when they condescend to you, darling."

"It isn't condescension. It's that we Anglo-Irish never fit their slots. We are not the peasants—or papists—they wish we were. They'd like to feel superior, but we have longer lineage and more money and better houses than most of them. And some of us"—he kissed her lightly—"have married out from under them the women they always wanted. Wouldn't you resent us?"

Before Pamela could reply, their children came running toward them. They had broken free of their nanny. Anne, who was five, was imitating her two-year-old brother's babyish salutation. "Da! Da!" they both cried. Soldiers made way for them and watched while Douglas stooped to take them in his arms. He picked them up together and buried his face in their squealing laughter. "Oh my ducklings!" he said, but then looked at Pamela. Her father was the one who'd called them "Doug's ducklings." Once more the loss of that good man hit him, and he felt a rush of hatred for the Germans.

The train's shrill whistle blew again, but this time it did not cease for a full sixty seconds. It was impossible to speak. One could only stand mutely, thinking here it was, the dread moment, at last. Pamela closed her arms around her husband and their children.

When the whistle stopped, Douglas put the children down, kissed them, then let the nanny take them.

This last moment was for his wife.

———

In the railway station at Gort at the end of that weekend at Coole Park nine years before, Douglas had managed to draw her aside. Her parents were already in their train compartment, but her father was holding the door open, waiting. Douglas wanted to take her hand but didn't dare. "May I see you again?" he'd asked.

"But isn't that impossible?" She seemed as saddened by the prospect as he was. They'd spent all day Sunday wandering the fields of Coole Park, glorious hours at the end of which Douglas had taken her hand and held it.

"Not if I come to London, it isn't."

"But you've just returned here."

"I'll find a way," he said. "I'll run for my father's old seat in Parliament." He grinned cockily, but what he felt was panic that he would never see her again.

Then, even in front of her parents, she took his hand, a small breach of the Victorian code, but to Douglas and Pamela an explosive one.

He remembered it now and took her hand in his. Now she would be the one watching a train pull slowly away. He said, "I'm nothing without you. I'm nothing until I see you again."

By now Tyrrell was the only soldier still on the platform. He began to back slowly away from her. She came with him. He pulled his hand, but it did not come free.

"Darling . . ." he said.

Steam hissed from the undercarriage of the nearest car. The railway man cried, "On train!"

Pamela started sobbing, a large breach of *this* code. "No, Douglas, don't!"

He tried to pull away from her, but couldn't. She simply would not release his hand. He felt a panic of his own, for this was completely unlike her. In nine years he had never seen her at this extreme of feeling, of need. Suddenly he saw his importance to her as if for the first time, and he too was overwhelmed. He reversed himself, going to her.

They kissed passionately and held each other.

"I love you," he said, and then broke away as the train began to move.

Soldiers hanging from the windows of the rearmost car hooted. "Don't leave her, Captain!" one called. "You'll be sorry!"

"I love *you*, Douglas!" Pamela called through tears she made no move to wipe. "I love *you!*"

He leapt aboard, then turned at once to face her.

She began to run with the train, reached out to his hand and touched him once more, for an instant, as if they were partners in a relay.

The train moved too fast for her, but she kept running until long after it made sense to do so.

Before she could properly breathe again, he would be halfway to the war.

As for him, he stared back at her, hanging from the carriage doorway, until even the perfectly poised twin cupolas above Victoria's mammoth vaulted roof were gone.

———

One image that the officers of the new British army then being fielded had of themselves was that they, unlike their stodgy professional predecessors, were a varied collection of fabulous personalities. It seemed so to Douglas as he made his way from compartment to compartment in the first-class cars looking for the Rangers he'd planned to meet. But something in the mood of those men made him uneasy. Subalterns in particular seemed given to raucous behavior as if they were on a school outing. In a way, of course, they were. One thing those men could all say for the war, it had put them back in each other's company, at the altar of which they had been taught to worship during their school years. The war had rescued the bond they had made with each other, rescued it not only from the anonymity of their mundane postschool lives in which even their clubs, if they had them, were pale shadows of those bright communities of boyhood; but even more to the point, rescued it from their women. That bond was precious because it allowed them to indulge once more—*puer eternis*—in the spirited camaraderie not of youth precisely, but of youth's license. Douglas was as appealed to by the *esprit* as anyone, but just then he was set apart by the fresh wound of his farewell and the attachment to Pamela that it revealed. He kept looking out the window, expecting to see, in place of the blurred landscape, her.

That a woman was his point of reference just then, instead of the brotherhood, made his perceptions somewhat different. He sensed the irony that these men setting off on a course of the most awful consequences should have had quickened a collective frame of mind that knows nothing of consequences. A pack of boys can do anything it wants because each member, by virtue of his membership, feels himself to be part of a life-force that is irrepressible, infallible, immune, destined to prevail. That was why on that train that day, once it had actually left London and its worrywarts behind, the men seemed deliriously happy. They laughed, joked, tugged at each other, tossed hats, and quaffed lemonade. They were not an army going off to war at all. They were a football team going to a tournament, and they couldn't lose.

"Tyrrell!"

It was Towne again. He was standing in the doorway of his compartment. Behind him four officers were playing Crown and Anchor.

"Hello, Peter."

"Here, come meet my friends." Towne turned to the others. They were all captains. "Gentlemen, welcome Mr. Tyrrell, my chum from Lincoln's. He prefers his Irish regiment to ours."

"Chacun à sa chacune," a portly officer said. The crack—to each man his own woman—seemed inappropriate, even though Douglas understood that the man's purpose was to impugn the masculinity of the Irish even while chiding him for disloyalty to the Inns. Douglas hardly looked at him but still noted that in the first days of the war the previous fall, such an overweight specimen would never have been commissioned.

"You're not a member of the London bar?" another asked without looking up from the dice game. This was his true offense, of course, to have proved himself worthy of the most exclusive legal circle in the world, *then* to have gone back to Galway.

"No, Dublin."

"I have to pee," a third said, slapping the dice on the table. He left without excusing himself or looking at Douglas.

Douglas and Towne turned away from the compartment doorway to face the open window in the narrow corridor. Douglas knew better than to take offense.

"There was something I didn't say in front of Pamela, Douglas."

"What's that, Peter?" Pamela, he thought, and once more his mind sank beneath the bright wash of her image. How he loved her.

"The latest from Ypres. Have you heard?"

Douglas shook his head. During his leave he'd deliberately kept clear of all war news. What London got was mostly rumor anyway.

"Jerry's put the push on again."

"As of when?"

"Two days ago."

"A big show?"

"We lost Messines, I hear."

Messines was the name of the ridge south of Ypres made famous in November when the desperate British held it.

"Christ," Douglas said. "We were well dug in there. We had lectures on Messines at Grimsby."

"Our C.O. told us our orders have been changed. We're going straight to Pop."

"Pop" was slang for Poperinge, the last staging town for Ypres. It was closer to the line even than Saint-Omer and orders there meant trenches.

Douglas brought his face around to look at Towne. Whatever had made them awkward with each other evaporated. Their eyes met, and each knew that the other was seeing the same thing, a fleeting vision of what this really was. For a moment the truth bound them.

All at once Towne fumbled in the side pocket of his tunic. "I'd like to give you something."

He pulled out a pair of rubber-handled wire cutters and offered it to Douglas. "I hear you might need these. That's why they don't issue them."

Douglas stared at the tool, not knowing what to make of it.

"Uncut wire, Tyrrell! Uncut wire!"

But the notorious barbed wire was supposed to be systematically mauled by artillery. At Grimsby, they said that by now artillery routinely obliterated wire before each charge.

"I have another pair. Take them."

"I'd better find my fellows," Douglas said. He hooked the wire cutters in his Sam Browne.

"No, you must conceal them, Douglas." Suddenly Towne was furtive, his eyes darting about. "They won't let you keep them if they see them. Wire cutters would be taken as a lack of faith in the gunner boys."

Douglas put the cutters in his side pocket and buttoned it, unsure what to make of his old friend now. Towne was afraid. "Good luck, Peter."

"Same to you, old sweat."

They shook hands briskly. Towne turned back to the dice game. Douglas adjusted the cutters in his pocket, to be sure they didn't crush the one photograph he had of Pamela.

———

At Folkestone, the port where the troops were to transfer from the train to the cross-Channel boat, there was a delay. The men waited on the dockside. The Tommies, Jocks, and Micks, in their impatience, grew even more rambunctious. Footballs were brought out of duffel kits and kicked about. Officers milled together, ignoring the hijinks. At last an aging side-wheeled excursion vessel, which had been impressed for transport, entered the harbor. Men began to notice it coming as it approached their pier. It had just crossed the Channel, and only as it drew closer did the mass of waiting men realize that its decks were crowded with soldiers returning from the line.

The hundreds on the pier grew silent—their footballs rolled idly—as the boat came aside and was made secure. Its passengers, though visible, were eerily quiet. Usually men on leave could not be contained. Were they wounded? Once the engines shut down, a new sound could be heard, a haunting, hollow echo they had never heard before, not moaning, not gasping, but something in between, a plain struggle of throats and lungs for air.

Gangplanks fell to the pier and slowly the procession of disembarkers began, first the litter cases, perhaps two dozen of them, stretchers borne by men who themselves wore bandages or limped. Then a strange line of zombies came, the men who couldn't breathe. Neither could most of them see. They held each other's sleeves as they stumbled down the gangway and followed the ones in front toward the railway platform.

Douglas and the men from the War Train stood silently by. When a medical orderly in white stopped near him, an officer asked the obvious question. Douglas heard the orderly's reply. "The accessory," he said. "These are the lucky ones."

Douglas looked to the man next to him, a veteran. The accessory? Clearly a euphemism, but for what? The man said, "Gas."

"Goddamn Germans," Douglas said, feeling the hatred once more. They'd been using chlorine gas since April. If it didn't kill you at once, it ate your lungs slowly, an interminable asphyxiation. Chlorine gas is a blistering agent that damages any tissue it touches, but where it wreaks havoc is in the lungs and eyes. The men disembarking before Douglas would all be dead in days. Yet soldiers dreaded gas not because they'd have preferred being mangled all at once by the splinters of an artillery shell or chewed up by machine-gun slugs or cooked by the liquid fire of a flamethrower—as if those weapons were more "humane"—but because a gas attack in which the very air is poisoned deprives a man of the one thing he needs most in war in order to keep from going mad—the belief that he might be the lucky one who isn't hit. Artillery, machine guns, flamethrowers, and bombs from airplanes pick their victims one by one or group by group, killing many but always sparing some. Gas gets everyone. It was the first mass weapon, obliterating individuality, and that was what made it horrible.

The medical orderly looked at Douglas. "No, sir," he said. "Not Germans. It was our own gas. The first time we tried it. The wind was wrong, and it came back on us."

Douglas stared at the man, trying to take in what he'd said. Then he looked at the gas victims again. Some clutched at their throats, a few emitting shrill, rasping sounds like the wheezing of bagpipes, and all of them gulping air like asthmatics.

What moved Tyrrell most was the way they clung to each other's sleeves.

He turned away and crossed the pier, to stand at its edge looking out at the Channel. It was gray and choppy, inhospitable. The thick line of the horizon—France was lost in the mist—served in his mind, as surely as if the earth were flat, as the exact border. Beyond it were the trenches. Beyond it was the war. He tried to think of Pamela, as he had repeatedly on the train. He tried to conjure her face, the fragrance of her hair. That he could not shocked him. From the depths in which his love for her was planted there arose only the question she had asked him: What will it be like? His training had not told him. The veterans had not told him. The wounded and dead had not told him. And now the throat of two seas was not telling him. Of course he was afraid, but it was not only fear he was feeling. Was it also awe? He was about to cross into a mystery.

The breeze on his face, blowing hard from France, reminded him of what the orderly had said about the gas. ". . . Our own gas," he'd said. Christ, Douglas thought, we're using it too. "The wind was wrong." He shuddered. Who controls the wind? "And it came back on us."

2

Sir Hugh Tyrrell had thrust his arm nearly up to its shoulder into the warm, bloody cavern of the whelping cow's uterus. As he'd expected, his groping told him that the unborn calf was tangled in its umbilical cord. In addition one of its legs had become snagged, and perhaps that was what had been preventing it from turning the last corner into the birth canal. The cord was garroting the poor creature, and as he worked to free it, blindly tugging with his hand, he knew he'd been right not to wait for the veterinarian doctor.

The cow had been crazed with pain and, though of a breed that was considered small as cattle go, only the weight of three of Sir Hugh's stoutest farm helpers had kept her down. Now she was stunned into quiet by the anesthesia of shock. Her passivity at this point was a sign of her distress.

Tyrrell's daughter Jane cradled the cow's head in her lap. Since the animal was on its side, Jane could see only one of its eyes, a black pool, but there was more terror in that one than she had seen in all the eyes of all the animals she had ever cared for.

Suddenly the cow jerked and Sir Hugh cried, "Let her go,

lads!" He was stretched alongside the cow's fawn-colored flank, and he rode up with her as she bucked once and fell back. His ear was by her ribs as if listening to the life struggle going on inside her. "Just there!" he cried, "Just . . . *there!*" He had succeeded in freeing the looped umbilical cord, and he felt the unborn calf turning. The cow's uterus contracted violently, crushing his arm. "Ahh!" he cried, then grimaced at his men. "A little love squeeze there."

One of the cowhands leaned close to Sir Hugh. "Always squeeze back, milord. It's what keeps 'em cows."

"Is that what the bull says, Connie?" Sir Hugh spoke through his gritted teeth.

Connie O'Brien had been undercutting his subservience with such knowing cracks since Sir Hugh's father's time. Now he faced away from his master, winking at the other boys and spitting.

While Sir Hugh waited for the contraction to pass, he looked up at Jane, whose eyes were fixed upon the cow. She was indifferent to the mess of her auburn hair which had fallen loose, obscuring her face. Sir Hugh sensed that she had calmed the cow by the touch of her hands, and that calm, more than his expertise, and more than the grunting presence of his brawny helpers, was what enabled him to free the calf. He did not take for granted her collaboration at such a moment, but neither could he imagine ever being without it. She was twenty-two years old, the only member of his family left with him at Crag-side and the only person in the world who loved it as much as he did. But of course she would, since she had been born there the year after he and Anita had come back, devastated, from London, determined to make their life in Ireland more than mere refuge, more than aftermath. Jane's birth, then life, had come as the seal of God's approval on their resolve.

The cow stirred and half rose up.

"All right now, lads, let's help dear mother push along." As the contraction eased and the pressure on his arm let up, Sir Hugh grasped the calf's awry leg and forced it in toward its flank, pulling as he did so. The calf shifted in the uterus and slid a bit toward home. "Good mother!" he said. "Good mother!"

The cow reared its head back and let out an ungodly moan.

"Give us your wee one now, missus!" O'Brien cried, and the other lads cheered her on. "Give us this day!" one shouted, half mocking his foreman.

The calf began to come. Tyrrell pulled his arm out quickly and rolled free of the cow, swinging around on his haunches. He moved with the agility of a man half his age. He was sixty-seven years old, but he was as lean and hard as any of his workers were. He liked to describe himself as a simple dairy farmer, but he had had extraordinary careers in the foreign service and in parliamentary politics. He had transformed Cragside from the horseman's showplace of his forebears to a working dairy farm, and though he'd left politics in disgust after the fall—and death—of his hero and friend, Charles Parnell, he'd spent much of the two decades since organizing dairy cooperatives all over the west of Ireland. He was not, in other words, a typical member of his class, and certainly today he was the only former viscount and the only present knight commander of Saint Michael and Saint George to have had his arm past its elbow inside the belly of a cow.

"Here it comes!" He slapped O'Brien's shoulder. "Look at that, will you, Connie?" The calf came out headfirst, smoothly, in a flow of water and of blood. O'Brien hopped back out of the way, dancing a quick jig as he did so. Sir Hugh bent to quickly peel the placenta membrane back, then tie and cut the umbilical cord. Just when he needed it, Jane was ready with the hot coal in pliers to cauterize each end of the stalk. When it was done and they drew back while the cow and her calf lay together, stunned, Sir Hugh and Jane stood each with an arm around the other, relieved and happy. One of the farmhands produced a jug out of nowhere and, when the foreman nodded, he took a swig, then passed it around, a communal toast. They watched gratefully while Sir Hugh drank, though the girl didn't. When the hands had withdrawn a bit for their second round of swallows, Jane said simply, "Doug should be here."

Sir Hugh squeezed his daughter. "I'm grateful you are." He looked at her, but Jane turned her face away and he sensed the cloud that had moved in to chill her heart. He stood in its shadow too. Douglas was in France by now and perhaps even at the Front. Not an hour went by that Sir Hugh didn't think of him, and though they hardly spoke of it, he was certain that Jane was as worried as he. He knew she felt bereft by all their absences. It had been one thing to lose Douglas to the army, but then, after the terrible news of the *Lusitania*, Pamela and the children were gone too. Cragside seemed empty without them. And when Jane felt the burden of her concern for her brother, she would have had Pamela with whom to share it.

Already the calf was kicking its legs, preparing for the great effort of standing. The instinctive fear of being left behind would have the creature on its wobbly legs within an hour.

Jane turned and walked out of the barn. It was a huge structure, having been built by Sir Hugh's father, replacing a smaller utility building, for two purposes—to store hay for his horses, but also, at one end, to house a squash court.

With cattle there was requirement for considerably less hay, and the squash court was gone. The barn was divided into milking stalls, and beyond it was a string of low structures that had been stables but now served as cowsheds. The complex of farm buildings was attached to the house—barn and cowsheds on one

side; remaining stable, garage, and storehouse on the other—
by a pair of curving columned ambulatories. All were built of
the same hewn blocks of dark gray local stone. From a distance
the farm buildings seemed to share one facade with the main
house; indeed, the barn and storehouse seemed to be separate
wings of it. The architect's idea had been to make the house
even more imposing than it was, more English. In England,
of course, the wings of such a house would have been a library
and a ballroom, not quarters for cows and horses, as the court-
yard between the wings would have been a formal garden with
sculpted boxwood and white pebble paths, not a rough, cobbled
apron that belonged as much to the animals as to the people.
No doubt, in the loneliness of that remote country, the original builder, Sir Hugh's great-grandfather, had been consoled
by having the livestock nearby. In ancient times one slept with
one's animals to protect them from attack, and that defensive-
ness had never become wholly inappropriate in such places. The
house itself was square, three stories high, with large multipaned
windows and a steep, balustraded slate roof, a classic Palladian
design. Still, it retained, with its dark stone walls, wrought-iron
wall braces, ponderous locks, and barred ground-level windows,
something of the feel of the castle from which it and all the great
Irish houses descended, for these buildings had always been and
remained centers of self-protection for a people who took for
granted the hostility of their less privileged neighbors.

Those neighbors happened also to be, for the most part,
their tenants whose rents made their greater privilege possible.
Sir Hugh Tyrrell had never managed an aristocrat's indifference
to the plight of the peasants who had made his family wealthy.
The year of his birth, 1848, had been the worst year of the first
Irish famine, but his father, Lord Turlough, was Galway's leading
opponent of the Tenant League, which was founded to help the

starving. By the time the second famine struck twenty years later, Tyrrell was just home from school, and he was scandalized by his father's willingness to force half-starved tenants, who carried only their bloated children, off the estate at sword's point. His quarrels with his father on the subject, rather than any true sense of vocation, were what led Hugh Tyrrell to enter the foreign service. He was assigned to Ceylon where his rapport with local people set him apart from other colonial officers. Eventually he was made governor general, was accordingly knighted, and at thirty-three was the youngest man to hold such a position anywhere in the empire.

When, upon his father's death in 1883, he returned to Ireland—now with his wife Anita, the daughter of a Raj official—he immediately set out to redress the wrongs suffered by his tenants. He was Turlough now, and he intended to use his status to change things. But it seemed hopeless. Men of his own background were offended by his efforts and they opposed him. Eventually he concluded that only the complete restructuring of Ireland's economy and government implied in the program of Home Rule would do. Not that Sir Hugh was a democrat. He felt that squires and tenants could live in harmony if each had what they needed to live decently within their own traditions, and that was what the Anglo-Irish reformers like Parnell proposed to give them. So Tyrrell became one of them. And when, eventually, Parnell asked him to stand for election to Parliament to swell the votes for Home Rule, Tyrrell agreed, even though doing so meant renouncing his peerage as Viscount Turlough. Using his status had failed to bring about the great reform, and then—because reform was tied to the fate of Parnell, which was tragic—renouncing his status failed to do it too.

The gulf between the classes in Ireland had become too extreme. She lacked that solid yeomanry, that self-satisfied middle class, with its tidy villages and sweet Tudor cottages with kitchen gardens, that, in England, stood between the rich and the poor, mitigating the arrogance of the one and the resentment of the other. In Ireland, until this century, there were only hovels and mansions, nothing in between. Anglo-Irish efforts at reform came to nothing, finally, because that fundamental economic inequity was never addressed. It undermined even the land-owners' position, and the lives of the peasants did not improve. It dulled the edge of peasant anger not at all if by 1915 nearly every great house, including Cragside, was in decline, begin-ning to crumble at the corners more quickly than the owners could repair them. The ivy that had clung so decorously to all those walls for more than a century had also been eating them, and now that ivy, in many places, was all that held the walls up.

But today there was little evidence of the imminent decay. Jane stood in the middle of the cobbled yard, halfway to the house, and in the distance behind her was the brilliant blue of Galway Bay and, beyond, the softer hue of the Connemara hills. On the other side of the house, the view opened to the Atlantic itself. Wherever one turned at Cragside there were breathtaking vistas, and when the weather, as then, was fine, one forgot how lonely the place was, how remote, how hard. To Sir Hugh it could seem like paradise. He did not allow himself to think that its beauty could be lost on someone he loved, not on Pamela or Douglas, certainly not on Jane.

She waited while he crossed to her. Her white cotton blouse, sleeves rolled to her elbows, was soaked from contact with the cow. Her dark skirt, tight at the waist, long to the ankles, was badly soiled. But to her father her beauty was always empha-sized by the ways in which their life rubbed against it. He'd have hated having a girl who never left the sitting room.

When he joined her he said, "Thanks for helping out."

He knew it was peculiar that he should thank her, as if her attending to the cattle were unusual, and he thought he'd somehow offended her when he saw an expression of abject sadness on her face. She worked at gathering her hair and pinning it up. She worked at not looking at him.

"What's wrong?" he asked.

She shook her head. "Are we still going to Lady Gregory's? I was going to bathe and change."

He took his pocket watch out. "We'd be late."

In the good weather Lady Gregory hosted picnics at Coole Park on Sundays, always an assemblage of interesting characters. Since Tyrrell had joined her in widowhood, their friendship had deepened. She was a great supporter of the co-op movement and a constant defender of his among their peers. Still he did not feel at ease among the eccentric company she gathered at Coole Park. Sir Hugh was not a literary man, but Augusta fancied writers above all others, especially if they were related in any way to her beloved Abbey Theater.

"I'm afraid we've missed it," he said, snapping the watch shut.

"But Captain Gregory will be there. He will have seen Douglas."

Augusta's son had joined the Fourth Connaught Rangers some months before Douglas had. The leave that Douglas had spent in London with Pamela, Robert Gregory had spent at Coole Park. Now, presumably, he would be joining the Rangers in France.

Sir Hugh saw in his daughter's expression the intensity of her longing. Any description of Douglas's situation would relieve her because its reality had to be more benign than her imagination of it.

Lady Gregory and Sir Hugh had these young people in common. The young people were what made their friendship deepen, for Pamela was like a member of Lady Gregory's family. When she married Douglas it was as if the Tyrrells and Gregorys had become related. Indeed, when Pamela's father died the month before on the *Lusitania*, his companion, also drowned, was Lady Gregory's nephew. They were returning from America, where they'd been raising money for the Red Cross. So now, Sir Hugh remembered, they had that grief in common too. They *were* one family. The visit would soothe an ache in him, he realized.

"You're right," he said. He brightened, an act of will. "We should go. It might be fun. Someone will read a new play, no doubt!" They turned toward the house. Tyrrell put his arm around her as they walked, and he felt the tension in her body. He stifled his question—Was it only Douglas or was there something else?—and he laughed loudly. "Another birth! Cow in the morning, bull in the afternoon!"

———

In order to get to Coole Park they had to go through Kinvara, a fishing town at the head of Kinvara Bay. Sir Hugh had been driving their phaeton at speed, but the pair of horses slowed automatically when their hooves struck the cobbles of the pavement as they entered the town. Even at a lessened pace it should have taken only a few minutes to cross through Kinvara, but just as they approached the town center, the doors of the Catholic church broke open and a crowd of villagers poured out into the street. The Sunday mass had just ended. Sir Hugh had to halt the horses as the men, women, and children swarmed around them, and at first the animals reared up uneasily. Tyrrell had to jerk the reins to control the horses, but by then they had frightened the nearest people, who were forced by the crush of the other mass-goers closer to the animals than they'd have liked. Most Catholics had no experience of horses and frightened easily. They glared rudely at Sir Hugh. There was nothing he could do but sit and wait for the crowd to disperse. It engulfed them like a tide. Their phaeton, a single-seat carriage, was modest by gentry standards, but its polished black wood gleamed and the leather shone. It surely seemed lavish to the Catholics, many of whom eyed it and the pair of fine horses with obvious, sidelong glances. Some scowled at Sir Hugh and his daughter—unchurched heathen that they were—but most tried pointedly to ignore them. They seemed in their frayed serge suits and their black-shawled dresses like somber, unhappy people.

"I never understand why they're rude to you," Jane said quietly, "after all you've done for them."

"These are fishing folks, Jane. Our friends are farmers. You know that."

"They know who you are. They know what Cragside is."

Sir Hugh shrugged. "We can't complain, can we, if they treat us like they treat each other? Their lives have made them mean."

At that moment the pastor appeared in the doorway of the church. His eyes met Sir Hugh's. "Their lives and their curates . . ." Sir Hugh said while touching his hand to the brim of his cap, a salute for the priest, who did not acknowledge it. "He knows who I am," Sir Hugh said quietly. Priests disliked him because they considered his co-op organizing among Catholic dairymen to be encroachment. Wealthy Protestant creamery owners with whom the co-op men competed disliked him for that too, but the priests claimed to be on the farmers' side.

He said angrily, "These people have been cursed by God in the religion He's given them. That's what keeps them down, if you ask me." He checked himself. He did not want Jane to take his remark as mere bigotry. It wasn't bigotry. He'd had enough experience with the parish priests to have come to a rational conclusion that the bleak subservience required of Catholics as a principle of moral theology was the single most important factor in the permanence of their plight. It wasn't England that oppressed them finally, but the narrowness of their own lives, and that narrowness—more than the touted faith, hope, or love—was the chief product of their overbearing religion. England merely took advantage of it. Century in and century out they had failed to muster the meager will it would take to claim their island nation for their own. Even now they remained inert while others tried to do it for them. Worse than inert! These people made Tyrrell impatient for the way in which they cooperated—not with each other—but with the ones who kept them down. Else why hadn't they rallied to Parnell when he was about to accomplish their liberation? Because he was a Protestant, that was why! Like himself! And the bloody priests joined hands with diehard Unionists to bring him down. And the fall killed him, his dear Parnell.

But Parnell, Parnell, that was other times, he told himself. He clucked his horses and snapped the reins, for the way had opened up.

The unpaved avenue leading into Coole Park was more like a tunnel than a road, for it was overhung with the leafy branches of dozens of sentry ilex trees through which sunlight filtered only intermittently. The cool air engulfed Tyrrell and his daughter, and only then did he realize how warm he had become on the bright road. The speed with which he had driven the carriage had kept wind in their faces, but the sun had been harsh nevertheless, especially for early June. His daughter had neglected to wear a bonnet, and her dress, which covered her from ankle to throat, must have soaked in the heat.

But when he glanced at her she seemed as fresh as she had

when she first appeared in the doorway after bathing and dressing. When she was gotten up like a proper lady her beauty was perhaps less apparent to Tyrrell than when she showed the effects of the rough-and-tumble, but it was then that he saw how much more handsomely made she was than Anita had been. What she had of Anita's was that fragility, layered over now with dogged toughness, as if Jane had implicitly resolved to be stronger than her mother had been.

They came out from the canopy of trees as the drive curved toward the house. On their right was the high garden wall and on their left was the grassy open plain on which years before Robert had organized his cricket matches but in which now a dozen scattered sheep blithely grazed. Sir Hugh did not rein his team until they were nearly at the stately yellow house, when he pulled them in abruptly. The horses kicked up the gravel and the carriage slid, announcing their arrival.

A groom dashed out from behind the hedges to grab the horses' bridle. "Good day, your honors!" he said, but he seemed to be speaking to the horses, an habitual, implicit acknowledgment that what he and the gentlefolks had in common were the animals.

Robert Gregory, resplendent in his uniform, came bounding through the door. "Sir Hugh!" he cried in greeting. "Welcome!" But it was to Jane's side of the carriage that he strode. A handsome, mustachioed man in his middle thirties, in his officer's tunic and Sam Browne belt he was the epitome of dashing Britishness. "And this is Jane?" He flashed his incredulity. "This is the first time I've seen you without your governess."

Jane laughed. He still thought of her as a child, Douglas's pesty sister. They'd seen each other rarely enough in the past few years that each sight of her as a woman, an attractive, lively one at that, was a jolt to him. He was married, otherwise he'd have

surely revised his mental image of her, and otherwise she'd have
taken offense at his inability to do so.

She said jovially, "And this is the first time I've seen you in
uniform." She let him help her down from the carriage, then
cocked her head to admire him. All at once she stiffened. "But
that's not the Fourth Connaught uniform." The patch on his shoulder was different from Douglas's and the badge above his breast
pocket consisted of the crown between a pair of silver-thread wings.

"I'm in the Flying Corps now, Jane, as of last month."

"Flying Corps!" She'd never heard of it.

"Aeroplanes." He grinned. "It's great fun."

"You fly aeroplanes?" Her mind failed to grasp what such
exotic machines—she had never seen one or spoken to anyone
who flew them—had to do with the war. Fun? Robert Gregory
was a famous sportsman, a champion rider, a demon fast-bowler
who'd led the All-Ireland cricket team. He lived for fun. But
what had fun to do with the war? Jane tried to comprehend.
Why was Robert having fun when Douglas was at the Front?
Weren't they both Connaught men? Weren't friends supposed
to stay together in a war? Wasn't that a rule?

"I don't understand," she said. "What about Douglas?"

"I haven't seen Douglas, Jane. Not in months." Gregory
looked uneasily at Sir Hugh. What was this? Douglas Tyrrell
was on his own, as everyone was. What did they expect of him?
He said to Sir Hugh, "But the Rangers have gone across. You
heard that, surely."

Sir Hugh nodded.

"Well then . . ." Robert paused. When no one spoke he
began again with a forced enthusiasm, as if describing a jolly
new sport. "We use aeroplanes for artillery observation." He
grinned again. "And some of us bring along our own supply of
Mills bombs to drop on the odd Hun who sticks his head out."

"Have you actually done it yet?"

"Flown? Dozens of times."

"Flown in the war, I mean."

"No." He stopped abruptly. "I've been training, Jane. We've all been training. Our side of this war is only now begun. Our lads have been holding the line for us, but now the Rangers and the Flying Corps and a thousand other fresh battalions are on their way across. We're going to push that line, Jane, right back to the Rhine. Mark my word. The war will be over before Christmas."

Robert had spoken the rote assurance—the war was to have ended by the previous Christmas; wars were always to end by Christmas—thinking that it was all Jane really wanted to hear from him.

But she said, "Is it safer? Flying?"

He laughed easily, in the way that flyers would from then on. Jeopardy could only be treated as a joke. "Than what?" he asked. "It's not safer to fly across No Man's Land than to crawl—"

Just then his mother came out of the house behind him. Lady Gregory was sixty-three years old in 1915. Not tall, she was more bulky than lithe, and her gray hair was pulled back sternly from her face. She was dressed, as always, in black. These individual elements of her appearance combined, however, with merry brown eyes, a vibrant sunny complexion, and a gracefulness of movement, to make her seem an altogether stately woman. Her arrival just then brightened the scene, and no one welcomed it more than her son. Sweeping his arm toward her he went on good-naturedly, "—but it's surely safer than attending the opening of one of Miss Augusta's plays at the Abbey."

Lady Gregory tapped her son's shoulder as she passed him to embrace Jane. "Why, my darling chick! At last you're here!" She kissed her on each cheek, in the French style, then turned to Tyrrell and opened her arms wide. In the way they hugged each other, even without kissing, the bond between them was obvious. In Lady Gregory's dramatizing mind, she and Hugh, once childhood sweethearts, were lovers who had missed each other. Their bond in the end consisted in a poignant acceptance of the irony—all good theater is irony—that now their having missed each other all those years was what made them friends.

"I was afraid you weren't coming." She spoke with a slight lisp, but she ignored it and always her listeners quickly ceased to hear it. "Everyone else is in the garden eating lunch. Forgive me for not waiting for you." She managed to convey in those simple words the strength of her affection. Those who knew her were no longer jarred by the contrast between her permanent mourning clothes and her lightheartedness. Those who knew her well understood how she exploited that contrast. She paid tribute to her widowhood by not relinquishing its trappings, even after more than twenty years, because it had been the precondition of her creativity. Death's claim on her had released that startling life-force that so affected everyone who experienced it. Her vitality and courage, her enormous range of interests, from the details of her stableman's Gaelic stories to Tyrrell's farmers' co-op movement, her talents as a playwright and sponsor of the best Irish writing, her association with the brightest people of the age had all contributed to her fame as the mother of the Irish Renaissance.

When Lady Gregory turned from Sir Hugh to Jane once more, affection overflowing, Jane felt powerfully that rare acceptance. She had come here thinking it was her duty to check her feelings, to change them, to deny what they were telling her. But now, all at once, her feelings seemed as welcome as she was. Lady Gregory embraced her once more and Jane understood that she *was* her feelings. Since her mother's death no one had embraced her like that, and Jane felt that lack, what she'd been missing all those years, more powerfully than ever. Yet immediately the longing she felt for her mother seemed like a judgment against her father, and that wasn't what she meant. Despite herself, she began to sob.

Lady Gregory tightened her embrace. "There, there . . ." How was it that such nonsense words were soothing?

Robert Gregory watched uneasily. Was this his fault? Had his uniform reminded her of Douglas's jeopardy? Or had his levity upset her? He glanced at her father. Should I ask forgiveness for my boorishness?

But Sir Hugh was staring at his daughter, troubled and hesitant. Seeing the waves of emotion breaking over her, he felt inept. He grasped finally that more than worry for Douglas had brought her to this, but he hadn't a clue what. He wished Augusta would look at him with a hint of what she saw, what she quite clearly understood. But Augusta was focused on his daughter.

"You were right to come, Jane," Lady Gregory said softly. "I'm glad you wrote to me."

At those words Jane raised her face from Lady Gregory's breast to look at her father. Suddenly even to have written to Lady Gregory without his knowledge seemed already like the grave disloyalty she had till then barely allowed herself consciously to contemplate.

Her mystified father was looking at Jane not with the accusing question she expected—What did you write to her about?—but with such plain worry and love that for the hundredth time she changed her mind. She could not do it. She could not do it to him. She collapsed against Lady Gregory again, overcome now with shame.

3

"Of course you can," Lady Gregory said. They were alone in the library. The other guests, including now her father, were in the walled flower garden, where the wine and food had been spread.

The library was dark and cool, musty with the pulpy odor of old books. The French doors, which opened on the garden, were tightly shut and, to make their privacy complete, Lady Gregory had drawn the curtains. A pair of electric sconces flickered dimly on either side of the black marble mantel, but the book-lined walls of the room seemed to suck the light up before it actually illuminated the space. Reading would have been impossible in here, but it was just as well. Jane was reclining on the plum-colored Victorian chaise longue. At her elbow was a side table on which sat a pair of gilt-edged books, *Cuchulain of Muirthemne* and *Gods and Fighting Men.* They were the first two editions of Irish epics that Lady Gregory had published more than a decade before. These two exquisitely bound volumes had been gifts from Willie Yeats.

Lady Gregory was sitting erect in an upright desk chair she'd pulled close to Jane. Her dark figure loomed over the young woman, but not threateningly. On the contrary, her sympathy was powerful; Jane felt it as a kind of pure oxygen and, even in that closed room, she breathed more easily. At last she allowed her most awful thoughts to take the form of words.

"But I'm all that's left of him. If Douglas is killed—" She stopped, feeling the full weight of those words she had never dared speak aloud. Horrible, yes, but still only words, and they certainly had not killed him. "—Pamela and the children would never return from London."

"Has your father told you not to leave?"

Jane shook her head. "It's never occurred to him I might want to."

"But you do."

A long silence followed those three words that were as much conclusion as inquiry. The silence was reply enough. Jane was lying back like a patient in a hospital. She had unpinned her auburn hair and it was loose to her shoulders, a pillow beneath her head. The luminous gray fabric of her dress contrasted not only with the plum velvet and with the darkness of the room, but with the upright woman at her side. She said in a quiet, resigned voice, "If I don't go now, Lady Gregory, I never will. I haven't been apart from my family, not at all, not even for school like other girls. I've always had governesses at Cragside."

"I know that. I must tell you that I was the one who encouraged your father to keep you at home. But that was when your mother died. You needed your father and he needed you. Your brother had returned to London to read law. It was a lonely time for all of you. But that time of need is past for both of you."

Jane's hand fell to her collar and she began to toy absently with her gold locket. She said, "I've been to Dublin, of course, but never alone. It wasn't until Douglas went away that these feelings got the better of me. More and more I began to think of him as already dead, and I knew what that would do to my father. And I knew that, with Douglas dead, I could never leave him."

"But Douglas isn't dead, darling." Lady Gregory dreaded her own son's departure for the war. But she knew how important it was to resist living as if the worst had already happened. What had already happened that year was bad enough. One brother's only son had been killed at Ypres, and another's at Passchendaele. How could she not be terrified for Robert? But she repeated calmly, "Douglas isn't dead."

Jane closed her eyes. "I know, I know. But Pamela's father is dead. And Mr. Lane. That great ship went down just beyond our cliffs, and they weren't even soldiers! And then Pamela and the children had to leave. And that was when I began to grow terrified. Not only for Douglas and all those boys in France, but for myself. I saw all of my life before me *there*. And I knew that much as I have cherished it till now, from here on I would hate it and I would end by hating him." She sat up and reached desperately for Lady Gregory's sleeve. "Oh, I love my father! I love him as he loves me! But I cannot spend my life at Cragside! I cannot!"

Lady Gregory covered her hand. "I know your father better than you, my dear. He knows that you are a woman now and not a child."

"But he'll be heartbroken."

The older woman shook her head, smiling sadly. "Hearts as old as ours have been broken and put together many times. Your father will miss you, but he'll do well enough. The more important question is what will you do?"

Jane replied at once. "I thought to go to Dublin, to find work."

"There! You see! Dublin! It's only three hours by the Great Western. The train comes right to Gort. You'll visit each other often. It's not as though you're going to America."

"Father won't go to Dublin, Lady Gregory. You know that."

"To be with you?" She nodded dramatically, widening her eyes, a stage effect. Then she became serious again. "But you'll need a place to stay, and as for work . . ." She leaned toward Jane, full of a new thought. "You handle all the accounts at Cragside? Bookkeeping, correspondence, the lot?"

"Yes."

"And you use a typewriter?"

"Not rapidly, but I'm careful. I manage with few mistakes."

"Well, I could see a variety of positions for a smart girl like you. What would you think of serving as secretary to a famous folklorist?" She picked up *Gods and Fighting Men* and idly flipped its pages. "She's forever transcribing notes, an endless task, as endless as these stories are. A good typist would be invaluable." She put the book down, then clapped her hands girlishly at another idea. "Or you could work as assistant manager of a struggling Dublin theater, a job doing accounts and correspondence at which you've proved yourself already, though not also involving midwifery to cows." Lady Gregory laughed appreciatively. Hugh, in explaining why they were late, had said this girl could do anything, and she believed him. "And you'd be with people your own age. And after the west of Ireland, my chick, you'd find that refreshing. All the players at this particular theater are under thirty."

"I'd never find positions like that."

Lady Gregory stroked Jane's hand. "They're one and the same position. I've been looking for someone like you for ages. You'd be my general factotum."

"*Factota!*"

"And she knows the Latin!" The two women laughed. "If you started by living in my house in Merrion Square, how could your father object?"

A startled look crossed Jane's face.

Lady Gregory misunderstood it. "Well, you'd be on your own through the fall. I'll be out here most of the time, you know that. Coole Park in the fair weather is where I belong. After I brought you on, you'd hardly see me. The theater season gets under way in a month. Rehearsals begin this week. You'll be catering to the whims of self-anointed geniuses. Keeping them in shillings and tea will leave you exhausted, and when their audiences fail to appreciate them, your job will be to laugh loudly, weep audibly, praise the show at intermission, and at the end clap until your hands hurt. It's not the glory days of the Abbey when John Synge and Willie were slaying dragons every time, but our writers and actors are serious people. You could help them do their work better. It's a position in Dublin I'm offering you, Jane. Not here in the west. I didn't mean you'd be at my side. Where I need you is the theater. And you'd live in Merrion Square only until you found a flat of your own. It's not another parent's shadow I'm offering you."

"I know that. What I'm thinking for the first time is that I *can* do it. That's what makes me nervous. It's one thing to dream of going, quite another to see a way—Oh, Lady Gregory, I believe you! I can *go!* You're right. And my father *might* accept my leaving if it was to work for you."

"He's not much for theater or for folklore."

"But he's much for you."

"And would it be what you want?"

Without hesitating Jane nodded, then threw her arms around Lady Gregory's neck. After a moment she pulled back, embarrassed. "This is no way to behave with my employer."

"First I'm your friend," she said simply. She looked directly into Jane's eyes, and she liked the way the girl returned her hard, searching look. This young woman's confusion and distress were signs of the intelligence she possessed in sufficiency to recognize what a lonely life on the remote, unfriendly coast of Ireland would do to her. The love of her father might sustain her for a time, but one day he would be gone and then what? She loved the animals, the work, the land, but no aspect of Cragside—not even her idea of the place—reached to the core of who she was. That her longing for something else was undefined did not make it less urgent. And that this instinctive rejection of her family's hallowed tradition was implicitly forbidden did not make it less right. What? She should make Cragside the absolute center of her life, her only future? And if her brother *did* return to claim his place as heir and lord, a wife at his side as lady, what then? Jane's position was impossible. A life alone? A life as spinster aunt? It was strength, not weakness, to reject a life that someone else had chosen, no matter that that someone else was her beloved father. It was honor, not disloyalty, to prefer her will to his in the matter of *her* life.

Lady Gregory identified, in other words, with the daughter, not the parent, perhaps in part because her own son had never inflicted such a pain upon her. He'd never felt stifled at Coole Park because she hadn't wanted him to stay. Robert's departure had not been rejection but acquiescence. She'd wanted him to leave because, upon reaching his majority, he'd become the legal owner of the place and nothing threatened Lady Gregory more than that. Oh, the position of women was impossible! Coole Park was the center of the world she'd created for herself, for Ireland, for literature. Gracious as Robert and his wife Margaret would have been about protecting her prerogatives, she'd have felt usurped if he'd asserted his right in any way.

"You should walk with your father down by the lake. Tell him today, my dear."

"Will you tell him with me?"

Lady Gregory shook her head. "Your father and I have a history that would make it doubly hard for him."

"He never spoke of what happened between you. I knew there was a time after Mother died that he . . ."

Lady Gregory waved her hand in front of her face, a fanning gesture or a banishing one. But instead of shooing the memory she called it forth. "It was sad for both of us. He was ready to throw off widowhood, but I had grown into it. How could I marry again, even him?" She smiled that sad smile once more, and her brown eyes were flecked with feeling. "I'm Lady *Gregory*. It's who I am. But I love your father, and I know how difficult it is to deny him."

"I always assumed you and Mr. Yeats—"

"No, dear, not Willie. It isn't like that with us. My goodness, he's thirteen years younger than I am." She laughed. What people made of her relationship with William Butler Yeats always amused her, and in fact in their earlier days she had secretly rather liked the air of innuendo that attached itself to their association. Now the prurient gossip of strangers irked her. Friends knew, of course, that the love of Yeats's life was Maud Gonne, the nationalist and sometime actress. Her portrayal of Cathleen ni Houlihan, the mythic embodiment of a free Ireland, had given Yeats and Lady Gregory their first triumph. But that was more than a decade ago. Since then, in Augusta Gregory's opinion, Maud Gonne had squandered her beauty, her talent, and the love of that great man for a bizarre series of self-destructive flirtations with men and movements, the most recent of which was with the dreaming madmen of the Fenian revolution. But Lady Gregory owed Maud a great debt, for her steadfast, cruel rejection of Yeats had made him all the more dependent on Lady Gregory herself. "Willie is my confidant and my muse, my inspiration. We never know whether he's created me or I've created him, and now, after all these years, neither of us is anxious to find out." When she unclasped her hands to touch a finger to her lips, the damage of arthritis was apparent. Her hands had been her best feature, but now they were crooked, misshapen. Behind her hand she was smiling, though, and she seemed the most gently self-accepting person in the world. "Willie is my best friend, Jane. Your father is my special love."

Jane saw that what Maud Gonne was to Yeats, Lady Gregory had become to her father. No wonder he was reluctant to come to Coole Park. She felt a wave of sadness for him unlike what she'd felt before—it was not guilt this time—and now it did not swamp her.

Lady Gregory said, "After you talk to him, then I will. It's the right thing, my chick."

"I keep thinking of Cragside. Who will—"

"Do you think he loves Cragside more than you?"

It was a question she'd never dared put to herself directly, but now that this woman had put it to her she saw the answer. Her father's love for her and for Cragside were of different orders and each in its way was absolute. Yet her father wasn't the one who had to choose between absolutes. She was. But that was done already. Her anxiety fell away. Already she was gone. She was alone. And she was—this realization came as a surprise, a gift from Augusta Gregory—strong.

Lady Gregory drew artists and writers almost mystically, but if Coole Park was a Capistrano for two generations of Anglo-Irish swallows, there was something in the place itself too that brought them. The house, with its yellow mortar walls, its gracious bow windows, and the elaborate flowering vine that lay against the façade like a lace veil, was more a home than a castle. The lawns were modest. The orchards, gardens, and woods were beautiful but not extraordinary, and all that distinguished the lake were the swans that made their nests there and the distant view of the Connemara hills. Yet altogether—house, grounds, garden, and lake—Coole Park achieved a decorum which, set against that wild Irish countryside, never failed to soothe its visitors. And in the house itself they saw the relics of the best of their own tradition, for the Gregory family had lived at its pinnacle for a hundred years. On the walls were mementoes of service to the Empire: scabbards and shields, Oriental paintings, and the photographs, all signed, of potentates and generals and field marshals, but also of family friends like Browning and Tennyson. There was a framed letter from Edmund Burke and a mezzotint given by Gladstone. The men and women who, unconsciously at first and then with an overriding self-consciousness, were reinventing the meaning of Irish life came to the Gregory estate for the sense of continuity it gave them. It offered a past from which a future might come. Against the mixed-breed hating chauvinists on two sides, Coole Park stood as a self-asserting middle ground that would not be denied. To be there was to breathe in the "dreaming air" of the new Ireland to which nearly everyone who came was devoted. Coole Park refreshed them in their conviction that already it had come, if only they knew to look for it.

Passing time that day in the blooming walled garden was Yeats himself. Since 1913 he had been spending most of each year in Sussex, where he lived with Ezra Pound; but swallow that he was, he'd returned the week before to Coole Park, where he would stay for the summer. He was still a bachelor and, though an eminent poet for twenty years already, he still had the air, even at fifty, of a youthful genius in which achievement is far outweighed by promise. His clinging boyishness probably derived more from the still unsettled character of his personal life than from any want in his writing. For example, at this moment,

he was standing moodily away from the others, like an adolescent, having stalked from the table because his opinion had not
carried. Dressed in bow tie, waistcoat, and somber gray suit, he
was standing on the ledge of the small fountain in the center of
the garden, the toes of his black shoes overhanging the water.
Across from him, seated in the corner of a stout wooden
bench, was Gerorge Bernard Shaw, tall, skinny, white-bearded,
wearing dark glasses, a cap, and a belted jacket. His arms were
folded over his chest. His glasses obscured the fact that he was
asleep, though his breathing, rhythmic and faintly whistling,
indicated his absolute indifference to whatever else was going
on around him. Not quite sixty, his nature was the opposite of
Yeats's, for he seemed very old. His wife, a frail woman in the
other corner of the same bench, was intent upon her needlepoint.

On the oval-shaped pebbled terrace near the house was
a long wooden table covered with linen and spread with the
remains of lunch. Half a dozen people lounged in their chairs.
One was Augustus John, the painter, whom Lady Gregory had
asked to do a portrait of her grandson but who had spent the
weekend doing Shaw. His canvas and easel were in a corner of
the garden across from the bench on which the Shaws sat, but
he still wore his paint-spattered smock and there were blue
smudges on his face. Next to John was Sir Hugh Tyrrell. He had
maintained a preoccupied silence through the animated meal,
partly because the dominant topic until talk turned political
was Gaelic folklore. The others regarded the subject of ancient
Irish mythology with reverence, but in Sir Hugh's opinion it
was a trivial genre awash in superstition. He couldn't say so, of
course, because his hostess had herself almost single-handedly
established its respectability. The other reason for his preoccupation involved his hostess' absence from the table; he couldn't
get his mind off Jane.

Next to Sir Hugh, no doubt the reason Yeats had left the table, was Maud Gonne. At five feet ten inches, she was always the tallest woman and often the tallest person in any group; which led her detractors to feel justified in calling her an Amazon. Yeats had never forgiven her for condemning him to the conviction that he was short. Middle-aged now, the mother of a nearly grown daughter and son, she was still beautiful. In her day she had mesmerized theater audiences and royal audiences. When she was presented at court as a girl, the Prince of Wales had declared himself smitten, and she still had the perfect features and dark eyes that so beguiled him. Even the excessive drapery of Victorian clothing had not muted her sensuality, and still the curve of flesh below her chin, the veined white skin inside her wrists, the subtly revealing line of her bosom heightened her appeal more than the voluptuous display of later generations would. In fact, her appeal depended on contradictions. Her womanly flare, so inviting to men, contrasted absolutely with the harsh, anti-English histrionics that were the mark of her public appearances. Working for the cause of Irish freedom—not Home Rule but total independence—she had become in her own way a legendary match to Lady Gregory, particularly in the west of Ireland, where, instead of collecting ancient Gaelic tales, she was a leading organizer of peasant resistance to evictions. The peasants worshiped her not just because she was on their side but because she wasn't a peasant. She served the dispossessed, but she was a wealthy woman who always traveled with a maid. She was brilliant and self-disciplined, but her husband was a meanspirited drunk. It was the great humiliation of Yeats's life that, having rejected him, she should have married the vainglorious buffoon John MacBride. But wasn't that the point? She had rejected the ambivalent poet who sought to hold justice and truth in the same moment in favor of a diehard Catholic whose hatred of

England and willingness to act upon it were unqualified even by so basic—to him, base—an instinct as self-preservation. Maud had left her husband when his violence turned toward her, but she never divorced him. Yeats, for his part, never put aside his worship of her. Was it her radically univocal mind that drew him? Her rebelliousness? Had he never recovered from the shock of love when she'd brought his Cathleen—his Ireland—to life on stage? Or was it only her rare beauty that obsessed him?

Maud was outrageous in Lady Gregory's garden that day, not in her attitude toward Yeats—she hardly noticed him—but in her argument with Robert Gregory who, next to his stunned wife Margaret, sat across the table from her.

Sir Hugh listened in silence as the two went at each other with the fierce but simultaneously detached energy of people who have known each other and disagreed for years. Maud was older than Robert, and she had been a figure of such stature at the Abbey Theatre as he came of age that he always deferred to her as if she were fully of his parents' generation. But there was no deference in him now. He was an officer in the King's Army and it was, finally, his duty to defend the King's honor.

Neither spoke for Sir Hugh, though he could not look at Robert or hear his defense of the British position on the war in Europe—that was the issue—without thinking of Douglas.

"We supported the Boers against England, didn't we?" In her anger Maud's voice became quiet and her pronunciation became even more precise, more aristocratic. "Why should not right-thinking people be against England now?"

"The Gregorys did not support the Boers, Miss Gonne, I can assure you of that. My father was an officer of the Empire, as you know."

"My dear Robert, your mother stood with me in Dublin protesting Queen Victoria's visit when that war was over."

"Well, my mother wouldn't stand with you today."

Robert's wife touched his sleeve as if to say, Don't go on with it. She was offended by Miss Gonne's politics, but even more by her manners.

Maud said, "The enemy of my enemy is my friend, that's my credo. I really don't see why the Irish people should regard the Germans—"

Before she could complete her statement, Willie Yeats turned around at his place by the fountain and cried loudly, like a director crying from the back of the rehearsal hall at a mulish actor on the stage, "Maud!"

Everyone fell silent at once and looked at him.

Willie had loved the talk at lunch, lighthearted yet intelligent. Gaelic mythology was the wellspring of his inspiration and as such set him apart from all the other poets of his generation. It made his work impossible to emulate. He knew the subject as no one else did and nothing pleased him like sharing his enthusiasm with others, particularly Irishmen. Yeats was giving them back a long-lost past, although whether they could ever fully have it back had been the crux of that fine, midday conversation. Shaw had said acutely, "To revere the old tradition is to realize one's separation from it." But Yeats of all people should have known that in Ireland—this was a major theme of his—culture always leads to politics. And so the conversation had stumbled out of the Celtic twilight into the pitch dark of England's Irish policy, from which, as a topic, sensitive souls like Yeats had withdrawn utterly. Hadn't he been battered for years at the Abbey by the primitives on both sides? And hadn't that tension, culminating in the awful Abbey riots of 1907 when Synge's *Playboy of the Western World* opened, led to his severe nervous breakdown? He protected himself now by keeping his enthusiasms in check and by regarding his early idols with a certain disdain. He couldn't imagine how Lady Gregory maintained her interest in a Dublin theater. Dublin opinion of every stripe seemed crude. And so, frankly, he finally admitted to himself, did Maud.

What he could not admit was that his anger at her was not only about her insensitivity toward Lady Gregory's son—the Germans had killed three members of his family in as many months—but also about the slight he himself felt from her. He'd been stunned with happiness when Maud showed up unannounced in midmorning. He'd thought she'd come to see him, but her indifference had soon belied that. She hadn't known he was there. She was simply at loose ends, waiting to address a Fenian rally that night in Galway.

He said sternly, "You're disgracing yourself. You exalt the hatred of England above the love of Ireland." His eyes flashed at her, but eccentrically. He had a skew cornea that destroyed the symmetry of his stare. "Please consider what this family must feel today. Robert leaves for France tonight."

Maud blinked across the table at Lady Gregory's son. "Is that true? You leave for France?"

"Yes. I asked Mother not to mention it. I didn't want our picnic to be a wake." He smiled sardonically, fingering his Sam Browne belt.

Maud blushed. It was as if a man had announced his terminal illness.

Robert enjoyed her embarrassment. He lifted the flap of his tunic breast pocket and withdrew a cheroot case. He took one, then offered the case to Sir Hugh, who also took one. When his eyes met Maud Gonne's he offered it to her, and she took one too. "By God, Miss Gonne, I'll give you this. You're the only person I know who hasn't changed a thought in her head on the Irish question in fifteen years."

Maud leaned toward Sir Hugh to accept a light from him,

then inhaled a lungful of the rotten smoke. "I hate to say it, Robert, but my ideas on the Irish question became permanent when I played that part in the play your mother wrote with Willie."

"I wrote that play alone," Yeats said good-naturedly, returning to the table.

"That's right," Robert said, winking at Sir Hugh. "Mother only helped with the dialogue."

When Sir Hugh waved out the match, he asked, "What have they told you about things at the Front, Robert?"

"We held our own at Festubert. Since then it's just a constant bickering with grenades and mortars, Sir Hugh. I shouldn't expect much news until our lads are set for the big show. The reserves are positively pouring over. The Channel is glutted with ships. Soon we'll have in place the greatest army the world has ever known. Then . . ." he took his wife's hand. His cheer was what she lived for now. ". . . you'll hear about the race for the Rhine. Put your shilling on the Irish regiments." He grinned. "Meantime, everyone *wants* assignment to the trenches now that summer's here. Only in the lines can one rest properly. The reserves are employed in constant night digging."

No one spoke. Robert's display of optimism was to be expected, of course, but still it seemed anachronistic. Did he believe what he was saying? The British public had no direct access to information from the Front. Censorship was rigorous and correspondents were addicted to the high-flown rhetoric of official explanations. And the public, lacking any larger sense of the overall situation, had no way to evaluate the bits and pieces of information gleaned from letters or rumors. Nevertheless, everyone knew that since the losses of the previous winter, the government's effort to fill the ranks had been carried out with an urgency approaching panic. And as for Festubert, the costly battle of the month before, even civilians knew that the goal had not been to "hold our own" but to break through the German line. Festubert had been another British disaster.

Douglas had written his father that he was being dispatched to Saint-Omer, and that had seemed good news because it wasn't Festubert. From maps in his study Sir Hugh had concluded, however, that Saint-Omer meant Ypres. Trying to ferret anything from Robert, he said, though it wasn't true, "I read that we're turning up the heat at Ypres again."

Robert replied easily, "They say in the trenches that anything can be true unless you read it."

"But the Connaught Rangers are being sent there."

Robert looked directly at Sir Hugh. "I'm sorry, sir, I don't know that." But he wasn't convincing. All his chums were still in the Connaught regiment, and he'd have known everything about it.

Willie touched Sir Hugh sympathetically. "Is Douglas with the Rangers, Sir Hugh?"

"Yes."

Yeats gave Maud a look. You see, woman!

And suddenly Tyrrell realized that Robert was being reticent not to protect his wife from the grim realities, but because he regarded Miss Gonne as some kind of threat to British security, as if she would pass on what he said to German spies. It was so ludicrous he almost laughed. Robert, trying to live up to the cultivated image of his long-dead father, was the last imperialist, and he was as self-inflated as Maud Gonne was. These people, all of them, seemed mad and their smug certainties preposterous.

Since his retreat to Cragside after Parnell he'd felt an abiding repugnance toward the political realm, even while disdaining his own attitude as antinomian. But lately his feelings had become more pointed. He'd instinctively supported Britain's war in Europe, but only until Douglas's enlistment. Since then he'd tried to understand precisely what justified the mounting carnage. He'd begun subscribing to London newspapers again and had read their pathetic moral boosters—"How Civilians May Help: Be cheerful, Write to friends at the Front, Don't think you know better than Lord Kitchener." By the time Douglas's regiment received its orders for France, Sir Hugh was in the grip of a fatal skepticism. It was just as well his son had spent his few days leave with Pamela, for the last thing he needed was a blast of his father's disgust with the pronouncements of the politicians.

Farmers were what Sir Hugh wanted, not statesmen and not poets either. Theirs was the only real Ireland, as his was only Cragside. Nothing is less abstract than a cow giving birth, nothing less ennobling than the harsh work of mucking stalls, nothing less "national" for that matter than the obsessive love of a parent for his children. All of this was the soil of Tyrrell's life. Cragside was not just an ancestral home he preserved for tradition's sake, as if he were, like most gentry, an idolator of his dead relatives. Cragside was meaning itself for him, the opposite of what he feared most—and this is an Irish fear—the loss of rooted identity, the permanent drift of exile. The war was, of course, destroying already the rooted identity of Europe itself, and that was why, even if one's son was not at risk, it threatened absolutely. By June of 1915, after months of failed brutal offensives by both sides, the deadlock of the trenches was absolute. One needn't have been privy to the reports of spies to sense with an awful dread how the primeval mire of that conflict had begun to rise, a foul tide, against not only the high-flown rhetoric— Rupert Brooke on soldiers' blood as "the red / Sweet wine of youth"—but also against the conventional British cheer of men like Robert Gregory. That was why his estimate of the coming "show" was received at his mother's picnic that day, even by those great talkers, with silence.

Sir Hugh turned away from the table to tap the ash off his cheroot. As he did, he saw through the opened garden gate a maze of boxhedges and beyond that the towering copper beech that stood apart from the other trees. The burnished red leaves of the luxuriant boughs contrasted with the mass of green of the firs and catalpas in the woods beyond. What drew his eye was the pair of figures approaching the tree from the far side of the house. Instantly he recognized Augusta and Jane, the black and bright gray of their long dresses, and he watched as they crossed the lawn. At that distance Augusta looked like Victoria herself. In contrast Jane's figure was youthful and modern.

He knew well the tree toward which they were walking. In its rough bark Lady Gregory had for years been having her most important guests carve their initials. The autograph tree, as she called it, had begun as a whimsy but was by then a Coole Park institution. Bearing the initials now of W. B. Yeats, John Masefield, George Moore, Lady Margaret Sackville, the Countess of Cromartie, George Bernard Shaw, Douglas Hyde, J. M. Synge, Jack B. Yeats, and many other artists, it had become a totem of the self-conscious Irish literary circle, and Lady Gregory loved to show it off. Sir Hugh watched as she and Jane drew close to the relic, and even from far away he could sense the hush of their awe. But then, to his surprise, he saw the sunlight flash off the small blade of a penknife. Lady Gregory handed it to Jane, and she began to carve upon the tree too. The surprise was that his daughter should have been asked to join that company. He stood, excused himself from the table, and approached the gate, where he stopped to watch. What had passed between them? he wondered.

When Jane closed the knife and handed it back to Lady Gregory, they embraced. Sir Hugh was moved as the two women stood, immobile, in each other's arms. Oh Augusta, he thought, thank you! When at last they turned and began to walk toward the garden, he dropped his cigar and went through the gate toward them, strolling with a casualness he did not feel.

"My dear Jane," he said with a broad smile as they met in the middle of the open lawn, "you've joined Augusta's living legacy! What an honor!"

Jane lowered her eyes, but not before he saw how red they were. It would be a mistake to treat this lightly. He looked at Lady Gregory.

She took Jane's hand. "The initials *J.T.* will be the ones the scholars come to see. You watch."

Far be it from a girl's father to undercut such a compliment, but Sir Hugh was more mystified than ever. Lady Gregory saw that, and she handed Jane over to him, saying, "Why don't you two walk down by the lake? Tell me if the willow leaves are touching the water yet." She moved away toward the garden, saying over her shoulder, "My guests must think me awful."

Sir Hugh and his daughter, after a moment's awkwardness, dropped each other's hands and began walking toward the lake. "I don't think her awful, do you, Jane?"

"Hardly. She's like Mother."

"I'm glad you feel that."

They walked in silence. Sir Hugh knew enough about coaxing creatures out of corners to leave the initiative with her. His job, if anything, was only to point the way once she began to move. God knew he had questions enough for that.

At the water's edge, Jane stooped for a pebble and threw it toward a line of swans. They veered away.

Then she faced her father. "Miss Augusta has offered me work in Dublin, father," she blurted. Then realizing that wasn't it at all, she added, "I told her I had to leave Cragside."

Sir Hugh's mouth fell. With her he was incapable of the

stony impassivity that he had always shown opponents. "I'm sorry," he said, "but I couldn't have heard you—"

"You did." One could only do this brutally, brutally to him, brutally to herself. It was like cauterizing that cut umbilical. Exactly. "I'm leaving."

Tyrrell turned away from her. Now that she'd said the words, it was obvious. This was what he'd dreaded in every part of his being but his conscious mind. Jane was leaving him. He would be alone. If Douglas did not return—

He snapped his mind shut against that thought, but the pain he felt even short of that loss was too much. And he felt anger. Yet another absolute betrayal, and from the one person he'd never thought to protect himself against. Douglas had always been ambivalent about Cragside. He'd considered the west of Ireland too small a world, which was why he'd read law in London and why he'd married Pamela. But Douglas had surprised him by coming home. Now Jane had surprised him too, and for the first time. His daughter leaving him? What was the feeling, that she'd run him through with a blade? Worse. Had she cauterized his skin with white coal between pliers? No. She'd used the scalding pliers to pluck his heart out.

Only by a fierce, dutiful act of will did he turn his mind away from what this meant for him. What did it mean for Jane?

To Tyrrell the world away from Cragside was a shallow, dangerous place. Dublin? Had she said Dublin? It was impossible for him to imagine at that moment, his daughter, his child, living in that harsh, bleak city. Miss Augusta? She would work for Augusta? How could his old friend have done this?

"What do you mean, she's offered you work?"

"At the Abbey, as assistant manager."

"The Abbey!" He swung around to face her again. "The Abbey! You can't mean it! I refuse to believe you mean it."

"I'm going, father."

"But to be with these people? They're all gas, Jane. Or they will be until the gas blows up in their faces!"

"They're Lady Gregory's—"

"I've never stomached her coterie, and you know it. I won't have you becoming one of them. Your place is at Cragside. The theater's nothing to you! Why would you give yourself to that . . . that . . . ?" He dammed his emotion and stopped. She was giving herself to anything but Cragside. "Was this something you and she—"

"We never discussed it until just now, father. I told her that I had to go away. It was only then she offered me the work."

"But shouldn't you think about it? Shouldn't you have talked it over with me?"

"I knew what you would say. I knew how it would hurt you." Her voice faltered, and she lowered her eyes. "But that isn't why I'm doing it."

Her statement should have undercut his anger, but instead his anger bubbled over. He nearly grabbed her shoulders to shake her. Instead, he faced away. And, in a flash, he saw his own father doing the same thing, showing him his back. But his father had had good reason; this was the son who would renounce his title and sell off most of the ancestral land for nominal sums to the peasants who worked it. This was the son who would put cows in the squash court!

And how his father would be laughing now!

"Jane," he said quietly, "what they're doing at the Abbey will come to no good. It's part of a brew of plots and movements that you know nothing of."

"It's theater, father. It's culture."

"Culture leads to politics. Listen to these fools here. You're enthralled with them, no doubt. With the great Maud Gonne.

But Maud Gonne is playing a dangerous game, and she won't be the one to pay when the points are counted."

If you do this, he added to himself, you will be the one to pay.

"My mind's decided, father."

She seemed so determined. Where was his fragile vulnerable child? He looked at her again. His Jane was already gone. On an impulsive, ill-thought-out whim, perhaps, but gone. And now his duty was to accept it. To do better than his own father had done with him.

But he could not. He stared at her. Who was this tough-willed stranger? Tears streaked her face, but she was not sobbing. He realized with a shock that he wanted her to cry with him as she had with Augusta, to show him her anxiety, her fear, her ambivalence. But was that wish of his the unreferred-to obstacle between them?

Tyrrell had loved his wife precisely for her vulnerability. With his daughter the pretense was that their hard, west-of-Ireland life would make her strong. And so, apparently, it had. Would his wee child defy him so? Would his darling girl so confront him with the flaw of their life together? Yes, she had a kind of strength, but what he wanted now was weakness. He wanted her will to fall before his. He wanted submissiveness.

But submissiveness was what he hated in the impoverished Catholics. He hated submissiveness more than the high-flown romanticism of stage-bound nationalists. He hated—

He checked himself, and, suddenly thinking of Anita again, he blurted, "My weakness, Jane, was that I loved your mother in *her* weakness. But that's not how I've meant to be with you. Perhaps my . . . what do I call it? . . . protectiveness? . . . has been a disservice—"

"Don't say that, father."

"You had lost your mother. I was worried for you. If I've

held the reins too tightly . . ." He stopped. Why was he protest-ing? To prove that he'd clung to his daughter for her sake, not his own? *I had lost my wife!* His grief choked him. *Douglas and Pamela are gone now too!* He wanted to cry out at her, How can you leave too?

He said nothing. He knew enough to recognize that these feelings of his—his need—were themselves driving her away. Yet he was at their mercy.

"I can't accept it," he said then, simply.

Once more she lowered her eyes. She was mute.

She was gone. He saw it.

He turned slightly. On a nearby path, a pair of ragamuffin stablemen staggered past, drunk. Tyrrell stifled his repugnance. How little the lives of the desperate country folk resembled the lives of his rich friends. But no one was untouched by the world's cruelty. For once the sight of men like that did not leave him feeling blessed.

He looked again at Jane. She was unprepared for the world beyond Cragside. He was certain of that. If it hurt her he would rail against it more than ever, but he would know whose fault it was. And he would not forgive himself.

4

Douglas Tyrrell still could not think of himself as a soldier, and as he sat at a makeshift desk in the orderly room, formerly the kitchen of the mayor's house, looking out the window at his men, it amazed him that they were soldiers too. A hundred of them had formed a ring around a pair of teams engaged in a wild game of hurley, the Irish national sport, a ferocious kind of hockey. The teams coursed up and down the hemmed-in village square as one man after another, with considerable stick finesse, snagged and swatted the hard leather ball. The ancient well, squat in the middle of the square, was an obstacle they accommodated easily. It was ironic, these men in British uniforms at such play, because hurling had been forbidden in Ireland under the penal laws that were designed to subdue the Irish population by stamping out its indigenous cultural traditions. Those laws had cost Ireland her language and her literature, but her old games held on and so, of course, had her old religion. The Gaelic Athletic Association was an incubator for Irish nationalism, more than the Church, and even today hurling sticks were classified as weapons and regularly confiscated by

English soldiers in Ireland. The Irish naturally embraced the game with renewed enthusiasm when the English disapproved it, and among the Paddy regiments in the British army it was played as a kind of badge activity. They played it as fiercely as the lads in other outfits played their football. They had skillfully fashioned substitute hurley sticks by whittling the limbs of ash trees. Their real ingenuity, it seemed to Douglas, as well as their real national insolence, was in using for their play a cricket ball. Even if unconsciously, it seemed to him, they mocked the hearty schoolboyishness—"the crack of willow meeting leather"—of an army that went to war as to a cricket match.

This was the village of Longue Croix, five kilometers from the larger town of Bailleul. The Belgian border was another kilometer beyond that and the Front itself another ten. Longue Croix had been a central village for a few dozen surrounding farms, but it was unlike crossroads villages in the west of Ireland because here the main crop was cider apples, and the village was encircled by orchards. By now, like other settlements in the region, Longue Croix had been transformed into a staging site and, in the months previous, dozens of battalions like Tyrrell's had pitched their tents in the adjoining orchards and taken over its few buildings. The Fourth Connaught had been there nearly two weeks now and the men had uncovered everything Longue Croix had for them. In addition to the mayor's house, there were on the square half a dozen smaller houses as well as the church; the *hôtel de ville*, which now served as battalion cookhouse, canteen, and messroom; a blacksmith's stable, which was now the machine shop and quartermaster's store; and a bakery in the window of which was a crudely lettered sign reading, ENGLISH NOT BUY BREAD UNTIL NOON.

Tyrrell's battalion was one of four Irish units billeted in the locale of Longue Croix, and together they made up the

Connaught Rangers, one of a dozen Irish regiments in the British army at that point. The Fourth Connaught was a thousand strong, and Douglas's unit, C Company, included two hundred and fifty men. At any given time during the war there would be fifty thousand Irishmen in the British army at the Front. The names of their units were among the most distinguished; the Royal Irish Regiment, the Royal Munster Fusiliers, the Royal Dublin Fusiliers, the Leinster Regiment, the Irish Guards, and the London Irish were the most famous. Counting those dispersed in other regiments, more than half a million Irish would fight in the war all told. One in ten of those would fall.

Headquarters for the Fourth Connaught was a château on the hill just outside Longue Croix, but the orderly room in the mayor's house was where the real events of the battalion's life took place. Douglas and the other three company commanders rotated duty as orderly officers. It was late afternoon now. Douglas was on until six.

His eyes clouded over as he watched the game. As so often happened in those weeks away from her, his mind drifted back to Pamela. He pictured her at a window like this, watching soldiers not playing but passing in the street. She would be looking for him. He imagined himself breaking from the ranks and running to her, waving. She would cling to the sight of him and he—

He shook himself and looked around, like a man waking. However they consoled him, once gone such thoughts of Pamela left him feeling the full shock of his situation. Only those thoughts undercut the grim resolve in which he held himself.

Across the room, bent over a Corona typewriter, tapping efficiently, was Corporal Billy O'Day, a spectacled, redheaded young man who had been so intent upon his pages that he hadn't slowed his pace in an hour. Tyrrell shifted in his chair, away from the hurley outside, to watch O'Day work. He was

transcribing the signalers' reports of Morse traffic from the days
they'd spent in transit. Since coming to Longue Croix there'd
been few signals received. It was as if O'Day considered the
silence of the wires ominous, and so he was pretending the
outdated notes were current and of some value. It was hard
to imagine that the signal officer had actually ordered him to
type the notes. They'd make just the sort of records that Regiment would order left behind when the move-up came. Tyrrell
marveled at the man's diligence.

"You want to watch your eyes, Corporal."

"Sir?"

"Leaning on your machine like that. Why not take a break?"

O'Day blinked toward Douglas. Light glinted off his glasses
and it was impossible to read his eyes for some reaction. His
shoulder patch, bearing the signaler's crossed flags, was sewn
slightly off-seam.

"Go to the cookers for some tea if you like."

"Tea, sir?"

Douglas smiled. "I'll listen for the wire for you, Corporal."

"You know Morse, sir?"

"Yes."

O'Day glanced past Tyrrell through the window at the
hurley. Tyrrell guessed that the exuberance of the players and
rooters made O'Day uneasy. The men habitually ragged the
signals clerk as a lead-swinger, and if he'd crossed through their
match they'd have punctured his reserve with friendly but
pointed barbs. He was not the kind for games, which only
made him more vulnerable. In the British army games were
the constant point of reference, and behind the lines men were
pushed like schoolboys into matches of every sort, even hurling,
because the *esprit* of sport, its camaraderie, the prize of daring,
embodied what the army wanted. Some officers were reported

to have led their men over the top by kicking footballs into No Man's Land. O'Day would have done better with the Germans. Word was that, behind their lines they provided men with books, not balls. In some sectors Tommies had overrun Kraut trenches and found dug-out libraries.

"Captain Tyrrell, did you want tea, sir?" O'Day took his glasses off.

"No, Corporal. Thanks. I was thinking of you."

O'Day was afraid he'd missed the officer's implication, but he was also perplexed because technically a signaler was not supposed to leave the telegraph. He sat half in and half out of his chair, unsure what to do.

Douglas leaned back on the two rear legs of his chair. His own report could wait, involving as it did an explanation of his order to move a section of his company's bivouac from one field to another because the tent floors were getting soaked from runoff each time it rained. He leaned a little toward the clerk. "Tell me, Corporal, what was it you did in civvy?"

It was the question every conversation opened with, but conversations between an officer and an enlisted man were rare.

O'Day did not reply at first.

Douglas nudged at his reticence by saying, "To use the typewriter so well."

"I had several years' experience, sir."

Douglas tried to read his accent. It wasn't Galway. It wasn't anywhere out west. "In a firm?"

"Yes, sir." O'Day hesitated, then blurted out, as if in admission, "An insurance firm in Cork."

"Well, I must say, they trained you bloody well."

"Yes, sir." O'Day turned again to his typewriter.

"And you've moved along in the ranks, then, quick enough, I'd say, haven't you?"

"Yes, sir." He plunged back into his typing.

Douglas watched him for a moment longer, then faced the window once more. The game was going on as before, but now his eye was drawn to the burly figure in front of a goal, the Second Left, as the men called him, Tyrrell's adjutant, Second Lieutenant Bernard Keefe. Keefe was a hard, unfriendly man and Tyrrell didn't like him. But nerve and toughness were what one wanted in a helper at the Front, not personality. Keefe had yet to be scored upon in any of the hurling matches, and that alone secured the respect of the men. He was the only officer who played.

Village women could be seen peeping from behind curtains on the second floors of their houses, watching. There were almost no French men in villages this close to the line anymore. Mostly they were in Joffre's army holding the French sector beyond Givenchy. Douglas let his eyes drift above the rooflines of the houses and past the steeple of the church to the hills beyond the village. Apple trees with fresh green leaves, boughs tinged with the barest hint of brown, the vestige of spring blossoms, were arranged in orderly rows against the hill's contour. Up there, out of sight, was the elegant château where Douglas and his fellow company commanders, together with the colonel, the staff, and their batmen were billeted.

As if his having merely looked up toward headquarters had magically set events in motion, the telegraph sounder on the table next to O'Day, silent now for thirty hours except for checks, came crackling to life. As he sat forward, Tyrrell's chair slammed the floor with the sound of a gunshot, and that, more than the telegraph, made O'Day jump. As he left his chair, it fell behind him, but he ignored it to get to his pencil. He bent over the sounder, writing.

Douglas listened with his eyes closed. Each time the stop struck the anvil, he registered its meaning.

After only a moment the clicking stopped.

O'Day swung around. "Stand by for regimental orders!"

Douglas looked at his watch. It was 1645. The men would go to mess at 1730. Those who were on pass were counting on a canned-up evening in Armentières, the social center of the BEF. Army-sponsored jitney buses ran to it from all camps. A town of about twenty-five thousand people, it was beyond Bailleul, and the men wouldn't have ventured that close to the Front casually, but Armentières was already legendary. Its shops, *estaminets*, cinemas, and lewder entertainments had been unaffected by the fighting, and prostitutes conducted a brisk trade in its nooks and crannies. This order was bad luck for the men. If the standby had come an hour later, Tyrrell would have delayed enough to let them go. "Sergeant Major!" he called loudly.

From a room beyond, the regimental sergeant appeared at once. He had heard the telegraph sounder and was waiting to be called. He saluted smartly. "Sir!"

"Kit inspection, seventeen-fifteen hours. Cancel all passes. We'll be hearing from the colonel at any time. Expect orders to advance, but don't say as much to the men. Treat it as a drill until we know what's happening. And before you whistle, send in Lieutenant Keefe."

"Sir!" The regimental saluted, turned sharply, and left.

Tyrrell looked across at O'Day, who had faced the telegraph set again and was now staring at it.

"One wants to acknowledge, Corporal," Tyrrell said gently.

"Oh Lord, yes." He leapt to the key and tapped out his receipt and his ready signal. Then he looked sheepishly back at Douglas. "Thank you, sir."

Douglas watched through the window. The sergeant blew his whistle. The game stopped at once and the men listened to the order to assemble for inspection. If they'd been old soldiers or if this had been the training at Grimsby, they'd have groaned in protest. But their anxiety was not thickly enough encased yet and the silence with which they greeted the sergeant's words was fraught. More than one man felt relief, however, having decided that waiting for his fate was worse than meeting it, no matter what it was. In pairs and groups of three they dispersed, heading for their tents to fetch their rifles and don web belts and haversacks and wrap puttees around their legs. This would be a preliminary inspection of each man's personal gear. If the order to advance came, they would have to assemble the forty pounds of additional equipment—greatcoat, entrenching tools, ammunition—that each man carried on the march.

There was a sharp rap on the doorjamb, then Lieutenant Keefe came in, saluted. "Sir!"

Douglas stood and returned the salute.

Keefe was considerably the shorter of the two. A stocky man, nearly bald, he was also older, nearing forty from the look of the gray hair above his ears. He had the red, bashed face of a Celt, and its hue was exaggerated now from the exertion of the hurley. Sweat dripped from his chin, but he seemed oblivious of it. His brown shirt was soiled and the sleeves rolled; his tunic, Sam Browne, and gun holster were bunched under his arm. Tyrrell knew almost nothing about Keefe, only that he'd been commissioned from the ranks the winter before upon the recommendation of Colonel MacIntyre himself. Apparently Keefe had distinguished himself in civilian life as a member of a Galway fire brigade, which was counted in this new army, like police service, as prior military experience. The new army was most unlike the old in that, for the first time in British history, officers were now being drawn from the lower classes. Most of an entire generation of the upper class, all those public-school lads, had already received their commissions, been sent to the

Front, and been killed or wounded. Men like Keefe were needed to replace them. Some social democrats welcomed that development, if not the carnage that caused it, thinking that the ancient barriers would begin to fall when men of different backgrounds were thrown together as peers. Douglas already knew what tripe that was. Proximity and familiarity among such men were only going to heighten class resentment by emphasizing what really separated them. And what really separated the classes was nowhere more apparent than among the Irish: not accent, bearing, education, taste, or wealth, but history.

"Mr. Keefe, we're in a standby posture here . . ." Tyrrell nodded toward O'Day at the telegraph. "We must presume the orders to advance are imminent. I'm the orderly officer until eighteen hundred and I may be extended. I'll rely on you to carry C Company through parade at least."

"We'll be moving out before mess, so, Captain?" Keefe's accent, in point of fact, differed markedly from Tyrrell's, though they'd both been raised in the west. Keefe spoke with what, in the Irish regiments, was the enlisted man's brogue.

"I expect not." Tyrrell sat. "Can't expect the lads to march on empty stomachs, can we?"

"'Twill be the Front then, sir?" O'Day asked from across the room.

Tyrrell shook his head. "Who knows? We may be sent in behind to fill sandbags." He smiled at Keefe. "Which would you prefer, Lieutenant?"

"No preference, Captain." Keefe had yet to make eye contact. Tyrrell stared at him, waiting, but Keefe wasn't going to look at him.

The telegraph sounder began to click. O'Day began to write, and for two minutes Keefe watched him. Tyrrell used the time to fill and light his briar pipe.

When the last click sounded, O'Day tapped off his acknowledgment, then crossed the room to hand the message to Tyrrell.

He read it in silence, puffing his pipe, raising a cloud around
himself. Now when he looked up at Keefe, Keefe was staring
directly at him. Douglas said, "This is it. We pull out with gun
cart, mess cart, the lot. Horses stay behind." The men held each
other's eyes for a moment. Much separated them, but in this
they were alike in being novices.

Finally Keefe asked, "What time?"

"Parade at nineteen-thirty. Step off at twenty hundred."

"Destination?"

"Rendezvous with Regiment at Poperinge at midnight."

Poperinge meant Ypres. Midnight meant deployment for
operations at dawn. They wouldn't be filling sandbags.

Keefe stiffened. "We'd better get cracking, then."

"Right. The men needn't know where we're off to yet. If
the colonel wants to tell them, that's for him to do at parade."

"Yes, sir." Keefe saluted and turned.

But Tyrrell called him back. "Mr. Keefe, go first to Quartermaster, will you, please?" He paused, looked again at the order
and over at O'Day. O'Day had written the orders out; there
was no protecting him from this. "At kit inspection, Colonel
MacIntyre will want the gas helmets distributed."

"O Jesus, Mary, and Joseph," O'Day said involuntarily, as if
the words hadn't registered on him in the act of writing.

Keefe's eyes flashed suddenly. "Well, then, Captain, there's
no point, is there, in not telling the men our destination."

"That's for the colonel to do, Lieutenant, not you."

"It seems the colonel already did, sir, by putting it on the
wire. The men aren't children to be shielded, sir. They'd rather
know."

Tyrrell stared at Keefe unpleasantly. He saw the man's point, but he had pushed it improperly. "You may take your leave, Mr. Keefe. Rendezvous is not to be published."

Keefe left without saluting again.

Half an hour later the entire battalion was assembled in the square for the preliminary inspection. Lieutenant Keefe reviewed C Company as the other companies were inspected by their captains. Tyrrell, as duty officer, stood in for the C.O., who would repeat the procedure prior to step-off. Now was the time to be sure each man had his equipment straight.

Once the review was completed, Tyrrell had the sergeant major give the stand-at-ease. He climbed onto the hood of the Crossley armored car to be able to see the men as he addressed them. It was true they didn't need to be shielded, but neither did they need to be panicked.

"And two further things, lads," he said. "You've all heard rumors about chlorine gas. So has Regiment. Purely as a precaution and to help us rest a bit easier about these rumors, Colonel MacIntyre has ordered the distribution of the new gas helmets." A broad murmur, whether of protest or surprise or fear or all three, rose, a single sound, as from the throat of one large creature. Douglas waited for it to subside. "And two, the QMS"—Douglas had just made the requisition, overreaching his authority, but he didn't care—"will include a tot of rum with each man's tea tonight."

The men cheered, the first release of the tension they felt. As Douglas leapt down from the large mustard-brown automobile, he carried with him the faces of dozens of them as they were—stunned and worried—at the moment he'd first used the words *chlorine gas*. They weren't children, as Keefe had rightly said, and most of them were, if not older, more accustomed to life's hard edges than he was himself. Why, then, did he feel this overwhelming sense of responsibility for them, a desire precisely to shield them from what he knew was coming? Was it because, however else he felt alien in the army and how little like a soldier and however mystified by the entire enterprise of this transit into war, he had in fact—in this exact attitude toward his men—appropriated the essence of what it was to be a British officer?

———

Tyrrell's batman had packed his kit by the time he arrived at his quarters on the sloped-ceilinged top floor of the château. He ordered the servant to unpack his shaving gear and fetch a basin of hot water. Even as he drew his razor across his cheek, compulsively edging his mustache, he realized how ludicrous his impulse was. He imagined laughing while describing it to Pamela. But she knew him and she would understand. If he was going into the line tonight, he wanted to be clean.

He repacked his kit. Beneath a shirt he saw the wire cutters Peter Towne had given him on the War Train. With a twinge of guilt, as if they were contraband, he balanced them in his hand. Where was Towne by now? he wondered. He'd been ordered to Poperinge two weeks before. Were these wire cutters Towne's relic now? No, something else. As he slipped them into his tunic pocket, he knew they'd become his own fetish.

When he was dressed again—his servant had polished his boots while he was washing—he went down to the dining room, where the officers were assembling for order group.

The elegance of the room struck Tyrrell again. The château was originally a fortified building of the fifteenth century—there was still a moat—but it had been rebuilt in the eighteenth century when French gentry sought to imitate the opulence of Versailles. Elaborate plaster molding, much of it gilded, decorated the walls and ceiling. Ornate frames of otherwise innocuous paintings added to the air of luxury, and the windows were swathed in bright silks and velvets. The antlered heads of trophy animals hung on the walls too, however, along with plaques bearing their shins and hooves, and that was how one knew one was in the northern countryside and not in the Île-de-France.

The floors were of contrasting inlays of dark and light wood, and though the wear of the successive regiments that had been through the place in the last months showed most visibly in the dull, scratched finish, they were still remarkable. Dominating the room was a gleaming table large enough to accommodate several dozen diners. Inside a huge fireplace a fire crackled away, and on the far side of the table were four floor-to-ceiling glass doors that opened on a terraced orchard landscape. It sloped away as the formal terracing gave way to gentle hills. In the distance the failing sun cast a hue over the green valley and made the water ribbon of the River Lys seem gilded too. It was a far cry, this setting, from the swampy hollow behind the village down below, where the men were camped, as the château was a far cry from their damp tents and the muddy boulevards that ran between them. The men had an advantage, for their discomfort kept them in touch with the reality of their situation; they never forgot what they were doing there. The field officers, on the other hand, grouped around a familiar polished table in a room not unlike the rooms they'd taken meals in all their lives, could pretend that what had gathered them was the school, the club, the vestry, the board—anything but the war.

Colonel MacIntyre sat at the head of the table. Seated along each side were his half-dozen officers, the company commanders, including Tyrrell, their adjutants, including Keefe, the chaplain, and the battalion surgeon. If the men themselves were unknown to Douglas before the war, he'd known their names. They were the sons of the established Irish families. At gatherings like this Tyrrell missed Robert Gregory and had to stifle a small resentment that he'd gone on to the air corps.

"Orders, gentlemen," the colonel began in his aristocratic baritone. A thin, self-assured man, he was a striking figure whose long nose above a handsome cavalry mustache so dominated the other features of his face as to make him appear haughtier than he was. True, as a regular, he was inclined to regard temporary officers with a certain disdain. That was self-defeating now, however, since apart from his senior staff all of his officers were temporary. Colonel MacIntyre could adjust his attitudes when he had to. What was more important to him was the fact that all of his officers, like most of his men, were from the west of Ireland. He'd refused to have lumped in with his battalion the misfit recruits from elsewhere in Ireland or, worse, from the Irish districts in English cities. He'd been attached to the Rangers since the Boer War and he had seen its personnel turn over many times. That was why his devotion to the traditions of the regiment was absolute, and no tradition meant more to its particular *esprit* than the requirement that its members be westerners.

"Administration," he said, reading from his daybook. "D Company will police the march, taking special care that no lights show at any point. As we are leaving the horses behind . . ." He looked up from his notes to interject, ". . . including officers' horses . . ."

Several of the officers, thinking of another kind of war, had brought their thoroughbreds with them.

". . . C Company will haul the carts . . ."

Now Tyrrell winced. His men would grouse at having to do the work of animals. There were three Lewis guns to pull, the quartermaster cart, the cookers' cart, and the officers' mess cart.

Tyrrell looked briefly at Keefe, who made the notation in his daybook, then looked up with an expression that made Tyrrell uncomfortable. Were the horses being left behind because of the danger? It was an irony Tyrrell sensed too. Some Anglo-Irish mucky-mucks would try to spare the horses a fate they'd willingly march their men to. But Colonel the Honorable Charles MacIntyre wasn't one of those, though some like Keefe might have thought otherwise only because of his lineage. MacIntyre was the second son—therefore, by the unwritten rule of primogeniture, the one for the army—of Barnaby Fitzhue MacIntyre, Fourth Viscount Kilcoman, with estates south of the Shannon. His brother, now Fifth Viscount, was in fact famous as the Master of the Limerick Hunt. To men like that the great tragedy of trench warfare was that it made cavalry irrelevant. For a long time and at great cost, they refused to admit that irrelevance, however, and because of the horse officer's influence, the British objective throughout the war would be to achieve a break in the German line that cavalry plunging through ahead of artillery could exploit.

"A Company will stand regimental guard at Poperinge. Particular attention once more to the dousing of all lights." Colonel MacIntyre looked up from his notes. "Extended order drill. March at ease, but quick-march if necessary to make rendezvous. At Poperinge there are permanent camp facilities. The Rangers will break for tea and rest until oh-four-hundred. Do not permit the men to remove their boots as their feet will swell. Oh-four-fifteen, battalion will count off and stand by." His eyes flicked across the officers, looking for someone.

"Mr. Tyrrell," he said sternly, "the Rangers would surely have preferred that ration of rum at the end of their march rather than at its beginning. You did them no service by ordering it up at mess. And if your thought was to ingratiate yourself, mind the impulse. It won't help your men and it will ruin you."

Douglas blushed. MacIntyre rarely rebuked his officers in public. He seemed most of the time to believe that they conducted themselves quite capably, which might be why they did. As a group they were implicitly dedicated to protecting their C.O. from any disillusionment and so, unlike other bodies of men, they had no stake in each other's failure. On the contrary, Douglas was aware that his fellow officers were staring at him unsympathetically. He was particularly aware that Keefe was looking steadily at his notebook, and he couldn't read him. It surprised Douglas to realize that the disdain of the others mattered less than Keefe's.

"Any questions?"

For a long moment there was silence.

Then Captain Tyndale of A Company asked, "Is there anything to be said, sir, about chlorine gas?"

Tyrrell heard the question as, Will it be ours or theirs?

Colonel MacIntyre shook his head. "We have the gas-helmet order from Regiment. That's all." His manner made his point efficiently: I'm not exercised about gas, don't you be.

"Anything else?"

After another silence it was Keefe who spoke. His accent jarred in that group, in that room. "Colonel, I was thinking . . ." He began easily, almost intimately, and one recalled that it was MacIntyre who had commissioned him. ". . . that the men might like hearing mass once they've stood-down at Pop. Helps a lad, you know?"

The colonel looked across at the chaplain. He was a Church of Ireland minister and he wore a captain's diamonds. He cleared his throat awkwardly and said to Keefe, "There's no R.C. available to us at the present moment, Lieutenant."

Keefe looked slowly toward him with a pointed neutrality of expression.

The minister said, "I'd be glad to conduct a communion service, of course."

"I was speaking of the men, Captain." Keefe's implication—not of the officers—was clear. He turned to the colonel. "Between here and Pop we'll pass a dozen churches, all Catholic. Surely a priest from one of those—"

The colonel cut him off with a nod, a wave of his hand, and he said to the chaplain, "Arrange it, Mr. Curtis, if you please." MacIntyre craned his white eyebrows dramatically. "And if there's nothing else . . ." He snapped his fingers loudly. Behind him at once, the door swung open. Orderlies filed into the room bearing trays with bottles of champagne and shallow crystal glasses. The labels of the bottles read, *Perrier Jouet, Reservée pour les officers*.

A contented murmur rose and fell back like the airy liquid. When each man had a glass and the orderlies had withdrawn, the colonel stood, and then the officers followed suit. Each one could look at the others and feel cheered, for they were a group of striking men, intelligent, grimly determined, having the hard-willed self-possession that the well-bred bring to difficulty. Only Keefe, a bit portly, a bit short, awkward with his glass, seemed out of place.

"Gentlemen," MacIntyre intoned, elevating his glass liturgically, "I give you His Majesty the King."

"The King!"

Each sipped.

Major Bourk, with a nod toward the C.O., said, "To the Fourth Connaught."

"The Fourth Connaught!"

Sips again.

It was Douglas who caught the colonel's eye then, its implicit permission. "And here's to a death . . ."

What grim poppycock was this?

"... in Ireland!"

The men laughed and chorused, "Here! Here!" They drained their champagne.

The colonel, to their surprise, turned and flung his glass into the fireplace, and in a flurry of shattered crystal all the officers did likewise, an elemental impulse.

Then a strange, chastening silence settled over them as they stared into the fireplace. The flames had swallowed the glass. What had seemed in one moment a primitive act of defiance had become in an instant an omen of obliteration.

"Parade in twenty minutes, gentlemen," MacIntyre said abruptly, and then he turned and led the others out.

Only Keefe made no move to go. Douglas hesitated. He faced him and then saw on the table in front of him Keefe's champagne glass, half full.

Keefe looked at Douglas sadly. "It's not my way." He forced a grin. "A tot of rum would do me, Captain."

After a moment in which neither knew what to say or do, Douglas nodded and turned to go. Keefe touched his sleeve. "Captain Tyrrell, if I may say so . . ."

Douglas faced him.

"... the C.O. was wrong about the rum. Right now is when the lads needed their drink, just like the gents here needed theirs. Tonight they'll be too numb to miss it. You were right to order it up."

"I appreciate that." Nevertheless, Douglas felt a rush of shame to be reminded of the rebuke. He had a schoolboy's urge to lower his eyes. Instead he let them drift toward the windows and the twilit orchard. He said noncommittally, "But the C.O. had it right too. I wanted the men to think well of me."

"Nothing wrong with that, Captain. Where in the King's Regs does it say they have to hate us?"

"Us, Mr. Keefe?" Douglas brought his gaze back and stared at his adjutant.

And finally Keefe smiled, nodding slowly. "Ain't that amazing, Captain?" he said broadly. "Us!"

Tyrrell picked up Keefe's champagne glass and handed it to him.

And in one motion Keefe downed the liquid and swiveled to throw the glass into the fireplace.

———

Colonel MacIntyre was distinguished as a senior British officer at that point in the war by the fact that he did not regard the men under his command—almost all of whom had been recruited in the last eight months—with contempt. It was one of the worst consequences of that hasty summoning of the civilian militia to replace the decimated professional army in the early months of 1915 that the commander, whether of social or military bias, were convinced that the new recruits were unreliable as individuals and therefore capable only of strictly controlled massed movements. This meant, for example, that in assaults against German positions across No Man's Land, Tommies were ordered to rigidly maintain their lines, steadily advancing in units with the uniform posture of the half-crouch. They were forbidden to take individual evasive action like running in zigzags or ducking and crawling. Consequently, by the hundreds of thousands, and over four years, during which this method of advance was never altered, they were cut down easily by German gunners.

Within months of this day MacIntyre's men had been sheep-herders in the rough hills of Connemara and turf diggers in the boglands around Lough Derg and strip farmers in the flat central plains along the Shannon. They'd been fishermen off Clifden and butchers' boys in Galway. And nearly to a man they'd had one experience: their flocks, their plots of bog, their tillage, their tar-sealed fishing boats, and their butcher shops had been too small to support them and their brothers and their parents *and* their children. When the army recruiters showed up in their towns and villages, they lined up to hear them and listened dutifully to patriotic flourishes that meant nothing. And at the proper time they signed their names and collected their bonuses for doing so. Those sums of cash had helped their wives to pay rents or their sisters to buy passages to the States or their fathers to get out from under debts; their enlistments had removed them at once from larders, tables, rooms, huts, and finally land that were overburdened with people. Stunned visitors were always asking why anyone would want to leave the beautiful, placid west of Ireland. And why especially for the made-in-England nightmare of duty in France. Neither those men nor their children nor their aging parents nor their desperate siblings could eat the scenery, that was why.

MacIntyre knew who those men were. He had no illusions about them. They were not idealists or patriots or servants of the Empire. But neither were they rogue adventurers or mercenaries. They were not cynics. They were loyal men who, in enlisting, had put themselves second to the people they loved, and *that* qualified them, in his opinion, to march with the best men in the British army. His task as their commander was to pull on that sense of loyalty, to stretch it a little, so that, having become soldiers out of a kind of love, they could now act as soldiers out of it too. It was his job to help them believe in the importance to *them* of what they were about to do or, if they were unlucky, what they were about to undergo. They were lined up before him in perfectly dressed rows, and the sight of that thousand men moved him, their rifles slung behind their right shoulders, their gear hanging from belts, gas helmets in pouches on their breasts, water bottles on their hips, all khaki. They were at attention, waiting for him to speak in the last light of the day.

"Men of the Fourth Connaught!" His deep resonant voice carried from where he stood on the top step of the *hôtel de ville* all across the square. "Tonight, at last, we move into the line. I cannot tell you precisely what awaits us there because I do not know. We may assume that the effort to regain the ridges to the north and south of Ypres continues. You know what ridges mean in warfare. They mean visibilitiy and vantage. They mean withering artillery fire on positions below. They mean impregnable defense. And ultimately, in the rules of war, ridges mean the difference between victory and defeat."

MacIntyre paused. The silence was absolute, the men immobile. Beyond them the sun had sunk below the level of the orchards outside the village, and the silhouetted trees with their clutching fingers stood in dressed rows of their own.

"The worst thing in war is to be asked to risk everything for an objective of no real value, to move the line a few yards, to divert the enemy's attention for a moment, to delay his advance an hour. And the best thing in war, conversely, is to be asked to participate in decisive action, to make the critical difference, to turn the tide. And that, with the help of God, will be our privilege tonight. We know this, lads. Our objective is a ridge! This is what this moment of the battle is about, a ridge! And I have seen what you can do, and I know that if the ridge the Allies need has not been taken by the time of our arrival at the line, then we will take it. And when we do, Ypres will be secure for the first time in the war, and our forces will at last be in the position to outflank the Germans and move against submarine bases on the coast. They will hear of us tomorrow in Berlin. And what will they say? They will say Ireland did this to us! And the farmers and fishermen and shopkeepers and woodcutters all over France will hear of us, and so will their wives and children and their old people. And what will they say? They will say Ireland did this *for* us! And, my lads, think of it! In London they will say it too! Ireland did this for us! Think of it!" MacIntyre's arms were raised above his head and his hands were in fists. The thought had never consciously struck him before, and the blood of his Anglo-Irish ancestors surged through him, a rare if unarticulated acknowledgment of what even his kind had suffered over the centuries at the hands of England. "In London they will say Ireland did this for us!"

The men felt it too. It would be for each of them, the forever slighted aristocrats and the downtrodden peasants, the best revenge of all, England saying Ireland did this for us!

MacIntyre lowered his arms and caught his breath, paused to let his eyes graze over those men, touching their eyes, savoring what bound them. He sensed their unity as never before, a veritable communion, if not of saints then of true soldiers, and that was better. He had never spoken to his charges with such feeling before. Men under his command had never looked at him with such fealty before. Their bond itself seemed ominous suddenly. He said more quietly, "And in Ireland they will know it was Connaught! Thinking of the pride it brings them, of the honor, of the unabashed admiration at last of London herself, Ireland will say it was Connaught did this for us. Connaught! For *our* children. For *our* families. For our villages and towns. For that smallest of all the small nations, our own dear island home." His hands shot up again and his voice broke out across the countryside. "Connaught! For Ireland! And for Britain! And for God! He stopped and for a long moment looked at his men. He wanted them to see the regard in which he held them. Then he said calmly, "To Whom we now should raise our voices."

And with that Colonel the Honorable Charles MacIntyre turned away. His chief of staff signaled the regimental sergeant major and at once there was the drum roll introducing the national anthem. These were lyrics many of those men had spent their boyhoods refusing to sing, but not now. As the bagpipes and drums played the familiar melody, the entire throng joined in.

"God save our gracious King," they sang. "Long live our noble King, God save the King." The music filled the square of Longue Croix and gently rolled out into the hills and valleys.

Douglas Tyrrell remembered standing as a child with his hand in his father's hand singing that great hymn—for the Queen, though. Those had been solemn occasions at Westminster Abbey or Buckingham Palace or on the Horse Parade at Whitehall. Sir Hugh was only a Member of Parliament at the time, and a controversial one at that, but it had seemed to Douglas that he was the Queen's own counselor. The pomp and stately music and rank display were proof to a child of his father's transcendent importance not only to him but to Victoria herself. That feeling of pride swelled in him again as he remembered his father's strong, full-throated voice rolling out those very words.

"Send him victorious, happy and glorious . . ."

Douglas Tyrrell's memory, as powerful as it was pure, quickened his love. With what strange happiness he stood there at the head of his company. All of his affections—for his father, for his children, for Pamela, for Jane, for his country—had become one affection. It was for these men who had been entrusted to his care and with whom he most heartily sang.

". . . long to reign over us, God save the King."

5

Dublin was a dream city to her, and as she walked across Saint Stephen's Green she thought the sky was never so blue in County Clare and early summer never so full of promise. The formal park, with its pebbled pathways and trimmed hedges, lawns bordered with gold of daffodils, seemed like an enchanted garden. Jane had been in the city for only two days but already she had walked everywhere, savoring every sight, from the great beech trees of Phoenix Park to Wellington Monument to the stately columned buildings of the Four Courts and the Custom House to the towering Gothic cathedral where Swift had preached and Handel played. As she crossed the graceful footbridge that arched over the crescent pond in the middle of the green, she stopped to lean on the railing, not knowing why until she found herself staring down into the water at her own reflection. It was as if she were challenging herself: What do you see?

She felt so different since coming here that she would not have been surprised to see another's face on her own shoulders there below in the water. But it was her face, the soft hair, the white skin, the familiar brown eyes into which she looked directly. What will the others see? This was to be her first morning at the Abbey. She was to meet the players, and the ticket seller was going to show her the accounts. In the days before, she'd walked by the theater half a dozen times, eyeing it furtively, as if planning to rob it. She hadn't dared go in— the hand-lettered sign on the marquee read "DEIRDRE OF THE SORROWS," REHEARSAL IN PROGRESS—because Lady Gregory said they wouldn't expect her until Monday. Today. *Deirdre of the Sorrows* was a play she'd never seen or read. Her impression was that Synge had never finished it and it was rarely performed. But what did she know about it? She pressed her brow between both her hands as if trying to push knowledge in.

At Cragside she had never stared into her own face like this, not even before the glass in her room. The impulse that led others to examine their own images before mirrors or dark windows took the opposite form in Jane. She would close her eyes, a deliberate exercise, and try to conjure her face, its most particular details, the line of her brow, the faint cloud of freckles across her cheeks and nose, the tiny blemish on her lip, the color of her pupils and the way minute veins crossed them. For all her concentration she never could satisfactorily picture her face, and that inability had taken on an irrational but powerful meaning—she existed for others but not for herself.

Now, as if released from perverse constraints that had made normal acts outrageous, she was enjoying the simple sight of herself. It was not a matter of mere vanity, as if the pleasure she was taking were in her prettiness. She had been afraid to gaze into mirrors and pools because she was never quite certain she would see anything there.

But she now thought, Here I am. And, Here I am in Dublin.

Suddenly her face was obliterated, and for an instant Jane felt the shock of an assault, the pain of having been clubbed. Her happy mood vanished and, indeed, an overwhelming despair invaded her even as she consciously grasped that the shattering was of her mere reflection, not her face. Some object had plunged through the water just there. But her feeling of despair only intensified as the distorted, undulating water calmed itself and her image appeared once again intact, whole. She saw the fright in her face. As easily as that could her fragile new happiness be lost, as easily as that could she be.

Then she saw, also reflected in the water, craning from the footbridge as she herself was, the image of a man. At first she thought it was her father. The despair she felt was in actuality remorse over what she'd done to him. How could she have left him? Hadn't that question been stalking her? The novelty of the city, of her rooms in the Gregory house in Merrion Square, of her freedom, had kept her guilt at bay. And now her father had come to take her home.

No, ridiculous thought. And as for the man, the merest glance dispelled her fantasy, for wasn't he wearing the soft tweed cap one saw everywhere in Ireland, but never, perhaps because of that, on Sir Hugh Tyrrell's head?

She looked directly at him, though in the water. And he seemed to be looking back at her. Reflected like that it was impossible to discern his features distinctly, to guess at his age, but his shirt was open at his throat and he had a full beard the color of fire. He was a large man. He raised a hand to wave at her.

But no, he was not waving—he was throwing something.

A stone. It struck her on the cheek, her cheek's reflection, and once again her image collapsed in the concentric chaos of the splash. That easily could she be lost. For a moment she hated him.

When the water smoothed out this time, the man was gone. Jane straightened and knew at once he was approaching her.

"I'm sorry," he said.

She turned slightly, saw him reaching for his cap. He was not an old man, but his beard prevented her from seeing him as young. His coat was shabby and he looked like a laborer.

"I didn't realize . . ." He removed his cap, revealing hair as wild and red as his beard.

His voice seemed disembodied to Jane, as if his words, like his face in the water, came to her by some reflection. But that was a result of her emotion. She felt panic that she might have to speak to him. Was he daring to speak to her? She abruptly swiveled on her heel and walked away. She did not look back once as she crossed out of Saint Stephen's Green and into the street. She determined to reclaim her mood, and she began by putting the rude stranger out of her mind.

———

Dublin's day was just beginning and so hers could begin again. Merchants and shopgirls were opening their stores. Grocers were setting out their fruit, and tea ladies were arranging cakes in windows. Coaches behind plumed horses vied with chugging automobiles and two-wheeled handcarts in the clogged inter-sections. Claxons whined and drivers shouted, but to no effect. Jane's flight had become merely the determined stride of an urban walker, and she wondered that anyone would prefer a stalled vehicle to moving by foot through the glorious city. Soon she was crossing between the gracefully arched entrance of Trinity College and the austere mammoth Royal Bank of Ireland, with its curving Greek portico and soot-blackened columns. Her father had pointed that building out to her once, saying that it had been built as an Irish house of parliament and that Parnell had intended to return it to its proper use when Home Rule was won.

But the thought of her father stopped her. She stood on the corner of College Green, traffic whirling past, carriages and autocars, but also clanging electric trams whose wheels screeched with the curve of the crescent street. She pictured a tall man in a dark frock coat walking with a girl of eleven or twelve, her hand in his. It was there, in front of that building, that he'd first begun explaining about Charles Parnell. She remembered the thrill of the realization that her staid, dignified father was revealing himself to her. Much later, when he explained more frankly that Parnell had been identified in a divorce court as an adulterer, he told her that Dublin mobs had jeered him by waving female undergarments while cursing Kitty O'Shea.

Dublin mobs, she thought with a shudder, looking at the throng about her, somber people on their way to work, not the type to jeer. But jeer they had. Dublin mobs were a figment of hers, what bogeymen were to other children. Dublin mobs— she grasped this much at an early age—had utterly destroyed her father's hero and in some part her father too. A fresh wave of her anxiety rose and broke in her. What was she doing here? Now it wasn't only remorse she felt, but also loneliness.

She crossed the Liffey into the northern half of the city, where, at Nelson's pillar, the electric streetcars from several lines converged. Sackville Street, leading away from Carlisle Bridge, was a bustling thoroughfare with the great General Post Office, the Metropole Hotel, where she'd stayed with her father, and the stores she had so loved to browse in. But when she turned off Sackville Street the atmosphere changed at once. There were no fine houses in this part of Dublin. She turned another corner and left the sunlight behind, and the soot-darkened bricks of the run-down buildings loomed over her. This was a district of saloons, and it was alien to her. The odor of stale porter hung in the air. Dublin mobs, she thought again, and drunkenness.

It would not have been brought to the attention of someone like Jane except in terms of their disgusting behavior, but Dublin had one of the most desperate populations in the world. Three hundred thousand people lived in the city at the time, and more than half of them lived like animals. Twenty thousand families lived in one-room tenements, and the death rate, at twenty-eight per thousand, was the highest of any city in Europe. Worse even than Moscow, and Moscow was under the Czar.

Jane wouldn't have ventured off the main streets on this side of Dublin—what she thought of only as the wretched Catholic slums were just blocks away—but this was where the Abbey was.

In 1915 the Abbey Theatre was in a fallow period that came after its early heyday. John Millington Synge, whose six short plays written in eight shorter years, had quickly made the wildest dream of Yeats and Lady Gregory come true. Between 1902 and his death in 1909 Synge's art, which Joyce described as "more original than my own," had transformed English by infusing it with Irish rhythms; had transformed acting by giving players lines that, despite their beauty or because of it, were to be spoken rather than declaimed; had transformed, like Ibsen, the subject matter of serious drama by focusing on the lives of common flawed people. What Synge established at the Abbey survived his own death, Yeats's disenchantment with the theater a few years later, then a long spate of parochial, audience-pleasing efforts. Lady Gregory, more than anyone, knew the difference between Yeats's *The Countess Cathleen*, with which they began, or Synge's *Playboy of the Western World*, with which they'd touched the sky, and the plays, including her own, the Abbey had been doing recently. It depressed her that the audience didn't seem to notice. In fact, Dubliners preferred run-of-the-mill peasant dramas to the periodic revivals of the early masterpieces. What they loved was the Irishness of the plays they saw, and in their view Irishness was what qualified them as art. The great works of which the recent ones were banal imitations had Irishness too, of course, but always with an edge. *Cathleen* had Irish women selling their souls to the devil; *Playboy* had Irish men murdering their fathers. For that matter Yeats's *Cuchulain* had them murdering their sons. Irish propaganda this was not. Indeed, the great Abbey plays never fit in with prevailing pieties or politics, and that was why with shameful regularity the Dublin audiences made mobs of themselves and rioted. "No Irishwoman ever did it!" they cried in Stephen Daedalus's memory of one brouhaha. The same people who had waved women's underwear at Parnell went berserk when Synge dared refer to such an item on stage in *Playboy*. There is no record, however, that they ever objected to the performance of mediocrities.

In any case, Lady Gregory, like a parent administering medicine, forced the revivals on Dublin every year between new plays. She was going to keep those triumphant works alive however she could. When eventually the Abbey players began touring America, it was Synge's work she featured. Catholic congregations in New York, cousins to all those Dubliners, were told it would be mortal sin to attend, which may be why one who went in 1911 was an actor's son named Gene O'Neill, who later said Synge inspired him to try his own hand at writing plays.

If the writing wasn't always great, it stayed above the prevailing level of mustachioed-villain melodramas. Lady Gregory's commitment to the excellence of the acting company was unwavering. Her players were her chicks, and they knew better than anyone that her devotion to the Abbey was no abstract attachment to a memory or an ideal. It was as real as the festive barmbrack bread she brought up from Gort for every opening night. But there was the difference. In the early days Lady Gregory would not have ensconced herself in Coole Park while rehearsals ran, content to appear only for the opening. She would not have dispatched as her surrogate an inexperienced gentleman farmer's daughter who was too timid to look at herself in a pool of water.

The Abbey took its name from the street it was on; there is no record that those Protestant founders considered it ironic, but some Catholic objectors regarded the name of such an irreverent enterprise as one more impiety. Yeats and Lady Gregory had first called their theater the Irish National, emphasis on national, and it shocked them when the nationalists who were as opposed to complexity as the clergy were took offense at their renditions too. A converted hall that had also once served as the city morgue, the Abbey was small for a theater, made of drab gray stone, its façade distinguished only by a tacked-on art nouveau canopy. This was the site of such magnificent controversy? It was hard to believe.

Yet however unimposing it was, Jane Tyrrell approached the theater feeling awed, and not only because of its already luminous history. Because of her early trips to Dublin with her father, she associated the landmarks of that city with her attachment to him, none more so than the Abbey. After her mother died, that became even more the case. Excursions across Ireland to see Lady Gregory's plays, particularly when they were controversial and needed support, became a way of shaking the loneliness they both felt at Cragside but never referred to. As Jane grew older she took increased pleasure in those forays; she loved attending the theater as her father's lady. When Douglas married Pamela and brought her to live at Cragside, Jane's special intimacy with her father broke. It was a temporary intimacy anyway, impossible to sustain once she'd become a woman, as she'd only realized when Douglas and Pamela had gone away. So now the Abbey, before which she stood, embodied both the magical bond she'd once had with her father and also, since it was what enabled her to leave him, the abolition of it. That was why awe that had nothing to do with Yeats or Synge nearly choked her.

She was afraid the door would be locked, but it opened easily. The foyer was dark and she hesitated, but then went in, leaving the door ajar behind her. It was a simple but dignified lobby, with square-tiled flooring and handsome walnut-paneled walls. Portraits of actors hung above the wainscoting; she recognized them as having been painted by Mr. Yeats's father, whose work was everywhere at Coole Park. Directly opposite the door were a pair of grilled ticket windows, and to the left was a broad staircase going up to the theater proper. From that elevated doorway she heard voices and saw the faint glow of a light. With relief she realized the actors were there, at work already.

She turned to pull the street door closed, and as she did her eye was caught by a figure crossing from the opposite sidewalk toward the theater, toward her. His red beard and the wild hair ill-kempt beneath his cap were what she recognized. Involuntarily her hand went to her face as if to be sure it didn't disappear again. He had followed her—she saw this with a gasp of fear—all the way from Stephen's Green.

She pulled the door firmly shut, tried for a moment to lock it but couldn't, then turned and ran across the darkened foyer to the stairs. Stumbling once, she went up quickly and through the doorway into, not the theater proper as she expected, but the balcony above it.

The auditorium, including the balcony, held chairs for fewer than five hundred people, but in the darkness it seemed vast. Only the stage was lit. It was framed by rich red velvet curtains, pulled back by sashes, which contrasted sharply with the stark washed-out white emptiness of the playing space itself. There three men were pulling together chairs of the straight-backed kitchen variety. Two of them were laughing loudly. "Move your arse, Joe," one of them cried, the punchline of a joke? The third stood apart somewhat. It was to this latter that Jane's eyes went. Something about him so struck her that she forgot for a moment about her red-bearded pursuer. The actor was dressed like the others, in shirt and trousers, but his rich black hair was longer, covering his ears. Even under the harsh unflattering light, his face, delicate and pale, seemed almost beautiful, like a boy's. When he walked to the forward edge of the stage to peer out into the auditorium, hooding his brow, his movement had such rare dramatic quality that Jane thought for a moment he was enacting a scene, and then that they all were. But no, it was real. Their action was informal, natural, unrehearsed. "Give me the bloody chair, Joe!" the first man yelped, tugging at a chair, slapping his leg with laughter. The downstage actor, peering intently, was looking for her, Jane decided, and she almost spoke. But then the actor spoke instead. "Time enough," he said and turned to the others. "Where the hell is Curry?"

The actor, trousers and all, Jane realized then, was a girl. Her voice, clear, sharp, and feminine, had effected such an unexpected reversal in Jane's perception that she revised her opinion; it must be a play. The actress' clothing and short hair—the very hair that had seemed long before—were exotic now, highly theatrical. Even for the most difficult chores of dairy farming Jane had never worn trousers, and all at once she couldn't imagine why not.

"We'll start without him," one of the men said.

But before anyone moved, the loud bang of a door slamming back against a wall filled the theater. The sound had come from the entrance just below the place in the balcony where Jane was standing. Before its reverberation had quite faded a voice, resonant and strong, bellowed, *"Haec Dies quam fecit Dominus!"* This is the day the Lord has made . . ." He was walking down the side aisle toward the stage when he came into view, the red-haired man, arms outstretched, cap in one hand, folded newspaper in the other. ". . . Let us be glad and rejoice in it."

"It's about blooming time, Dan," one of the men said.

He leapt up onto the stage and embraced each of the men, saying each time with solemn self-mockery, *"Pax vobiscum,"* bringing to the actors' faces broad forgiving smiles. Then he turned to the girl, with arms outstretched.

But she waved him off. "Never mind, Curry."

Undaunted, he dropped to one knee before her. *"Mea culpa, mea culpa . . ."* He slapped his breast so hard that the sound carried to the balcony. ". . . *mea maxima culpa!"* He hit himself again and fell over, lying at her feet in a lifeless heap.

Despite herself, the actress laughed. "You take the biscuit, Curry." And she started to step around him.

But he grabbed her ankle and made as if to bite. "Biscuit! It's the tart I want!"

"Let's do this, Dan." One of the men spoke with abrupt authority. "You'd better know your lines today." He hopped off the stage and from a seat in the front row picked up a script. "Act one, beginning from Ardan's exit. Deirdre and Naisi are left alone." The director began to read from the script. "Deirdre is royally dressed and very beautiful—"

But Curry, on his feet now, held up his hands and announced to the dark house, "But wait! You haven't let me apologize!"

"Dan . . ."

He looked down at the director. "Where is she?"

Curry asked this with such a shift in tone, from the stage-boisterous to the real, that despite himself the director said, "Who?"

"Our visitor." Curry's eyes were searching the seats. Jane,

to be smaller, sat in the nearest chair, afraid he would see her. "The girl who came in before me."

"No one came in . . ."

"I followed her. I couldn't believe it when she came here. I was going to apologize." He looked out at the darkened house again and said in a loud voice, "I didn't see where the stones were landing until it was too late." Jane was afraid to move. She knew he hadn't seen her sitting there.

Finally, after long moments staring out, he turned back to the stage. While Curry shrugged off his coat, the other actor leapt down to sit with the director, leaving only Curry and the actress on the stage.

Curry suddenly swept his arm up toward the balcony, and Jane thought he'd seen her after all. But when he spoke, his voice was different, wholly lacking any hint of the smart aleck, laying bare a seriousness she had not until then suspected he was capable of. "The stars are out, Deirdre, and let you come with me quickly, for it is the stars will be our lamps many nights and we abroad in Alban, and taking our journeys among the little islands in the sea."

"Dan . . ." The director waited for Curry to look at him. "I said from where Ardan exits. It's not your line. It's Nora's. Please, friends, be attentive. Take it in half-time. I want you to listen to what you are saying."

Nora sat in one of the chairs and after a moment's silence raised her hand to Curry. "Come to this stool, Naisi. If it's low itself, the High King would sooner be on it this night than on the throne of Emain Macha."

Sitting by her, he said, "You are Fedlimid's daughter that Conchubar has walled up from the men of Ulster."

Jane sat forward in her seat in the balcony, forgetting to make herself small. She remembered the old legend: Deirdre, the king who wanted her, and the man she loved. She listened and watched intently and soon forgot that the red-bearded man was someone she'd been running from.

The girl in trousers, because of the way she sat in that simple kitchen chair and because of the haunting dignity with which she spoke, did seem like a young queen. She asked sadly, "Do many know what is foretold, that Deirdre will be the ruin of the Sons of Usna, and have a little grave by herself, and a story will be told forever?"

Her lover looked at her with a sadness that carried all across the empty theater, and Jane, recognizing it as a mark against which to measure her own sadness, forgot her own. She read nuances of sympathy in that bearded face—was it only his eyes that carried that meaning?—that she had never seen before. He said quietly, "It is a long while men have been talking of Deirdre, the child who had all gifts, and the beauty that has no equal; there are many know it, and there are kings would give a great price to be in my place this night and you grown to a queen."

———

It was midday before the rehearsal ended and before Jane came down from the balcony.

Several other actors had come in for various scenes, but they had not worked. The whole morning had been given to Deirdre and Naisi. Now the group stood putting on caps and sweaters. The director, still in his seat, was turning pages of the script, looking for a particular passage. Nora—Deirdre—was leaning over his shoulder. It was Dan Curry who saw Jane at the back of the auditorium and watched her walk down the sloping aisle. He was dumbfounded at her appearance now. Through the rehearsal he'd forgotten all about her.

"Good day," she said, approaching them. "I'm Jane Tyrrell . . ." The company fell silent.

". . . the new assistant."

Curry realized he had put her out of mind, thinking she was too beautiful to have been real. The new assistant? She carried herself like the lead actress in the company. She was wearing a long brown woolen skirt cinched at the waist by a broad leather belt, a plain white long-sleeved blouse open at the throat to display a gold locket. Setting off the face, a bare glimpse of which that morning had turned him into a moonstruck boy, were regal wisps of auburn hair that had come loose from their pin behind. Her eyes glistened, and that was what told him she'd been watching. Who could hear the tale of Deirdre and Naisi and not be moved? He put out his hand to welcome her. "Miss Augusta has finally answered our prayers."

Jane found it possible somehow to laugh lightly, turning him aside, "You pray to Lady Gregory?"

"Doesn't everyone?" Curry swept an arm toward the group. "There is no God but 'Gusta," he intoned. "And Willie is her prophet." The players hissed, Curry pretended to duck. "We're her non-profit."

Jane laughed despite herself and realized she would never be able to match the jovial banter of these actors. Would that matter? She put her hand out. "You're Dan Curry."

He took her hand, pleased. "You've heard of me?"

Instead of deflating him with the truth, which is what an actor would have done, she lied, nodding, but without an excess of flattery. "From Lady Gregory. She speaks so fondly of all of you."

They introduced themselves one at a time. Jane realized, as each one took her hand with genuine friendliness, what a fool she'd been to arrive afraid. These were young bright people, vital and happy in the way she hoped to be. And they seemed

to welcome her. Nora in particular impressed her. She had a
bohemian air that, to Jane's surprise, seemed natural and right.
After greeting her, Nora offered Jane a cigarette. Jane declined,
but only because she didn't want them to see that she hadn't
smoked before. It thrilled Jane to glimpse in them the person
she might herself become. In the meantime, and beginning at
once, she was determined to be of great use to them.

It was Curry who outmaneuvered the others to show her
around the theater. In the greenroom, the cramped but cozy
space a flight below the stage where the actors waited when they
weren't on, he said, "I meant it this morning when I apologized.
I know I gave you a fright at the footbridge in Stephen's Green."

Jane shrugged. "When you gave me a fright was at the door
of this theater." Jane laughed. "I thought you'd followed me."

"I had. I couldn't believe it when you came here. You might
have said something. We could have walked together. You
dawdled and made me late." She won't look at me, he thought.
Why won't she look at me?

The greenroom was furnished with couches and stuffed
chairs. It seemed suddenly an altogether too intimate place to
be with this man. His intensity was overwhelming and, as if he
consumed more of the small room's oxygen than proper, Jane
found herself short of breath. That in turn, because it seemed
girlish, embarrassed her and made her want to get away from
him. "And where is the office?" she asked with forced casualness. "That's where I'll be spending my time. I think Miss Cleary
might be wondering where I am."

"Behind the ticket windows. Follow me." But to get there
they had to go up onto the stage, and as he crossed it ahead of
her before that dark, vacant theater, he stopped suddenly, as if
despite himself. This was not his doing, but the muse's. Instantly
he became someone else, facing Jane with a purity of feeling:

"I see the trees naked and bare, and the moon shining. Little moon, little moon of Alban, it's lonesome you'll be this night and tomorrow night and long nights after, and you pacing the woods beyond Glen Laoi, looking every place for Deirdre and Naisi, the two lovers who slept so sweetly with each other."

Jane knew it was shameless of him, to recite such lines to her. Did he think the erotic implication would make her swoon? But in fact she was caught for a moment in the spell, not of Dan Curry's weaving, but the ancient one of those lovers. She had never stood in the middle of a lit stage before; it was to stand, once he led her into it, in a wholly other reality.

Curry sensed that Jane was affected, as he always was, by the stage itself, by the theater, by the primordial expectancy of the place, how it required from actors and, for that matter, audiences, things no one knew they had to give. He raised his arm in a broad sweep that took in everything, saying softly, "Yet it should be a lonesome thing to be in this place, and you born for great company."

To Jane's surprise she realized that, having heard Nora drilled in the lines that morning, she knew them herself now. Instinctively she answered, not altogether steadily, but more compellingly for that. "This night I have the best company in the whole world."

But Naisi turned away to say formally, "It is I who have the best company, for when you're queen in Emain you will have none to be your match or fellow."

"I will not be queen in Emain." She said it simply, definitively, the way Nora had.

He faced her abruptly, amazed. "Conchubar has made an oath you will surely."

"It is for that maybe I'm called Deirdre, the girl of many sorrows . . ." Jane stopped. How she wanted to go on, to say what that girl said, to give flesh to those extraordinary feelings, that miraculous decision, but she could not remember the lines. She could feel the spell melting away.

In a completely different voice than Naisi's, Curry prompted her. ". . . for it's a sweet life . . ."

Jane caught it at once. ". . . you and I could have, Naisi. It should be a sweet thing . . ." She stopped cold again.

And again he fed her. ". . . to have what is best . . ."

". . . to have what is best and richest, if it's for a short space only."

Naisi took her hands—Curry had taken Nora's hands—and said with distress, "And we've a short space only to be triumphant and brave!"

Jane had never before been looked at the way he was looking at her now. She felt as though her survival depended on not meeting his eyes with her own. It did not matter that it was artifice, that he was acting. In some way she was acting too, even as she shyly looked away. She had been acting since leaving Cragside, but if that was so, why did this moment seem more real—more full of threat, but also promise—than any moment of her life before? She took her hands back and said, "I found it very moving, watching you."

Her compliment, tribute to his art, Nora's and Synge's, broke the spell absolutely.

He stepped back from her awkwardly.

"You know the play?"

She shook her head and smiled. "But after this morning, I know the first act." She looked at him for a moment longer. He seemed to be blushing. She couldn't think what else to say, so she led the way across the stage. Gathering her skirt, she prepared to leap down, but he went ahead of her. From the floor, he reached and took her by the waist and swung her down. They parted pointedly and walked up the aisle not quite side by side. The lobby was deserted but brightly lit now. Voices could be heard coming from the office behind the ticket windows.

Curry felt that when she went into the office he would lose her again. He stopped her. "In the second act she kills herself rather than go off with the king, who killed her lover."

Jane looked at him blankly.

"She's a figure for Ireland, don't you see? *That's* why this play is so important. She would rather die than give herself to England."

Jane shook her head, shocked at this interpretation. "I don't know the play, but I know the story of Deirdre. Every girl in the west of Ireland knows it. She and her lover fled the king, yes. But Conchubar is based on Conor, king of Ulster, and where they fled was to Scotland. When her lover dies and Conor takes her, she kills herself because she hates life without her lover, even if it's in Ireland with an Irish king. It has nothing to do with England."

"You're being literal. Synge, thank God, was not. *Deirdre of the Sorrows* is about Ireland's rejection of England. Believe me, Jane, it is."

"One rejects England by killing oneself. Some rejection."

Curry shrugged. "That's Synge for you. All his plays are about the same thing. First you get free, then you die. But that's because he was dying when he wrote his plays."

Jane knew they couldn't stand in the lobby and continue this. She had to get into the office and meet the ticket seller and learn about her duties. But Curry clearly was going to go on as long as she let him. She was not oblivious of the fact of his attraction to her, nor was she indifferent to it. But she was far from knowing what to do about it. And equally far from knowing how to handle her attraction to him. The man was simply overwhelming.

Having decided that she had to get away from him, she made no move to do so. Instead she said, "What moved me was Deirdre and Naisi. I don't care about the larger meaning." Jane said this as if she was admitting something. And to herself she was. If she identified with the mythic figure of Deirdre, it was not in the obvious way—a girl who must for her own reason desert the beloved realm in which she was raised, no matter the consequences. Jane was not a dramatizing girl, but she had often walked along the cliff's edge at Cragside watching the sea crashing onto the rocks below and feeling the forlorn piquancy of her fate. In the Druid legend, Deirdre is doomed from birth to be alone, and nothing she does changes that.

Loneliness came as a great surprise in Jane's life; it came not with birth but womanhood. It was a new role, one written just for her—Cragside, her father, the loss of Douglas and Pamela, the few men of her own background whom she might have befriended gone to the war, a life of resigned but pleasant spin-sterhood—but she refused to play it. Deirdre may have been born to sorrow but Jane wasn't. No daggers by her own hand into her breast, thank you. She regarded her situation as unique, but in fact all over Europe, women of her generation were coming of age in a whole new way, because no matter how widely their circumstances varied otherwise, they all had one crucial fact in common: they were women without men. Most of them always would be. Their adjustments to that given, carried out instinctively, bravely, and often, by necessity, rebelliously, were beginning to accomplish the twentieth century sea change in the place of women in society. The irony was breathtaking: the liberation of that generation of women presupposed the obliteration of that generation of men.

So of course the story of the tragic lovers—Deirdre is the primordial European love story; "Tristan and Isolde" is based on

it—would be what moved Jane. That did not make her senti-
mental. Like women everywhere in Europe, she knew already,
though not consciously, that what had been forever the tragedy of pairs was now becoming the tragedy of an entire race.
That was larger meaning enough for her, however far she was
from being able to give expression to it. As for Dan Curry's
larger meaning, it seemed frankly trivial. Jane sensed that this
big red-bearded Catholic found the theme of Ireland in mate-
rial the way his peasant forebears found crosses in the trees and
apparitions in sunlight filtered through the clouds.

Jane turned away. Peasant forebears? What had just happened?
An unwilled visceral disdain for Curry gripped her. For Curry as
a Catholic, as a Gael, as the son of peasants. She felt ashamed. He
was looking at her the way he had when they'd stood together on
the stage, when she'd encouraged that way of looking by seem-
ing to return it. She had welcomed that emotional storming of
their differences. The thrill of their enactment had been wonderful. But that moment was artificial and it had passed. Now she
wished he would look away. She knew that she was blushing
and she knew that he would take that as yet another sign of her
being girlishly overwhelmed. But what she wanted was to get
away from him. This was a mistake. He had thrown stones into
her reflection and she had disappeared. She stood there, blood
in her skin, unable to move, like a frightened doe.

A long moment passed in which the only sound in the bright
lobby was of their breathing. Even the voices in the office had
been quelled.

As she feared, Curry had completely misunderstood her
silence and her obvious confusion, as she knew by the soft,
caressing tone of his voice when he said, "The only truth the
wave knows is that . . ." He paused meaningfully.

Jane forced herself to make his theatrical hesitation into her opportunity. She turned on him, feigning playfulness, pointing her finger at him. "Are you testing me?"

"What?"

"You want to see if I can finish the line. That's why you paused."

"Well, can you?"

She composed herself dramatically, then wryly imitated him, even to his Dublin accent. "The only truth the wave knows is that it's going to"—now she paused—"get all wet!"

"No, no, no! Going to break!"

When Jane smiled mischievously, Curry saw that he'd been had.

"You knew it," he said. He laughed, realizing he'd made a fool of himself. "Well, at least you've read *Playboy*. I'd begun to fear for your literacy."

"The only truth I know is that I'd better get into the office."

"But you can't." He almost touched her. "You haven't called me Dan."

"Do I know you that well?"

He opened his arms; no secrets.

Suddenly he seemed completely harmless. Jane felt herself relax. "Good-bye, Dan."

As if she had granted a rare wish, he folded his arms and bowed.

He was just an actor. She was foolish to let him put her in a state.

But when he straightened, he took her by surprise again, now by breaking into song. "Magnificent life," he sang, and began to dance happily about the lobby. He repeated the phrase. "Magnificent life . . ." He had a rich bass voice and he played each word out elaborately with great musical flare. He was a rough-hewn man, but now, instead of either her previous disdain or her fear of being overwhelmed, Jane felt awed by his large-spirited exuberance. The people she knew well were trim and self-possessed to the point of clenching compared to this. "Magnificent life . . ." again and again. Curry was the size of a longshoreman and carried himself like one, but at that moment he moved across the polished lobby floor with the lithe grace of a waltzing prince. "Magnificent life, the fruit . . ." She had thought him insensitive, but now remembered those moments on the stage, the ones she'd watched from the balcony and the ones she'd shared. As an actor and singer he possessed an elegance he had no right to. She had resolved to dismiss him because he was so unlike her. But what she saw in him now was a delicacy of character, a vulnerability, she thought, exactly like her own. That, not his studied charm, seemed irresistible.

". . . the fruit of some frenzy of the earth." He looked over his shoulder slyly and said deadpan, "I'm singing Synge." Then he danced, humming grandly, toward the door. At the last moment he turned and waved his cap at her, and then he was gone.

6

On Sackville Street a crowd had gathered around a stalled tram and Curry pushed closer to see. But the tram was draped with large-lettered posters and bunting, not the usual advertisements for Pears Soap or the Guinness Brewery. A large banner ringing the top, like a crown, read, IRISHMEN ENLIST TODAY! The tram wasn't stalled, in fact, but was positioned on a stretch of lesser-used track. Across the front of the car, below the headlight, were huge red letters reading, RECRUITING OFFICE. And on the side below the windows another banner read, FOR THE SMALL NATIONS AND FOR IRELAND, HOW CAN YOU SAY NO?

Dark-suited men were lined up, waiting their turn, and others, like Curry, had pushed in close to watch them file onto the tram to stand before the British soldiers for their interview. The observers were passive, almost sullen, but they looked on without jeering. What shocked Curry wasn't the recruiting— for weeks posters had been appearing all over Dublin saying, KITCHENER WANTS YOU—BAD TEETH NO BAR—or even the willingness of Irishmen to enlist. Many befuddled boyos had done so and many more would. What surprised Curry and, in a

way, offended him more, was the British appropriation of an
ordinary Dublin streetcar. Was nothing immune from their
impressment? It was a simple reminder, of course, that trollies,
belonging to the city, belonging to the county, belonging to
the nation, belonged like everything on that damn island first
and foremost to bloody England. His resentment bubbled, and
Curry suddenly thought, To hell with working on Naisi's lines;
and he turned, pushed back through to crowd to the sidewalk,
and went into Mc-Mahon's, a Sackville Street pub.

At first the darkness blinded him. The pub was jammed with
the last of the lunch crowd, and it took Curry a few moments
to make his way to the bar. "P.P.," he called, a Dublin joke, not
about urine but about parish priests, and the bartender served
him a pint of porter. He raised his glass to the man next to him.
"To the bloody fools outside," he said and drank thirstily.

His neighbor lifted his own glass, removing a blackthorn
pipe from his mouth to drink. Then he looked quizzically at
Curry. "Where's your patriotism, man?"

The man's sarcasm registered. He had a familiar face, with
its heavy nose, sensitive mouth, skin even paler than most Irishmen, thinning hair carefully combed, but Curry couldn't place
him. He guessed he was thirty-five, ten years older than he was
himself. The man chomped down on his pipestem again.

Curry concentrated on his pint, trying to shut out the feelings stirred up by the permanent British insult, but also by
the noise of the boisterous drinkers around him. Naturally the
tram—recruiting office outside was the subject of the heated
talk. Everyone in the pub had his opinion about it and everyone seemed determined to state it at one and the same time.
Curry closed his eyes. This wasn't what he needed, not at all.
He hadn't had five minutes to collect himself since leaving the
Abbey. He hadn't been affected like this by a girl in a long time

and he wanted to think about her, to hold her image in his mind, turning it this way and that, like a precious stone, eyeing facets, appraising, deciding, as it were, whether to cut or polish.

But wasn't that a pompous, self-aggrandizing metaphor? Curry's rejection of it cost him his ability to remember Jane Tyrrell with any precision. He'd loved the way the wisps of her otherwise tightly pinned hair framed her face, but now he couldn't quite conjure the face itself. But if he fancied himself a jeweler, that was as it should be. The thought of holding her up to the light embarrassed him. Was that lithe, lovely girl only an object to be examined? And anyway, was he even remotely a connoisseur? On the contrary, like most of his kind when it came to women, he was a man without much to admit to. Furtive encounters with Tyrone Street prostitutes—they were naked under their coats so no time was lost fumbling with clothes—only compounded a fellow's insecurities with what one soon came to think of as the other women, as the normal women, or, in good Irish fashion, as the good women, the ones with clothes. But Jane, he sensed, fitted neither category, and that, perhaps, was why she fascinated him.

But wasn't he an actor and a rakish one at that? In his year at the Abbey and, before that, as a member of the drama club at the university, where he'd gone after quitting the Catholic seminary in Maynooth, Curry's reserve had evaporated in every aspect except one. His ill-chosen and unhappy stint in training for the priesthood had brought him to the threshold of manhood even more confused about the female than other Irish boys. Where the others threw sullenness or impassivity over their confusion, he threw the cloak of his great personality. With women, particularly the lovelies who were actresses, he played the role of the Gaelic extrovert and it never failed to charm them, but only to a point—the point at which, as if by prior agreement, they always withdrew from one another. Nora Guinan, for example, the actress playing Deirdre. His passionate flirtation with her for a few months early in the year had been wonderfully circumscribed by the fact of her marriage. The truth was that big Dan Curry, though he could not admit it—hell, he could hardly believe it!—was afraid of women. He thought it was because he'd been stunted in the seminary, but he was just like most other men of his class and background. If chastity didn't stunt them, poverty or obedience did. Ireland itself was their seminary.

Curry knew all of this, of course. And that was why it horrified and humiliated him that, despite the public and personal triumph of his success at the Abbey—he was a professional actor, by God!—and despite his own steadfast refusal to accept it as a spoiled priest's inevitable lot, he had not overcome this one unreferred-to but monumental inhibition. When he'd quit the seminary he'd adopted the pose of the gregarious but also mysterious, even ascetic loner. At twenty that had had its charm. But at twenty-five he was just another Irish bachelor waiting for Ma to die before taking up with someone else.

He looked around the pub: a roomful of them! Even the married ones were bachelors! Curry had to stifle a sudden repugnance for the coarse, argumentative, brew-swilling men. Men like him.

Someone yelled in the heat of an exchange, "They'll give us our nation six feet at a time!"

Curry turned to the fellow next to him. "But they'll still want their rent."

A bantam Irishman leapt up onto a chair and sang, "Full steam ahead John Redmond said / that everything was well, chum; / Home Rule will come when we are dead / and buried out in Belgium."

The drinkers cheered, and so the little man sang it again.

The man with the blackthorn pipe looked around at them, saying quietly to Curry, "We either stand in line to join their army or we stand on chairs to sing drunken songs against them. How King George must shiver at the thought of us."

The man's eyes met Curry's, and their weighty sobriety, in that context, prompted Curry to ask, almost despite himself— why should he take Ireland's bondage seriously when the others didn't?—"What else are we to do?"

The man answered with a long stare. When at last he spoke, his words were like a footnote to what his expression had conveyed. "Stop playacting."

"What?" Curry felt defensive at once. He hadn't expected to have his profession attacked.

"We must stop playacting. It's become our national pastime. Redmond with his Irish regiments in the King's army plays the role of an English lackey so they'll give him Home Rule as his reward. Carson with his Orange bullyboys plays the role of the snarling villain who keeps the maid of Ulster tied to the tracks. James Connolly has his Irish Citizen's Army and a home-grown honest-to-God militant class struggle, but what the lads really want are those fancy Australian bush hats, Sam Browne belts, and trousers with stripes down the leg. Eoin MacNeill is the C-in-C of the Irish Volunteers and what is their duty? Why, begorra, to defend the shores of Ireland from foreign invasion!" He laughed bitterly but didn't stop. "And then there's Arthur Griffith and the Sinn Fein, who claim the name Ourselves Alone but want a dual monarchy like they have in Hungary. And there's Pádraic Pearse, who's he, then? Why, he's the unrepentant poet of the Irish Republican Brotherhood, bloody phantom revolutionaries, heard but never seen. And lo, Doug Hyde of the venerable Gaelic League still parading about in the native Irish kilt, blathering jibberish, and the GAA still handing out hurley sticks behind the nation's hedges. Oh, how they must quake at Dublin Castle! And never forget the Irish National Literary Society, which gives us the sacraments of our new religion, and its cathedral, the Abbey Theatre, where at least they have the grace to admit that all they do is *pretend* that the freedom of Ireland means a damn." The man stopped now, his eyes burning at Curry.

Curry's impulse was to slink away from him. Instead he said, "I'm with the Abbey."

The man nodded. "You're Daniel Curry."

Ordinarily such recognition would have flattered the actor, but in that context it made him realize that the man had a purpose in speaking to him like this. "Who are you?"

"Pearse."

Hadn't he just mentioned Pearse? Pádraic Pearse of the IRB? But Curry recognized him then. The high forehead and pale skin of a schoolteacher. Yes, Pearse. In true Irish fashion his scathing contempt for the competing movements of Irish nationalism, as impotent as they were flamboyant, was self-contempt. Pearse's writing appeared regularly in *Irish Freedom*.

Curry deflected the awkwardness he felt with an easy but pointed comment. "I must say, Mr. Pearse, you do spread the blame around fairly, including yourself, I mean."

Pearse was staring out of the pub window toward the tram-recruiting office, toward the line of men waiting to sign up. He shook his head. "I don't blame them. Their children are ill-fed. Black tea and dry bread are what they feed their families. They'll sign the paper in the streetcar there, and at once their kippers are on the royal payroll and they'll go home tonight with milk and butter. With luck, they'll die in France and their families will get the pension and have milk and butter for as long as

Ireland is part of England." Pearse laughed and raised his drink, gesturing around the pub. "A damn long time, if these blokes have anything to say about it. These are the ones I blame." He let his eyes drift back to Curry while he drank. Then he wiped his mouth with his hand. "But you're right. What's the point of blame? Aren't the priests always telling us it's hopeless? And if it's hopeless, then we sin if we do something real about it. It's a perfect system when Dublin Castle joins hands with the Pro-Cathedral."

"The priests have never gotten over Wolfe Tone's thinking well of the French Revolution."

Pearse raised an eyebrow at Curry. "They taught you that at Maynooth?"

Curry channeled his surprise that this stranger should know such a thing about him into a show of looking around for an invisible prompter. "Mr. Pearse, do I take it you've been talking to my mother?"

Pearse smiled thinly. "I'm sorry if you think me overpersonal. It's true that I've made an inquiry or two about you. But not of your mother."

"My mother would tell you what a disgrace I am to her, for having quit Maynooth. She never forgave me."

Pearse shrugged. "We're all in that boat, boyo. We were all born to be priests. But that's all right. Our mothers were born to be disappointed."

Curry laughed and felt consoled.

Pearse said, "The difference between you and most of the rest of us is that you had a moment of selflessness. You were capable of handing yourself over to an ideal. I understand why eventually you didn't want the priesthood, but whatever happened to that original selfless impulse?" He waited for an answer. When there was none, he said, "You're a large-hearted man, Mr. Curry. You'd have made a good priest. You've a way of kindling fervor in your audience. Fervor not for God, but for the cause of Ireland. You were magnificent in *The Deliverer.*"

Curry searched his face for a sign of sarcasm, but saw none. The play was Lady Gregory's great work about Parnell. "Thank you. That's an example of what playacting, as you call it, can do for the cause."

"But only sensitive souls ever see it, five hundred at a time. Who attends the Abbey but the likes of me?" He gestured toward the recruiting tram. "Not those fellows out there. That's the fervor that needs kindling, and I don't mean for wee Belgium. What's the point of a priest preaching only to the choir?"

Curry lowered his eyes. "I'm not a priest."

Pearse stared at him, reading the depths of his feelings. Then he said quietly, "But you do care for Ireland."

"Indeed I do." He raised his face to meet Pearse's eyes.

Pearse lifted a finger to the bartender. When he'd brought two more glasses, Pearse clicked his own against Curry's. "When I watch you on stage you make me lay aside my awful inbred cynicism. I'm so weary of thinking ill of my fellows. Yet I never think ill of you. I saw you in *John Bull* and *Riders to the Sea* as well. And I confess that each time I began by thinking, Here is more talk, talk, nothing but talk. Sometimes I think Ireland will float away on talk, like one of those French balloons. Listen to them."

He stopped long enough to let the pub noise swell. The drinkers and smokers were going to do this and that to the bloody English. They were going to bring a halt, by God, to the obscene blasphemy of British recruitment outside these very doors. But first they'd have another nip.

"But your talk, Mr. Curry, won me. What was your fellow's name in *John Bull?*"

"Keegan."

"Ah, Keegan. Right. As he put it, our Ireland is the dream of a madness. But it's the only dream there is for the likes of us. You helped *me* to take it up again. You kindled *my* fervor. So I'm wrong, aren't I, about the choir? I said, watching you, This man believes it! This man lives it! You convinced me, Mr. Curry. Or was it only that you fooled me?" Pearse faced Curry aggressively. "Is it more than talk to you? I have to remind myself that by profession you're a man who seems to be what he's not. What kind of profession is that, sir? Forgive my asking such a question. But you see, I think the Lord sent you in here today, to sit by me, so that I might put it to you. That question and this: can't you do more for the cause you claim to worship than make the Anglo-Irish gentry squirm with guilt while their ladies bathe in an ocean of warm feelings for you?"

"I think what I do is more than that."

Pearse shrugged.

"What are you saying, Mr. Pearse? I should join the IRB? The phantom revolution?"

"The IRB isn't run by Protestants."

"What has that to do with it?"

Pearse shook his head, as if it was too fundamental to explain. But he said, "You are their servant. You're a tenant on their estate. Don't you see that?"

"You said yourself that—"

"I said you kindle fervor, aye. In the plays of all those Prods. But Shaw, Yeats, Synge, and Lady Gregory are like their cousin John Redmond. They think *they* are the heirs to England, not us. They want the King out, of course. They want the Irish Parliament, true. But whose parliament do you think it will be?"

"Ireland's, Mr. Pearse. Ireland's."

"But Ireland is Catholic. You're a Maynooth man. You know that."

"Yes, I do. But I'm an Abbey man now, and I've seen that Protestants can love Ireland as dearly as we do."

"Which is why we make alliances with them. But we mustn't forget what our purpose is. To the Protestants Ireland is a vast estate, rolling hills, lush with grass for grazing their horses in. But to us Ireland is the hovel and the slum in which our people starve. Is it more than talk to you? Begob and begee and the divil for Inglind. Erin go brah and Ireland forever. But for whom? Forgive me, Mr. Curry. It's my obligation to put the question as directly as I can."

"I don't know what you're asking."

"What can you do for us?"

"Besides wear a stripe down my trousers?" He shrugged. "I'm in costume all the time as it is."

Pearse shook his head. "Don't misunderstand me. We let the boyos playact militia because there'll come a time when they leave the theater for the streets."

Curry looked around. "I think your problem is getting them out of the pub, Mr. Pearse. Not the theater."

But just then, as it happened, a shabby small man, clearly drunk, began shouting while making his way to the door, "To hell with Belgium! To hell with John Redmond! To hell with bloody King George!" The others opened an aisle before him and began to cheer him on. He banged against the door, and the glass rattled as it bounced open. He stumbled out into the street, staggered while his eyes adjusted to the blinding glare of the afternoon, then righted himself. When he straightened to his full height and puffed his chest out, the evident contrast between the fierce image he had of himself at that moment and the pathetic figure he actually cut was heartbreaking. He strode forward, only to stumble at the curb. Even on the street, men made way for him, and he kept up his shouting—"To hell with small nations!"—as he approached the recruiting tram.

Pearse and Curry moved to the window with the others,

and the crowded pub grew silent. Everyone craned to see what would happen.

As the drunk drew closer to the tram, three large, helmeted policemen appeared—two from beside the streetcar, one from inside it—to block his way. They held their heavy batons menacingly. But the drunk ceased neither his provocative ranting nor his unsteady march toward the makeshift recruiting office.

Curry said, "Christ, they'll murder him." He turned to Pearse. "We can't let him do this."

But Pearse, a man to whom any manifestation of England's oppression was welcome, did not take his eyes from the scene.

Curry pushed away from the window, through the men by the door, and out into the street. The crowd had filled in behind the drunken outrager and Curry had to shove mightily to get through them. They had become relatively quiet too. "To hell with the fucking King and Queen and all the fucking princes too!"

Curry was only feet behind him when the drunk arrived at the tram. The police had not come to meet him, and they didn't strike at once. The man surprised them by veering at the last minute toward the banner beside the door. He seized it—HOW CAN YOU SAY NO?—and ripped it from the streetcar.

Then the police, joined by two others, fell upon him. All five bluecoats clubbed the drunk, who went down like a scythed sapling. The police continued to strike him.

The sounds of their clubs against the man's head and body carried loudly. The crowd had shrunk back in stunned silence.

Curry pushed into the open circle. "Stop! Stop! He meant no harm!" But a policeman swung around at him and lunged with his baton, catching him as he came forward full in the stomach. As Curry fell, another policeman clipped him on the side of the head, above his ear, not squarely. He hit the pavement hard and covered his head with his arms against more blows.

The bloodied drunk had sobered fast, and the distraction provided by Curry gave him the seconds he needed to roll under the stationary streetcar, across the tracks, and out the other side, where he disappeared into the throng.

The police let up on Curry when they saw the first culprit escaping, and he too rolled away. The bystanders had not come to his assistance, but now they closed around him as they retreated. "Good man yourself!" a voice cried. "Shame on them!" another yelled, and then a third one, brave after the fact, cried, "Fuck England!" Curry got unsteadily to his feet, then stumbled and fell.

But now someone caught him.

Blood was streaming from the cut above his ear, matting his beard. In his red hair the blood seemed black. The man who'd caught him applied his handkerchief to the wound. Curry looked up at him. It was Pádraic Pearse.

"Are you all right?"

Curry touched his head and winced. He took Pearse's handkerchief and began to do his own nursing. "You're like all the others, Pearse. A race of spectators. You know what an Irish hero is? The fellow that stands by with bandages."

"It's not heroics we need, Dan. That's not what I was asking for. Come along . . ." Pearse led Curry away from the crowd. Half a block away, in front of a horse's watering trough, was a wrought-iron bench. "Sit here," Pearse said. "I'll get something for that." He disappeared into an adjacent chemist's shop.

A few moments later he came out with iodine, sterile cotton, and tape. "Bandages, you say?" He smiled. The moroseness that had made him so bleak in the pub had evaporated, replaced by a cheerful agitation. He daubed Curry's wound, then closed it with the cotton and the tape. "This will sting when you take it off, but the thing now is to close it up and keep it clean."

Curry let him finish. "Thank you," he said. He felt better.

"You're a good man, Dan. And you've got the stuff. But you shouldn't waste your time running at them when they have the clubs."

"That's the definition of it, though, *n'est-ce pas?*"

"Not for long. Things are changing fast now. A few of us have decided across the lines of our separate movements that when the moment comes we'll act as one. There hasn't been an opportunity like this in seven hundred years and that is what unites us. You know as well as I do that if we Irish ever stopped fighting with one another, the fight with England would be over in the twinkling of an eye." Pearse winked. "It's a short time only, isn't that what Synge said?"

"In which to be triumphant and brave. Yes. John Millington Synge, the Anglo-Irish Protestant."

"A case in point, my friend. Because the opportunity I'm speaking of is given us by the war in Europe. England's misery is our bliss, but do you think your Anglo-Irish friends feel that? They're the ones leading the poor buggers down Sackville Street here into the British army. And if the poor ignorant bastards have a religious qualm at the last minute about swearing allegiance to a king who claims to be head of the Anglican Church, then the slick recruiting officer says it's a war for Belgium and France, a war for Catholic nations. Sign here in the name of the Father and of the Son and of the Holy Ghost."

"I've heard that said."

"And if your friend Synge was alive, he'd bemoan the war like all civilized people do, but we rejoice in it. The war makes all the difference. Don't you see? London is desperate. That's what recruiting offices in the trams of Dublin mean. London is up against it for the first time since William the Conqueror came across the Channel. Her boys are falling like wheat falls in autumn. And we say, the more the merrier. Am I ghoulish?

On this point, yes. As the going gets worse for England, it gets better for us."

Curry said nothing. He felt bent by the weight of the man's hatred. For once the rhetoric of nationalism seemed ugly, and that was how Curry knew that this talk, talk, talk was true.

"When the time comes, Dan, you could make a big difference. Men would follow you if you spoke to them from off that stage."

Curry couldn't look at him because it was true. He was a modest man, but he knew he had a gift. He'd watched squirming audiences freeze at his entrance and he'd heard the rhythm of their breathing alter because of the way he used his voice. When the passion of his own conviction joined, the way meaning joins with words, the passion of the great Irish speeches, his power to move and to convert and to inspire was greater even than the power of priests.

"I'm telling you, Dan. You should be one of us."

Curry heard Pearse's statement as pure command. There was recruitment, but this was conscription. The church he was called to serve was Ireland herself.

Most nights of his working life—"I cannot leave my brothers when it is I who have defied the King!"—he enacted the ritual rebellion. He knew how this was done. In Pádraic Pearse his own dear nation had touched his shoulder, and now it was his to say *Adsum*. He faced Pearse and nodded, deliberately and slowly, showing with his eyes that he understood what he was doing. "All right," he said—a modest bit of antirhetoric, just what the moment wanted.

———

Curry knew that she would have to cross the Liffey on the Carlisle Bridge, so he loitered there. As wide as it was long, this was the main span over the river, a graceful arched bridge with columned marble railings the perfect height for leaning on. The streetcar tracks neatly bisected it between lanes of carriage, cart, and automobile traffic, and the eye naturally followed the tracks down Sackville Street. The confiscated tram was just a block and a half away. Curry stared at it. From that vantage the crowd around the recruiting office seemed less mammoth. All up and down the boulevard, one of the grandest in Europe and in fact the widest, people were pointedly going about their business. The wheels of carriages and the hooves of horses clattered on the cobblestones. It seemed Dublin was determined to ignore the affront of the British recruitment. Well, for a few moments so could he.

He turned to face the river, and, like a corner boy, spit into it automatically. The muddy water failed to reflect the sharp blue of the sky. It was a rare afternoon for Dublin, warm and sunny. Such weather always filled him with a poignant nostalgia. By a trick of his memory the days of his childhood had always been sunny like this. A form of selective repression, no doubt, for he'd lived in squalor on the bleak, dead-end Henrietta Street just a few blocks north of this very river. His eleven brothers and sisters, his parents, and a wet-brained uncle had shared two rooms in a dilapidated tenement that had been built a hundred and fifty years before as the Church of Ireland's Archbishop's mansion. In Curry's day the former drawing rooms, parlors, dining hall, corridors, and even the former chapel housed three hundred souls who'd have thought themselves sinners had they known their home had been asperged by a Protestant divine. Good weather alone had rescued them from the stench and darkness of the place, and that was why Curry remembered his childhood days—a favorite game was chasing rats from lane to lane—as sunny.

Where was she?

He watched the figures of the people crossing the bridge, hoping to see a brown skirt, a white blouse, a dark shawl, a woman with graceful posture, long neck, confident walk, and no hat—Jane Tyrrell. He'd taken refuge from his anxiety in thoughts of her. He'd left it with Pearse that he would come to a meeting the next day. Before they'd parted, Pearse had made him solemnly swear an oath of secrecy, and that was when Curry had become afraid.

But there was no sign of her. He looked downriver again. From Carlisle Bridge, because the Liffey gently curved just there, he could see the Custom House. In that distance the waters of the river seemed tranquil and blue, and he could just make out the shimmering reflection of the stately Palladian building. Curry was not unmindful of the irony that Dublin's distinction as a city was the result of Anglo-Irish genius and enterprise, not Gaelic. Its magnificent public buildings, of which the Custom House was the masterpiece, were embodiments of Ascendancy virtues—restraint, symmetry, mannerist detail, devotion to classical themes, intellectual rigor. Only a primitive could be unmoved by their beauty, but an Irishman could still experience those places as alien, indeed had to, and in that case the perfection of such buildings as the one he was looking at— how the color of the dome, a robin's-egg blue, matched the sky today—only compounded the feeling that foreigners were choking him. Everywhere in Dublin the message was the same. The two great cathedrals, Christ Church and Saint Patrick's, were monuments of the Gothic genius that brilliant Irish monks had inspired throughout medieval Europe. The two soaring cathedrals, so exuberant in their worship of God, so enthused with what they wanted men to think of themselves, epitomized the high point of Catholicism, but the Protestants had made them their own, leaving the Catholics to squeeze into the drab, undistinguished Saint Mary's Pro-Cathedral—false Cathedral—in North Dublin. The Four Courts, designed by the same Englishman who built the Custom House, and the huge Phoenix Park obelisk named for Wellington, and Nelson's Column commemorating Trafalgar, the Bank of Ireland, the former Parliament, and Dublin Castle, the military headquarters, and the somber arches of exclusive Trinity College all cast cold shadows on the filthy streets and collapsing hovels that alone belonged to the vast population. The people cowered, never daring to consider the great buildings of Georgian Dublin as their own, much less to enter them. On those buildings was engraved a coat of arms, English lions joined with Irish harps, and inscribed, *Quis separabit?*, Who shall separate them? Curry thought of that seal, staring downriver at the Custom House, and he said to himself, We shall.

"Hello."

He turned quickly, surprised that his thoughts had left her and disappointed that he hadn't seen her coming.

"What is it with you and bridges?" Her smile was dazzling.

He started to answer, but the words wouldn't come. He was so pleased to take in her beauty again. His fantasy had done her an injustice. He shook his head. "What?" He adjusted his cap, to hide his bandage.

"In Stephen's Green this morning, that bridge."

"Was that only this morning?"

She joined him at the marble bridge railing, leaning on it with her elbows as he'd been doing, letting her happy eyes take in the sights along the river.

He studied her quite openly. The sleeves of her tight-wristed blouse fluttered in the breeze, and she pulled her shawl about her primly. Wisps of hair feathered her face, but she ignored them. He sensed she was aware of his staring. How could he make her understand all that was happening? And how could he explain that since he'd first seen her that morning it seemed that doors had opened inside of him, loosing a cavalcade of feelings the way sunny days had turned loose tenement children on the north side of Dublin.

Due north, that's what she had seized in him, so that the needle of his concentration, even after spinning wildly between Deirdre and Pádraic Pearse—the old fate of Ireland and the new—kept returning to her. That was why he'd stopped here to wait. What he had for bridges was her. Irrationally, he had been convinced that this woman had come in the morning to teach him what Naisi felt, and now he was convinced she had come to prepare him for his encounter with Pearse.

But she and Pearse were opposites. No, more than opposites. Curry suddenly shuddered with the recognition that Jane Tyrrell and Pádraic Pearse were enemies.

7

Already they were saying it was a war of inches, but after their notorious April gas attack the German inches had been adding up. They had succeeded through the month of May in pushing the Front three kilometers back toward Ypres, and every day threatened to bring the breakthrough. Whenever the British forces had stopped their drive, the Germans had come back at them again, determined to eliminate the salient that protruded well into German-held territory. The threat at Ypres to the Germans was that the British would be able to use that bulge in the trench line as a jumping-off place to attack the U-boat base at Ostend and even to control the other crucial North Sea ports. That was why, since the autumn, this point had loomed above all others, and why British commanders were willing to suffer losses indefinitely to hold it. The salient was their one advantage.

Every German push there was met head-on. But the first gas attack, which had so astounded and frightened the British, had given the Germans a momentum that was rare in that stalemate war. That momentum could still be felt when Douglas Tyrrell and his regiment joined the battered line of men who'd been trying for nearly two months to overcome it. By the middle of June the salient had been cut in half and the Germans had pressed to within two kilometers of Ypres.

At Poperinge the Fourth Connaught hooked up that night, as planned, with the rest of the Irish regiment. To the troops the rendezvous had seemed chaotic and disorganized. Rations had been haphazardly distributed and the order to move out had come even before the men had had tea. Even the Catholic mass that Lieutenant Keefe had proposed was canceled. The men had to stifle the feeling that after weeks of monotonous waiting, they were being thrown into the line hastily, with none of the measured grandeur Colonel MacIntyre's speeches had led them to expect. They were a part of a divisional force numbering more than fifteen thousand, and though they knew the division was moving against the ridges south of the town, they could hardly appreciate how little the real movement of such a group into battle itself resembles the graceful, swift flow of arrowed markers on the maps they all carried in their imaginations.

The northernmost tip of Messines Ridge, the part nearest Ypres, was designated Hill 60. The Germans held the hill and the Rangers were ordered into position immediately below it. As they approached in the darkness, they could have no sense of how it loomed above the valley, its sides running steeply up to a narrow pinnacle from which German artillery units had been freely operating. The hill had long since been denuded of trees, so that the men could see the awful flashing of the guns. But that seemed like fire in the sky, and since those guns were targeted on Ypres itself, they did not threaten them. In fact, by then those guns had nearly leveled the historic Flemish town, although not the deep, connecting cellars beneath it that still functioned as Second Army Headquarters. The German guns fired at will on the fixed British lines up and down the sector, and their artillery positions were well dug in, defended with heavy machine guns and fortified just below the crest of the hill, at the steepest part of the slope, with rolls of barbed wire.

Once soldiers dug in, the constant artillery turned them into a paralyzed mass of burrowing creatures, and the orders to attack the superior German positions that had been regularly issued in the previous weeks had been intended as much to ward off that paralysis as to preempt the German assaults. Waves of Tommies, Jocks, and Micks had been ordered up Hill 60 dozens of times in that period, and all had been thrown back. Between assaults, the bodies of the fallen had been scrupulously removed by night crews—out of respect, of course, but also to prevent the next wave of attackers from guessing what had been happening there. Soldiers will obey an order not to stop to help the wounded, but they won't dash across a carpet of their dead and dying comrades.

The trenches in which the Connaught Rangers were to take up their positions were immediately at the bottom of Hill 60, half circling it for nearly two miles. They were extremely vulnerable to rifle-fired grenades, mortar, and musketry from above, but they were in no danger from the heavy artillery because those guns, even if they weren't aimed at Ypres, could not have closed the angle of the hill. Still, the noise of their firing was so relentlessly terrifying that Tommies were relieved to be ordered out of the trenches even if it was to attack.

But the Irish soldiers' fear was at a pitch even before they got to the trenches, because a kilometer from the Front, less than an hour ago, they'd been ordered to don their black-snouted gas masks. They didn't know that theirs was the only regiment in the division to receive that order; neither were they told that the reason for it was not the expectation of a gas attack that night, but the fact that the Rangers were occupying a position that had been heavily gassed three days before, wiping out their predecessors in the line. The Germans could lob gas canisters down on them with impunity; but even if they didn't, the poison from three days before would linger in the trenches for at least two weeks, in the present rain-free conditions. But the pressure on Hill 60 had to be kept up.

The men knew none of this, of course. They knew only that in the most frightening hour of their lives, their fear and discomfort had been multiplied a hundredfold by having to wear the suffocating, foul-smelling face gear. In that pitch-black period before dawn they made an eerie sight: dark silhouettes against the sheet-lightning flashes of the guns, monstrously masked, crouching instinctively though to no purpose, moving one after the other along the Ypres-Comines Canal, which led directly to their position.

When the five thousand men of the Irish regiment had at last taken cover in their poisoned trenches, some of the men collapsed with relief as if a rest-easy order had been given. Some took their masks off and gulped at what they thought was fresh air. Those poor bastards screamed at once as the gas residue attacked their lungs. They desperately tried to replace their masks, but it was too late; they writhed in choking agony while their helpless comrades realized fully for the first time that their nightmare had begun. The officers went up and down the ranks, evacuating the gas casualties and enforcing discipline. Soon, just as the first light appeared in the east above the German lines, the British artillery barrage began, and now the worst noise wasn't of guns firing but of shells exploding from beyond the crest of the hill above the German position. Everyone knew that the order to go over would come within the hour.

———

Douglas Tyrrell watched a French priest, gas mask above his soutane, move along the line. The lip of the trench was only a foot above his head, but he felt no need to crouch. Each man knelt as the priest came to him. In their gas masks real talk was impossible, and they didn't share a language anyway, so Tyrrell wondered what kinds of confessions they could be. The priest seemed satisfied that they were real enough, because after a moment or two he absolved each man of his sins by waving his hand in the sign of the cross above the penitent soldier's bowed head. For once the mindless Catholic ritual, perhaps because in this form its mindlessness was too obvious to be denied, did not seem bizarre to Tyrrell. In fact, to his own surprise, he envied the men the consolation their religion gave them.

When Lieutenant Keefe touched his arm, Tyrrell turned to face him. Keefe spoke, but because of their masks, Tyrrell missed what he said. Keefe repeated himself in the strange hollow voice: "All in order, sir."

The men had properly assumed the passive, hunched position—ducking shells—that was the near-permanent posture of infantry on the forward line of the Western Front.

Tyrrell nodded, and his eyes drifted back to the priest, who, after ministering to another soldier, straightened and faced the officers. To Tyrrell's surprise Keefe at once crossed to him and fell to one knee. The priest bent to put his ear by Keefe's mouthpiece, and a moment later blessed him. Keefe pressed the priest's hands against his gas mask, and after a moment Tyrrell realized that Keefe was kissing them. Then the priest stood and faced Tyrrell expectantly. Tyrrell shook his head briskly and felt embarrassed as the priest approached him. It was unthinkable that he should kneel before this man, but also that he could possibly explain that he meant no disrespect. The French priest had probably never met a Protestant before and he probably didn't know that Ireland had plenty of them. Tyrrell put his hand out, surprising the priest. But then they shook vigorously and Tyrrell said in that otherworldly, amplified voice, *"Merci, mon père."* The priest bowed, then moved along the line.

Tyrrell looked at his watch: 0527. The barrage would lift at 0600, whistles would sound up and down the line, and they would go. He stretched himself up to his full height, then mounted the fire step to look up at the hill, which now, in that faint light, loomed several hundred feet above them. It was a gray mass with no surviving vegetation or other detail apparent, like a huge pile of slag from the coal fields or like a black pyramid, tomb of a king. The German artillery had stopped firing, its crews having presumably dropped into bunkers when the British shells began to land. At that point in the war British guns still threw, almost exclusively, shrapnel shells that were unrivaled at killing troops in the open but were useless against field fortifications. They wouldn't dent the pillbox gun emplacements but, in theory, shrapnel shells would obliterate the belts of barbed wire ringing them. That was what the Rangers, like all their predecessors, had been promised. The big guns cut the path for you, chums. Tommies had to believe it; how else could they throw themselves "toot sweet" across the fields at walls of barbed wire?

Despite the noise of the British shells exploding on the hill above him, Tyrrell was aware suddenly of the drumming hollow echo of his own gas helmet, like the "ocean" resounding in a conch shell, and it made him uneasy. Whatever feeling of security against the dreaded gas those masks gave them, they heightened the sense of disorientation, of being suspended in an unreal inhuman world where even one's mates were monsters. To ward off an unexpected wave of his own anxiety, Tyrrell moved down the line of his men, touching their arms and shoulders reassuringly. "Good luck, men," he said again and again. He was filled with admiration for them, their stoic patient courage. They stood along the crowded trench shoulder to shoulder, instinctively leaning against the forward wall, clutching their bayoneted rifles, resting their faces and heads, which were covered only with soft cloth hats. Until the order to stand-to was given, they would stay low like this, bridging the fire step or sitting on it. Tyrrell could see only a couple of dozen men at a stretch, for the trench bent sharply in a series of kinks in the line. He remembered the theory: such angles, per regulation, were to prevent an enemy force that succeeded in taking one part of the system from firing down the length of it.

The trench just here had been well house-kept, the walls had been lined with sandbags, and the parapet had been reinforced with timber. Duckboard flooring had been laid on top of the ubiquitous mud and water. Even when it hadn't rained, as now, the trench floors were always wet because the water table in the Flemish fields was high. Duckboards were a luxury, and the condition of flesh rot caused by their near-universal absence had already passed into the language as "trench foot." But Tyrrell knew little of that. In training at Grimsby the mock trenches had been sandbagged, neatly cut, and protected by well-constructed breastworks. In the reality of Belgium and France, most British trenches were squalid, ramshackle places because their occupants were always led to believe that the great offensive breakthrough was imminent and they would be moving east to new positions. On those rare occasions when they survived their movements east, overrunning German trenches, Tommies were amazed to discover clean, well-built timber-lined dugouts, domiciles the defenders had intended to occupy indefinitely. Tyrrell didn't know enough to take the exceptional condition of his own section of trench as an ominous sign; the men who'd built it and occupied it prior to the introduction of chlorine gas, had assumed they were going to be there a long time because the German fortification above them was invincible.

With an absurd regret, Douglas realized that, given the trench's poisoned state and the timing of their assault, he would not be able to organize the by-the-book routine that would have had his men on a proper cycle of front, reserve, and rest. The Western Front was known for stasis, but his regiment's experience since leaving Longue Croix was of constant movement. Bizarre though it might seem, he'd been encouraged to look forward to the trench routine. Officers of Tyrrell's rank were senior in the trenches, since field officers and staff stayed back on the GHQ line, and they took pride in maintaining conditions that kept their men safe and sharp, if rarely dry. However short their time was in it, this was Tyrrell's first trench, and the two hundred and fifty men stretched along the three hundred yards of it that formed his company's section were his now in a way they never were in training or in transit. Colonel MacIntyre and the other commanders who up to now had been the experts were suddenly the amateur observers miles to the rear. Tyrrell was the expert here or had better be. But alas, this trench, seat of his authority, was a bare stopping place. He checked his watch again; in half an hour they would be out of it, scrambling up that hill, and then each man would be his own expert.

At the end of his company line, he turned back the way he'd come. How he wished his men weren't wearing respirators. He longed to see their faces. Their goggled eyes followed him like animal eyes following a flame in the dark. At an intersection where a trench from the rear joined a frontline trench—in the argot, where a communication trench joined the fire trench—Tyrrell came upon the signals officer and with him Corporal O'Day. Instead of a rifle, O'Day carried a wooden box with air holes drilled in it: the pair of homing pigeons. Once the Tommies overran the German position on top of the hill, the marked birds would be released. Within minutes the pigeons' arrival at GHQ would announce the regiment's success, and reinforcements would be sent forward at once. Reinforcements were reserved for the purposes of securing victory, not of compounding losses in defeat and not of tilting the balance in a close fight either. Tyrrell clapped O'Day's shoulder. "Fly your pigeons well, Corporal." O'Day nodded but said nothing. Even through the mask Tyrrell could see that the lad's eyes were out of their sockets with fear.

Farther along he came upon a man hunched over the well-creased white page of a letter. They all carried letters like that. *My Darling Son.* The boy had it out now because, if his mother was near, what harm could come to him? It seemed to Tyrrell that those words were scrawled on the dawn-lit air above them all. My *Darling Son.* He carried no such letter himself, but, at that moment his personal thoughts overran the defenses he'd built against them to leap toward both his father and Timothy, whom he pictured as an infant curled like a loaf in his arm. It had been two years since his son was that size. Like turning the page of an album, he pictured his father holding his baby son on the bright lawn of Cragside. The boy wears a tiny cricket cap.

For an instant Tyrrell allowed himself to feel a quiet fatalism. He would not see them again, not Sir Hugh or Timothy, not Anne or Jane. He would not see—and this certitude cut more brutally still—Pamela. *My Darling Wife.* His lips moved around the words, soundlessly.

———

Pamela was sitting on the terraced lawn beside the trimmed hedges. Beyond were the shimmering bay and the curving hills. Her black hair framed her face, which glowed with happiness to be looking at him. Her legs, covered, were bent under her,

her body leaning upon her extended right arm. With her left hand she grasped the ankle on which she sat. She was relaxed, complacent in the repose of a weekend afternoon. On the grass of that very lawn, just beyond that very hedge, he had made love to her once. She had pretended to be scandalized, covering his mouth with her fingers, to silence him. Yet she had been the one to make noise, laughing. Now, sitting there, demure, in his mind, she was quiet. And suddenly Tyrrell thought she was too quiet. Then he realized he hadn't conjured a memory of his wife at all. She was sitting on the lawn beside the hedges not as she had in life—why couldn't he picture her beyond that hedge, her stockinged legs around his hips?—but as she had now for months in the photograph he carried. He panicked to think that his memory had taken second place to a mere reminder. But he told himself it didn't matter if his mind dulled so long as this feeling didn't. *My Darling Wife!* It was not a photograph he loved, it was she.

Tyrrell, the officer, should have told the man to put away his letter, but he left him alone.

———

He didn't realize he'd returned to his own position in the line until he came upon Keefe, who was on one knee, as he had been before the priest. Keefe was blocking the way. At first Tyrrell thought he was praying, and a qualm filled him. Of all people, Tyrrell was counting on Keefe to match him in maintaining the detached soldierly calm the other ranks needed to see in their officers.

"Keefe?"

Keefe turned and looked up, and only then did Tyrrell see that he was not praying, but rather adjusting his puttees.

Puttees? An officer's service dress did not include puttees, the woolen strips wound spirally around ankles and calves. Officers wore riding boots or leather leggings. But Keefe's leggings were lying next to him, discarded, and he was wrapping the second of his legs with cloth. Tyrrell had noticed that Keefe wore straight trousers instead of the trimly cut riding breeches he and his colleagues favored, but he'd assumed that was because Keefe hadn't the money to properly outfit himself. British officers were still paid as if they all had private incomes and many of the "temporary gentlemen" ran up such bills at military tailors in England that the tailors as a group were even more attentive to published casualty lists—and almost more appalled by the rate at which junior officers fell—than the officers' mothers were. Keefe, though, had no tendency toward sartorial flare and no physique for it; he hadn't run up bills at any tailor's. Now, when he stood, his trousers bloused at midcalf in the oafish manner of other ranks, and it was easy to see the Second Left as one of them.

"What are you doing?"

Keefe pointed at Tyrrell's knees and said, "The Germans tell their gunners to aim at the ones with thin legs. Our lads call it 'dandy-fire.'"

Was this a display of fear? Tyrrell strained to read Keefe's face, hidden inside his respirator, the infernal device. He said, "You're afraid to look like an officer, Mr. Keefe?"

Keefe stared back at his captain rigidly, then bent to make a last adjustment of one puttee. Only when he straightened did he say, "I'd prefer to look like a linden tree, if the truth be told. But that's not what I'm after. I don't want our lads afraid to have me next to them when we're running up that hill."

Their exchange seemed unreal because their muffled voices sounded so strange. Tyrrell realized that Keefe's pragmatism was far more to the point than his own priggishness. It humbled him, suddenly, to have reacted like a sixth-form prefect. Tyrrell abruptly put his hand out. "May I have the glasses, please, Mr. Keefe?"

Keefe handed the binoculars over and Tyrrell turned and stepped onto the fire step to peer over the parapet. Adjusting focus he could just see through the dust the crescent of rust-colored belts of wire near the top of the hill, untouched by their own artillery fire. This was not agricultural barbed wire; razor points gleamed as the early sunlight struck them. But apart from the wire he saw nothing of the German position. Did the fact that the machine guns were not visible mean that the men would be able to scale most of the hill before coming into range? He saw dust billowing from the incessantly exploding shells. When the artillery lifted, it would be a deadly race, his men up the long slope against the German gunners up from their bunkers. The Rangers' only hope was that the machine guns were even then taking hits, that their ammunition belts were being broken, their tripods collapsed, their muzzles jammed into the dirt—anything to slow their crews in mounting them.

Tyrrell handed the glasses to Keefe, who'd joined him at that parapet.

Keefe stared up the hill for a moment, then mumbled something.

"Crown of thorns," was what Douglas thought he heard him say.

———

At 0550, ten minutes before breakout, Captain Tyrrell, like company commanders all along that two-mile stretch of trench line, gave the order to stand to arms. As the word passed, the men uncomplainingly took their positions and, with what seemed to their captain heroic forbearance, they waited. My darling sons, he repeated to himself. My darling sons.

He unsnapped his holster and drew his pistol, then reached into his tunic for his brass whistle, which he fit through his mouthpiece like toffee. He touched his other pocket, where Pamela's photograph was.

He placed his arm under his chin, propped on the parapet, so that he could watch the sweep hand of his timepiece. Repeatedly over the next few minutes he thought the thing had stopped, and that, more than the knowledge of what awaited them, nearly made him cry out in panic.

At 0600 the barrage was supposed to lift, but it did not. At 0601 the shells were still exploding beyond the lip of the hill and no one in the line had moved.

My darling sons.

He sensed a difference in the noise; the steady din of explosions faded as shells began booming singly, the last rounds. Heard individually like that they seemed louder. They reminded him of the solemn dong, dong, dong of Big Ben's bell beat, and suddenly he saw the chimney pots of the Inns of Court, the view from his window at Lincoln's Inn, where for three years he'd marked the time by those gongs.

As if the guns *had* been striking the hour, on the sixth dong— he'd have sworn it was the sixth—the barrage lifted. The noise stopped. An absolute silence, a blanket of silence fell. But the mind corrects; it was not silence, only a pause. The sense of pause brooded above them. Tyrrell gulped a quick intake of breath, preparing to whistle, but then he waited. The pause lengthened, as if for a period of thoughtful consideration, and in that instant of the neither here nor there, all of their faces came once more into his mind, a tumble of red noses, bashed foreheads, spotted teeth, grinning cheeks, freckles, and, because of their haircuts, ludicrously oversized ears. They were west-of-Ireland faces, the faces of men who'd worked his father's farm and who'd come to Douglas himself with legal problems; they were the faces he passed on the road to Gort and the faces of the fishermen in Bally-vaughn. He shifted slightly, and his eyes met those of Bernard Keefe, the Galway fireman. But Keefe's eyes, like everyone's, were disembodied. In that mask he was a man without a face. That was the horror of the moment—that all those men, his darling sons, even the older Keefe—were going now into the infinite jeopardy of the mad charge without their faces.

Far away a faint whistle sounded. It grew louder, working its way up the line. The two officers were still staring at one another, and for Tyrrell the signal came when Keefe's eyes, like a starter's flag, fell.

He blew with all the force he had, as if that shrill screeching were a voodoo act meant to frighten the evil spirits across whose border his men now nobly threw themselves.

Tyrrell kept blowing his whistle as he ran, emptying the contents of his mind into the air. He thought of nothing then, having become, perhaps for the first time in his life, purely physical, a creature without consciousness. Some men have the capacity to lose themselves entirely in the act of sex. He didn't. He had never lost himself entirely in anything until then. All at once he was capable of no perception, reflection, or experience. He was running and blowing. He forgot Keefe and all the others. He forgot the discomfort of his mask, the threat of gunfire, the racing Germans. He forgot Pamela. He was aware only of the shell-plowed ground. It required an unusual dexterity to run across the pits and craters without stumbling, and he had it. As he dashed higher and higher up the slope, the act seemed so natural, so easy really, that it didn't occur to him to wonder where the machine-gun fire was.

Gradually, as shortness of breath and the increasing steepness of the hill slowed him, he became aware once more of the other men. They were on both sides of him, matching his speed and finesse, all having instinctively employed the numb suspension of mind that makes such "courage" possible. Tyrrell was aware of them now not as his "sons" or even as his "men" but as his mates; this was the hurley game again, but now he was playing too. Having lost himself in the pure act of pumping legs, he was lost now, also for the first time, in the communion of the charge. It didn't matter what he gave himself over to—running, camaraderie; the point was to keep his mind at bay until this was over.

He stepped into an old shell crater that was deeper than he expected, and he fell. This was an instant before the moment when the German gunners got to their machines, so that when the opening burst of gunfire broke across the hill, he, nearly alone of that first wave of Rangers, was not hit. Sprawled on the ground, he saw the men above him fall like ninepins.

He had had the wind knocked out of him when he'd hit the ground, and the sight of the lads tumbling over each other ahead of him knocked it out again. Instinctively he tore at his gas mask until it was loose, and he flung it aside. He rose firing his pistol, and resumed running up the hill.

The machine-gun emplacements were plainly visible from that point on the hill, and some of the Rangers had stopped the insane running toward them and were now prone, in marksman's posture, squeezing off aimed shots. Again and again, the Germans were hit, the gunners and the belt tenders and then the reserve gunners and tenders who rushed to take their places. Even from that distance the silhouettes of their spiked helmets struck Tyrrell. Those helmets were always featured on British recruiting posters, emblems of the "Hun." But that worked against the British now because those helmets made their wearers seem even more barbaric and therefore more invincible. It was yet another fear to overcome. The Germans fired their rifles individually down at the Rangers, but the prone Irish marksmen remained fixed on the two machine guns. They succeeded for long seconds, then moments, in keeping them silent.

Tyrrell felt nothing but the manic movement of the men around him; motion, everything was motion. Constantly, they fell, picked themselves up, clawed through dirt and over rocks, pushing each other. At one point the ground below him sank sickeningly and he realized he had stepped on someone's corpse, which only made him climb faster.

The immobile wall of men's backs just ahead confused him. Why would they stop? Tyrrell was in a frenzy as he approached, screaming at them to keep moving, furious that just below the crest of the hill his company should freeze. They could be taking it! It was a miracle they'd gotten this far! He wanted to crush through them, pushing them aside, the bastards, the cowards; why had they stopped?

But as he drew closer he saw. The men were bunched two-and three-deep across a section of ledge forty feet wide, and the front rank of men—dozens of them—were writhing on the barbed wire they had attempted to crawl over, or into which they'd been pushed by the now panicking men behind them. Their hands and faces were bloody as they continued to rip at the wire. From only a few yards on the other side, the Germans at one position were firing at the mangled bodies from behind sandbags.

"Bombs!" Tyrrell cried. "Bombs!," thinking of Mills bombs, the hand grenades, as if someone could explode one there to open a swath in the wire. It was nonsense. If the artillery hadn't cut the wire, a Mills bomb wouldn't.

Behind him waves of Rangers were bunching up, having successfully mounted most of the hill, and to the left and right, as the ledge spilled off into a broad plateau, other Irish soldiers were running from side to side looking for a gap in the wire.

The German machine gun finally opened fire with a deafening noise, it was so close, and for a moment Tyrrell's men fell in groups. But then the German gunners must have been hit again, for the machine gun stopped. His men were screaming as the panic spread. Most of them still wore their gas helmets, and that made their hysteria all the more frightening. One turned and began to run back down the hill. Others acted equally out of instinct, but differently, to stand there and fire up at the Germans.

Tyrrell did not know how he came to be on the wire, how he'd forced the men to make way for him. He didn't know that he'd dropped his pistol and pulled out of his tunic pocket the wire cutters Peter Towne had given him as the War Train pulled out of Victoria Station. He didn't know that his picture of Pamela had fallen in the mud. With a steadiness that had nothing to do with his inner agitation, he clipped at the wire, snapping through the steel, while someone at his side bent the wire back as he cut through it. He looked once at the man. It was Keefe.

When the gap was opened he didn't have to give an order; the men poured through less like water through a broken wall, since this was upward, than like smoke through a window. Someone handed him a rifle or he picked it up, and then he too was tossing off shots. Despite the mass frenzy, Tyrrell was lucid enough to grasp at once, as they crested the hill and stormed the gun emplacement and the trench behind it, that the Germans were less prepared for them than they should have been. His soldiers swarmed over the position, taking it. Resisters came at them, but futilely. His men careened across the top of the hill, knocking out the other positions that were facing the other slopes.

Tyrrell, running full tilt, jammed his bayonet into the belly of one German, but then couldn't pull it free. The blade had lodged in the man's skeleton, and as he fell he took the barrel of Tyrrell's rifle down with him. Tyrrell fired, and at once the gun recoiled and came out easily.

When the last of the resisters was subdued, Captains Tyrrell and Tyndale, Lieutenant Keefe, Tyndale's adjutant, and two platoon leaders conferred briefly. Hill 60 was separated from the main part of the Messines Ridge by the dip of a valley, and that separation isolated the hill from the larger German force just enough to confine the action. Their momentum might have carried the Rangers on to the next position, but the valley stopped them. Having taken the heights, they knew instinctively not to leave them. About three hundred men from all four companies had made it to the top, and a stream of others, many wounded, kept coming. They had overcome a German force of perhaps one hundred. In addition to the pair of machine-gun emplacements C Company had run up against, there were two artillery bunkers and four other pairs of machine guns at various points on the hill. Those guns, having fired more efficiently, had been overrun only from behind by Tyrrell's men. Looking back down the hill, his eyes clouded over at the sight of all the fallen. Most were bunched at the belts of barbed wire where they'd been so easily cut down. The only gap in the entire semicircle of wire was the one Tyrrell had cut. Most of the regiment lay dead or dying on the slope. At the bottom, where the trenches were, dazed men could be seen walking, half stooped, clutching their throats. Having discarded their respirators in the charge, they had fallen back for cover into the poisoned trenches, and now the chlorine gas was attacking the tissue of their lungs and eyes.

The officers mustered the men into various detachments, securing prisoners, dismantling the artillery, manning the machine guns, and posting perimeter guards.

Keefe hauled out a German major who'd been caught at the field telephone in the dugout. Tyrrell had never before seen the odd German helmet close enough to read what was emblazoned on its seal: *Mit Gott fur Koenig und Vaterland.* With God? How could the enemy claim God too? The major sputtered in German, and when Tyrrell looked at him uncomprehendingly, he said in smooth, accented English, "Those trenches below were gassed. Who would put his own men in there?"

And Tyrrell understood why the Germans on Hill 60 had seemed less than prepared for their assault.

————

One of the wounded who staggered to the pinnacle just then was Corporal O'Day. The left side of his body from his shoulder—that skew signalers' patch—to his hip was awash with blood, and what was left of his arm hung lifelessly. But under his right arm he clutched the air-holed wooden box, and when the sergeant major asked him for it, he refused to let go of it. He was weeping when Tyrrell approached him.

"Good man, Corporal."

"Captain, sir then . . ." O'Day's body folded. Tyrrell caught him, bloodying himself. The box fell.

"Release the pigeons, Sergeant Major." Tyrrell gently lowered O'Day to the ground. He propped O'Day so that he could see. "Look, Corporal!" The two birds leapt free, fluttering, climbing into the white sky. Those pigeons would get them their reinforcements. The sun, fully risen from that vantage, was bathing the countryside, which stretched all the way to the smoking

ruins of Ypres itself. From that hill they watched as the pigeons
swooped, rose, and fell, flying back across the trenches toward
GHQ. The words of Colonel MacIntyre filled Tyrrell's mind,
as if the birds were criers declaiming for all that Belgian countryside to hear. "Ireland did this for us! Connaught did this for
us!" And he was overcome with proud exhilaration at what his
men had done, at what O'Day had done. When he looked down
at him to say so, O'Day's eyes had rolled back. He was dead.
Tyrrell lowered his own face to put it close. The stench from
O'Day's wound was sickening, but he put his lips on O'Day's
brow and kissed him.

   "Captain! Jesus, Mary, and Joseph, Captain! Look at this!"
Tyrrell let O'Day down, then stood, facing the ridge.

   Then he saw. Six, perhaps eight columns of German soldiers,
winding in more or less parallel, yet oddly twisting lines, were
crossing the valley that separated Hill 60 from the ridge. What
Tyrrell felt was anger: they couldn't do this! The columns
stretched back as far as he could see, several thousand Jerries,
streaming at them. "To arms!" he cried. "To arms!" He looked
wildly about. The defenses of the hill were wrong, geared as they
were for attack from the west and south. "Remount the guns,
Lieutenant!" He slapped Keefe's shoulder. But just then a deafening noise cracked over them and the hill shook as the first of
the German shells landed. The German artillery, on positions
along the ridge, had adjusted easily for this new target. The men
dove for cover, tumbling one on top of the other and on top of
German corpses into the dugouts and bunkers.

   Tyrrell watched, remaining in the open. He saw the earth
jumping, soil shooting into the air, craters being churned into
new craters, and he understood that this artillery barrage would
"walk" a few dozen yards ahead of the approaching columns of
German infantry. His men had no choice but to bury themselves,

and he saw at once that when the Black Marias stopped firing
at the last moment to allow the attackers to sweep up onto the
hilltop, with no barbed wire to slow them and no properly
mounted machine guns to cut them down, his men wouldn't
have a chance. He turned to look back toward his own lines
beyond the trenches below. The country was a wasteland of
holes and ditches, long lines of trenches at right angles and
parallel to each other. It was like seeing the entire Front at once.
The battered steeples and jagged rooflines of Ypres in the far
distance seemed to beckon teasingly like a vision of home, like
London or even Dublin. In the cellars and tunnels of that town
majors and colonels bent at the map tables, and in the luxuri-
ous châteaux above Poperinge and Bailleul the generals bent at
theirs. Tyrrell knew they would never dispatch reinforcements
in time. O'Day's noble birds would arrive with the news of their
triumph just as the Germans arrived to undo it.

He was the last one standing exposed. Shells exploded
around him. Debris flew and the bodies of the fallen bounced.

"Captain!"

He turned.

In the entranceway of the well-built dugout, Keefe was
waving at him to take cover. Tyrrell crossed to him and went
in. In the noise, even in that dark chamber, it was impossible
to talk. Each man was alone in a world of ear-splitting terror.
Tyrrell was content to slump against a wall of sandbags, letting
exhaustion take him under at last. Like the others, he made a
casing of his arms to protect his head and made himself small.
The earth moved under them, but the dugout held. His mind
went blank and, but for one faculty, he might have been asleep.
Only his hearing functioned, and only the segment of his brain
in which he would know by the first alteration in timing and
pitch when the barrage was coming to an end. These last living

members of his regiment were no one's sons now, not the major's, colonel's, or general's, but his. His darling sons. He had it in his legal and moral power to spare them. And he would.

The moment came, either hours later or minutes.

As the last shells fell he forbade his men to move and ordered Keefe to give him his service revolver. He holstered it, then climbed out of the dugout alone. The sun blinded him and he wanted to shield his eyes, but instead he held his hands high as the first Germans surrounded him. Their helmets were what he noticed again, but now they seemed ludicrous, not terrible, as if the spikes were candles balanced on their heads. He waited impassively until an officer came, then he saluted smartly and handed over his pistol as the emblem of their surrender.

8

Jane sat in the darkness watching Dan and Nora as Naisi and Deirdre for the hundredth time, and still the play enthralled her. Not still, but more. The longer she'd been at the Abbey the more the power of Synge's work and the marvel of theater itself affected her. Every night she'd found herself pulled deeper and deeper into the mystery of suffering. Deirdre's, of course, and, somehow, her own; but also Ireland's. Curry had been right to underscore that meaning, and Jane had not been immune to the entire company's passionate reading of the play as a national lament. They'd been trained as Irish actors and, as such, to seize hold of their misfortune and by simultaneously protesting it and accepting it, to turn it into the source of their art. With Synge, because his perfectly tuned rendition of their experience matched their passion perfectly, the Abbey players accomplished the rare miracle—what brings people into the theater in every age—every time the curtain rose.

In her six weeks at the Abbey, so many things had been quickened in her—her sense of freedom, of womanhood, her feeling for dramatic expression—it was hard to single one out as dominant. True, the Abbey had sharpened her perception of Ireland's plight as more than an abstraction, more than the myth of Charles Parnell, more than the stale, rehearsed complaints against England, and more even than a losing cause her father had embraced when he was young. Her sense of it as *her* plight had begun to take hold. But of course, if she was honest, the Abbey meant so much to her, first, because this was where she could see Dan.

He had not made himself available to her exactly. On days the theater was dark she rarely saw him, and the other days he rarely came in before noon. But when he was at the Abbey he seemed to make a point to find ways to be with her, surprising her by bringing tea to her at her desk, for example, then boosting himself onto the large oak cabinet to sprawl above her, talking. "Here's something you should read," he'd say, and she never knew whether what he pulled from his pocket was going to be a *United Irishman* political pamphlet or an essay written by Cardinal Newman or the copy of a new play he wanted for the Abbey. Then, a day later, he would question her at length about it. He seemed to value what she thought. She was sure he held her in more than casual regard, but she was also aware that he kept himself somewhat in check. He'd never troubled to make explicit exactly how he felt. He'd made such a strong impression on her that first day, particularly in their spontaneous recitation on the naked stage, but he hadn't been that expansive or direct with her again. Thus, with Curry she was always more expectant than fulfilled, and of course that sharpened the edge of her attraction to him. She had concluded that he was inexhaustible, and she sensed that if she had come to occupy a place of even slight importance in his life—why else that constant tea?—she shared it with other things and people. That was his advantage, of course. Dublin was his city, and its causes, crises, charms, oddities, and occupations were his in a way they would never be hers. For all her happiness at having come here, she was alone, still a newcomer at the Abbey, a stranger on the streets and a visitor in her own rooms at Merrion Square.

And that was why when her father had arrived at the theater unannounced this very afternoon, she'd felt at once that a terrible pain was being soothed. It didn't matter that she'd barely acknowledged having it, even to herself.

She was so pleased that he'd relented. She'd pleaded with him to visit her in Dublin and had even asked Lady Gregory to encourage him to do so. That at last he had was a great relief to her. Wasn't part of her pain the guilt she felt at defying him, and wasn't her loneliness at bottom the result of her estrangement from him? Apparently he felt those things too.

Now he was sitting next to her, watching the play. She wanted him to approve it as if she'd written it or mounted it, and that feeling alone made her realize how attached she'd become to the Abbey. However tangential her contribution to the players' effort was, and no one was more aware of the modesty of her role than she, Deirdre and Naisi were still what she had to show for herself. And, she felt, if they didn't justify the breach of her having left Cragside—only youth under the spell of theater would feel this—nothing she ever did would.

Jane watched him for his reaction. Perhaps the half-light of the theater was what made it difficult, but she was unable to read what was written in his face. Even at those moments when audiences, including this one, invariably gasped or laughed or even wept, Sir Hugh sat immobile and unresponsive. She did not understand how he could be unmoved, particularly by what to her was the infinitely masculine struggle of Dan Curry's Naisi. How could any man resist it? Her father was in no way like Curry, lacking utterly that raw, unpolished energy, but his reserve now, in the face of the tragedy unfolding before him, seemed like a failure of character to Jane. What a rare thought for her! And then she realized that where her father's response as a young man to such a conflict as Naisi's had been to withdraw from it, Curry's would be to stay to the end, even if that meant dying.

Her father had seemed aloof on first arriving this afternoon, but Jane had assumed he shared the awkwardness she felt to have him for the first time ever on what amounted to her side of the island. But he hadn't relaxed. When she walked with him to the places in Dublin she'd come to treasure, he seemed distracted. She'd hoped to hear his stories about his days in Dublin, but his remarks had been offhand and trivial. When she suggested his seeing *Deirdre of the Sorrows* with her he'd demurred, but she insisted. This was the last performance of the play; she simply had to be here for it. His coming today had seemed like a reward for all her work—the accounts at the Abbey had been terribly neglected and she'd been at her desk constantly—and it was inconceivable to her that he not see it.

But now, as the play was drawing to its stunning conclusion—"Deirdre is dead and Naisi is dead; and if the oaks and stars could die for sorrow, it's a dark sky and naked earth we'd have this night in Emain"—Jane sensed with distress that it really had left him unmoved. That this was the last performance made it seem doubly like death to her. They each sat fixed to their chairs even as the applause faded and the audience members around them rose to leave.

She forced a certain cheer into her voice to say, "Will you come with me to meet the actors?" The audience filed out, many still folding their handkerchiefs. Jane and her father were sitting in the very part of the balcony where she'd sat, transfixed, that first morning; it was where she always sat. They were the last seats sold in any case, but Jane felt the magic more powerfully from there than any place, and now, from there, she felt the loss.

"Certainly," he said.

She was afraid to ask him what he thought, so they sat in silence until the theater emptied. Then Jane led the way down through the main part of the theater, up the short flight of stairs, through the curtain, across the dark stage, and down the winding metal steps to the greenroom. The actors and various crew members, a dozen or fifteen people, were sprawled about on the couches and chairs or on the floor. They were smoking and passing glasses of wine and plates of sponge cake in ritual observation of the play's closing. Nora had already changed into her trousers, and she was the first to greet Jane. When Jane introduced her father, everyone stood. The men shook his hand and Sir Hugh found it possible to compliment them graciously, but still it was awkward. Jane realized she'd breached an etiquette by bringing her father back on that night. Only Dan Curry could have dispelled the unease—he'd have done it with a gesture, a toast, a reference to Lady Gregory's own well-known affection for Sir Hugh, or perhaps even a pointed but ingratiating joke about a night to meet a knight. But Dan Curry, Jane realized with surprise, wasn't there.

"Where's Dan?"

Nora and the actress who played Deirdre's nurse exchanged a quick look. "He had to hurry off. Probably has a meeting." The edge in Nora's voice seemed unkind.

"At ten o'clock at night?" Jane checked herself. She'd scrupulously avoided displaying exceptional interest in Curry. She hadn't realized until now how very much she wanted her father to meet him. It was why she'd brought him to the greenroom.

Their exit—it was unthinkable that they should stay—was as awkward as their entrance, and by the time Jane and her father left the theater, she felt devastated.

The city streets were nearly deserted. A light rain was falling, but it was the end of July. These were the weeks in which the soft Dublin rain was not bone-chilling, but warm. Sir Hugh took his daughter's arm as they crossed Abbey Street. "Come on, we'll go to my hotel." Sir Hugh was thinking that Merrion Square was too far to walk, and there would be taxis at the Gresham.

Neither would have minded the rain, actually, and at Cragside they'd have thought nothing of being out in it. But pressed by their mutual unspoken disappointment, they hurried with lowered heads as if it were the weather that curdled their mood. Jane felt defensive and found herself rehearsing her explanation. "I am twenty-two years old and for the first time in my life I have felt real passion and I have inspired the interest of admirable people and I can imagine growing old without being dependent, yet at the same time alone. At Cragside I'd have become a hard, disappointed woman, and eventually even you would have made me feel unwelcome." She imagined saying all this with great heat, fists clenched, the way Nora would have.

She said nothing, of course, but she was certain that her father's continuing resentment of her desertion was what caused his unhappiness.

But for once, Jane was wrong, and finally at the hotel, sitting next to her in the empty lobby, having been served tea by the night porter, he found it possible to tell her. "When you asked about Douglas this afternoon, I wasn't able to be honest with you. I mean, I wasn't quite prepared to be, and I'm sorry."

She froze, her teacup halfway to her mouth. "What do you mean, father?"

"I came from London this morning, Jane, not Cragside. I've been there a week, I was there a week last month."

"In London!" Her father hadn't been to London since

Douglas's wedding. Even more than Dublin, London represented the life he'd turned his back on.

"Douglas is missing, darling. I've been haunting them at Whitehall and at Westminster to make the army find him."

Jane lowered her cup, channeling her emotion into the act. "I scan the lists every day, the dead and missing list in the *Irish Times*. I never saw his name."

"Those lists are far from complete, Jane. We don't get the half of it."

She placed the cup in its saucer without making a sound, and then she put the cup and saucer on the end table by her corner of the settee.

"When?"

"Mid-June at Ypres. The Connaught lads were handed a hard acre to plow. Only half of them came through it. The Germans took a sizable group prisoner, but they haven't released the names. Douglas could have been captured. If he was killed, no one survived who saw it, and they haven't found his remains." Sir Hugh took his daughter's hand. He made a conscious decision not to refer to the reports of chlorine gas. "I'm sure he's alive."

The shudder that went through Jane at his words could easily have become an earthquake, toppling the rigid structure of her defenses, but she shook it off at once. She insisted, "There would have been news of this, father. The papers say everything's been going well at the Front. There's been nothing about Irish losses, about the Connaught—" As she spoke she pressed his hand with both of hers, and her tremors grew back toward that earthquake.

Her father interrupted. "The newspapers aren't telling us anything, Jane. What I'm telling you is true." He said it with his old authority, and it stopped her.

As she exhaled deeply, she sank against him, her face upon his shoulder. "But you're not telling me what it is. Douglas is dead, isn't he?"

He held her away and said, too fiercely, "We mustn't say that!"

Jane heard his reaction as pure denial, but understood. Their saying it could make it true. Like the newspapers: if they didn't report the carnage, had it really happened?

Jane stopped thinking of herself. She couldn't imagine—literally could not picture—anything of Douglas's situation. A German prison? A hidden grave in Belgium?

Slowly she realized what pain this was for her father. Like all daughters of her class and time, she accepted, or thought she did, the primacy of sons. Douglas's death was simply the worst thing that could happen to her father, worse than anything to do with her. She shifted slightly, altering her posture so that he was as much in her embrace as she was in his, and she held him tightly to let him know that of course she understood and that of course, now, she would do anything he asked.

But then her thoughts flew to Pamela, to Timothy and Anne. She drew her face back. "Does Pamela know?"

Sir Hugh nodded. "I stayed with her. She's quite . . . distressed."

Only months before, that woman had lost her father, and now Douglas, who was the center of Pamela's life, was gone too. What had seemed the infinite grief of Deirdre for Naisi now paled, for this death was real, and Jane discovered that her capacity for feeling the pain of Synge's doomed lovers was nothing compared to what she felt now for her brother's wife. "I should go to her," she said, yielding again to the pull of what she'd been raised to. Women went to each other at these moments, the way fathers went to Whitehall. Grief and worry—real grief and worry—implied a role she knew by heart, and it was unthinkable that she would not play it.

At eleven o'clock the Gresham bar emptied and a dozen men filed across the lobby, several of them unsteadily. They ignored Sir Hugh and Jane as they crossed in front of them toward the hotel door.

"I should be seeing you back to Merrion Square."

"Just show me to the taxi."

Sir Hugh smiled at his daughter, though her instinctive reassertion of independence saddened him. It wasn't to dominate that he'd offered the traditional courtesy, what he'd have done for any woman in his company. But he sensed how inappropriate it would be to push it. They'd agreed to meet for the midday meal the next day before his train to Gort. They stood to go.

"Jane!"

The sound of her name abruptly called out startled her, and when she turned to see Curry crossing toward her from the bar, two men trailing behind him, she thought of the war cry of a Gaelic chieftain. His beard and hair had never seemed wilder. The pleasure she felt at the sight of him—and at the obvious enthusiasm of his greeting—pushed hard against the gloom she felt about Douglas. But the gloom didn't budge and her pleasure fell away.

Curry overrode her mood to take her hand. "I wanted to see you."

His companions stood awkwardly back.

Jane said, "Dan, this is my father."

Curry was thrown by her announcement. In point of fact, he had barely noticed that she was accompanied, and now his mind refused to work its way past that word *father*. He knew Jane was the daughter of one of Lady Gregory's blueblood friends, but he had never really allowed the fact to register, underscoring, as it would have, the enormous differences between them.

Sir Hugh offered his hand, but spoke coldly. "I admired your performance tonight very much."

"Thank you, sir," Curry said, still flustered. "I had to leave immediately after . . ." He glanced awkwardly at his companions, one of whom was Pádraic Pearse. He turned to introduce them, but to his further surprise Jane Tyrrell's father preempted him.

"Hello, Casement," he said to the other.

"Sir Hugh!" The gaunt bearded man shook off his surprise to take Tyrrell's hand. He was older than Pearse and Curry, though somewhat younger than Sir Hugh. That they had a history with each other was obvious, but there was also more than a hint of a recognition that they'd gone their separate ways.

Tyrrell indicated Jane. "This is my daughter. Jane, this is Sir Roger Casement, late of the Foreign Office, like myself." Tyrrell smiled briefly at Casement. "We shared the honor."

Casement bowed over Jane's hand and kissed it. She did not attempt to mask her confusion—a titled former colleague of her father's in a Dublin pub with Dan Curry—which was then compounded when Curry introduced Pádraic Pearse. When Curry had pressed his poems on her, they had seemed rather too pious to her, and his anti-English essays had seemed quite shrill.

After a stilted handshake with Pearse, Jane's father turned to Casement and spoke with scarcely veiled irony. "Or have you renounced the honor yet?"

"No, Sir Hugh, I haven't."

"I find that strange, frankly, given your views."

"My views, Sir Hugh, are widely discussed but little understood."

"You actively collaborate with Germany. You and Childers trade with them for arms."

"If you're referring to the paltry cache of antiquated muskets we brought in on Erskine's yacht last summer, that was before hostilities commenced between His Majesty and the Kaiser. As you must know, sir."

"German guns nevertheless, Casement. To use against the Crown to which you, unlike your colleagues, swore allegiance."

Casement reddened and tried to cover the embarrassment he felt by waving his hand dismissively. "It's not force we want, Sir Hugh, but only the threat of force. Nothing more than what Carson and our Orange cousins in the north intend. You, better than any, should understand how the game is played. We want what Parnell wanted. You should be with us. Men of our stamp . . ." Casement hesitated. It was a gaffe to acknowledge the common bonds of class, background, religion, and profession that he shared with Tyrrell—with the late Parnell, with Childers—because he lacked such bonds with Pearse and Curry. It wouldn't do now to quicken their feelings of inferiority. ". . . Well, we could use you, Sir Hugh. Many of us have often wished you'd join the fray again."

"My mind, frankly, is on a larger fray right now."

"What, the war to save defenseless Belgium? Forgive me, Sir Hugh. I did my service in the Belgian Congo, as you no doubt recall. I saw in particular detail how defenseless that little nation is. The Belgians are colonial murderers even beyond what the British are, and Leopold is himself a monster. Don't talk to me about poor Belgium. Let them fight their own battles, I say. And the same for England. Let her arm and drill the sickly population of her slums—" Casement had begun a speech and even he heard it as such. He stopped.

Pádraic Pearse twirled his hat casually, as if he'd not noticed the tension, and smiled ingratiatingly. "Mr. Tyrrell," he said, "I've been hoping to set up a meeting with a few of the Galway Cope fellows"—*Cope* was the informal word for the Agricultural Cooperative movement—"and I was thinking you and some of your Burren dairy boys might like to come. We have a common cause, you know."

"Talk to me when the war's over, Pearse."

Jane wanted to look up at Dan Curry, but she couldn't. Why didn't he say something witty and charming to end this nightmare scene? She had never before sensed helplessness in him; perhaps that was why she felt so devastated now.

"And, Casement," Tyrrell said, "as an old friend I feel bound to warn you. It is one thing to oppose Ireland's participation in the war, quite another to take up the part of His Majesty's enemy. You are still liable to be called to serve. The Foreign Office has a hold on you."

Casement bristled. "Not for long. I'm off to America."

Tyrrell eyed him skeptically. "Why?"

Casement leaned toward him confidentially. "Because the fate of Ireland will be decided there."

Pearse took Casement's elbow. "That's enough." Pearse, it was suddenly clear, was the man with authority. He put his hat on, doffing it to Jane. "It's been a pleasure meeting you, miss." Without a further look at Tyrrell, he walked away from the group.

Curry waited for Jane to look at him. When she didn't, he glanced at her father and was undone by his unkind stare. He nodded awkwardly, then left to catch up with Pearse.

Casement hesitated, and Sir Hugh said quietly, "Roger, be careful of your associates. They are not wise men."

Casement's eyes were sad. "They're what's left, Sir Hugh, because men like you stay home." He put his hat on and grinned. "And, Christ, they love having a Protestant along!" After a pause during which Tyrrell made no move to shake his hand, he said, "Good-bye," and turned.

"Before you go . . ." Sir Hugh hadn't intended to say this, but the impulse overwhelmed him.

Casement waited.

"My son is a German prisoner or else he's dead."

Casement stared rigidly at Tyrrell, saying nothing for a moment. Then his shoulders sagged. "Good God, Hugh. I had no idea. I'm sorry."

"Just think of him now and then, will you? It isn't all Belgians, Germans, or English over there. It's an Irish war too, Roger, like it or not. When you're meeting the German ambassador in Washington, think of my son. Think of the thousands of Irish boys who want nothing now but to live through this damned war."

Casement blushed. The second time in five minutes.

And that told Tyrrell he'd guessed right; he *did* know how this game was played. "You want a treaty with them, don't you? And the Germans no doubt want one with you. 'The IRB loves Fritz.' If Germany commits itself to the liberation of Ireland, then goggle-eyed Irish-Americans will rally round. Isn't that the thought? What will Germany give you to keep America out of the war?"

"Since you raise the issue, Sir Hugh, they'll give us special treatment of Irish prisoners, for one thing. They already do."

Tyrrell's emotion flared and he half stepped toward Casement. "Don't you dare barter for Irish prisoners, you faithless—"

"Father." Jane took his arm.

"Casement!" Pearse called from the doorway, an officer summoning his dallying subordinate.

Casement turned at once and walked away. He and Pearse left the hotel together. Curry hesitated long enough for Jane, finally, to show him what was in her eyes, so that when he went out into the rainy night, it felt like shelter.

———

Under the awning of a shop a block away the three men stopped. Pearse turned on Casement. "What did you tell him?"

"He guessed it. I didn't tell him."

"About Washington?"

"Yes. But that's all. He has no idea I'll be going on to Germany." Casement looked awkwardly at Curry. They hadn't discussed Germany in front of him.

But Curry was impassive and Pearse seemed unconcerned about him.

Casement shrugged. "If Tyrrell knew, he'd have asked me to find his son."

"What do you mean?"

"His son's been captured, if he's alive."

"Christ, man, that gives him all the more reason to oppose us!"

Casement shook his head. "The man was trained, Pearse. But he's only thinking of our agenda for Irish-Americans. He thinks we're merely waging a campaign for popular opinion. Let him."

"You fool. That's enough to take him to Dublin Castle in the morning, and by afternoon you're detained."

"Not if I leave tonight. There's a ship out of Cork in the morning. Murray can get me on it."

Pearse stared at him for a moment. "All right, I'll cable Devoy in New York and have him meet you. And if von Bernstorff accepts the terms of our proposal, let me know at once. I'll want someone from the council to meet you in Germany, to help with arrangements there."

"Who?"

"It isn't decided yet. I'll keep Devoy informed."

"I didn't need help in Germany last year, Patrick." Casement refused to address Pearse by his Gaelic name, the way Pearse refused to use the prefix *sir*.

"You were making a few purchases, not negotiating an alliance. It's more than guns we're after now, the way it's more than popular opinion." Pearse slammed his fist into his palm. "It's an honest-to-God Irish army!"

"I know what it is we're after, and I can get it."

"Not alone."

The two men stared at each other for a moment, their grim silence a tacit recognition of the impasse they'd come to.

Given what he'd done for the cause, Casement resented the fact that the men of the IRB still refused to trust him. He was an Ulster Protestant who had repudiated the provincialism of his own people, but he equally abhorred the sectarian impulses of the Gaelic Catholics. It was everything he could do to keep the likes of Pearse from lumping him in with Redmond.

Casement looked out into the darkness. The rain was falling heavily now, and Sackville Street glistened. He remembered the Russian maxim "Faith in the peasants in proportion to one's distance from them." He would never have accepted the humiliation of such treatment, but peasants like Pearse controlled the movement now, and the Germans knew it as well as he did. Casement was nothing without the endorsement of the IRB, and he would undercut his own good opinion of himself to keep it. He had no choice. Having already lost the good opinion of his family, his oldest friends, his former colleagues, he had nothing left but his will to work for Ireland and his dream of leading her through nights like this to freedom.

"Good luck," Pearse said finally, and offered his hand. Casement took it. Then he shook hands with Curry and hurried off into the rain.

Curry and Pearse watched him go.

After a long time Pearse said, "You knew her."

It took Curry a moment to understand. "Jane Tyrrell?" He looked at Pearse, who only continued staring down Sackville Street. Not far from there was the place where the recruiting tram had gathered its crowd the day he'd met her. "I know her from the Abbey. She's the bookkeeper."

Now Pearse looked at him. "I wondered if there wasn't more to it than that?"

Curry shook his head. But at once he felt a pang of guilt. Of course there was more to it than that. Curry felt as if he'd spent this summer sleeping in a stranger's bed, dreaming his dreams. If he'd been in his own bed, he'd have wanted Jane Tyrrell with him.

"And did you know her father?"

"No, I never met him."

"He was one of Parnell's people."

Curry smiled. "I don't remember Parnell, Pádraic."

"You make me feel old, Dan. I'm only thirty-six." Pearse laughed. Then he lit a cigarette. For the first time he was letting down, relaxing. He looked at Curry with a rare show of affection. "You're new to the movement and you're still wet behind the ears. What can you do but stand on stages and rant at mobs? You don't remember Parnell!" He shook his head in disbelief. "Why do I trust you so?"

Curry shrugged. But he was pleased at the admission.

"I trust no one, Dan. You know that. Not Connolly, Larkin, Clarke, or Murphy. Not labor, not the hurley boys of the GAA, not your literary chums of the Gaelic Revival, not Redmond and not Casement either. They're all my allies, but I never let them behind me. Men I've known for years. Men who've given everything for Ireland. And I don't trust them. But I trust you, Dan. Why is that, do you suppose?"

Was there something sinister in the question? Curry tried to focus on Pearse's implications, while saying easily, "Because we've become friends, Pádraic. I've been at your side. And you know me."

"But not so well. Perhaps there's the key." Pearse took a deep drag on the cigarette, eyeing Curry through the smoke. "I think it's that you've a gift for the truth, Dan. It's why we believe you when you're up on stage. But what if you had to play a role that wasn't so noble?"

"I wouldn't do it."

"Not even for Ireland?"

"What are you driving at, Pádraic?"

"I want you to go to Germany."

Curry, though stunned, said nothing.

"I've brought you into the secret now, Dan. We've a new William the Conqueror on our side, only he calls himself Wilhelm."

"What's that to do with me, Pádraic?" Curry was hardly breathing.

"If Casement gets the agreement with von Bernstorff, you'll meet him in Germany. Everything hinges on the Irish prisoners. If we can convince a sizable group of them to come over to us, then we have"—he ticked points off on his fingers—"leaders to train our recruits, officers and sergeants to staff our army, experts to show us what to do with what the Germans are already committed to give us—heavy cannons, rifles, pistols, and hundreds of thousands of rounds for them. Weapons, Dan! Real guns! More than we can use. And beyond that, not least, we have a bold manifestation of Germany's goodwill toward the Irish Republic. We have an army instead of a boy's club, America has a reason to stay at home, and England has a fight on her hands here."

"Christ, Pádraic . . ." Curry shook his head. ". . . I prefer taking England on one to one."

Pearse snorted. "One to one they've killed us for a thousand years."

"Maybe, but there's something rotten about throwing in with Germans and you know it."

Pearse stared at him. "Like I said, you've a gift for what's true. I've a gift for what's necessary. We won't be shoulder to shoulder with Germans, Dan, shooting at our cousins. Don't you see? England won't fight us. She can't bring an army to Ireland now. All we have to do is make the show. You know, Dan— Irish National Theater. The Irish Brigade of former prisoners, the German guns, the German troop ships landing our lads on Kerry Strand. We declare our independence and England, under pressure to demonstrate goodwill, accepts at once. And we therefore declare ourselves nonbelligerent and neutral. Germany expects a U-boat base in Cork harbor, but we don't give it to her, although Casement thinks we're making a solemn commitment to it. Casement is ready to trade his English master for a German one, and that's why we must rein him. It may be that we'll decide as free men—but *only* then—to do what we can for England. If we won't be John Bull's lackeys, we certainly won't be Jerry's. But, short of that, Casement is right. We play them off each other. It's the perfect moment, the perfect plan."

"Then let Casement carry it through, Pádraic. Rein him afterward. He'll run better for us, given his head. He doesn't want me clucking him."

Pearse poked Curry's chest. "Dan, if you were in the British army now sitting in a German camp in Hamburg or somewhere, what would you think when Kraut guards showed Casement in? He's the ghost of all the landlords and all the constables and all the rent collectors who ever stood with their boots on your mother's throat. If you *did* harbor doubts about fighting for England, would they be appealed to by a man who's so confused about the meaning of being Irish he still calls himself 'Sir'? Would your highest virtue be summoned forth by a man who's betrayed an oath? Wouldn't you wonder if it wasn't the old Protestant Ascendancy cleverly looking for yet one more way to dominate the mass of the Irish people? How does Sir Roger Casement stir up a Dublin butcher's boy's longing for an independent Irish nation? For a Catholic nation united by the old faith? What they need, Dan, is the true gospel preached to them by one of their own."

"I'm no preacher, Pádraic." The slightest reference to his status as a spoiled priest made Curry bristle.

"But you know what I mean. You've a gift for making people see the truth of Ireland's need. That's all I'm talking about."

"But I've no gift for asking men to condemn themselves in the sight of God. You talk about Casement. What about the soldiers? They took oaths too, you know, when they joined the army. Oaths to the Crown, solemn ones."

Pearse had had to face this question himself, and he responded at once. "But were they valid oaths? Didn't they teach you at Maynooth that oaths, to be binding, have to be sworn to freely? Is it free when a man's motive is to put a crust of daily bread on his children's table? Is it free when he thinks he's joining an army to defend Irish shores, but then is sent to fight a nation far away with whom Ireland has no quarrel?"

"You sound like a Jesuit. There were no Jesuits at Maynooth, Pádraic."

"This is what I asked you before. Would you play a role even if it wasn't noble? Are you so accustomed to being a hero? Perhaps it's not only our lives we must be prepared to sacrifice, but the purity of our consciences."

Curry stared out at the night. "I've got to express my reservations, that's all." He tried to picture himself making speeches at German camps, but couldn't.

"Is it because of her brother?"

"Whose?"

"The girl's. Tyrrell."

Her brother! The connection hadn't registered. This was why Pearse wondered about his feeling for Jane. But he hadn't even known she had a brother in the army. The war and her family were things they'd steered clear of. But what *did* he make of her brother? Pearse had made it sound as if the prisoners were all butchers' boys.

Jane Tyrrell's brother was neither here nor there, but was Jane? The pain he'd seen in her face as he left the Gresham had made him miserable, but that pain had to do with more than her brother's plight. She was caught between walls that weren't of her building. If the walls were closing in on her, still he did not know if she wanted out from them. He did not know nearly enough to justify the rush of guilt he felt. He'd taken no oaths. They'd avoided all of this, except in the large sweeping arcs of talk that everyone around the Abbey mastered. If politics and religion and family were kept to the margins, no wonder what held sway between Dan and Jane were the simple facts of themselves. But wasn't the charged air between them, the fact that each inhaled it and thrived upon it and had come to need it like a personal form of oxygen—wasn't that a kind of commitment? There is a baptism of desire; are there such oaths?

"If you have a thing for her, it wouldn't do for you to cross paths with her brother, as you could if Casement gets the agreement. The Irish prisoners will all be brought together."

"Her brother's not the issue."

"What is?"

"You've asked me at last to leave the ranks of the melancholy sentimentalists who have an excess of patriotic fervor, but also of domestic obligations. They thrill at the talk of risings and at the risings of their elbows. They drift from meeting to meeting like atoms of fog that cover the fact that nothing ever happens." He grinned. "As for me, I like my revolutions on the stage. You want me to leave it for the real world in which to do something real for Ireland. Of course I'm reluctant."

"But you'll go?"

"My play closed tonight, Pádraic. I need the job."

"And as for the qualm of your conscience?"

"I didn't have Jesuits at Maynooth, but I had them at the university. My conscience will come along."

Pearse flicked his cigarette into the night. When it hit the wet pavement, it sizzled. He said, "Will you tell me, man, without irreverence that you'll do this and that I'm right to trust you?"

Curry took Pearse by the shoulders, a rare act of familiarity. "I love Ireland, Pádraic. Let me make my solemn oath to her through you."

They parted after midnight, at the Liffey. Curry was walking back to his lodgings near Christ Church Cathedral, feeling agitated, but also relieved. The elements of his life—his hard tenement boyhood, the long seminary apprenticeship that led to nowhere, the ruthless, self-imposed regimen of study at university, and the exhilarating but finally unsatisfying work of theater—had always seemed jarringly discontinuous to him. But now they had fallen together into what seemed a wholly woven pattern of preparation. Preparation for this. Preparation for a serious, potentially decisive role in the birth of a new Ireland. His relief was what a man feels when he discovers that without knowing it he has already become what he'd always hoped to be.

At College Green he was crossing the street toward Cork Hill. Because of the rain he hurried with his head lowered, and because his mind reworked furiously what Pearse had told him, he did not notice the hired carriage bearing down on him until the horse veered. The driver shouted.

Curry would have ignored the carriage and gone on his way, but it stopped. He felt a rush of energy. Was the driver going to challenge him? The man, having spent his evening waiting by a call box, would be drunk, and Curry would have the devil's time turning aside his insults.

He faced the carriage, ready. But the driver didn't move from his perch.

Curry waited in the middle of the street, rain dripping from his beard. On one side of him was the black, pillared hulk of the Bank of Ireland and on the other were the gates of Trinity College, graceful but also—to a Catholic—forbidding.

The door of the carriage opened. That was all. It simply opened. No one alighted and no one leaned out. The curtains were drawn and it was impossible to see in.

Curry approached the cab slowly. The rough cobbles beneath his feet made him feel unsteady.

At the carriage door he looked in. The sole figure in the far corner was wrapped in darkness, but he knew at once it was Jane.

The horse reared, the carriage rolled roughly back, and the driver cursed while struggling to control it.

Curry imagined himself saying to her, I'm not the man I was before. Not even that.

But he felt a current coming from the corner of such pain and such longing that he was forced, at last, to recognize his own. He climbed into the carriage. When he closed the door behind him, the horse heard its slam as the signal to bolt.

9

Ireland's was a religion of sacraments. Outward signs, the catechism called them, instituted by God to give grace. The most common gestures and materials carried the weight of transcendent meanings; water, bread, fire, oil, signs of the cross all pointed beyond themselves to the eternal, ever-living triune God Himself. Into the service of this rubric even the humble shamrock had been impressed. Signs of the sacred were everywhere and in everything. The idea of sacraments, in other words, was at the heart of that perennial Irish oversensitivity that made too much of too little. If a splash of water on one's forelock could make the difference between eternities in heaven or hell; if a few mumbled phrases in an archaic tongue could wipe the soul's slate free of the most grievous sin, then a man and a woman who, out of primitive needs for warmth and consolation, took shelter in each other had no right to complain that the briefest, basest mingling of flesh had been made to mean too much.

Perhaps the Reformation, in rejecting sacraments, had rescued Protestants across the north of Europe from this overloading of the mundane—preferring to make things and acts mean too little than too much—but not in Ireland.

Not, at any rate, if you asked Jane Tyrrell. She did not concern herself with abstract concepts, but she had a signifying mind that habitually saw shadows of the world beyond, not a faerie world or a spirit world, as the peasants had it, but a world in which the substance of things was only barely hinted at by surfaces. But since surfaces were all one had to go by, they were crucial. One could almost say sacred. She might as well have been a Roman Catholic. The implication of that moment, for example, as she sat in the formal front parlor of Lady Gregory's house in Merrion Square watching Dan Curry build a fire meant far too much to her. But wouldn't it have to others? How could she ever have explained to Miss Sweeney, Lady Gregory's aged housekeeper asleep in the garret room, how she'd come to bring him here at this hour? How exactly did she explain it to herself?

At the hotel her father had said she was pale, unwell-looking, and he hadn't wanted her to leave alone. Of course she was upset. He'd made it seem as if Douglas were dead, and the more he denied it, the more she felt sure of it. It made her think of her mother. She should have been seeing Douglas and Pamela and the babies, but instead she saw her mother in the plain white apron she wore in her garden, the great crop of ripe gooseberries in the basket she cradled, gooseberries for jam that Jane still could not taste without crying. She was buried under an avalanche of the old grief, and the only way out from under it— she couldn't breathe!—was to leave her father. He had his grief too, but she had finally admitted to herself that she could not ease his pain until she eased her own. It was awful, she knew, but she had to be alone.

But then, as if there were holy ghosts and guardian angels, as the Catholics said, Dan Curry had appeared. The small kindnesses she'd had from him over those months had suddenly, irrationally loomed as the only truly soothing events of her time in Dublin. The books he'd given her, the sonnets he'd recited for her, the boiled-egg lunches he'd arrived with, the rose he'd left once on her desk with the note "You and this flower must be related"—these tokens of his, exactly like sacraments, seemed in memory transcendent, acts that had lifted her into a realm of grace. As quickly as her relief at seeing him had come, it faded when those other men appeared with him in that lobby. She felt the curtain of her old neurasthenia fall between herself and those contending men. They made it seem as if Douglas didn't matter, her grief didn't matter; and Dan Curry was one of them. But he'd looked at her with such feeling before leaving, and his message was, The realm of grace is the realm of danger.

And then, like the ghost or angel himself, he'd appeared out of the night rain in the shining street.

Grace, yes, but danger also. That was what she felt. Having on impulse brought him here, she was sure that the wrong words, gestures, and acts would have transcendence enough to destroy her. But she felt at the same time—this was why she'd surrendered to her impulse, why she didn't regret it even now—that the right ones could save her.

From her vantage she could have taken him for a broad-shouldered servant, so dutifully bent at the fireplace was he. She was touched by the frayed sleeves of his wet coat. He'd been so intent upon his effort to coax the flames that he had not acknowledged her when she entered the parlor carrying the tea tray. She'd moved about the kitchen quietly, as if Miss Sweeney would hear her from four floors away. She sat and was now pouring.

When he stood, watching the flames licking at last up around the logs, she said, "You should take your coat off and hang it there."

He looked around at her without turning fully.

"To dry it." Panic rose in her. In the carriage they'd hardly spoken. Everything that had occurred to her to say seemed wrong, and he had been content to sit across from her in silence.

She splashed the tea onto the table, then made it worse stabbing at it with a napkin.

He took his coat off and draped it on the back of an upright chair, drawing it close to the hearth. He watched the fire a moment longer, then, satisfied, faced her.

At once his eyes soothed her, and an easy smile brightened his face as he tugged on the hem of his waistcoat, saying, "A fellow feels underclothed without his coat in such a grand house. I've always wondered what these places were like. May I smoke?"

"Of course. Lemon?"

He shook his head, lighting a cigarette. He crossed to her for his tea. Then, saucer and cup in hand, he retreated to the fireplace. He put the saucer on the mantel, flicked his ash into the fire, and sipped his tea. "That's lovely, thank you." He stared into the tea as if studying the room's appointments in the liquid's black reflection.

But it was Jane's conceit, not his, to think he was always looking at reflections. She let her eyes drift around the room, trying to see it afresh, the way he must have. If using the black circle of his tea as a reflecting-glass, he'd have been struck first by the decorative plasterwork on the ceiling, an intricate design of *fleurs-de-lis*, scallop shells, and cupid heads. Would he have considered such rococo display tasteless vanity, as she was herself inclined to? The plasterwork was dingy and badly in need of refurbishing, though Curry showed no sign of having noticed it.

The floor-to-ceiling curtains were drawn, closing out the city. Not even the sound of heavy rain came in. Only one lamp was lit, the green-shaded one on the graceful, fringed-cloth-covered oval table by her settee. It was the light she read by at night, though the light it threw left much of the room in shadows. The fireplace too now threw light, but it was still impossible to make out the details of the various framed objects hanging on the walls. Curry would recognize the Jack Yeats portrait of Lady Gregory. Mr. Yeats had painted it to hang as the center-piece of his Abbey portraits, but she'd refused to hang it in the theater lobby, saying it would make her feel dead to see her portrait in a public place. The other ill-lit pictures of ancestors and country scenes, faded photographs of children, the original of Lady Gregory's bookplate, and a gilded Chinese fan would register with Curry only as so much bric-a-brac. As for furni-ture, in addition to Jane's own deep-red plush sofa, its end table and artfully arranged matching sofa and table, there were half a dozen upright chairs of various styles angled in such a way as to accommodate one large conversation. Lady Gregory did not entertain in Dublin as she did at Coole Park, but she often had the backers of her theater to tea in this room. On the dark Catalonian refectory table against the wall beside the doorway were piles of playscripts and pamphlets from past years describ-ing Abbey seasons.

"I was under the impression that you'd have been here." Jane spoke nervously. "Doesn't Lady Gregory invite the play-ers, her beloved chicks?"

"Oh, I *have* been here. I've been in some of the grandest houses in Dublin. I've come up." He laughed and replaced his cup. "But I'm still the bloke from Henrietta Street, and it always seems like the first time to me." He looked around the room, now taking it in the way Jane had. "Fifteen of us lived inside a pair of rooms half this size where I grew up." He said this not with bitterness but with amazement, as if the arrangement of his family's life had been a physical feat he could not believe in now. As, in a way, he couldn't. He moved in rooms and circles—a world—his parents, uncle, and siblings would not have believed existed in their own Dublin. As, in a way, it didn't.

Jane said, "Where I grew up the rooms didn't matter. What mattered were the sun and the fields and the sea."

Curry picked up his tea again. "You might have told me that your father was a deputy to Parnell. I assumed your people were Unionists."

"You might have told me that you're in Irish politics yourself. A friend to Casement and Pearse? You claim to be a plainspoken man, Dan Curry, but you've held back on me."

"So there we are."

Jane leaned back against the settee, cup in hand. The curving form of the sofa's armrest and back, from where Curry stood, called to mind the curve of a woman's hip. He let his eye fall across her body. She was wearing a printed white cotton dress with a shawl collar that displayed her throat. As always, her locket on its chain hung there. He wondered if it held a man's picture. "What else haven't you told me?" But then he was afraid she would read him too accurately and know he was asking about her loves, if she had them. He added, "Politically, what are you?"

"I don't know what I am. But I know what you are."

"What?"

"An actor."

"You make it sound like a failing."

"I only meant you have the knack for playing what's given you."

Curry bristled. "I'm not playing tonight, Jane. Not earlier and not now."

"No, Dan, you misunderstand me. I admire that you're an actor. I envy you. I envy everyone at the Abbey. I never met such people before. You live more deeply than the rest of us."

"But we read the lines others hand us. Isn't that what you meant? And, of course, it's true."

"No, it isn't true." Her eyes were locked on him. "You take those lines and transform them. Nothing exists until it passes through you."

"Like dung through a horse."

At once Jane blushed and looked away.

Curry's impulse was to cross to her and apologize, but he checked it. Next thing he'd be on one knee. This was not a night on which he needed to romanticize the profession he'd just abandoned. Hence his ugly remark. But neither did he need to disparage it, much less insult this woman. Sometimes he loathed himself. Instead of going to her, he remained where he was, waiting for her to look at him. Oh Christ, he thought, here was one more woman with whom he'd have gotten so far and no farther. But this one, he knew, would leave him feeling bereft. He envied his friends who didn't give a tinker's damn for what was hidden in the corners of their minds. He envied men who could say, Hell, she stopped her taxi for me in the middle of the night. What else was there to know?

He dropped his cigarette in the fire. If he left now he would never see her again. Was he going to spend the rest of his life punishing himself for having fallen short of his first ideal? How long was he going to do this to himself?

Curry forced himself to pick up his teacup again and cross the room. He took a seat on the second sofa, opposite her. He put his teacup down next to hers. The saucers almost kissed. "Jane, all I meant to ask before, when I said, 'What else haven't you told me?' was about your locket. I've long admired it. But you've never let me see whose picture's in it."

Without speaking or looking at him, Jane raised her arms to unclasp the chain behind her neck. The press of cotton stretched across her bosom emphasized her womanliness; he imagined her stepping from her bath, arms like that to pin her hair. He imagined her naked. Curry had never been with a woman in that way, watching her casually while the air dried her skin, while the blush of heat faded in the cool breeze as she toweled herself. This woman was a wholly other creature than the bitter whores, those few, whom he had furtively watched in the shadows of those awful rooms in Talbot Street. Yet the lustful feeling was the same. It shamed him, how he wanted to ravish her as he had those prostitutes. When he saw a flash of her breast inside the collar of her dress, he averted his eyes prudishly, and he felt mortified. What was it the Austrian psycho-doctors spoke of, the Holy Mary complex? Even the scent of her perfume—honeysuckle?—assaulted him. Custody of the senses, they called it in the seminary: what he had just lost.

She offered him the chain, and dangling from it, the locket.

He took it, let the smooth, gold heart rest in his palm, studying it with a detached air that had nothing to do with the agitation he felt. If this was a scene, he'd have focused everything on that object as a method of control. It is her heart, he'd have said to himself, and she gave it to me.

But this was no scene. She'd given it to him so that he could open it. Not her heart, but one of its secrets.

He fumbled at the catch and his counterfeit detachment failed him. He looked up at her anxiously, as if his opening it were not what she'd had in mind. "May I?" When she nodded, he did open it.

And *his* heart sank.

He saw the small photograph of an impressive-looking man, not her father, his hair dark and slick, sharply parted, his brow strong, his mustache perfectly shaped above a pleasant mouth and chin. Even in that tiny image the patrician features and the inbred air of self-possession made it evident to Curry that this was the sort of man he would never be. Yet it wasn't resentment he felt, because the photograph also conveyed, somehow, the man's decency. One sensed his kindness. Curry imagined meeting the man, exchanging a hearty handshake with him, and liking him at once. The thought doubled his chagrin. He imagined strolling the Liffey quays with the bloke as he described the great fun he and Jane—would he call her Janey?—had had as children. They'd have been second or third cousins, and on one of their estates, his father's or hers, they would have shared a playhouse in which Janey kept her dolls and he his tin soldiers, and it would have been built to scale, down to children's size, but still larger than the hovels in which their fathers' tenants lived.

Curry cursed himself for a fool, and now his resentment surfaced, a geyser of it. In all those weeks of seeing her at the Abbey, he'd never seriously entertained the thought that she was spoken for. She hadn't misled him. On the contrary, in all their encounters she'd been careful, almost reserved. If he had never quite pressed initiatives past the casual or sought to broaden the context of their friendship beyond the Abbey, neither had she. She was less flirtatious, in fact, than Nora Guinan, and Nora *was* married. So who the hell wouldn't be confused? Especially when eventually he decided that her reserve was a matter of something else. She simply seemed innocent of the sort of history a man's photograph in her locket implied, and she always, despite her shyness, made him feel she valued his company more than anyone's. He'd thought the bond between them, while not erotic precisely, was potentially so. And if he had not just in those weeks been swept by Pádraic Pearse into the great struggle, he'd convinced himself it would have flowered.

She had told him that her mother was deceased; now that he thought of it, one of her few personal revelations. And he had told himself from then on that it was her mother's image she treasured in the locket. But he was the one with the mother complex. He looked up at her, trying to keep his peevish feelings at bay. What business had she stopping him tonight and bringing him here?

"It's Douglas," she said.

Douglas?

"My brother."

Curry directed his surprise into the act of slowly lowering his head again to look at the tiny picture. He raised the locket for light then, eyeing it the way a jeweler does a gem.

What was he doing to her and to himself by being here? First he'd regarded it as fatal that the locket held the picture of her lover; then, on learning the good news—not lover, only brother—he discovered how much more fatal good news could be. This was Pearse's point, the one he'd refused to hear. Her brother was a prisoner of the Germans. The Germans, friends to Ireland, to whom he had within the hour agreed to serve as emissary.

Decency required that he say something, but he couldn't. Any sentence he began on the subject would end as a lie. He could imply nothing of what he'd promised Pearse, not because of his oath, but because she would hate him. At that moment the most important thing in the world, more important than his solemn secret and its hold on his immortal soul, was that she not.

Decency required that he leave.

He snapped the locket shut. "Thank you," he said, handing it back to her. She took it shyly. Suddenly he felt a rush of sympathy for her, and his urge to leave faded. She wasn't the object of his desire now, but a shattered girl. "You must be so worried for him."

"I'm sure he's dead."

"Is that why your father came, to tell you?"

"Yes." When she looked at him now, tears spilled out of her eyes.

And he saw why she'd stopped for him in the street: she couldn't carry this grief alone. Before that recognition fell all his reasons for pulling back. For the first time he surrendered the center of his own preoccupation to her. Jane needed help. And she was asking for it from him. Jane had been moving through the events of that night like a sleepwalker, thickly aware of things said and done by others, but focused mostly on her dream. It was a dream of Pamela screaming, striking blows, and refusing to believe that Douglas was dead. While she herself stood mutely by refusing to believe he wasn't. Even in the dream it was a question: Why should she be so certain that the worst had happened? The evidence wasn't in. "Missing," her father had said. "In a German camp," he had said. But to Jane, Douglas was as dead as their mother was. One of the two unmovable margins of her existence—her father was the other—had simply vanished, leaving that side of her exposed. She knew from before that the world from that side—Douglas's side had been her mother's side—could do anything it wanted to her.

The world—what an enemy to have. Jane had grown up thinking of it as that broad but limited stretch of grass between the great cliff of Cragside and the embracing Palladian house. The house and cliff were immutable, more reliable to her than any of the ideas—God, Britain, Ireland, the Church—on which others depended for their stability. But if Douglas was gone, the ancient house was gone or the eternal cliff was; half of what protected her was gone. Douglas had stood between her and death. Now she understood why she had panicked after he and Pamela had left Cragside. Even with her father there, she was all too vulnerable; no, more vulnerable than ever. What if he died too? She'd fled to Dublin to find other cliffs and houses, other break walls with which to hold back the swelling indifferent world.

When she looked at Curry she knew her tears would spill, but she didn't care. "I came to Dublin because I knew he was going to die. I knew it when he went to France."

Curry wanted to ask, How did you know? But he said nothing. He looked at her steadily to show that he was not afraid of her abject fatalism.

She said, "And when I met you I realized how little I know about everything, and I began to think that I *could* live without my family if I had to."

"We all need our families, Jane." Even as he said this, the sadness of his own situation choked him. His family, even his hard-shell brothers, had utterly rejected him when he'd quit Maynooth. He turned slightly to stare at the fire. After a moment he stood, crossed to it, adjusted the logs, then returned to the sofa opposite Jane. She had composed herself somewhat. He said, "I understand the feeling you have, but you should remember that you don't know he's dead."

"You're right. I'm going to stay with his wife in London. There's no point in doing that if I'm just going to drag her down."

Curry felt a stab of disappointment that she was leaving. But so was he. That wasn't the point just now. "Not everyone who goes to France gets killed. And if he's a prisoner, I'm sure that's safer than being at the Front."

Jane looked at him incredulously. "But imagine what the Germans do to them."

Curry shook his head, knowing he should skate away from that, but it was the crux of his own issue. "The Germans are no worse than the British, Jane." He forced a laugh, determined to lighten their mood. "The Kaiser is King George's cousin. They went to the same kind of schools and they play by the same rules. One rule is to respect the enemy's officers. Douglas is an officer, isn't he?"

Jane nodded.

"An Irish regiment?"

"The Connaught Rangers."

"Then that's another point for him. There's reason to think the Germans will treat the Irish well."

"Why?"

Curry buried his anxiety in the act of lighting another cigarette. She watched him intently the whole time, waiting for his answer. He shrugged and said as casually as he could, "Because their argument is more with England than with us. The point is, mourn the dead, but pray for the living."

Jane reached for her tea. She hadn't prayed for Douglas because she didn't know how. "Do you pray?"

"Yes. I wanted once to be a priest."

Jane's surprise showed.

Curry laughed again. "We've known each other how long? And you don't know that? It's the most important thing about me. I studied for the priesthood for nine years, from the age of twelve. Then I chucked it."

"Why is that the most important thing about you?"

He slapped his forehead dramatically. "I keep forgetting you're a Protestant. A Catholic would never ask me that."

Jane blushed. Had she been rude? She said helplessly, "I don't understand."

"It marks me for a failure. It always will. Which is why I don't talk about it."

"Do you mind talking about it now?"

He shook his head no.

"Why didn't you go through with it?"

"Because . . ." No one had ever asked him this. In case they had, he was always going to say, Three reasons: poverty, chastity, and obedience. But it was unthinkable he should be flippant with her. He said simply, "I couldn't face a life alone."

"That's why I left Cragside. Which in my world, since I'm unmarried, was equally out of the question."

"A pair of exiles, then?"

She nodded. For the first time that night she smiled. "Curious isn't it, how marriage features. I was supposed to get married and you weren't."

"Why didn't you?"

"Nobody asked me, sir," she said.

"Go on. The Dublin Horse Show is a parade of men for your picking, Jane."

"I haven't been to the horse show for years. My world was Cragside. I was happy there." Her smile faded and her eyes filled again. "I loved it. I still love it. But it isn't a place for me anymore."

"What is?"

"I haven't got a place, Dan. Unlike you. It's one of the ways we're different."

"Me!" He'd been thinking they were alike.

"You have Ireland."

"You think I'm Naisi? You think I'm Cuchulain?"

"No, but isn't that what it means, that you were with Pearse and Casement?"

He eyed her steadily. "Yes, I suppose it does. I won't be going back to the Abbey, Jane."

"Dan, you can't mean that. Isn't the Abbey for Ireland? You mustn't leave the Abbey. It needs you."

"You said you have to go to London to be with your brother's wife. Events compel you, Jane. It isn't a question of choosing to go. In certain circumstances one simply goes. It's the same with me."

"How do they put it? You'll be working for Ireland's freedom?"

"It doesn't matter how they put it."

"But what will you be doing? There's nothing to be done until the war is over. And then Parliament has already passed the law giving us Home Rule. It's a *fait accompli.*"

Curry saw now how unthinkable it was to her that England's war should take second place to anything. "Not if you ask our friends in Ulster or their friends in Parliament. We'd be fools to take Home Rule for granted, Jane." He veered from his next thought, that Irishmen like her brother had been fools to think of earning Home Rule by joining the British army. It was a typically lame-brained Irish idea, that blood in the dirt could seal an otherwise impossible contract. But how could he say such a thing to her? Or should he just insult her outright by deigning to explain why England would never succeed in defying Carson's Ulsterites on the issue? The futility—and by now stupidity—of Parnellite dreams of Home Rule were either too obvious or too complicated. Either way, it was irrelevant. He went on abstractly, without conviction, a conversationalist no longer listening to himself, "Maybe Home Rule has been the problem, that so many of us on our side have seemed willing to settle for it all these years, while in the north they've refused even to discuss it. Home Rule is Rome Rule, and all that."

"You mean, we force Ulster into thinking well of Home Rule, which preserves some link with London by beginning to demand absolute independence?"

"That's one thought." He laughed. "Or, as Cardinal Newman put it, 'Lead, kindly Light, amid the encircling gloom; / Lead Thou me on!'" He stared at his cigarette, thinking, What delicate distinctions we're trained to make. The wish for Home Rule is gentlemanly in the south but treason in the north, while one can loyally defy Parliament in the north, but in the south the idea of defiance is obscene. Clearly Jane had yet to think past her father on the question. She hadn't gathered that the knot was tied more in Belfast now than London, and Belfast was where the British navy's ships were made. Because a primitive and simple notion of Home Rule had been the outer limit of her father's ambition for Ireland, and no doubt it was a notion built on the dream of a restored Ascendancy, Home Rule remained the crux of the issue for Jane. He felt obliged to at least indicate that something separated them. "We're not singing in unison on this one, Jane."

"I know."

"Does it matter?"

"No."

"Nor to me."

What then? What possibly then? Snuffing his cigarette, Curry said, "Speaking of Newman, not that we were . . ." He managed this as if he'd never been less disconcerted. ". . . As you know he founded the university here. There's a statue to his memory in the Jesuit Garden, and I went to see it. I passed a caretaker. I knew where I was going, but out of a need to acknowledge him I said, 'This is the way to Newman's statue, no?' John Henry Newman who in the decade since his death emerges as one of the most glorious writers to have graced Dublin since Richard Sheridan and one of the greatest bishops of the Church since Fisher. And the caretaker nods at me from his shovel and says. 'The convert?'"

Curry laughed hard, remembering how at the time he'd felt obliged not to. But Jane didn't laugh. Curry grew silent and waited for her to look at him. When she did, she said, "May I say something personal?"

"Of course."

"I envy you your belief, Dan. I don't believe in anything."

"Don't say that, Jane. It isn't so."

She smiled vaguely and fussed shyly with the bow below her collar. "But you said I could say it."

He panicked that she thought herself chastised, and he wanted to go to her, to take her hand. She seemed so young, so open to be hurt.

She said quietly, "It is so. It's why I can't pray for Douglas and why I feel he must be dead. I never could pray for my mother. Where you have your faith, in that place in me I have just emptiness."

"But you have Christ."

"Is it so unthinkable to you that I don't?"

And of course it was. But had he ever discussed such things with Protestants? And wasn't it a Catholic conviction that Protestants held their thin creed the way they held their teacups, with two fingers only, and not a fist? The faith was for good weather, not bad. But in good weather, who needed it?

Her neck was bent like a swan's. She was intent now upon smoothing the cloth of her dress across her lap. He sensed that she was incapable of taking delight even in her own loveliness, and suddenly that was what seemed unthinkable. There seemed to be more truth in the hold her beauty had over his senses than there ever could be in her despair. Isn't despair what the absence of faith amounts to? Curry had been taught that faith was a gift from God, freely given, and that it could be just as freely taken away. "Lead Thou me on!" he repeated to himself. "The night is dark, and I am far from home; / Lead Thou me on!" Once he'd have recited such lines aloud in that circumstance, full of his own flamboyance. But he was full now only of her pain.

"I believe, Lord," he said quietly. "Help Thou my unbelief."

Jane looked up sharply; how she hated Bible quoters. "Why do you say that to me?"

"Because I want to help you. That's a prayer you can say, isn't it? It's a prayer of someone whose faith is shaken."

"But I don't believe, Dan. I don't believe at *all.*"

"You believed in me, Jane, enough to stop your carriage."

She lowered her eyes as if she regretted that, as if it made her ashamed.

He crossed to her and, as he sat, he put his hands on her shoulders, turning her. The feeling gnawed at him until he called it by its name. "I love you, Jane." She fell against him, and then her body convulsed as she surrendered at last to the worst grief of her life.

————

At a certain point they lay absolutely still, stretched on the floor, fully clothed. Curry felt the pressure of her hips. Slowly he raised himself to his knees, then pulled her up after him. In their first burst of passion neither had been aware really of falling from the sofa. Now he craned past her for the lamp and turned it off. The room was washed by the flickering light of the fire, but it was a relative darkness and just what each needed to lay aside an inhibiting modesty.

They undressed in silence, separately, without their eyes meeting.

Curry had no more experience with this than she had. Men helped women to disrobe, he knew, unless they were whores. But her garments were a mystery and she hadn't looked to him. He was naked before she was, and he stood apart, painfully conscious of his erection. When she stepped out of her shift, it was toward him. Her breasts gleamed and her hips flared around the furrow between her legs. He stared at her while she raised her arms as she had before to undo the locket chain. Her breasts flattened across her chest, but now not under the deceiving cloth, and he felt the pitch of his arousal climbing. She unclasped her hair, and with a quick shake of her head, it poured down over her shoulders.

As she went to him, raising her eyes for a look of confirmation and finding it, the scent of his skin was what moved her, an earthy, unperfumed musk. When he took her into his arms now, brushing her face with his soft beard, she was surprised at his tenderness. He was kissing her, not roughly as he first had, but gently, all across her face and neck, into her hair and down to her breasts. His beard was like feathers, and the sensation was so light, so delicate, so unbearably sweet, she realized she had never felt her own skin as a distinct part of herself before. And the same was true, she saw, of sexual desire; neither had it seemed like hers until now.

———

Later, after they lay motionless in each other's arms, he made as if to go. Was he disappointed, embarrassed? He had ejaculated all too quickly, so that her own first experience of real arousal had taken her nowhere. Even Jane knew that lovemaking was meant to be more. Still, that seemed unimportant to her. She held him, but he pulled away. She was sure that he was leaving her.

But a moment later he was above her, brushing wisps of hair away from her face, pulling her upright, turning her so that she faced away. She would always be his, she felt, to move as he willed, to shape.

She did not realize what he was doing until he lowered the locket from above her head, encircling her throat as if it was a prize. He deftly hooked the ends of the golden chain at the nape of her neck. The locket on her bosom was so cold it made her realize how hot his skin had been. His heat inside her, deep and wide, had made her know she was not empty. As she touched the locket, she understood that he had read what was written in her. The sensation—to be at once absolutely exposed and absolutely embraced—filled her with the awe of a lame person healed, one blind made to see. She turned to him.

Curry could never have said to that woman, Let me give you back your brother, yet that was his great wish. He could never have said, Let my love give you faith and hope. He was unworthy for once of words. It had nothing to do with class or politics that he felt unworthy at last of her.

Once more they kissed, and more slowly now, their young bodies having learned, they became one sign to each other again, giving grace.

10

Trier is the oldest city in central Europe. At the juncture of three rivers and close to the points where Belgium, France, and Luxembourg each touch Germany, it was a natural site for the large complex of camps that the Germans used as a clearing station for their prisoners. Thousands of French and British soldiers were brought through Trier. Most remained for only a matter of weeks before being transported by train to camps east of the Rhine, in the heart of Germany. But one group of prisoners remained there, segregated from the rest—men of the Irish regiments. By the fall of 1915 there were more than a thousand of them, including nearly three hundred from the Connaught Rangers. It was fitting that Trier should have been the site of their incarceration because, before it had served as the seat of the ancient Roman government for Western Europe—the Romans left behind in Trier the famous ruins of baths, the great bridge across the Mosel, the amphitheater, and the massive Porta Nigra, which was the northern gate to the entire empire—Trier had been settled by Celts.

The Celts left behind little more than a legend. It concerned the Leuk waterfall, a seventy-foot cataract, an overwhelming downpour of water that ran in a furious stream from the hills beyond Trier down to the Mosel, two miles or more away. The Celts believed it to be the flow of tears of gods who had lost their children in the wilderness of forest and mountain through which the river ran.

The compound in which the Irish soldiers were kept was in sight of the waterfall. The hill beyond, down which the water rushed, was crowned with the ruins of a castle just visible above the glorious red-and-gold spread of leaves on the turning trees. In that castle had lived the archbishops of Trier, who, as electors of the Holy Roman Emperor, had been for a time some of the most powerful men in Europe. Now the ruins of their hill fortress and the hill itself in its autumn splendor and the cascading river that had seemed sacred to the first settlers all combined in a rare, timeless beauty that seemed wrong to men who had to view it from behind barbed wire.

As likely as not, their idling gaze would go the other way, toward the main body of prison compounds, tent settlements arranged in neat squares and spread across the valley away from Trier itself. There were dozens of house-sized tents, encircled with barbed wire and set off from one another by muddy avenues through which streams of vacant-eyed prisoners were marched. The Irish soldiers could see with their own eyes that conditions in the main camp, from which they were set apart, were vastly inferior to their own. The Irish had true huts, not tents. They were on higher ground and so it was dry. Yet the avenues between buildings were paved with duckboard. They had laundries, an infirmary, a broad playing field with chalked boundaries, and a large mess tent in which they were served food that surpassed what they'd grown used to from their own cookers. Discipline was maintained not by harsh, spike-helmeted guards, but by their own officers. The Irish officers alone among the Allies had not been separated from their regiments, and as a group they made the men feel protected from their captors' whims. Yet all of this, particularly as it contrasted with what went on in the rest of the internment camp, left the Irish prisoners feeling more guilty than grateful. What had they done to merit their relative privilege? No one was more sensitive to inequity than a foot soldier, and every Paddy understood why every Tommy and Jock would hate him for his exemptions. But as Irishmen they also felt that hatred as yet another undeserved English insult.

It was the middle of October, early morning, and the men were gathering for the day's first muster in the large open yard between the mess tent and the high fence that separated the Irish prisoners from the others. The chill air had them slapping their shoulders, and their breath came in small white puffs. Tyrrell stood with Keefe by the fence while the men formed their ranks. After inspection Keefe would take them through their exercises, then Tyrrell, as senior of the seven officers, would address the men. His biggest problem had been to think of ways to occupy them. Today he was announcing a mandatory program of study of the Irish language. It would be conducted by the several dozen Gaeltacht lads for whom it was their native tongue. The nationalists among the men, who'd enlisted in the first place to help achieve Home Rule, would welcome the idea, but the men from Ulster regiments, about a quarter of the prisoners, would groan. Tyrrell himself cared nothing for the Irish language, but the men had to do more with their time than police the camp, play football, hurley, or surreptitious games of Crown and Anchor in which the betting was for cigarettes. However foreign the intellectual exercise would be for most of them, they would need it, particularly as the weather turned colder. The Germans had agreed to supply chalkboards.

A detachment of recently arrived French prisoners could be seen filing along one of the main camp avenues. They still had the drooped, resigned look of battle-shocked men, and paid little heed to the German guards who nipped at them like sheep dogs. Keefe said, "More Frogs. Every day this week, they bring in Frogs."

Tyrrell watched the prisoners. "But still no officers. I keep waiting to see officers over there."

"But if it's French they're bringing in, maybe that means things have eased up at last on our line. Maybe Wipers is over."

"If the fight at Ypres is finished, Keefe, it's because we lost it. In that case, we'd be seeing our boys by the lorryful over there, not Frenchmen. We haven't lost at Ypres yet, don't worry."

Keefe laughed. "Did I sound worried?"

Tyrrell laughed too. Keefe was not indifferent. He was simply stating the obvious, that his concern did not manifest itself as worry. He was a pragmatic, steady man. Tyrrell had come to value him beyond any officer he knew, and he sensed that Keefe reciprocated, though a studied and mutual formality still formed the structure of their relationship.

Tyrrell fixed his stare on the distant row of copper trees that formed the far border of the internment camp. The stream from the waterfall ran down to them, and beyond those trees, invisible, was the next slope of land that fell off to the Mosel River. "Beech trees," Tyrrell said. "I've been staring at those trees for four months and only now realize that they're beeches."

"You haven't been thinking about the trees, Captain."

"Oh really, Mr. Keefe? What have I been thinking about?"

"The river."

Tyrrell looked at Keefe, but said nothing.

Just then Riley, the regimental sergeant major, presented himself. "Ready for roll call, sir."

"Very well, Sergeant Major." Tyrrell looked back at the men. They were standing easy in loose ranks, drably outfitted in what remained of their uniforms. Some had blankets draped around their shoulders against the chill. "Get those blankets back to billets, Sergeant Major. This is kit inspection, not slumber time."

The NCO nervously looked back at the ranks. "Those men have no tunics, sir. I thought what with the cold . . ."

"Do they have shirts, Sergeant Major?"

"Yes, sir."

"And are there surplus shirts in the quartermaster's store?"

"Yes, sir."

"Then give them second shirts. We'll wait. We can't have men on parade looking like beggars, can we?"

"No, sir." The sergeant major saluted and turned briskly.

When he was gone, Tyrrell said to Keefe, "I don't know what we'll do as the winter comes. Fritz won't be handing out greatcoats."

"If we all wear blankets, Captain, then there's no affront."

Tyrrell let his appreciation for his adjutant show. "You've a knack for solutions, Mr. Keefe."

"Blanket solutions, Captain." Keefe grinned, then abruptly assumed his more characteristic neutrality of expression. "In point of fact, sir, Jerry might very well offer us a supply of over-coats. Mind you, not that I expect it. But I didn't expect meat once a day either."

Tyrrell nodded and stared out across the main internment camp. "It's a question of balancing the needs of our men with the solidarity we owe those other regiments. They're not getting meat out there. Should I be refusing it for our lads, do you think?"

"No, sir. We should take what we can get, as long as we haven't sold ourselves for it."

"I keep thinking the Germans will be moving us along too, but now I wonder. I don't understand what they're up to."

"The men think you and Captain Tyndale have pooled your family allowances to bribe the German commandant."

Tyrrell laughed and said, "We're so rich," although he knew that Tyndale's family fortune was vast. "I think it's as simple as the fact that our situation is standard. These other prisoners are deprived because they're still in transit camp. Perhaps, in contrast, this is our final destination." Did he really believe this? He offered the argument to Keefe as if he did. "When they are settled, as we've been, their rations will improve, as will their facilities. Their officers will be reassigned to them. Their camps will be like ours, in other words, but they won't have a clearing station full of desperate cases abutting them, undercutting their ability to savor their relief at having survived the trenches or to enjoy the few essentials—dry feet, meat, fresh bread, chalkboards—the Krauts dole out like luxuries. It bothers me that our lads should have to look across this wire and be made to feel like corrupted beneficiaries by what they see." He watched the desolate column of French prisoners disappearing into the center of the shabby, makeshift compound. Suddenly, Tyrrell said bitterly, "Their suffering is not our doing, damn it. Our lads have what little they have by right, not charity and not bribery either. When the winter comes I'll *demand* overcoats for them! I'll demand them now!"

It was another day like that one, though a week later and somewhat colder, when an open German staff car drove into Trier. A German officer sat in the front seat next to the driver, his peaked hat strapped to his chin against the wind. From the fender in front of him fluttered a large square flag bearing a black Maltese cross in the center of which reared a talon-flashing black eagle.

In the backseat of the large tan car sat the bearded figures, one dark and one red, of Sir Roger Casement and Daniel Curry.

Curry could not bring himself to look at the faces of the citizens they were driving past. No one was more conscious of the impact of his appearance than he, a redheaded Irishman in a country where all the men were black-haired or blond. But in fact few of the people they passed on the streets of Trier were men. Like most cities in Europe by then, Trier was populated mainly by women. The contingent of troops who served as guards at the burgeoning prisoner-of-war camp was made up largely of soldiers who themselves had been subjects of disciplinary action, and they were permitted to leave the camp barely more often than the prisoners were. Trier proper therefore seemed tranquil as Casement and Curry were driven through it. Their guide turned from his place in the front seat to point out the antiquities. A German officer named Bremer who'd accompanied them from Berlin, he carried himself as if he held great authority, but he wore the uniform of a Landsturm colonel. The Landsturm was the German reserve force made up of those too old to serve in the Regular Army. They counted for nothing, but one wouldn't have known that from Bremer's friendly self-assurance. On the train he and Casement had argued about Richard Strauss's *Elektra* in a way that had made Curry feel excluded.

"A grotesque sensation, my dear Sir Roger," Bremer had said mildly, flourishing his liberalism. He was no vulgar chauvinist, compelled to defend everything German. His informality with the titled Casement indicated a place of some rank in the rigid social caste of Imperial Germany.

"I saw Strauss himself conduct *Elektra* in London," Casement replied. "The barbaric English disgraced themselves. I agree with Shaw, who said that anyone who disliked *Elektra* is an anti-German hysteric."

Bremer, sitting opposite Curry in the train compartment, had exchanged a quick glance with him. He sensed Curry's sympathy and sought to nudge the conversation his way. "You, Mr. Curry, have you seen Herr Strauss's work?"

"I fancy Johann," Curry said, "over Richard." The Austrian over the German was the unspoken comment. He smiled.

Casement reacted as if Curry had insulted him. "Waltz music! What is that? The masses love waltz music!"

Casement's haughtiness irked and embarrassed Curry, and he was moved to bring him down a notch. "English audiences aren't the only ones to disgrace themselves. We've a tradition at the Abbey: we can always tell a masterpiece if the people riot."

"My point exactly," Casement said. "Strauss is the German Synge."

Bremer leaned toward Curry. "You are associated with the famous Abbey Theatre? In Berlin, we often compare the Freie Bühne to the Abbey."

Curry had heard of the German theater, but his contrariness carried over, making him want to deflect Bremer's compliment. "At the Abbey we were inspired most by the Théâtre Libre."

"Ah, yes," Bremer said easily, "of Paris." He smiled vaguely. "They riot in Paris too. Stravinsky, Diaghilev, Nijinsky." He checked himself. It wouldn't do to seem superior, yet who could think of an occasion on which a German audience had misbehaved?

Now the staff car was passing a large cathedral. Bremer turned from his place in front and pointed to it. He was a stout man, and the simple act of facing backward seemed like contortion. "The Liebfrauenkirche, one of the oldest Gothic cathedrals in Germany. In its treasury you will find the Holy Robe of the Lord, the seamless cloak which was given to the Bishop of Trier by Saint Helena, the mother of Constantine the Great. She brought the garment here personally from the Holy Land. We Catholics venerate the relic above all others."

Curry understood the man's heavy-handed purpose—to ingratiate himself with these Irish Catholics. Curry resisted the impulse to refer to Germany as the home of Luther, but he couldn't stop himself from turning to Casement. "What would Protestants make of the Holy Robe, Sir Roger?"

Casement seemed not to hear him.

As the car left the massive Porta Nigra behind, Bremer said, "Of course, when the Emperor Augustus came to Trier in fifteen before the Lord, he is not beginning the city. You say that, 'beginning'?"

"Founding."

"*Jah*, founding." Bremer smiled broadly, flashing a gold tooth. "Because it is that Irish people are already here." When neither Curry nor Casement reacted, Bremer nodded vigorously. "Is true."

What will he claim, Curry wondered: that the Irish settled Germany or that Germans settled Ireland? Sure, wasn't theirs an alliance made, if not in heaven, in its anteroom?

In the journey from Berlin, Bremer's obvious efforts to ingratiate himself had offended Curry, but it was Casement who disturbed him. Until their rendezvous two days before in Switzerland, Curry hadn't seen him since that July night in Dublin. He'd been prepared to hear a stream of objections from Casement about his having been forced on him by Pearse, but Casement had seemed at first too distracted to grasp that Curry had been assigned with him to the same mission. Casement had been furtive with Curry, and at their meetings with Berlin officials, he had been unfocused, taking for granted a German commitment to arm, outfit, and train a large Irish force. But it was ludicrous, because the Germans knew as well as Curry did that such a force did not, as of yet, exist. Not in Ireland, anyway. Casement, having just come from the States, claimed there were thousands of Irish-Americans—the Clan na Gael—ready to come to Germany, and he spoke of the Paddies in the British army as if their transformation had already occurred. There was, in other words, an air of exaggeration, if not of unreality, about him, and it didn't help that Casement had introduced himself to each German official, including Bremer, as the commander-in-chief of "the Irish Brigade."

And now, as the staff car crossed through a ring of hills outside Trier into the gently sloping plain on which the vast internment camp had been erected, Casement reached forward and touched Colonel Bremer's arm to say, "When you introduce me, call me Commandant."

———

"The Mosel runs into the Rhine at Koblenz, here." Tyrrell planted his stick, but then raised his eyes from the ground for an instant, distracted by the flag-bearing staff car in the distance. He watched as it approached the headquarters compound, then disappeared into it. He dropped his eyes again, poked at the earth, and continued. "A straight run, downstream. But there's a problem." He had drawn in the dirt a map of the intersecting rivers. Captain Tyndale, Lieutenant Keefe, Lieutenant Clark, and a pair of platoon leaders named Fitzhugh and Desmond were grouped loosely around the dirt scratchings, smoking idly, facing away from Tyrrell, but managing to watch his pointer with sidelong glances. Tyrrell continued in a low voice. "There are locks to accommodate the barge traffic."

"Locks?" Clark asked.

"For passing barges from level to level. Every lock is a place where you'd be at risk, and they may not operate at night."

Clark could barely disguise the relief in his voice. "So much for a small boat creeping along under cover of darkness."

Captain Tyndale absently tossed a pebble at a nearby tree, watching the guard who passed beyond the barbed wire on his regular patrol. He turned to Clark for a light. "But that was precisely the thought, Lieutenant. Commandeer a fishing boat, a skiff, a dory. Hide by day, drift downstream by night." He blew his smoke toward Clark. "It was a lovely thought." He glanced at Tyrrell. "Quite compelling, really. But one doesn't drift through locks, does one?"

"What are the barges?" Keefe asked.

Tyrrell had traced and retraced his rivers, but now he poked the ground aggressively as he said, "Coal from the French mines in the Saar Valley, here. The River Saar joins the Mosel ten miles upstream from here. The Germans control that part of France and they are working the mines around-the-clock. They ship so much coal through here now, the cook said, that the river has turned black."

Keefe said, "If they're mining around-the-clock, then the barges run through the night. The locks must operate." Keefe looked at Tyndale. "So you hop a barge, Captain, instead of a dory. Free ride to Koblenz. If you're lucky, it goes down the Rhine to Cologne or further."

Tyrrell scratched his stick along the ground, extending the mark that represented the Rhine. "All the way to Amsterdam."

"And then what?" Desmond said. "Pick tulips?"

Tyrrell cast an impatient glance at the subaltern. "The Netherlands remain neutral, Mr. Desmond. One proceeds, therefore, to the British Embassy for assistance."

Tyndale shook his head. "It's impossible, Douglas. From here to Amsterdam must be two hundred miles."

"Two hundred and sixty, by my estimate."

"Well, then."

"With luck, you could make it. The Rhine must be jammed with shipping. Once you got there, you'd practically be home. I think you could safely take six men."

Tyndale looked sharply at Tyrrell, for the first time directly. "I'm not inclined to do so."

Tyrrell stared back at him. He said without rancor, "I'd give it a go myself, George, but my responsibility is here with the men."

The two captains continued to stare at each other; then Tyrrell began to kick at the dirt, obliterating the map. That was it. The officers drifted apart, but Keefe lingered. When they were alone, Keefe said to Tyrrell, "I think it's worth a try, Captain. I'd take a few lads who didn't mind coal on their faces."

Tyrrell turned his back on him, thinking, Not you, Bernard; I need you. In fact, he had never addressed Keefe by his Christian name. He said, "So you're thinking Captain Tyndale didn't want to soil his tunic, eh?" Keefe said nothing. Tyrrell couldn't face him. "Tyndale's probably right. Who knows what they could pick up in Koblenz or Cologne? And all we've talked about is the river." He looked out across the separate compounds. "First they'd have to slip this bloody camp. And with no weapons . . ."

Keefe ignored this new reservation. "With coal on our faces they'd think we're Turks and they'd send us along first-class. What do you say, Captain?"

Tyrrell had no choice but to encourage Keefe. The escape attempt had to be made by volunteers, including the officer leading it. It almost didn't matter if they succeeded. If even only half a dozen men broke out, or tried to, it would remind the other thousand that they were soldiers. It was like Keefe to want to try it. Tyrrell turned around. "All right, Lieutenant. Begin sounding out the men. When you have the right six, let me know. One of them should be an NCO, but not Riley. If you're gone, I'll need him more than ever." And that was as explicit as Tyrrell's acknowledgment of his dependence would get. "We should go to dinner," he said, slapping Keefe's shoulder, turning him. As they walked together, Tyrrell swung his stick as if it were a riding crop.

The men went to dinner in four shifts because the mess tent, though the largest structure in the compound, accommodated only three hundred table places. But on that day one of the Germans announced at the end of each of the first three shifts that the men were to return to the tent at the end of the fourth for assembly.

It was nearly midafternoon by the time everyone had finished the meal, a comparative feast of bacon, boiled potatoes, beets, and cake. The men from the earlier shifts crowded back into the mess tent. Tables were pushed against the walls to clear the space for them. The mess tent was actually a wooden structure with solid flooring and half-walls. Only the roof was canvas, and it muffled the sound of the boisterous men. They were keyed up, like schoolboys waiting to hear the headmaster's lecture.

When the entire cohort of Irish prisoners had crowded into the tent, the German kitchen crew began passing among them bearing trays that, to the Paddies' joyous amazement, held clay steins of wine. Finally they were getting to taste the local vintage, what in Ireland they'd have called "hock." Some men tried to think what holiday it was, and others said the war was over. But most just gulped the wine down and happily grabbed for more. For twenty minutes the Germans kept the wine coming, and the men furiously slaked their thirst.

Tyrrell had not been notified ahead of time of this assembly. It was unprecedented. A garrison lecture, he thought, or the announcement that they would finally be moving out. He sat, perplexed, at the officers' table in one corner of the room. His fellow officers were as intent upon the wine as the other ranks were. Tyrrell's stein was untouched.

He watched the door, for, though the Germans had never addressed his men en masse, preferring to convey their orders through him, his instinct told him now that the camp commander or his deputy would be making an appearance. For one thing, a small, portable stage several feet off the floor had been installed against the wall, just inside the door. Was he to believe that wine had been provided to give his men pleasure? Was that what Tyndale believed? Across the table, he saw him swilling the liquid down, and Tyrrell had to stifle a feeling of disgust.

Sergeant Major Riley was standing nearby; he too was holding himself aloof from the celebration. Tyrrell raised a finger and he came over. Riley had to put his ear by Tyrrell's mouth to hear him. "Sergeant Major, watch the door flap. When the German officers appear, call the men to attention, just as if it's our own brass. I want proper military display."

"Yes, sir."

Only moments later the canvas at the entrance was pulled back from behind. No one entered, but after a pause a German NCO barked out the order for attention. The prisoners ignored him. He repeated himself more loudly, and still they paid no heed. He nervously looked back through the doorway.

Then Riley's voice boomed once, "Atten . . . tion!"

The men stopped talking. Half of them stood to attention while the others gaped in confusion above their wine. Riley stood rigidly immobile before them, just in front of the platform, and it was clear he had no intention of repeating himself. Soon every man in the mess had come to his feet. Given the fact that many held on to the precious clay mugs, they achieved only an approximation of the proper posture.

The camp commander entered, a medium-sized man in a severely starched gray uniform with jodhpurs, polished riding boots, black gloves, and the elaborately emblazoned Prussian helmet: *Mit Gott* . . . Below the legend was a crowned eagle holding in its claws a scepter and a globe. The collar of his tunic came high on his throat, and his shoulder boards displayed the insignia of his rank and the silver braided knot of his unit. He was a colonel of the Prussian Guards and his name was Adler. On his breast was pinned a black-and-silver Iron Cross. He went directly to the platform and mounted it. He pointedly took in the sight of the crowded tent, then turned back toward the door and signaled with a slight nod. Colonel Bremer, Casement, and Curry entered and took up positions against the wall next to the platform.

"Guten Tag," Colonel Adler began. "Speak English, Jerry!" someone muttered loudly. Adler ignored him, but in fact went on in English. "Good day, my good Irish soldiers." He smiled in an appealing way. "I trust it is that you have found the humble drink of our region to your liking." He raised his eyebrows and paused, expecting some response. The men were taking their cue from Riley, who stood impassively at his place on the opposite side of the platform from Bremer, Casement, and Curry.

Tyrrell was staring at the two civilians. One seemed familiar to him, and the other's red beard and ruddy face made him seem an unlikely German.

Adler said, "We are privileged today to have with us special guests . . . You could perhaps to stand at ease . . ." He looked toward his own NCO.

"Ausgehanzug!" The sergeant said, but no one moved. Colonel Adler looked at Riley, then back at the men. "Stand at ease!" he said.

Riley didn't budge and therefore neither did the men, although a few braced themselves more properly now that the Germans had made an issue of it.

Adler let it go. "To make an explanation and to introduce these guests, let me hand you Oberst Humbert Bremer, who comes from the Commission of National Defenses in Berlin." He stepped down and Bremer replaced him on the platform.

For some moments Bremer simply looked at them. His uniform was ill-tailored compared to the commander's. With his gray tunic he wore a shirt and tie, not a Prussian collar, and instead of the helmet, he wore a soft-peaked hat with visor. He removed it, revealing a head of white hair. Only now was it apparent how very old he was. In one hand he held his hat, and in the other a sizable brown envelope. He began in a voice that seemed quiet, but which no one in the tent had trouble hearing. "Men of Ireland, I salute you!" He paused to emphasize this greeting. "Even in Berlin we know of your valor. Had you been in the vanguard, racing our armies to the sea, we know that our advance would have been impossible. And we know with full appreciation that the soldiers of Ireland, alone in this war, have no military ambition. Even we Germans confess to military ambition, as must your English rulers. Your ambition is peace for your own fatherland, and the German people understand you and we are prepared to support you."

Bremer paused to pull out of the envelope a letter-sized document that he held up for all to see. In one corner was a wax, beribboned seal. "This is the sacred treaty drawn, agreed to, and solemnly sworn between the German people and the people of Ireland." He slowly turned, displaying the paper liturgically. The soldiers were stunned, and as one body they stared in silence, trying to grasp what this could possibly mean. "Your place is not in Germany, nor in France, nor Belgium. Your place

is in Ireland, where the moment of your deliverance has arrived."
He referred again to the document. "Signing this agreement for
the Government of Germany with the authority of the Imperial Diet and the Kaiser himself is the German ambassador to
America, Baron von Bernstorff. For Ireland, the president of the
Clan na Gael, John Devoy, and the envoy plenipotentiary of
the Supreme Council of the Irish Republican Brotherhood and
the commander-in-chief of the Irish Brigade, Commandant Sir
Roger Casement, Knight of the British Empire." Bremer swept
his arm toward Casement, then stepped down.

Casement blinked out at the men. Did he expect them to
cheer? Aside from a momentary buzzing as they exchanged startled expletives—"Who's this bastard?"—they remained silent.
Curry sensed Casement's hesitation. He leaned into him and
whispered, "Don't lionize Germany and don't slander England.
Speak of Ireland, man."

Casement mounted the platform. His height and thinness,
his unornamented black clothing, and his ill-kempt beard set
him apart from the fastidious Germans. His eyes flashed as he
began to speak, stiffly at first, with an orator's formality. "I have
been sent by your people to speak to you of the new day that has
dawned in Ireland. Even now, events undreamed of only months
ago have begun. The Irish people have followed the American
example and the urgings of her martyrs to declare her independence from England. She will pay no further taxes. She will offer
no recruits to Imperial forces. And she will accept no services
from Westminster. This means, of course, terrible suffering and
the prospect of reprisals from the callous British—"

Suddenly Casement was interrupted by a single voice:
"Boo-o-o-o-o!" Others joined in, and then someone cried out,
"What the hell is the Irish Brigade?"

"You are!" Casement's arm shot out at them. The ferocious

will with which he cried this silenced them. "You are the men who must now put yourselves at the service of your own families, not England's. When British police come to arrest your mother for merely reading the leaflets she's been handed by one of our boys, what will she think of you?"

"Keep your leaflets to yourselves!"

"To hell with you, man!"

Casement ignored them. "I have come before you to invite you to join the Irish Brigade—"

"The Kaiser's Irish Brigade!" someone jeered.

"No!" Casement raised his hands. "Ireland's. Join with us. We are mobilizing a great force to return to the sacred shores of our small nation. When you joined England's army, to fight her wars, Ireland wasn't ready for you. But now she is."

"Join Germany, you mean!"

"No! No!" Casement's eyes bulged and his skin reddened. He teetered on the edge of the platform. "This war we renounce. It is not our war. It has nothing to do with Ireland. We are neutral!"

"You have a treaty!"

Then someone else cried, "Traitor! Traitor!"

"*You* are traitors," Casement screamed back at them. "You are enemies to your own people."

There was an explosion of hooting as the men began shaking their fists at Casement. "Fucking liar!" they yelled. "Bloody fucker!"

Sergeant Major Riley looked over at Tyrrell, who nodded. Riley barked out his command and it was heard even over that din. "Attention!"

The commotion ceased at once. Now the men had dropped their steins and they stood rigidly at attention, some palpably bewildered, some angry, but most with a stern impassivity.

Tyrrell raised his forefinger so that Riley could see it, and he twirled it in a small circle.

Riley nodded, then boomed, "About . . . *turn!*"

The men turned on their heels in perfect unison, and once again they were absolutely still.

Sir Roger Casement, blushing, stepped helplessly down from the platform.

No one moved.

Then Daniel Curry, on a desperate impulse, leapt up to the platform. "My friends! Brothers! I'm Dan Curry from Henrietta Street in Dublin. You've misunderstood us. We meant only to speak to you of Ireland. Our purpose is noble because her cause is just. You have to do what you think is right, but so do we! Don't turn your backs on Ireland, men! Let me make her plea to you now!" Curry had never so wanted to move an audience, but the sight of their stolid, indifferent backs, a thousand of them, made his heart sink. What a terrible miscalculation this was! How far they were from understanding each other! He intended to go on—perhaps with the lines Yeats had given Cathleen ni Houlihan to woo the young man to the thorny cause of Irish destiny—but all at once the grand rhetoric failed him. So much for Tone and O'Donovan Rossa, Pearse and Connolly, the Sinn Fein and the IRB. He'd given one and the same speech in all the counties, save Ulster's, of Ireland, but now he couldn't remember a word of it. He searched across the figures in front of him, looking for one man who showed any sign of readiness to listen. One man, he felt, would redeem this blunder. But if any in that throng harbored the usual Irish resentment or felt in his breast the ancient Celtic fervor, Casement had squelched it.

Curry veered from blaming him. For once it wasn't his high-toned foolishness that had stymied them. He had ruined the dream that had brought them here only by bringing it out into the cold light of actual utterance. Curry saw what his uneasiness with this scheme from the beginning had been a signal of. They were wrong to have come here; England's war with Germany was an entirely other question than theirs, and its moral complications were of another order. These men were Irish, yes, but he and Casement had come at them as if they were farmers in want of the Land League or workers looking for Socialist reform. They were captives, Curry saw finally, properly concerned with their own survival and properly contemptuous of anyone in league with their captors. Ireland's liberation would not and should not be born in a German internment camp.

He stared at the brawny necks, wanting now only some sign that they might understand at least that he and Casement had come in goodwill. The last thing they wanted was to make the prisoners' lot harder. He sought some sign that they hadn't taken offense.

But still, all he saw were the shoulder seams of their brown tunics. All, that is, until he turned toward the officers' table, where he saw, waiting in ambush expressly for him, the face he knew from the gold locket and eyes he knew because they resembled Jane's in every way. But how they hated him.

11

Jane Tyrrell. For four days in July and early August they had been together, the most blissful four days of Curry's life. Jane's burden had weighed on him, but not nearly enough to keep him from feeling that at last he was giving himself to a woman fully and without reserve. He was free of the hold his detached and hesitating second self had on him. That that second self, observing and commenting, as it were, from his shoulder, had made him a gifted actor by taking him into every experience far enough to imitate it, though never far enough to claim it as his own, seemed of no consequence when he lost it. Curry was no actor now. Ironically the capacity Jane had freed in him had, in her absence, enabled him to embrace more fully than ever the cause she disparaged. His country's moment had come, and by giving himself over to the movement as he had to her, it had become his moment.

What else could he have done to channel the extraordinary fissure of energy his feeling for Jane had cracked open, particularly after she, unable to postpone her departure, had gone to London? After that they exchanged letters every three or four days. He'd been ordered to hold himself available to go to Switzerland at any time, but he hadn't idled. He'd spent those months traveling Ireland, recruiting for the cause and organizing the cell groups that would anchor the rebellion. But no matter where he was, he'd managed to return to Dublin twice a week to get his mail, and he always answered her letters at once. In that too, something new had been released in Curry. He'd never allowed the expression of another to take on such importance. Like the man newly out from the cave that he had taken for the entire world, he felt alive to sensation of every kind. He was awed at the way her words could make her present, but also profoundly disoriented by her absence. But the larger experience was that his deepest disorientation had been ended. He was in love.

And that was why this moment in the mess tent was like the climax of a nightmare, as if Jane herself had turned those eyes on him. She was obsessed with her brother's welfare. Not a letter had come that hadn't referred to it. And now here her brother was, not merely alive and well but, if Curry's sudden dread was any measure, strong as the iron of the weapons he and Casement had come for.

He turned away from Tyrrell. But the backs of all those Irishmen hit him then, as if there too Jane were present, rejecting him.

———

Casement, Curry, Colonels Bremer and Adler filed out of the mess tent while the prisoners were still faced rigidly away from them.

Tyrrell crossed to Riley and said, "Hold the men here." Then he followed the others outside. They had just climbed into Bremer's staff car, which gleamed in the crisp afternoon light. Tyrrell said, "Just a moment, please."

The four looked at him.

He addressed himself to the camp commander. "Colonel Adler, I protest with utmost vigor this attempted sedition. It violates every norm set down by the Hague Conventions of 1909 concerning treatment of prisoners of war."

Adler looked at Tyrrell, but without haughtiness. Events in the mess tent had left him humiliated and flustered. It had been his task over the late summer and fall to win the goodwill of the Irish prisoners. No one had told him that a commissioner from Berlin would be coming. No one had explained their purposes to him. And here was this impertinent Irish captain daring to humiliate him further. "I saw you make that order, Captain. That was your doing!" he said, as if it mattered.

Tyrrell turned to Casement, who was sitting between Adler and Curry. "You have a bloody nerve, Casement! Do you think these men are like you? Have you no morality?"

Casement stared glumly ahead.

Curry was on the far side of the car from Tyrrell and thought he would be spared the main blast of his fury, but he felt it as a wave of heat when Tyrrell leaned into the car across Adler to grab at Casement. "You traitor! Get out of here!"

Adler gave an order to a pair of sentries, who leapt on Tyrrell from behind. He struggled, but only briefly. He said to Adler, "We demand to be treated like all British prisoners! We are British soldiers! We demand to be sent to British camps! Don't bring these dogs near us again!"

Only then did Bremer intervene from his place in the front of the car. "Don't worry, Captain," he said smoothly. "You will be treated like a prisoner now."

He snapped his fingers at the driver. The car lurched forward, leaving Tyrrell in the grip of his fury and the German sentries.

Keefe, coming out of the mess tent, took one of the German

guards by the elbow. *"Herr Ober,"* he said. "All is *nicht gut?"* The
sentry, a boy not yet twenty, displayed his anxiety. The other
guards, including the NCOs, who might have told him what
to do, were still in the tent. Without direction from their own
superiors, the two accepted Keefe's kindly but firm gesture as
permission to release the British officer.

Tyrrell watched the car speeding through the narrow lanes
of the internment camp. "The bastards thought they could have
us if they gave us meat once a day."

Keefe laughed. As he followed Tyrrell back into the mess
tent, he said, "Maybe now they'll give it to us twice."

———

The four rode in silence back to camp headquarters, apparently oblivious of the gauntlet of haggard dull faces watching
from behind barbed wire. It was a translucent afternoon, and
in the open car the air that whipped at their clothes was cleaner
than what they'd had to breathe in the overcrowded tent. Curry
welcomed the rush of wind because it made talk impossible, and
he needed to think. In his mind everything was coming clear.

For all their self-proclaimed sharp-eyed realism, Pearse,
Connolly, and the others were as addicted to the green fog of
Irish dreams as all the failed rebels who'd gone before them.
The fabled uprising would never exist outside the Irish imagination so long as it was easier to conjure a horde of highly
trained, Gaelic-speaking revolutionaries returning en masse from
German prison camps than it was to do the hard, thankless work
of winning over the corner boys in Dublin and the shepherds,
small farmers, and turf diggers of the remote countryside. They
alone were the ones who had the power to throw off England.
Shovels and hurley sticks in their gnarled hands would threaten

London far more than German carbines in the slim fingers of Casement's figments. It had been warning enough that the plan was spawned and prepared for not in Ireland, but in America, where Irishmen had become expert at waging war with words. The lesson for Curry was that he should have voiced his misgivings weeks before.

Even before the car had quite stopped, Bremer was standing to dismount. He hit the ground moving, a deft maneuver for a man his age, and it was clear he expected the others to follow him. The commander's quarters was the only true building in the entire set of prison compounds, a fieldstone house that had belonged to the sheep farmer whose pastures had been confiscated. The sky-colored stone, that peculiar Mosel slate, made the house seem like a work of nature, and though the window frames needed painting and the roof sagged, it seemed a place of substance. For a century and a half it had been a farmer's modest dwelling, but now the tents and huts surrounding it made it seem like a manor. As Bremer approached, the door flew open ahead of him: Adler's orderly.

In the front room, which once would have had overstuffed chairs and a woven-reed rug and a shrine to the Virgin—this was Catholic Germany—there were three straight-back chairs arranged in front of a desk on which books and papers were stacked as by a straightedge. The uncarpeted wooden floor had been painted gray and waxed, and now shone in the bright light that streamed into the room at a steep angle through the immaculate glass of three windows. The walls were freshly whitewashed and nothing hung on them but a tinted photograph of Kaiser Wilhelm. The artificial green tone of his skin made him look deathly ill.

Casement was the last of the four into the room. Bremer slammed the door and turned on him. "You have completely misled us! You have made us think the Irish wanted this!"

Casement snapped out of his lethargy. "They do. It's the officers who resist." He pointed at Adler. "He shouldn't have left the officers with them. Without officers their own natural leaders would have emerged. Their leaders would be with us."

Adler protested to Bremer, but in German. However, it was easy to guess that he was citing his orders: all the Irish were to be kept together, officers included.

"The officers are Englishmen. They're not Irish," Casement said. It was the IRB line about men like himself. Casement said it as if he believed it.

But Curry interrupted him. "Don't you know who that was? Didn't he seem familiar?"

Casement looked blankly toward Curry, as if trying to remember who *he* was.

"Tyrrell. Sir Hugh Tyrrell's son."

The others could see how that revelation shocked Casement, but then he turned it around. "That's my point precisely." He waved a finger at Bremer. "Recusants like him, what do you expect? Get rid of the officers."

Curry spoke to Bremer. "It won't make a damn bit of difference. There wasn't an ounce of rebellion in that room. It's not how men are in such a circumstance. Give them wine. Give them goblets of whiskey. Then put the choice to them, the Kaiser or the King, and they'll take the King no matter what they'd say at home. If I was one of them, I'd feel the same way. We were mistaken, Colonel. That's all."

"No!" said Casement. "You've no authority in this, Curry. Disregard what he says! You should segregate the officers at once. It's the common men we want, the Catholics; they're the ones who hate the English. They're the ones we must work on."

Curry took his colleague's arm and spoke softly. "We should go back to Ireland, Casement. This isn't—"

"Not without my army!" He pulled roughly away from Curry and crossed to Bremer, almost touching him. "We have an agreement! Uniforms, rifles, an Irish Brigade, ships to land them on the coast of Kerry. We have an agreement!"

"But have we the men?" asked Bremer coolly.

"Get rid of the officers, get rid of all the Protestants, get rid of the Ulstermen. There were Ulstermen among those prisoners! I saw their badges. What stupidity!" He glared at Adler. But why should the Germans have known to observe such distinctions? Casement was a Protestant Ulsterman himself. "What we want are the men with divided loyalty, and then we appeal to the side their mothers are on." Casement, ever more manic, leaned yet closer to Adler. "Do you have priests?"

"Not for prisoners."

"Give them a priest. A German priest. Have him hear their confessions. Tell him to preach about a man's God-given duty to his own people. Tell the priest to preach to them about loyalty to the Pope."

"Good Christ, Casement," said Curry. "Listen to yourself." Curry remembered that Bremer was a Catholic.

Casement ignored Curry. "They'll take whatever the priest says as the Word of God."

Bremer spoke to Adler in German, an efficient set of directives aimed, apparently, at implementing what Casement proposed. But, of course, Bremer would be in no hurry to return to Berlin with news of this disaster.

Casement waited until the German fell silent, then resumed, as if briefing juniors. "And after a few more weeks and after additional new Irish prisoners have been brought in from the Front, I shall return to address them once more. You'll see the difference."

Curry said, "The difference will be that I'm gone."

"Good," Casement replied, and he flashed an eccentric smile at his colleague.

Curry felt his palms moisten as he saw his dilemma. His impulse was to undercut Casement and the entire dishonorable project of inciting Irish prisoners. Eventually, no doubt, Casement would come up with a handful of converts, but who could trust their motives and what difference could they make to Ireland's struggle? But what was the point of arguing with Casement in front of the Germans? And wasn't Bremer as prepared to pervert his own religion in this cynical manipulation? The poor Irish bastards had been seduced first by the godless English, and now devout Germans would do the same. And what had become of the noble cause of Irish freedom in all of this?

Bremer asked Curry, "What is your meaning?"

"Only that Commandant Casement can carry on without me. Isn't that right, Commandant? I should report to Dublin that the process of recruitment is under way, but it will take a little longer than we expected."

Casement nodded. "And say the delay works for us because every day the invincible German army brings in more prisoners. The brigade will exceed a thousand!"

Bremer looked from Casement to Curry noncommittally. Finally he clapped his hands sharply once and said to Curry, "*Jawohl!* Then you will return with me to Koblenz. You can make railway connections to Geneva. And you, Commandant . . ." He faced Casement. ". . . Oberst Adler will find accommodation for you in Trier, no? Is it not useful for you to stay nearby?" Bremer looked at Adler, ignoring his obvious distress at this proposal, and spoke to him at length in German.

Casement drew Curry aside and said quietly, with a sobriety he had yet to manifest, "Tell Pearse the Germans need reassurance. They're wavering. The Irish Brigade must have their full support.

It's the centerpiece of our plans. The Germans will never trust our alliance with them unless our break with England is total. *That* is why they want the brigade. Nothing else is certain without it." Casement leaned in on Curry; his breath was foul. "Tell Pearse I won't return until I have the brigade. I know you don't agree with me, but you must tell him. The guns, the ships, all their support depends on our getting the brigade. Will you tell him?"

When Bremer faced them, he was displeased to find the Irishmen talking out of earshot. There was a heretofore disguised arrogance in his eyes to match Casement's new display of cool sanity. As Bremer came between them, Casement obliquely watched his compatriot for his answer. A test of loyalty. Curry nodded.

———

A day later the brilliant autumn weather had already begun to fade as a mass of cold wet air pushed into the Mosel Valley from the hills. It would be winter in a week.

Tyrrell thought for a moment and glanced quickly again at the approaching figure of Colonel Adler before saying to Keefe, "Get Riley and Tyndale. Go to the latrine and wait for me."

Adler strode down the duckboard, trailed by two rifle-bearing guards. In the distance beyond the stretch of barbed wire was the mythic Celtic waterfall and its dramatic stream running down toward the Mosel from the castle-peaked hill. Only moments before, Keefe had said sardonically, "Everywhere I go in Germany, I see castles and waterfalls." The man used irony, Tyrrell had come to understand, to distance himself from his experience, which was a reason he was so useful to Tyrrell and a reason they hadn't become better friends. Two facts for which there were other reasons, too.

As Adler drew near, Tyrrell pocketed his briar pipe, braced, and saluted. The German returned his salute. "Captain, it is my duty to inform you that you and . . ." His eyes darted downward. In the palm of his hand he held a cribsheet. ". . . Captain Tyndale, Lieutenants Clark, Keefe, Fitzhugh, Roy, and Desmond"—he looked up, blinking through his spectacles—"will be making transport to an officers' detention on the morning at eight hundred of the clock. Please to inform your officers to be in readiness."

"Tomorrow morning? Impossible. My officers are responsible for the organization of the camp. We need a week at least to—"

"*Tomorrow* morning, Captain!" Adler started to turn away.

"What about the transfer of my men? I want them with British regiments!" Tyrrell grabbed his sleeve. "I refuse to be transferred until my men are in with British regiments."

One of the guards slammed the butt of his rifle against Tyrrell's head while the other followed Adler out of the Irish compound.

Tyrrell slowly stood, brushing the blood from his eye. "Fuckers," he said.

At the latrine, a lean-to behind the mess tent sheltering a roughhewn commode bench with a dozen places, Tyndale, Keefe, and Riley waited. Keefe immediately went to Tyrrell's eye. "What the hell happened, Captain?"

"Tripped on a tent rope, Mr. Keefe."

Keefe ignored Tyrrell's attempt to turn him aside. Tyndale soaked a handkerchief at a nearby wash spigot and handed it to Keefe. "We should shoot the buggers," he muttered, daubing it clean. Tyrrell's eye was swelling fast.

Finally Keefe stepped away from him.

Tyrrell touched his face gingerly. "Thank you."

Keefe smiled. "Always said you've blasted cheek."

Everyone grimaced but Tyrrell. "I'm going to need it. I'm breaking out."

"What?"

"Adler just told me the officers are being moved along. We're being scooped in the morning, all seven of us." He turned to Riley. "The lads belong to you now, Sergeant Major. It's what I expected when I demanded that we be treated like the others. The men will be in good hands with you."

"But what are *you* doing?" Keefe asked.

"I'm going to London. The War Office would like to know what Casement and the Germans have in mind, don't you suppose?"

"But it will never work," Riley said. "The Irish regiments will never join Fritz, sir."

"There's more than one way for the Germans to use the Irish malcontents, Sergeant Major. The point is, the rebels have made their alliance. The Germans are taking them seriously. Colonel Bremer didn't come here from Berlin on his own authority. To our great shame, London must needs look over her shoulder now." He paused to let the statement sink in. Yes, shame. But then Tyrrell grinned suddenly. "Besides, why should I go to a prison camp where I'm not senior?"

"Don't be foolish, Douglas," Tyndale said. "You can't travel the heart of Germany in jodhpurs and riding boots, with no weapons, no language, and alone."

"He won't be alone, Captain," Keefe said, then faced Tyrrell. "If you'll have me, sir?"

"Captain Tyndale is right about the risk, Lieutenant."

"I don't feature an officers' camp, Captain. That's a lot of Protestants in one place. Anyway, I haven't got your problem with riding boots."

"Excuse me, sir," Riley said, "but how in the name of Jesus are you getting out?"

Tyrrell led the men behind the latrine shed. A space of six feet separated its back wall from the fifteen-foot barbed-wire fence that encircled the compound. He pointed to the water-fall across what remained of the sheep pasture. From where the men stood, it was a distance of only a hundred yards to the cascading stream, but two heavy belts of barbed wire at an interval of thirty yards blocked the way. "By tracking the stream," he said. "It will take us down to the Mosel. From there we hop a barge."

"But the wire."

Tyrrell bent down and loosened his left boot to pull out Peter Towne's wire cutters. He held them up in triumph. "Remember these? Don't talk to me about my boots," He looked across the field. "We go after dark. We can be across the barrier in ten minutes. The guard goes by only every thirty."

"But he'll see the cuts in the wire, even in the dark. They'll be after you before you get a barge."

Tyndale said, "Not if you and I go out with them, Sergeant Major, and then return, splicing the wire." He looked at Tyrrell. "That way you'd have 'til morning before they know you're out. We'd need your cutters, of course, to twist the wire."

"I'd want you to have them in any case. You might want to try a break of your own later." Tyrrell stared at his colleague, reading his fear. There would be no break attempt by Tyndale. Tyrrell touched his arm. "George, I appreciate it." Tyndale looked awkwardly away and Tyrrell turned to Riley. "Sergeant Major, I want you to make it plain to the men that I'd never have left them if the Germans weren't moving me on."

"They know that, Captain."

"Good." He clapped Riley's shoulder, then looked at his

watch. "I'd better see what I can do about these jodhpurs, then, eh? What do you think, Lieutenant Keefe? Can our catch-as-catch-can quartermaster make us look like a pair of river rats?"

———

The easy part was crossing the field. It was a pitch-dark night and the only sound was the snapping of the wire cutters. To the four men it seemed like bell gongs, but in fact the clip-clip couldn't have been heard a few dozen yards away. They crawled as quickly as they could. Tyrrell and Keefe wore soot-darkened identical clothing: the brogans, trousers, and multiple shirts of other ranks; they'd blackened their faces. At the second belt of wire, in brief ceremony, they shook hands with Tyndale and Riley, who set about at once retracing their path into the compound, stretching and fixing the wire as they went.

Tyrrell and Keefe crawled to the low brush that lined the edge of the stream; then they got to their feet, crouching low at first, and ran. Each had strapped to his waist, wrapped in oilcloth, a bundle of bread and cheese, as well as kitchen spoons, the one utensil the prisoners were allowed. But these spoons had been flattened and sharpened into oval knives. Tyrrell wore a coiled thirty-foot length of rope like a belt.

They followed the meandering stream with cuts and darts, as if racing the rushing water. The land sloped steadily downward.

Within a quarter-hour their course had brought them to the edge of a forty-foot sandstone cliff that overhung one bank of the Mosel. The stream funneled down into the river in yet another waterfall, and it was only by an act of urgent braking that the two, having given themselves over to a rush like that water's, held back from jumping with it into the dark below.

The view that presented itself beyond the dark slash of the

river, even in the moonless night, required a different kind of eyesight than the hazards at their feet. Tyrrell and Keefe stood in silence, except for their ragged breathing, waiting for their eyes to adjust to the vista. Immediately beyond the river the land shot steeply up, the famous Mosel wine-growing hillsides. Just on the far bank stood a pair of eerie cone-shaped structures like haystacks, but made of stone.

"What the hell is that?" Keefe asked. Everything unfamiliar was a threat.

"Medieval cranes," said Tyrrell. "For unloading cargo, long since obsolete. And if you look closely there, you can see the line of the towpath that parallels the river. Barges have been plying this water since Caesar. They used horses on that path to haul the vessels upstream. Still would, probably, but horses are pulling carts in the army now or have been slaughtered for meat. Traffic on the river is probably all powered anyway."

"How do you know about it? Have you been here?"

"On the Rhine, student days. Enchanted river; its hills are full of monks, dragons, castles, robber barons, and lovelorn maidens. Everyone did the Rhine."

Not in my school, thought Keefe.

As if reading him, Tyrrell slapped his shoulder. "Now's your chance, Lieutenant."

Each stared hard at the strange world below them.

"Look!" Tyrrell pointed downstream at lights.

"A village," Keefe said.

"No, the lights are moving. Navigation lights. They're moving away from us. That's a sizable barge, Keefe. Just what we want to see."

Tyrrell traced the line of the river with an acute focus of mind and eye. Finally, pointing upstream, he said, "There it is." A mile away loomed the black silhouette of an enormous bridge.

From the shape of its eight arches, two of which spanned the navigation channel, he knew it was the ancient Roman bridge. One side of it was anchored on the bluff of the same red sandstone cliff on which they stood. Above the bridge the faint glow of sky marked the city of Trier.

Keefe said, "The openings between the pilings of that bridge seem too bloody narrow for coal barges to get through."

Tyrrell pointed at the lights again. "But there goes one now, Lieutenant. It cleared the bridge. The bridge is what we need. We can do this dry."

"Thank God, Captain, because I can't swim."

Tyrrell led away from that revelation by turning and heading upstream, along the cliff's edge.

More than once he stumbled, or Keefe did, causing the other to reach quickly. They stayed close together, and at certain points when they had to descend the steep sides of ravines, then scale them, they held on to each other physically. When they climbed up onto a deserted roadway that ran up to the bridge, they collapsed against a stone wall to rest. Tyrrell looked at Keefe, his blackened face streaked with oily perspiration, his weariness apparent. It was one of the few times Keefe's age registered. In truth, he wasn't that much older, but the exertion was taking more out of him than out of Tyrrell. That relative weakness in an otherwise strong man moved Tyrrell. Keefe met his eyes and Tyrrell felt their friendship open like a blossom.

Keefe grinned. "We're going to make it, Captain. I can feel it."

Tyrrell nodded, but he had to look away. An unfamiliar emotion choked him, and he thought of Pamela. Her image calmed his anxiety. Realizing that he would see her and Timmy and Anne, that he would see his father and Jane and Cragside again, he felt released from a grief he had never acknowledged.

Throughout his time on the Front and in the camp, he had assumed their deaths. Not theirs, he saw at last, but his own. "Let's go," he said.

They stole up the steep approach road, gaining even more altitude above the river. The tower of the *Hauptmarkt* in the town square came into view on their left, and at the point where the approach road joined the main road running from the city to the bridge, they could see into the heart of Trier. Before venturing onto the road they hid in the shadows, watching. A few dozen yards to the right, where the bridge proper began, was a small guardhouse, but it was dark and silent. In Trier there were a few lights showing, but no vehicles, and, in a period of five minutes, signs only of two or three citizens, heads ducked, hurrying home. The city was asleep. In silhouette, above the rooflines of the houses, were the market tower, the looming mansard shape of the *Rathaus*, and the great spires of the cathedral that held Christ's cloak, the prize of gambling soldiers.

Tyrrell motioned at Keefe, then darted into the roadway toward the bridge, Keefe following. Though they stepped lightly, their boots made muffled sounds on the cobblestone road, and that was what gave them away.

Just as Tyrrell was about to draw even with the guardhouse, he heard a loud bang from it and then a further noise, and then startled voices that were cut short at once. Tyrrell and Keefe instinctively leapt over the stone railing onto the grassy edge of the sandstone cliff. They were just short of the point where the bridge soared away from the cliff on its own timeless supports. They crouched, dead-still, against the stone, on top of each other. Tyrrell was immediately aware of Keefe's breathing as too loud, and he had to check an impulse to order him silent. They waited.

For some moments there was nothing.

Tyrrell raised his head far enough to peer between the stone balustrades. The door of the guardhouse opened tentatively, and all at once a figure dashed from it, a girl clutching her skirts and running back toward Trier, disappearing into the night like a Rhine River nymph. Tyrrell nudged Keefe so that he could watch too as her lover then followed, a boy struggling with the straps of his lederhosen as he ran after her.

"Holy Mother of God," said Keefe.

Tyrrell laughed quietly and whispered, "You Catholics! How do you know that's who it was?"

"She's still a virgin, Captain, from the look of pain in that fellow's face."

"He'd be Joseph, then. An apparition!"

Keefe pressed Tyrrell's arm, an unprecedented familiarity. "I told you we'd make it."

They leapt the railing and scurried out onto the bridge, staying low. Their silhouettes above the balustrade would have been visible up and down the river. Even in the lee of the railing, as they moved along it, the wind from the river valley tore at them, and the cold air sliced their lungs. When Tyrrell stopped, Keefe ran into him.

Tyrrell craned over the railing, then retreated half a dozen paces toward Trier. "Here we are."

The bridge towered seventy feet above the water, but even from that height the whoosh of its passage was audible. They were positioned above the center arches, which spanned the channel. Tyrrell pointed down at the base of one pillar. "A buttress, see it?"

"Yes. Twenty feet above the water."

"The thing is pointed like that to break up the ice floes in the winter, to keep the ice from building."

"It should do us nicely, Captain. There's ample ledge there."

Keefe traced the formidable stone face of the pillar, spying the crevices between the enormous blocks of purple stone. At regular intervals on the corners, he saw strapping iron clamps. He was looking for foot- and handholds. Directly below them was a strange form bulking out from the vertical surface.

"What the hell is that?"

"We've had Joseph and Mary," Tyrrell answered. "That's Jesus."

"What?"

"A stone crucifix. You see them on bridges where boats have gone down. Those pillars obstructing that current have finished off more than a few, you can bet. I never knew whether they hung their crosses asking God to remember the dead or to spare the living."

Keefe, ever sensitive, heard the hint of condescension. Tyrrell spoke about the river piety as if it were a strange cult of primitives.

He said, "It's enormous, Captain. It looks to be more than life-size. We can use it for a ladder, right down to that ledge." He grinned at Tyrrell. "If it's not against your religion."

"Jesus saves, Lieutenant, that's what I believe." He efficiently uncoiled the rope from his waist and secured an end of it around the solid stone balustrade. He threw the other end over and they watched it fall in a slow curl until it snapped out at its full length. "God damn it!" said Tyrrell when he saw that the rope was a good ten feet short of the crucifix.

"Close enough," said Keefe. "We can drop. It's a stout-looking cross."

"Right. I'll go first. Wait until I'm down."

"Wrong, Captain. We both go now." Keefe pointed toward Trier. A lorry with glaring head lamps had appeared in the roadway and was picking up speed as it approached the bridge.

Tyrrell went over. At first he tried working his feet into the crevices between blocks of stone as he lowered himself, but it was too slow. He gave all of his weight to the rope just as Keefe joined him on it. The rope groaned but held.

As he knew it would, the rope played out well above the mammoth stone crucifix. Tyrrell dangled from the end of the rope, his shoes a bare five feet above the *Christus*. Seen close, even from that angle, it was clear that the figure was half again life-size and it made an easy target. Its head was tilted to the side over the left shoulder, the classic posture. Tyrrell swung his weight slightly in that direction and then dropped. His legs straddled the head of Jesus, instead of landing on it. He caught the stone protrusion full in the crotch, and the pain of the jolt was made infinitely worse by the carved spikes of the crown of thorns. The pain was gone in an instant, though, replaced by fear as he started to fall backward. He clutched the shoulder of the statue, swung down across its chest, and held, but he still felt himself falling. The crucifix itself had begun to give.

But then it held too, and he realized he was safe. Gingerly he shinnied down the cold naked figure, and from its bent, bloodied knees he dropped to the six-foot triangular ledge of the pointed buttress. Another twenty feet below that was the raging black river. A fine spray hit Tyrrell's face, cooling him, and only then did he realize how, even in that chill, he'd been perspiring.

He looked up and saw Keefe dangling from the end of the rope. "Go gently," he called. "That cross . . ."

Keefe dropped at that moment in much the way Tyrrell had, but when the mass of his body hit the head of the *Christus*, its rusted iron clamps ripped away from their bolts and the entire stone crucifix pulled from the pillar, Keefe riding it.

As it fell away, he reached back for the bridge, but there was nothing to grab. Tyrrell saw the mass of stone coming down on him, a great hulking, hideous monstrosity, arms outstretched, face tormented, wounds gushing, chiseled mouth agape to shriek. And then Tyrrell saw at the last instant those powerful legs of the stocky Irishman shoving off from that pillar, pushing the mass of stone out over the river so that when it fell, it would not hit him.

There was no shriek. Keefe fell without screaming—Tyrrell would always be certain of this—because his scream would have given his comrade away. There was nothing for Tyrrell to do but flatten himself against the smooth sandstone pillar, lest the statue crush him. It and Keefe missed by inches; if Keefe hadn't pushed away from the bridge, Tyrrell would surely have been crushed. As it was, a corner of the crucifix struck the narrow ledge on which he stood, and for an instant he thought the miracle had happened, that Keefe had landed safe.

No. Like that the massive stone figure and Keefe were gone. The swirling river swallowed them without a splash. At once Tyrrell was on his hands and knees, leaning out from the ledge, stretching down as far as he dared. He saw nothing. But he knew what the men knew who'd hung that cross centuries before: whatever went into that water was never coming out.

Without a thought for its futility or its risk, he began to cry as loudly as he could, "Bernard!" He cried Keefe's name like that. "Bernard! Bernard! Bernard!" But the name, like the man, was soon swallowed in the empty vastness below him.

———

At some later point, in the middle of the night, a laden coal barge came down out of the Saar Valley fast. The bargemaster had to maneuver his huge vessel expertly if he was to slide beneath the arches of that bridge without smashing into its buttressed pillars. *Kalter Druck*—cold pressure—is what they called it, the

phenomenon by which a heavy craft slides without friction along
a watery decline at an even faster clip than the river current.

He had to stare ahead at the flat prow of his barge from
his vantage at the helm high in the stern of the vessel. He was
aiming for the dark hole of the center span, darker than the
others because it opened on the far distance of the river. He
thought he was on course, but as he drew nearer it disoriented
him terribly when he could not see the ancient crucifix. By the
time his careening vessel had lurched into the fierce whirlpool
just above the bridge, where the water blocked by the buttresses
ran back against itself, the absence of the cross terrified him.
Like his father and grandfather before, he had never passed
through the hazard of Trier without reverencing God's name at
the sight of His Holy Son.

This meant the barge was going to hit. The current would
throw it sideways into the bridge, and in minutes it would be
smashed to pieces and he would be drowned.

For the barest instant he closed his eyes.

The stout rag-and-rope bumpers on the starboard prow
of the barge kissed the buttress, but made the channel, sliding
home like a ferry into its slip. The bargemaster registered the
triumph in his spine, and he let out the traditional yelp—"Holla
ho!"—as he soared through the center arch of the bridge.

The cross on the pillar was truly gone, but he doffed his cap
and blessed himself anyway, crying, *"In Gottes Namen!"*

Had he seen the black figure when it leapt onto the pile of
coal in the body of the barge before him, he'd have been certain
it was God's Son down from His cross, risen once more from
the dead and come at last to punish him for all his sins.

12

Hyde Park was London's way of being in the countryside. Its lawns were tailored to look like the lawns of paradise surrounding the great rural houses for which every Englishman, whether as lord or servant, felt an innate nostalgia. This morning the earth still smelled of rain from the night before and the wet leaves clung to each other in sodden piles instead of frisking about in the late October wind. The chill air sent the park animals scurrying about; the mad but pointed hoarding of nuts and berries had begun. Animals always feel an autumn panic for food, and this year the people of London felt it too. First the young men had disappeared, and then the groceries had. Vendors in London no longer filled their shelves. Fresh fruits, meats, and vegetables were sold by subscription now to the upper classes, and the display of provisions served no purpose if it was all spoken for. At the markets of Covent Garden only damaged produce was offered to the population at large, and each evening the scraps discarded between farmers' carts grew more meager as the scavengers contending for them grew more numerous. The fine ladies and older gentlemen on their way to the nearby Opera felt assaulted by the pitiful scenes that they found more and more difficult to ignore. Even in Hyde Park, now, one saw old ladies collecting chestnuts in their aprons, shooing squirrels.

Pamela and Jane were sitting on a bench watching Timmy and Anne chasing pigeons. The grass was wet and the children's shoes would be wrecked, but who had the heart to rein them? Though Timmy at three was two years younger than his sister, he had a boy's wildness, which gave him the initiative. Anne imitated all his moves, careening from one bird cluster to another, scaring them into flight, but she lacked his fierce abandon. He had given himself over to the chase because he believed in it. His sister knew full well they would never catch the birds, and that knowledge, like a dirty secret, inhibited her.

Jane and Pamela, by contrast, sat quietly. They were alike in appearance. At twenty-seven Pamela was five years Jane's senior, but each dressed the part of a modern young woman, without Victorian flamboyance. They wore somber, unplumped, form-fitting ankle-length skirts, shades of blue and brown but decidedly not black. Pamela's long kid gloves gave her a citified air that Jane lacked, but her relative sophistication was undercut by the toy bear she held. The fur on one of its fists was sucked smooth.

Since coming to London, Jane had taken to varnishing her nails. Her nails had become a rare vanity, in fact, but that was because in all her years at Cragside—all that manual labor— she'd never had long fingernails. She was staring at her nails now, thinking that her life in London as Pamela's companion and the children's bonny aunt could easily have been her life in Cragside, less the work: it was that cozy, that comfortable, that small. It hadn't begun to depress her until Dan Curry's letters had inexplicably stopped coming three weeks before.

"Oh, he nearly got that one," Pamela said delightedly. Timmy had come within inches of snagging a pigeon. "He's rather wonderful, isn't he?"

Jane agreed, and the happiness Pamela took in her children always gave Jane pleasure, but her heart was with Timmy's earnest sister. Jane knew how difficult it was for a girl to be forever measured against a gifted male. She said, "He's just showing off for Anne." Jane had believed that Douglas's great feats—pitching stones cricket-style to hit particular fence rails, then later coaxing horses to leap those rails—had been performed for her benefit, even when he didn't know she was watching him. Douglas was years older. To her he was the young god who came home from school twice a year. And because of their sudden progression from total strangers to fast friends, she was always heartbroken when it came time for him to leave. In truth, she did not know him; she worshiped not Douglas but the image she created of him in his perennial absence. That was the difference between her and Pamela—she took the loss of her brother for granted. To Jane *this* absence of Douglas seemed, if not natural, inevitable, and so did the pain of her loneliness. Unlike Anne, Timmy, or their mother, Jane had been raised to solitude, and what had made her know it, and feel it, were those rare periods of her brother's company. These memories stabbed her into thinking of Dan, and they made it seem inevitable that her main experience of him should have been his absence too.

"But he's so fast and surefooted." Pamela sighed, and Jane sensed that the sight of the child put her sister-in-law in mind of Douglas too. Here they were, a pair of women whose men were gone. Why had they been unable, she wondered suddenly, to comfort each other?

Pamela's sighs had filled the house in Chelsea. Her sighs had weight, and their accumulated density, when added to that of Mrs. Wells's curdled silence, had made even that spacious mansion too small for Jane. Pamela's sighs seemed to consume Jane's share of oxygen, leaving her choking with claustrophobia. If she and Jane were to sit together for long, it had to be outside like this; not even the Chelsea garden would do. It was Jane who insisted on Hyde Park, because there the fear of suffocation left her. She wanted an expanse of grass like the one that ran in Cragside between the house and the cliff above the sea. In that open air she could once more admire Pamela for not being near tears all the time, as she was herself, and for not clamping down morosely as her mother had. Away from Chelsea, Jane could marvel at Pamela's level of cheer, an ample brightness based on her resolute expectation that Douglas would return. This was not hopefulness on her part, or mere optimism. Pamela was simply incapable of imagining a life without Douglas, although Jane knew she was already living it. Hence that unconscious, constant stream of sighs, her one expression of desolation. Pamela's sighs were driving Jane insane. She would never have said so.

A policeman walked by in his blue-black helmet and white gloves. He saluted the women without stopping.

Why did he look so pleased with himself? Jane wondered. Nothing embodied the prosaic sobriety of the English better than London bobbies. They were the perfect emblems of the triumph of rationality over passion, which was the central fact of English supremacy. Ever since the Romans defeated the Druids, organization had been defeating feeling, and that was why England ruled Ireland yet. Jane had never considered herself fully Irish, but since coming to London she'd sensed that she was even less English. There were feelings in her heart that nothing could defeat, and here that seemed somehow wrong. It seemed un-English of her to hurt so, to be at the mercy of her longing, and to need to express the chaos of her emotions. Expression was under interdict. If England caught on fire, she thought, it would find a way to swallow the smoke. There would be no scream, no cry. There would be, she saw, a national sigh, the sound a ship makes before slipping beneath the sea.

Jane pointed at the policeman. "Did you read about that ship sinking in the Channel, how the sailors, as they went down, aimed the searchlights at the flag? If London was sinking, they'd aim the searchlights at the bobbies."

Pamela gave her sister-in-law a look. "That's a strange comment, Jane."

Jane touched Pamela's sleeve. "I meant only what symbols they are, don't you think?"

Pamela let her eye follow the policeman. She said absently, "They're the same as the police in Dublin."

It was true. How little Jane had understood before. The police in Dublin, though native-born Irishmen, were English too. She said, "We've become dear friends, Pamela, but we've never discussed the fact of my being Irish, how it sets me apart."

Jane's hand still rested on Pamela's sleeve. Pamela covered it with her own. "That isn't so. You aren't set apart. I don't believe that for a minute. You aren't really Irish, Jane. Any more than Douglas is."

"But we *are*, Pamela. Don't you see?"

Pamela shook her head. This was a conversation she had had dozens of times with her mother, who'd disapproved of Douglas for this very reason. Pamela tried to keep impatience from her voice as she used one of her old arguments. "The Duke of Wellington was born in Ireland. Lord Kitchener himself was. That doesn't make *them* Irish. Is George Bernard Shaw Irish? Or was Oscar Wilde? Or Edmund Burke? Or Jonathan Swift? Really, Jane, some of the best Englishmen come from Ireland. The Irish are the Catholics, you know that."

"And if I was to become a Catholic, what would that make me?"

Pamela pulled away. "Don't be silly."

"I'm serious, Pamela."

"What, about becoming Catholic?"

"No."

"I didn't think so."

"About being Irish. You mustn't deny it. You think of Cragside as if it were on the coast of North Devonshire. It's in County Clare! You think of my father as if he were an honor's-list pensioner away for his retirement. He's an Irishman, and he's at home, Pamela. Our people have been in Ireland for four hundred years. If my ancestors had gone to America, we'd be Americans by now surely. Why can't we be Irish, then?"

"Because Ireland belongs to England. America doesn't. You'd feel differently, Jane—I'm older than you, I know these things—if you'd gone to a proper school. Your father should never have kept you—"

"School has nothing to do with it!" Jane said this so angrily that Anne stopped running where she was and looked nervously back at them.

"Please, Jane."

"I'm sorry." Jane knotted her hands in her lap and fixed her eyes upon them, upon her varnished nails. Whose hands are these, she thought?

Pamela put her arm around Jane, while pressing her son's toy bear to her own breast. She said softly, "I have only one ambition, Jane darling, and that's to have Douglas back. He can come back as an Australian aborigine, as long as he comes back. I don't care if he's Irish, Jane. I don't care if you are. I love him and I love you."

That's not what I meant, Jane thought. But she rested her head on Pamela's shoulder, and she let her strong, resilient English sister-in-law hold her, even though she felt no real comfort in her words.

———

Their carriage was waiting for them on North Carriage Drive between Marble Arch and Speakers' Corner. It was nearly noon by the time Pamela, Jane, and the children approached from the sprawling green park. Jane was carrying Timmy piggyback, and Anne for once was the one to run ahead. She was drawn by the high-pitched ranting of a stout, red-faced, bald-headed man who stood on an upended crate behind a crude, hand-lettered sign that read, ROME THE HOME OF BEELZEBUB!

Timmy tried to slide down from her shoulders, but Jane held him. An old woman thrust a pamphlet at her: *The Healing of Christian Science.* Because she tried to decline politely, she was distracted from her effort to hold Timmy, and he succeeded in slipping out of her grasp. He ran after Anne toward the fiery antipapist. There were half a dozen orators, each declaiming to the broad gray weather: South Africa, Christian Science, the antipapist, Salvation Army, and a woman denouncing whiskey. Pamela said, "I'll get them," and she went after her children, leaving Jane momentarily alone.

It was then that a ragamuffin boy ran by her, then came back to stop in front of her. "Hello, ma'am. This is for you." He held out a small piece of notepaper. She wasn't going to take it, but the boy said, "The gentleman give it to me." She took it and he ran off.

Jane was instinctively furtive, turning aside to open the

note. It said, in his familiar hand, "Find a reason for staying in
the park. Your Dan."

———

Curry watched from a hundred yards away. He was dressed
in a dark suit, tie, and a bowler hat, and he carried a mackintosh over his arm. His hair was cut short and, for the first time
in five years, his face was clean-shaven. His unweathered skin
was raw and pale. He had arrived at Southampton on the liner
from Genoa the night before. His papers identified him as an
insurance salesman from Cork who'd traveled to Switzerland
for treatment of a mild consumption. He was on his way back
to Ireland now. He had no justification, counterfeit or real, for
having come to London.

Jane was stooping to kiss the children. She straightened
and then, one guessed, began explaining herself a second time
to the other woman. Curry admired the slim line of her figure.
From that distance he couldn't make out her face clearly, though
he recognized the particular angle at which she held her head
when she was being earnest. He remembered the slight tremble of her gestures when she was being unsure of herself, and
he thought he saw that in her hands and arms now. She kept
glancing around, looking for him, he knew.

At last the woman relented and, kissed Jane lightly on the cheek.

Curry began to draw closer.

With her children on either side of her, the woman backed
away toward Carriage Drive. The children waved while the
woman eyed Jane impassively. Then they mounted their carriage
and a moment later they were gone.

Jane turned and looked for him.

He ran toward her. She saw him coming but didn't move.

As he drew nearer she still did not react, and he slowed his pace. It hadn't occurred to him she wouldn't feel as he did. Her eyes were fixed upon him, but she hadn't so much as lifted a hand. He stopped, perhaps a dozen yards away. He was oblivious of the nearby orators, their few listeners, the lunchtime strollers. The wind had picked up and clouds had moved across the sky, throwing a blanket shadow over everything.

All at once her hand swept to her mouth and she cried, "Dan!," running to him.

He took the full force of her weight as she threw herself on him. His hat fell, but he ignored it.

"I didn't know you," she said. "How could I not know you? How could I not know you?" She clung to him.

After a long time of simply holding her, he said quietly, "You didn't know me without my magnificent beard."

At once she pulled back to look, her mouth agape, wet eyes like saucers. "Good God! You've shaved!"

He laughed and hugged her anew, but she pulled back once more to look. Amazement, wonder, and delight filled her face. "You're handsome! What a chin you have!" She swung about, hanging from his hands. "What cheeks! And your mouth! I never saw your mouth before! It's beautiful!" And then she kissed him.

When he drew back to look at her, holding her face between his hands, he thought she looked like the Madonna come alive. For him God's mother was a measure of beauty. Her transparent eyes seemed to offer him access to what was inside her; what he saw was the love she bore him. He touched her neck, then her shoulders, which, even through the bulk of her coat, seemed thinner than before. She seemed altogether frail. "You've lost weight. You've been unwell."

She shook her head. "I've missed you. That's been my illness."

And you've been worried for your brother, he added to himself. Since leaving Trier he'd been aiming for this, to tell her, He is alive! Your brother is alive! But now that the moment had arrived, he could not say it. Concern for himself intruded. Once her first happiness at the news faded, then what? He should tell her the rest? Your brother's captors are my allies? The hope of my nation? I stood with his keepers who let me look at him through the bars of his cage? Concern for himself, exactly. She would hate him.

"Why are you here, Dan?"

"Because of you." That at least was true, and it was relief to say it. He grasped instinctively how important it was that he not lie. "Because I . . ." He stopped and looked away.

She caressed his smooth chin with her fingers. "Where have you been, darling? I'd begun to be afraid for you too. Your letters stopped."

Why couldn't they have come to this hours from now, days or years from now? Why couldn't he have been with her quietly for a time, strolling with her, in a bright room with her, lying with her? The image of her nakedness filled his mind, but no sooner did he picture her bare, astonishing breasts than he remembered the gold locket hanging between them.

He took her hand from his chin. His eyes blazed into hers, as if he could burn himself onto her, like the mark of a brand, so that she would never be without him. But, of course, she would send him away once he told her. Still it was unthinkable that he should not. "I've been in Germany, Jane," he said simply. And then, not giving her a chance to react, he said the rest so that he would have done it. "I'm on my way back to Ireland. I've come here to tell you that I saw your brother. He's alive and he's unhurt. He's in a prison camp near Trier and they are treating him well."

It was as if he'd filleted her, and he understood that emotionally he had, slicing flesh from bone, cutting her into a perfect butterfly of contradiction, the best news and the worst. How could she possibly take in either?

She fell away from him. A peasant woman with such an expression on her face would have blessed herself to ward off the ghost of what she saw. "What? I'm sorry, what?"

He stepped toward her.

But she held up her hand. "No, just tell me again what you said. What did you say?"

"I said, your brother is alive. I saw him."

It was like looking now not at a madonna, but at a nun, so little could he see of her: no hair, no eyebrows, no ears, no neck. Only those hard, heartless eyes that made him feel like a mulish pupil who could not make himself understood.

"Listen, take them one thing at a time. Douglas is well. Just take that for now."

"Did you talk to him?"

"No."

"How can you be sure . . .?"

"You showed me his picture. When I saw him, I inquired. Captain Douglas Tyrrell, Fourth Connaught Rangers. He was captured at Messines, near Ypres. He's well, Jane. I was as close to him as we are to that bench."

Having seen the bench, they moved toward it and sat. A space of a yard separated them.

"I've come here, Jane, to tell you that Douglas is alive because I knew how sure you were that he was dead."

"When did you see him?"

"Six days ago."

"And he wasn't hurt?"

"He looked fit."

Whatever relief she felt, Jane did not display it. And Curry could feel nothing but despair. Only the prospect of her happiness had made possible his ruining himself with her, but her happiness was keyed as much to him as to Douglas, and Curry's mistake was in not grasping that.

"Why were you in Germany?" She wouldn't look at him.

He watched her, wanting her to raise her eyes. "I was looking for something."

"What?"

He shrugged. "My country's place among the nations."

"Did you find it?"

"No."

Now she did look up, sharply.

Curry wished for pebbles to suck, to moisten the stuck dry prow of his tongue, to launch it. With an intake of breath he said, "I went as Ireland's emissary, Jane."

"To England's enemy."

He nodded. "Ireland is England's enemy too."

"Not all of Ireland, Dan."

After a moment he said, "I saw your brother because I went among Irish prisoners to ask them to join us." He paused, relieved to have admitted the one thing that seemed shameful to him. "To their credit, the Irish prisoners would have none of us. They were right, and I see that now. They're men with comrades at the Front. They took oaths. They've cast their lots for now with England and it was wrong to ask them to break faith."

"So you repudiate having gone?"

"No. The arrangement with Germany stands and I support it. There may or may not be an Irish Brigade, but we will have other German help. We haven't a hope without it."

She looked away from him. "You shouldn't speak of this to me."

"If you tell me not to, I'll never mention it again."

"In all your letters you said nothing of what you've been doing."

"Did you think I was shearing sheep?"

"But England is losing, Dan." She whipped around to face him. "England is losing the war."

"I know she is. We're counting on it."

"How can you say that?"

"Don't you remember when we first met? What did you think it meant to me when I pranced about that stage saying, 'I'd give a lifetime to be in Ireland, a score of weeks, for there's no place but Ireland where the Gael can have peace always'? I've only one loyalty, Jane. And it's not to England. Her defeat means our triumph. Not her defeat, her mere distress. Just distress is enough. I don't wish her worse than that."

"Well, there's plenty of distress."

"I didn't come here to add to yours."

"Did you think I'd be grateful for what you've revealed to me?"

"That your brother's living? Yes. I couldn't go back to Ireland without you knowing. And I wanted you to know that I wish him no harm."

"Just distress."

They stared hard at each other. He saw a stoniness in her he'd never suspected was there, and it frightened him. He said, "Was I mistaken, then, to come?"

When, after a long time, she did not answer, he smiled and said softly, "Just then you called to mind the nuns I had as a boy. We never saw anything of nuns' faces, did you know that? Only their eyes, which were cold eyes, and hard. To tell the truth, darling, your eyes are cold like that now, and your face might as well be in a starched white helmet for all it shows

me. Fancy you, a nun, an Oblate of Mary or something." He
laughed, but there was nothing light in him, nothing amused.
"Imagine, and you a Prod."

"And me a Prod," she repeated. Suddenly she turned on the
bench dramatically, throwing her head back. "I have a little key
to unlock the prison of Naisi! Keep back, Conchubar! For the
High King who is your master has put his hands between us!"

"Don't say that!" Curry grabbed her wrist.

"Why?"

"Because Deirdre's 'little key' was the knife she plunged
into her heart."

Jane sank, deflated, and she fell against him. "I only know
how unthinkable it is that I should live without you. That's what
Deirdre felt and it's what I feel."

But he sensed how wounded she was, and so even her sharp
declaration did not cut the knot of his anxiety. He ran his fingers
through her hair, touching his nostrils to it, inhaling her. "Jane,
I have so longed to be with you. You are more important to me
than anything."

"Than Ireland?" she asked promptly, without raising her
face to him.

And just as promptly he said, "Yes," surprising himself as
much as her.

"Then I shall not be jealous of her if she has you." She closed
her arms around him. "Oh Dan, my love, let me hold you. Just
let me hold you."

And he did.

After a long time he said, "And you, love, what will Ireland
be to you?"

"My heart's in two places, Dan. You know that."

"Days are coming, Jane, when it won't be able to be. I
want you with me, darling. You should be with Ireland, not

just because she's yours and was your father's, but because she's right. It's a question of morality."

"The morality of it, Dan, is all a muddle. I don't see how it's moral to go against England in her time of need. My father doesn't do that. While the war is on, we can have no argument."

"But will you be coming back to Dublin?"

She shook her head. "Pamela needs me. It's not only Douglas. Her father died on the *Lusitania*. Her mother is failing. I can't leave them, at the soonest, until Douglas is safe."

"But you can tell them he's alive."

"And how shall I say that, exactly? I heard it in Hyde Park, at Speakers' Corner? Or should I say the truth, that my lover went to recruit my brother for the Kaiser?"

"Say what you like."

"What I like?" She pulled away from him. "Oh Dan, it's impossible! Impossible!"

"If you won't have an argument with England, don't have one with me!"

"It isn't England! It's my family! I love these people too! I loved them first! You make it sound like I'm choosing sides with Henry the Eighth, the great adulterer. You use the word *England* the way that lunatic on his soapbox over there uses the word *Rome*. There's a sneer in your voice and I won't have you using it with me. And what's so venal about England anyway? Saint Patrick was from Britain, Dan. The Book of Kells was written on Iona. Your own Pearse is the son of an Englishman from Birmingham, while Ulster's Carson was born in Dublin. It's all a muddle, I tell you! What's the point of hating England so? It's all mixed in together, as it should be. I'm Irish, yes. *And* I'm English. So are you. Listen to the words we're using. We're speaking English, Dan, because that's who we are too!"

Curry responded to her outburst rigidly. "Don't start on the language, Jane. It undercuts your case, since, as you know, our own language was the first victim of this war."

"No! Our reason was, and our common sense! How can anyone think it's Germans we belong with? I'd rather be ruled from London than from Berlin."

Curry abruptly stood; this was too much. "And what of Dublin? What's wrong with wanting to be ruled from Dublin?"

"Wait until the war's over, and you will be! Home Rule has already been passed."

"Home Rule is dead, Jane. Carson killed it, wherever he was born. *He* killed it." Curry pointed at the ranting antipapist preacher. "'Home Rule is Rome rule'! They think we learned our subservience from our priests, but it's our priests who have kept alive in us our dream of freedom. Without our religion we wouldn't have survived as a people, and that is why he hates it. Should we let such idiots and bigots control our destiny? You are not paying attention! The war has put Westminster at the mercy of men like that, and their one ambition is to keep men like me their slaves!"

"That's a bit extreme, Dan."

"Oh, Christ." Curry wheeled away from her, cursing himself, but then abruptly turned back again. "Yes, it's extreme! I'm extreme! I haven't swallowed my soul like you have! Where's your fire, Jane?"

"What you mean is, where's my hatred?"

"Yes, God damn it! Yes! I hate them. Whom else should I hate for what I saw growing up on Henrietta Street? There were times when my mother cooked rats, Jane! She served their meat to us, swearing it was chicken. And we pretended to believe her so that we could swallow the awful stuff—we were that hungry. And going out from my own experience, yes I hate the landlords who've starved our peasants, and I hate the vicars who've stolen our churches, and I hate the servants of the King who've taken our children. It's extreme of me, is it, to say 'slavery'? When the parents of Catholic families were murdered or starved, do you know what happened to their children? To hundreds of thousands of them? They were shipped as slaves to the West Indies, the *British* West Indies!"

"That's history, Dan."

"Yes, it's history. What else do we have?"

She stood up and faced him squarely. "Then what about the history of Parnell? Whom do you hate for his destruction? Wasn't it your own church that brought him down? You people did that! Catholics had at him like jackals, and the fiercest of all were your noble priests. And then what became of the Irish party? Then what became of Dublin rule? That's what sent my father from the fray—not the English, but the Irish themselves and their hatred—yes, hatred!—for the one who'd have set them free!"

He stared at her. "'You people'? What's that phrase refer to, Jane?"

"It refers to all of you who think the test of a person's passion is how heartily they hate. English or Irish, Protestant or Catholic, that mad Orangeman on his box over there denouncing the Pope, or you cursing the servants of the King—what's the difference? I've seen both sides of it. My people have a history too, a history in the middle, neither English nor Irish, but something needed by each side. But instead of letting us be the source of healing, both of you revile us, English and Irish alike. I don't have to recall Parnell or Wolfe Tone. I don't have to appeal to John Redmond or Lady Gregory or your own Synge to find an Anglo-Irishman who wanted only peace and freedom for his people, only to have them turn him out as surely as the English ever did. I have my father for that. He taught me the meaning of loyalty, Dan, and it's a broader, truer meaning than yours. And he taught my brother too."

"You can't serve two masters, Jane. It's that simple."

"Nothing's that simple."

"To me it is."

"Well, then." She stared at him furiously.

He had never seen such stone in a face before, and it filled him with despair. He went to the bench to pick up his hat and mackintosh. As he fingered the rim of his hat he said, "I feared it would lead to this if I came to you."

"Yet you came anyway."

"Because I love you."

"You can't love me, Dan, and hate my people."

"But can I love my own people unless I do?"

Neither answered his question. They stood opposite each other, opposites truly.

Then she said, "It was arrogant of us to consider ourselves immune from this."

He nodded. Yes, he thought, this far and no farther. The woman he was born to be with, and now never again. Curry had heard the truth of her accusation. He knew full well how rampant hatred could poison even the most righteous cause, even theirs. It was what he didn't like about Casement, a man whom hatred had made mad, and it was his own main fear for himself. But now, there in the cockpit of London, he knew that he suddenly had a more grievous cause of hatred than any he'd had before. That England had murdered his people was one thing, but now she'd murdered his love.

———

Before either had mustered the will to say good-bye, there was a commotion at North Carriage Drive beyond the Hyde Park preachers, near the Marble Arch. A carriage behind two foaming horses came hurtling to a stop.

Curry didn't recognize it as Pamela's carriage, but Jane did.

The wheels were still turning when the door was flung open and the figure of a man leapt out. He turned to help a woman dismount behind him; then they were both running toward Curry and Jane, waving wildly.

Involuntarily Curry stepped back. The man wore the uniform of a British officer. He was grinning like a boy.

Jane reached for Curry, a reflex of her own, pressing the varnished nails of both her hands into his arm, as if he could save her from the approaching apparition, which, far from rejoicing her soul as it should have, filled her with fear.

Pamela, the flawless façade of her stoic composure cracked at last to smithereens, was crying at the top of her voice, "He's home! He's home!"

And at her side, happy as she'd never seen him, was their dear Douglas.

13

Tyrrell plunged toward his sister like a diving kite. He hardly registered the face of the man she was with, but he was aware of his presence. Even as he took Jane into his arms, an act of pure emotion, his intelligence worked to assess the man's importance. Importance to Jane, was the first thought, of course. She had been holding on to him like a frightened child, which was how Tyrrell knew to take him as more than a stranger.

He turned the question aside, allowing Jane's familiar scent to fill his nostrils, to work together with his other senses—the feel of her bones in his embrace, the sound of her fevered greeting—against the dread suspicion that all of this was fantasy. He'd been in London now less than two hours. A day earlier he'd arrived in Amsterdam, rotten with the filth of four days in the holes of barges and the black alleys of Rhine River waterfronts. And now, clean, fed, in shimmering London, he had found his wife again and his children, whose deaths he had assumed in assuming his own death. And here was his sister, her eyes brimming for him, her hands clawing at his shoulders with what he recognized as panic that this—his survival—wasn't real.

He had lived for days like an adventurer in dreams, afraid to sleep, certain that when he woke he would see the faces of his guards above him. The faces of his guards. In a cruel reversal, the very thought of those men made him think of another man, Bernard Keefe. Before his mind grasped Keefe's relevance, making explicit what he knew viscerally already, that Keefe was somehow linked to the man his sister was with, the thought of his dead adjutant unleashed Tyrrell's grief. "Bernard!" He'd hurled that name into the midnight river like a stone. "Bernard! Bernard!"

He buried his face in Jane's hair. This was not Bernard. This was not the stranger a glimpse of whom had snagged him. This was Jane, his own darling Jane.

"Jane! Jane! Jane!" He cried her name the way he'd cried Keefe's, feeling himself on the edge of a great precipice, clinging to his own life, holding on to the earth by holding on to her. He knew what he had done: On the cold stone of that bridge buttress, he had sunk to his knees and pressed his face against the darkness. He had groveled, kissing the feet of death, unable to help himself. He had been desperate to bring back Keefe, because only Keefe alive could have covered over again the hole in his heart that he'd hidden from for years.

He had been twenty-two years old when his mother died. He had fled the pain of that loss, never facing it, by going to London to be with Pamela. His mother's death, despite how he loved her, had barely touched him because he hadn't allowed it to. The mystery was that the death of a Galway fireman, a roughhewn "temporary gentleman," a Catholic with whom he had nothing in common, should have so unleashed these long-battened feelings. The death of Bernard Keefe embodied the deaths of all the men who'd fallen beside Tyrrell, and only now did the full horror of what he'd been through hit him. Only now did he feel the full range of his need.

But Jane was holding him and his need was being met. As if he had just been born, but with an adult's awareness, the power of his own life surged through him. He was alive!

The pristine joy of that knowledge should have possessed him utterly, but it didn't. Memory nagged at him again, tossing up now the face of Roger Casement, that sinister, gaunt, black-bearded bastard, the first man Tyrrell had ever truly hated. He tried to pull away from Jane, but she held him.

Not Casement, he thought, not Casement. He knew it made no sense that the image of Roger Casement should have taken over the field of his concentration, and he tried to shake it off. The feeling was that Casement had caused Keefe's death.

Not Casement. His mind stumbled toward recognition as he opened his eyes, but Jane clung to him still.

The man to whom Jane had been clinging before—it was *his* face he had to see. But now his sister was pushing him away, preventing him from turning to look. Jane? But what are you doing, Jane? Who is this man, and who is he to you?

Tyrrell succeeded in pulling back from her, and he saw, first, in her eyes an expression of utter quandary, like a night animal caught in a hunter's light, unable to decide which way to flee. Then he turned and saw that the man whose face had finally come between them was walking quickly away.

———

Curry had seen Tyrrell coming down the path the way bystanders saw Lazarus crawling from his cave, the linen death-wrap dangling from his chin. Lazarus made for his sister, whose tears had so moved the Lord. God knows what the others did.

By the time Curry recovered from his initial shock, Tyrrell had reached Jane and enveloped her. It didn't matter to Curry that he was just a man like himself, any more than it mattered to the friends of Lazarus that he would die again. At that moment Tyrrell was a ghost to Curry. How had he come from Germany? It couldn't be Tyrrell, but Curry knew it was. Tyrrell had come for him, the way his eyes at that assembly had sworn they would. But how had Tyrrell known? How had he found him here?

Curry reined his agitation, falling back instinctively on an actor's artificial rationality. My fear is groundless, he told himself. He has not come to find me. He hasn't even seen me. He won't recognize me without my wild hair and my full beard. I wouldn't have recognized him if not for Jane. He'll never know it's me.

His actor's technique kept him rooted for the seconds it took to realize that headlong flight would be a grave mistake, a rank admission. Play the role, he told himself. You are a trespasser caught inside a locked gate. An actor's exercise. He could hear a director barking at him—Normality! Give me normality!

His only chance lay in the appearance of casual nonchalance, and so, as unobtrusively as a minor character making his exit while the principals enact their great scene, he put his hat on, touched a finger to it, turned, adjusted the draped mackintosh on his arm, and walked away.

I am late for my appointment with my solicitor, otherwise I'd never hurry off so rudely. The young lady was kind enough to point the way for me; I have no other business here. My further presence would be an intrusion.

He spoke such sentences to himself through jaws painfully clenched against an absolute impulse to run from everything he had done and said and prayed for and desired since leaving the Abbey Theatre; no, since meeting Jane.

"Hello."

Curry pretended not to hear.

"Hello!"

Tyrrell was running after him.

Curry's mind worked quickly. If he pretended to be English, there would be the problem of his not being in the service. If he was Irish, the deadly nerve would be exposed. He was dressed incorrectly for an American.

"Hello! Sir! Please!" Tyrrell had nearly caught up with him now.

Curry stopped and turned, blinking. "I beg your pardon." He was Thomas Broadbent now, a solemn, earnest civil engineer just back from Pretoria, where, on His Majesty's behalf, he'd inspected rubber plantations as part of the urgent effort to find new sources to alleviate the killing wartime rubber shortage. He was a buoyant, likable Englishman of the sort who'd have carried a Union Jack handkerchief if he had a bigger nose.

Tyrrell stared at him.

Curry made a show of pulling spectacles from his pocket, donning them, then peering at the officer with good-natured curiosity. He said in a high-pitched, English voice, "Did you want a word with me, Captain?" He smiled. Light glinted off his glasses.

Tyrrell backed off. "My sister . . ." He indicated Jane, who remained where she was, several dozen yards away.

"Ah, the young lady who stumbled. It was my honor to help her to her feet. No thanks necessary, Captain. My perfect privilege, sir."

"She stumbled?"

"Well, anyone would have. Those ruffians with their dogs off the leash. They cut right in front of her. Where *have* they gone to?" He looked about. No sign of the culprits. He showed a sudden concern. "I trust she's all right. I assumed as much when you arrived. She seemed so . . . relieved. I deemed my further presence a slight intrusion, and I'm due at Whitehall . . ." He withdrew his pocket watch and deftly snapped it open. "If you'll excuse me, Captain, unless I can be of further service, of course, to the young lady . . ."

"No, no. You've been most gracious. Thank you, Mr . . . ?"

"Broadbent, Thomas Broadbent." Curry smiled. "Civil engineer. Ministry of Munitions, Captain. Office of Mineral Resource and Supply." Curry blinked eccentrically throughout, anything to avoid letting Tyrrell hold his gaze under the glass of memory.

Tyrrell looked about awkwardly, as if someone could explain the tricks his mind was playing. He nodded. "Indeed so. Keep up the good work, and thank you, Mr. Broadbent." Tyrrell saluted him informally and backed away.

Jane had turned to Pamela, and they were holding each other. It was unclear who was consoling whom, but Tyrrell sensed what a shock his return was to them, and he chastised himself for leaving them alone. He retraced his way up the path, pausing only once to look back at Broadbent.

Curry resumed his brisk but perfectly controlled escape. He gave thanks now to George Bernard Shaw for creating Broadbent, the absurd hero of *John Bull's Other Island*—and to the Abbey, where he'd played him.

————

"The sight of the man filled me with shame," Curry said. "We were wrong to ask those prisoners to join us."

"I warned you, Dan." Pearse craned across his desk. He was taking Curry's report in his cluttered office at Saint Enda's, the Dublin school he had founded to teach the young the Irish language. Pearse was dressed in a sober black suit and tie that contrasted starkly with his pink skin. With his garb, his complexion, his hunched shoulders, he cut the precise image of a dreary schoolmaster, but his blue eyes were fierce, capable of peering into the very souls of people, eyes that had become the source of his power not only over schoolboys but over the hardest men of his generation.

Now those eyes were lit with anger. "This is what comes of your unchecked romance. What are you, a moonstruck boy? You had no business in London! It was a gross act of insubordination and you'll have to account for it."

"Is that so, Pádraic?" Curry had anger of his own. Pearse had sent him off on a harebrained mission with a half-mad wild-man. "How can you bring me before the council and charge me with defiance for not coming directly home from Germany when you've kept MacNeill and Connolly in the dark about the German treaty? And now I understand why you've done so. MacNeill and Connolly would never approve it."

Pearse shook his head and leaned back in his creaking wooden swivel chair. "That isn't why, Dan." He eyed his subordinate carefully for a moment, then softened and said, "You look better without the beard. You'd have broken all the female hearts in Ireland, if you'd been ordained."

"All but my mother's, Pádraic." Curry grinned. "But she doesn't have one."

"Sit down, Dan."

Curry sat in the stiff wooden chair opposite Pearse's desk. Appropriately it was the chair in which stubborn Saint Enda's boys were disciplined.

Pearse swiveled slightly to look out the window. A steady rain was falling; the gloom of the weather matched the liturgical calendar, for it was All Souls' Day, the day of the suffering souls. He said quietly, "MacNeill and Connolly are in the dark about our German arrangement for the same reason I brought you into the light about it." He looked sharply at Curry. "Security,

Dan. Absolute security. Only a handful of people know of our alliance with Berlin. While the British keep their sights set on the Volunteers parading in Dublin behind Eoin and the Citizen Army on display in Cork under Jim, we work in secret to prepare the invasion in Kerry and Clare and Galway. That's why *you* were the one I sent to work with Casement. Because you're *not* MacNeill or Connolly or Clarke or Plunkett, because you can move about without attracting Castle attention. Or you could before you went so carelessly to London."

"Tyrrell didn't know me."

"You knew him."

Curry shrugged. "It's irrelevant now, Pádraic. The invasion is a figment of yours. It'll never happen. That's what I've come to tell you. I watched a roomful of Irish soldiers curdle with contempt for us. No one will sign on with Casement but the kind of men we wouldn't want."

"What kind is that, Dan?"

"Men with no morality."

"You've a priest's sense of certitude, Dan. Once the die is cast, niceties of moral theology take second place to bringing events to a swift and proper conclusion."

"What die is cast?"

"We've set the date. We're committed now to full revolution."

"When?"

Pearse answered only with his stare.

Curry smiled. "Absolute security, eh?"

Pearse nodded.

"It's a classic mistake, Pádraic. The Irish have always struck with too little. I've just told you there will be no Irish Brigade."

"The Irish Brigade is neither here nor there, never has been. Our agreement with Germany goes far beyond equipping and landing a few malcontent Micks." He leaned forward and laid it out. "Cork and Dublin will fall easily to the Volunteers, who are already well armed and drilled. Our problem will be countering the army garrisons elsewhere in the country and preventing the British from sending in heavy guns or frontline troops. That's where the Germans serve us. We'll have perhaps fifty thousand men, but only eight thousand rifles. Everything depends on redressing that inequity. Therefore"—he began to tick off items on his fingers—"the Germans will land arms and ammunition to be distributed to units in place in Clare, Galway, Limerick, and Kerry. In addition, the Germans will land a contingent of experienced, English-speaking officers who will assist our forces in the west. Simultaneously, they will support the Rising with diversionary raids on the east coast of England and over London with Zeppelin raids. And most important, they will send U-boats into Dublin Bay that will cut off British gunboats and reinforcements. Once the scope of the Rising is evident, the police and constabulary will collapse because Irishmen won't fight us when they see we're going to win. We'll be up against the present army force, fewer than fifteen thousand third-line troops. Ireland will be ours in a week."

Pearse stopped abruptly, his eyes flashing in triumph, as if he'd just described what had already taken place. Curry was as awed by the plan as Pearse, and for the first time he saw the real possibility of Ireland's freedom. Curry's doubts were less power-ful than Pearse's certainty.

But then he remembered what Casement had said, and his own promise to report it. "But, Pádraic, you've dismissed the Irish Brigade. Casement told me to tell you that they are more central than ever. The Germans don't trust us to break with England once we have our freedom. They regard the willingness of Irish soldiers to betray the Crown as a symbol of our breach with England and as a guarantee of our compact with Berlin."

Pearse stared at Curry, not at all pleased to have his magnificent strategy questioned. He said nothing.

Curry pressed. "You said it yourself, that rainy night in a doorway on Sackville Street. You pounded one fist into the other and said, 'Everything hinges on the Irish prisoners.' You convinced me against my own judgment to help recruit them, but they wouldn't be recruited. So now you say they're neither here nor there. But Casement thinks they're still the crux of our alliance with Berlin."

"Casement is full of himself. He's in this for his own glorification, not Ireland's. He sees the brigade as his way into authority we'd never give him otherwise. It's an illusion. Casement is not in command."

"Neither are you, Pádraic. MacNeill is the chief of staff of the Volunteers, and he's committed to waiting out the war. You talk to me of insubordination. You've done all this without authority."

Pearse flushed with anger, but immediately checked his emotion and assumed the obviously counterfeit demeanor of a patient parent. "Dan . . . Dan, the Volunteers are what's visible. Preparations for the real Rising must be invisible. When the moment comes, Eoin will yield to me. He'll have no choice. His men will greet the day with alleluias, and then so will he."

An awkward silence fell between them. For the first time Curry understood the Germans' problem, how impossibly complicated the Irish rebellion would seem to them, the Sinn Fein, the Volunteers, the IRB, the Citizen Army, Pearse, MacNeill, Connolly, Casement—all claiming to speak for the cause, yet each refusing to trust the other. Of course the Germans would need some guarantee. And a substantial force of Irish soldiers under *their* control would provide it. But now the brigade was "neither here nor there." Curry studied Pearse, wondering what would be neither here nor there at the next phase? The man was not nearly as steady as he seemed.

After a time Pearse said, "And what of you?"

On the wall beside Curry's chair was a large map of Ireland, a sharp, rich green. Curry's eye moved to it, took refuge on it. In his mind the island took on the shape of a human head, facing away from England toward the vast emptiness of ocean. He was aware of his welling emotion, as if the island were a desperate person with a claim on him. As, of course, it was. Ireland was his mother, and she was staring off after all her sons and daughters who'd abandoned her to the cruelest fate a nation knows. And now, through this pale schoolmaster, she had put to him at last the momentous question: And what of you?

He faced Pearse. He spoke with a cool edge of analysis that had little to do with the complicated, ambivalent, tumultuous emotion he felt. "My commitment to the cause is firm, Pádraic. But the means give me trouble. If it all went according to plan, and I admit it's impressive, the Germans would have us at their mercy."

Pearse shook his head. "The Germans are playing a game called Keep America Out of the War. They must abide by our agreement or America will have her first true reason for coming in. America is our surety."

"But Germans need surety too. That's Casement's point. You told me yourself that once we're free, we could well declare neutrality."

Pearse lit a cigarette and put a foot on his desk. "Did I say that?"

"You know damn well you did."

"I believe in taking one war at a time, Dan. What do you think, this is a ritual act with directions for each step outlined in red ink on the margins of the page? There are no rubrics for rebellion, Dan." He made a show of inhaling his cigarette, eyeing Curry all the while. "You referred to that night on Sackville Street. You made a statement of your own that night, as I recall. You said, 'My conscience will come along.' It hasn't, has it? Is it your conscience, Dan? Or is it the girl?"

"The girl! Christ, I *ranted* at the girl about the nobility of our cause. I told her the time for divided loyalties is past. She sneered at me; she said it's all a muddle. Casement's a Protestant from Ulster fighting for the Catholics of Dublin; Carson's from Dublin fighting for the Orangemen of Ulster. She said the famous Patrick Pearse is the son of an Englishman! What could be more chaotic than that? I know it's a muddle, Pádraic, and I'm not waiting for the water to clear. It's just that . . ." Curry stopped. What *was* it? He felt panic rising inside himself. Was this a crisis of conscience? Was this loss of nerve? Why hadn't someone taught him to distinguish the two? He sat forward in his chair. "Is that true, about your father being from Birmingham?"

Pearse nodded.

"And you feel no qualm about the course you've set?"

"None. You've qualm enough for both of us, man."

"Pádraic, I can't help feeling that your cool intelligence is in the service of a decision you've already made on other grounds."

"Be that as it may, the decision is made. We've informed Berlin through Washington. They have to trust us and we have to trust them. There's no turning back. The question now is you, Dan. How can I trust you to go back to Germany and represent me as the preparations go forward when you're so lacking in conviction? That woman has undercut your fervor, and it's fervor that will carry us through."

"I'm showing you nothing new, Pádraic. This is who I've always been."

"Which is why you've always fallen short."

Curry felt his face redden. "What do you mean?"

"Why you quit the priesthood. You've no gift for seeing a thing through, Dan."

Curry stood. "I offered myself honestly, with a want of certitude, that's true. The Church requires certitude to the point of blind stupidity. Is that your requirement too?"

"I require absolute loyalty and absolute obedience."

"I've given you those."

"You went to London without authority."

Just then Curry felt the most acute panic of his life. Pearse had reached a hand into the cavity of his chest, squeezing his lungs, making breath impossible. Loss of nerve? Pearse had found the nerve in Curry that he could never ignore, and he had twisted it around the most awful question there was. Had he the capacity for solemn commitment or not? Nothing had ever drawn from him such feelings of loyalty as Ireland herself had, not the Church, not his family, not the theater. Not Jane. He had thought to give himself over to Ireland utterly, but he hadn't. He had clung to his reservations and to his doubts exactly as he had in the seminary, not because they were true or relevant but because they spared him the burden of having to truly give himself over to something else—anything else. If he lived like this, he would end up alone and useless, a shell of the man he'd hoped to be. In a voice lacking in bravado he said, "I've given myself to Ireland, Pádraic. I made a vow through you and I intend to keep it. I'm with you until the end."

"And what of the woman?"

Curry read the meaning of the question—not question, but demand. "I won't see her again." Even as the words left his mouth, Curry felt himself sag inside. But he forced himself to believe that it didn't matter. Jane Tyrrell would never have spoken to him again in any case. If he couldn't win her, then he could perhaps win Ireland instead.

"Swear it."

"I swear by the blood of Christ." And like that, she was gone. He would be a divided man no more. Hadn't he once embraced a life without all women for the sake of purity? So what was a life without one of them if his purity could be restored? If he'd put his hand into a flame just then, he'd have felt nothing.

Pearse watched his cigarette smoke rise to the ceiling. His fierce, punishing intensity weighed on Curry absolutely, all the more so because he had forced such obeisance while lounging back casually in his tilted chair, foot still on his desk, one hand back of his neck and the other, from which the smoke curled, at his chin. "But I still can't send you back to Germany," he said mournfully. "And you can't stay in Dublin if Tyrrell has seen your face. The Brits will let the boyos wear stripes on their trousers but they won't tolerate intercourse with the enemy. You're an honest-to-God traitor to the Crown now, Dan. Congratulations." Pearse smiled, but only for the moment it took his crack to fall flat on Curry's silence. "So you'll be my man in the west." He plopped his chair forward and stood to cross to the wall near Curry. He stabbed his finger at the map of Ireland, sequentially at several points along the west coast. "Tralee, Kilrush, Ennis, Galway, and Westport. Those are the five centers. Until now the service units have operated independently, reporting to us here. We can't draw them together into one command yet because MacNeill would try to control it, but it's time to get them ready. I want you to move informally among them, get to know them, choose the best men without regard to MacNeill's selections. See to their drilling if only with hurling sticks, tools, and branches. Make them understand in general terms that they'll be the first to receive rifles, and when the time comes they'll seize and hold all harbors from Kerry to Donegal, giving us a dozen places to unload German ships. Let the English obsess about Sackville Street Jackeens. The marches and demonstrations will keep them in Dublin and Cork, but it will be in the hard, pure Gaelic west that we prepare our great blow against them, and when the time comes, you'll be in command of it." Pearse randomly placed the palm of his hand against the map and leaned on it while watching Curry's reaction. "Am I a fool, Dan, to trust you with this?"

"No. It's what I want."

"It's your old job back again, what drew me to you in the first place when I saw at the Abbey Theatre how you can win the people over, making them believe that the ancient dream is coming to pass. That's all we must do now, Dan, is make them see that the liberation of Ireland is truly possible. It's been talk, talk, talk for so long now that many simply cannot conceive of it as anything else. But you must bring them word of something else now, and I mean *action!* You must show them how to take it!"

"You've already set the date, you said."

"That's right. The bread is in the oven. The bread is rising."

"When will it be done?"

Pearse faced away from him, leaning all the more heavily against the map, his full weight on his hand, as if pushing. If he could push the map through the wall, couldn't he push Ireland out of England's grasp? He studied the west coast for a moment, then said, "You'll want a motorcar to cover all that area. I'll get you one." He looked over his shoulder at him. "Can you drive, man?"

Curry nodded. "What's the date, Pádraic? How much time do I have?"

"You know I can't tell you that. There's time yet, Dan. You'll be the first to know. It won't be this month."

"This year?"

"Don't press me, Dan. You've just become a military man. You don't press your commanding officer."

"Should I salute?" Curry smiled.

Then so did Pearse. "You'll have rank and so will I, but that won't be the point between us, will it?" Suddenly Pearse took his hand off the map and offered it to Curry. The two men shook warmly.

Curry felt a swell of gratitude. He felt simultaneously unworthy of this man's friendship and affirmed by it. His qualm was stifled now, swallowed without aftertaste. He wanted to say a word of thanks to Pearse, but it would have been an overly emotional one just then, and such expression was strictly beyond the limit of his otherwise exuberant Irish manliness. He channeled the impulse into the heartfelt handshake. Neither made a move to end it for a long time.

Finally Pearse turned away, went to his desk, and began rifling through a pile of papers.

Curry's eye went to the map, to the stretch of Irish coast that would be his. The place against which Pearse had leaned was darkened by a palm-shaped perspiration stain. It marked the rugged peninsula that ran below Galway Bay from the Cliffs of Moher up to the site of Cragside.

Pearse found what he was looking for and crossed to Curry with it, but instead of giving it to him, he led Dan to the door and out of the office. As they walked through the corridor of the school, Curry wondered what Pearse had to give him. A pamphlet, he thought, with some of the orator's great rhetoric: "Ireland unfree shall never be at peace!"

More than any other event in years, this man's speeches had undermined the inbred Irish subservience on which the English had always depended. Curry had been present for the great oration at O'Donovan Rossa's funeral and would never forget it: "The fools!" Pearse, the frail man of learning and of letters had raised both his fists and become Cuchulain himself, branding England with his scalding words. "The fools! The fools! The fools! They have left us our Fenian dead, and while Ireland holds these graves Ireland unfree shall never be at peace!"

That autumn Pearse had begun to touch crowds the way he had already touched Curry in the summer. Masses of Irishmen—young and old, male and female, tradesmen and peasants, gathered on corners, in graveyards, in parks and playing fields—were made by mere words to feel that mere words were no longer enough. The pressure on Pearse became enormous, and no doubt his compulsion to act outran the impulses of other rebel leaders because his speeches had begun to condemn speech itself. It was a dangerous position for an orator to take, for the better his talks became the more insufficient they became too. But Pearse depended for his power neither on logic nor political analysis nor military insight nor anything that might have prepared him to act successfully. Ironically he depended on the one thing that, when the time came, would be of little use—the fire of passion. But short of that time, Gaelic fire from the teacher of Gaelic not only seared Britain, it burned through the crust of Ireland's ancient passivity. Dan Curry's own conversion was his best reason for believing Pearse; and if it could happen to Curry, it could happen to a whole people.

At the main entrance to Saint Enda's, a former convent on the edge of Dublin, Pearse stopped. The doorway's pointed Gothic arch loomed above them, lending the moment of their parting a staged solemnity. Outside the rain was falling steadily. Pearse handed a sheaf of pages to Curry shyly. "I want you to read this. I was thinking of you when I wrote it."

Curry looked at the top page, a title page. "The Singer. A Play About Ireland's Struggle. By Pádraic Pearse."

Curry was speechless. When had he been so honored?

Pearse layered their awkwardness over. "It's a translation. I'd rather you read it in Irish, but . . ."

Curry grinned. "I didn't go to a fine Irish school like this one. Now, Latin and Greek . . ." He put his hand on Pearse's shoulder. "Thanks, Pádraic. I'll read it right away."

"Take it with you. I don't want you in Dublin a moment longer than you have to be."

Curry put the pages under his coat, donned his hat, hunched forward, curling his collar up, and, with a last nod at Pearse, dashed out into the rain.

Before he'd gone a block, he was soaked through. The rain only intensified. He didn't want to get the play wet. He nearly knocked an old woman down when she cut across his path. He started to apologize, but she ignored him, heading into a church just there. He remembered what day it was, and that he hadn't been to mass yet. He followed the woman into the dark shelter of the church. The vestibule was puddled, but the church proper was dry and warm, crowded with worshipers, and it was a relief to slide into a pew in the rear. The mass had begun moments before, but the priest, in his black fiddleback vestments, was faced away from the congregation. Like the adolescent he would always be in that setting, Curry was grateful that the priest couldn't have seen him come in late.

The priest intoned the *Dies Irae*, the Gradual verse between scripture readings. Curry closed his eyes and began to recite the Latin psalm to himself. *Dies irae, dies illa, Salvet saeculum in favilla.* Day of wrath, day of anger, time melts into ashes . . .

The rhythm of the verses—that familiar singsong—soothed Curry despite the grim prophecy they contained, and tension drained out of him as he sank into the comfort of the church. All Souls' Day, the commemoration of all the faithful departed, was the perfect Catholic observance, for the religion that made no sense and seemed only calcified and priest-ridden in the light of the day—say of a dry, fun-filled summer afternoon—became an exquisite consolation in the dank shadow of early November, when, in the mean cycle of time, death had come around again. The place of Catholicism in Ireland depends on the facts that early November lasts ten months of every year, and that only the departed are considered faithful.

On a clip on the pew-back in front of him was the day's holy card. Curry took it and squinted at the picture, a black figure, hooded like death and with an upraised accusing arm. Beneath the figure was the prayer for All Souls' Day. "Thou Who didst raise Lazarus fetid from the tomb; Thou, O Lord, give them rest and a place of pardon. Thou Who art to come to judge the living and the dead and the world by fire; Thou Who didst raise Lazarus fetid from the tomb."

Curry's hand shook at the memory of that moment, seeing Tyrrell coming at him. Now Curry knew why the sight of Jane's brother had been so awful. Not for mere human reasons, that Tyrrell might have caught him. Tyrrell was one sent from God, come to accuse him. But of what? His treason? His ambivalence? His failure? His lust? His having left the priesthood? His qualm about Ireland's struggle? Even now Curry did not know what his sin was, only that it was mortal and he had yet to repent of it. He knelt on the hard wooden slat and buried his head to pray. I'm sorry, I'm sorry. But the words he spoke in his mind were addressed not to God—he recognized this at once—and not to Pádraic Pearse either. He was addressing Jane.

At the end of mass he sat in the church for a long time, his mind empty. He felt the sublime relief that came, for Catholics, in the backwash of an abject admission. "I am a worm," he'd been taught to say with Thomas à Kempis, "and no man." And that was how he felt. Now all thoughts of Jane were gone. It was like giving himself over—and wasn't this how his Irish sin could finally be purged?—to Pearse, so that Dan Curry, the man, could be molded again.

He picked up the pages beside him and opened them at random, the way an Orangeman opens his Bible. Even in near-darkness—the sexton had doused the lights—he could make out Pearse's careful words.

"One man can free a people, as one Man redeemed the world. I will take no pike. I will go into battle with bare hands. I will stand up before the Gall as Christ hung naked before men on the tree."

Curry raised his eyes to the cross, his beloved Jesus standing on His nails, and with happiness to have given himself away at last, he wept.

14

The girl rapped quietly on the door.

Pamela opened her eyes at once, surprised that she'd slept after all. She was curled inside Douglas, and the feel of his body naked against hers shocked her. Because he was behind her, she couldn't see him, but then she realized his hand was on her breast. She raised the blanket slightly to look at his hand, confirming with her sense of sight that this was real, he was real, he had come home. They'd made love repeatedly through the night. Dawn had come without their having slept. Then, apparently, they'd drifted off in weariness and contentment.

And now Margaret was at the door with their breakfast tray. "Come in," she called.

Douglas stirred, but then held her closer, cupping her breast more snugly. She pressed the blanket down at her throat as the door opened.

"Good morning, ma'am." Margaret put the tray on Pamela's dressing table, then curtsied. "Shall I draw the curtains back, ma'am?" The servant drew the curtains before Pamela could ask her not to. The morning light spilled into the room, through the dull filter of rain. Pamela would happily have stayed inside her husband's snug embrace, but it was just as well. He had his appointment this morning. Margaret curtsied once more and left, closing the door behind her without a sound.

Pamela listened to Douglas breathing. He was asleep again. She wondered if he was dreaming. Would he believe it, when he awoke, that he was with her? She pushed the curl of her body back against him, then turned inside his arms. She savored the long, still embrace, but her leg brushed against his erection, which aroused her in turn. She kissed him in a sisterly way, lightly on his cheek and brow, and when he opened his eyes she kissed him more sensually, forcing her tongue into his mouth. His knee went between her legs as he kissed her longingly in return.

It was only in entering her that Douglas fully awoke. The night before he had ravished her repeatedly, but now the rhythm of their stroking was different. She too moved more slowly. They watched each other's faces. As they began, physically, to rise and fall, they did so together, quietly and unfrantically.

Afterward Douglas served Pamela her breakfast. While she sipped at her coffee and milk, watching him, he stood at the dressing table, above the spread of newspapers. She waited for him to speak, but when she saw that he was reading pages for the second time, she said, "The newspapers tell you nothing."

And a good thing, too, Douglas thought. Last month we lost at Artois, and this month at Loos, with the Germans inflicting twice as many casualties as they took. Why should newspapers tell wives and mothers that? He did not know what to say.

"So, of course," Pamela continued, "we think the worst."

"It isn't the worst, darling. And it isn't the best. It's somewhere in between." Douglas said this absently, while staring at an item about the Mediterranean fleet. Two battleships, *Exmouth* and *Venerable*, had steamed into the Aegean, and others were to follow. Douglas guessed that the long-awaited withdrawal from Gallipoli was under way. Like all British officers in France and Belgium, he hated those responsible for that second pointless front. The shells and soldiers wasted in the Dardanelles all through the spring, summer, and autumn could have made the difference not only at Ypres, but at Neuve-Chapelle and Festubert. He clenched his fist and nearly cursed out loud, but he didn't. Gentlemen did not inflict the disasters of their wars or businesses upon their wives.

He picked up the newspaper, fixing upon another item. "Parliament's going to pass the Military Service Act." He looked up at her. "Conscription."

"That's good, isn't it?"

"It's because no one's volunteering." He crossed to the bed and sat, adjusting his dressing gown, reading all the while. "Asquith says the spirit of patriotism must be what motivates us." Douglas laughed, thinking, But what if the reason no one's volunteering is that we're all dead? The irony of the conscription debate struck him, and the outrage of it. It was the surest sign of England's jeopardy that these waistcoated old men, safe in their paneled chambers, should be preparing for the first time in the nation's history to force boys into battle against their will. England's first sons, her best and bravest and most brilliant, had failed utterly to counter the German thrust, and now the geniuses of Westminster were going to send catchers out with nets to snag the ne'er-do-wells, cowards, and alley cats to see what they could do. By November of 1915, in fifteen months, England had gutted herself. How great could Great Britain be now if she had to force her sons to fight in her defense? "The living shield," they called the army; now it would be the unwilling one.

In the *Times* account of the conscription debate he came across the name of his father's old nemesis, Sir Edward Carson, the Irish M.P.—the man Hugh Tyrrell regarded as a mob-baiting bigot who depended on the fear and hatred of Ulster Protestants for his power. Douglas remembered that the only time Carson had ever spoken well of Catholics was when he'd teamed up with them to bring down Parnell. And now he was approaching the peak of his power because Asquith, the Liberal prime minister, needed his support to maintain his party's majority. Asquith had introduced the Irish Home Rule bill in 1912, but to appease Carson, he had backed off. It was obvious that Carson's plan was to use the emergency of the war to scuttle Home Rule altogether. Now, in the conscription debate, he was once again using England's plight to beat down Ireland, arguing that conscription should apply to Irish men as well as English. Nothing would inflame revolutionary sentiment more, of course, and Carson's wild speech alarmed Douglas as he read it. The man intended more than simply filling the ranks with new recruits. And Douglas realized that, to Carson, the trenches of France would seem the perfect place to resolve the age-old Irish problem.

"Good Christ," he muttered.

"What, darling?" Pamela reached across the bed to him.

Staring at the text, he said, "Sir Edward Carson."

Pamela nodded. "One of Jennie Churchill's beaux."

Douglas looked up sharply. Carson's love life was irrelevant. It pained him that his wife was more aware of the figure Carson cut in London social circles than of his central role in the growing Irish crisis, and once more he realized how very much separated them. To her, Ireland would never be more than her husband's losing wicket.

"This is what Carson says about the war." He read the line aloud, with unveiled bitterness, thinking of the boys he'd ordered out of trenches, thinking of Billy O'Day. "'The necessary supply of heroes must be maintained at all costs.'"

The Admiralty anteroom in which Douglas was asked to wait looked out on Trafalgar Square. He stood at the windows, staring through the gloom of rain at Horatio Nelson's pillar. In Dublin its miniature stood on Sackville Street. He was struck by the contrast between his own situation and the heroic ideal of Admiral Nelson, the embodiment of England's glory. Tyrrell was an Irish army officer about to make his formal report on the treason of a knighted Irish foreign-service officer. Below the surface of his shame were layers of a deeper shame, and he dreaded revealing any of it to the board of officers before whom in moments he would be standing. He could picture them easily, stolid, impressive Englishmen, older versions of his Oxford classmates or of the Lincoln's Inn barristers and benchers who always managed to convey, without ever being rude, their assumption that Douglas, for all his winning ways, was of a separate species.

He stared out at the bustling midday crowd that swirled through Trafalgar Square. All those Englishmen in their carriages, trams, and automobiles, all those clerks on their way to stools in the City, shopgirls to counters in Piccadilly, war bureaucrats to desks in Whitehall; all those Englishmen whipping past the huge gray pillar on which their hero stood. But they weren't heroes, were they? Just Englishmen. Whatever their class, background, or function, everyone in that square took for granted a note of identity that Douglas Tyrrell permanently lacked.

But now his first question nagged again. He was army. Casement was Foreign Office. The issue was Ireland, which should have meant Home Office, but he'd been ordered to appear here at Admiralty Arch, in the offices of the navy. Why was the navy involved in the question at all? He stared out at the stone figure of Horatio Nelson, as if he would answer. Nelson was posed like Napoleon, hand in his blouse, eyes on the far horizon. Douglas remembered reading that Nelson had made a point always to bring with him his coffin, which he'd had carved out of the mast of an enemy ship. To carry one's coffin with one, Douglas thought, was it grim madness or only prudence? Eccentricity or a wise, moderating reminder of one's mortality? Whatever it was, Nelson's habit was justified when he was laid out in his faithful casket at Trafalgar. Tyrrell shuddered and then had a strange thought: Ireland is England's coffin, and that's why she must cling to her.

The door opened behind him.

"Captain Tyrrell?"

Douglas turned around. A navy lieutenant was waiting for him by the open door. As Douglas crossed toward him, his eyes went past the navy man to the room beyond, an ornate gracious chamber with a large Persian rug and a delicate crystal chandelier. Its candles had been electrified and were now illuminated. Below the chandelier was a broad table along the far side of which sat half a dozen men. They had all raised their eyes to watch Tyrrell enter.

The man seated in the center he recognized at once as Lord Kitchener, the secretary of state for war, whose staring face, eyes wide apart above a drooping walrus mustache, was familiar from all those recruitment posters. His presence at the meeting shocked Tyrrell and made him understand that the concern was with more than the fate of Irish soldiers in a German prison camp, more even than the disgraceful behavior of Sir Roger Casement.

He strode to the center of the room and stopped in front of the table before saluting smartly.

"Be at ease, Captain." Kitchener nodded at the navy aide,

who brought a chair. Douglas sat. None of the other men were familiar to him. Two wore the uniform of navy admirals. One other besides Field Marshal Kitchener was dressed as an army general, one as an army major. The last man wore civilian clothes.

Kitchener leaned toward Tyrrell and spoke in a resonant, articulate voice, "Captain Tyrrell, my personal compliments. Reports of your conduct precede you, and speaking for my colleagues, I salute you." Kitchener threw glances left and right. Several of the men nodded and one tapped the table in front of him. Kitchener continued, "Let me begin by making the introductions. You know of me perhaps." He smiled.

"Yes, my lord."

Kitchener indicated the others in turn. "This is General Lovick Bransby Friend, the general officer commanding the army in Ireland. Major Ivor Price, the military intelligence officer for Dublin Castle. Admiral Sir Edward Hamilton, naval intelligence chief. Admiral Sir Neville Gates, commander-in-chief of the home fleet, and finally, here at my left, Undersecretary for Ireland, Sir Matthew Nathan." Kitchener put his hand on Nathan's arm. "An august gathering, wouldn't you say?"

"Indeed so," Nathan chirped, but his eyes looked vacant behind thick spectacles.

But for two exceptions, these were the quintessential Englishmen that Douglas had expected to face, and they eyed him with a certain implicit hauteur. The exceptions were Kitchener himself, a would-be Nelson, the closest thing England had to a hero in the nightmare Boer War. Douglas suddenly remembered what one never saw referred to anymore, that Kitchener himself was Irish-born, and wondered if that explained his presence here. The other exception was Nathan, the man in charge of administering the Irish executive from Dublin Castle, and what made him different was the simple fact of his being Jewish.

Kitchener cleared his throat, and from a file that included, no doubt, a copy of the report Tyrrell had submitted, he withdrew a photograph.

It would be Casement's photograph, Douglas guessed, and he realized that this must be a formal hearing for the certification of evidence. If Casement was to be cited for treason, Douglas would have to make the charge. As Kitchener slid the photograph across the table, Douglas was aware of the irony—a pair of Irish-born servants of the King leading a third up the King's scaffold. "Captain, would you look at this photograph, please?"

Douglas took it. To his surprise it was not Casement or even Casement's Irish accomplice. It was the fat-faced German who had escorted them. "I've seen him, yes."

"He was with Casement?" Hamilton asked.

"Yes."

Hamilton glanced at Kitchener, triumphant satisfaction in his expression. "As we thought. If Admiral Bremer is orchestrating this, it's everything we fear."

"*Admiral* Bremer?" Against protocol, Tyrrell expressed his surprise. "The man wore the uniform of an army colonel."

Hamilton shook his head. "He's navy. He works for Tirpitz. The German-Irish conspiracy is a navy project."

"I'm sorry, sir . . ." Tyrrell looked at Kitchener, whose nod gave him permission to speak. ". . . My understanding is that German lines between the branches are quite severe, and the army has responsibility for prisoners."

"We're not talking about prisoners, Captain," Admiral Hamilton said. "We're talking about the German invasion of Ireland. If the army was laying out the plans for it—General Alfrink, for example, or Ludendorff—there would be reason to treat the entire matter as a feint to get us to commit troops to Ireland, weakening our position on the Western Front. But the navy would not concern itself with such a strategy." Hamilton faced Kitchener. "It's Bremer and Tirpitz, my lord. We must regard it as a deadly serious prospect."

"With your permission, sir, but I made the point in my report that the German effort failed utterly. Not one of my soldiers volunteered for the so-called Irish Brigade."

General Friend, the commander in Ireland, spoke. "Doesn't matter, my dear Captain. There are other camps than yours. And now, of course, even at your camp, one presumes the Germans have sweetened the offer. Lord Kitchener"—Friend craned past Hamilton—"you simply must disband the Irish regiments, or at the very least put them under the command of English officers. We can't have them used in this way."

"General, we *refused* to be used. That is my point . . ." Douglas failed to keep the edge out of his voice.

No one else commented on Friend's remark. It was impossible to tell whether the stone-faced Kitchener agreed or not.

Admiral Gates of the home fleet, a lethargic man, had preoccupied himself with the grain of the mahogany table. Now he spoke without raising his eyes: "Whether the Germans succeed in recruiting prisoners for their Irish Brigade is of no relevance." Gates paused, shifting in his chair, but his eyes remained fixed upon the table. "If an invasion were to succeed, an Irish Brigade would function as a rallying point for imbecile Irishmen and their cousins in America. But if an invasion succeeded, the Germans would do quite nicely with or without the support of the Irish people and we would have a far graver problem than the opinion of the Americans." Gates stopped abruptly and a long, charged silence followed.

Tyrrell stared at the men, baffled, while Gates resumed his play with the surface of the table. Douglas noticed for the first time a brass plaque fixed to the edge: "This table, made from the wood of the *Golden Hind*, was presented by Sir Francis Drake."

Finally Kitchener leaned forward and looked at Hamilton. "If we're going to ask Captain Tyrrell to help us here, perhaps it would be in order, Admiral, to explain things to him."

Hamilton coughed, then stood up. He crossed to a large map of the British Isles that included all of the North Sea and much of the North Atlantic. Pins of various colors representing ships dotted the blue stretches, with a heavy concentration of black pins in the sea between England and the northern coast of Europe. Hamilton studied the map for a moment, then turned to look past the other officers at Tyrrell. "Captain, your report gives us the first confirmation we have that the initiative for an invasion of Ireland lies with the German navy. Therefore, we know that the aim of such an invasion is neither to draw off our strength from the Front nor to influence opinion in America by forming an alliance with Irish nationalists, though both of those consequences could follow. The aim of a German invasion is the establishment"—Hamilton stabbed at the map—"of a major U-boat base in the west of Ireland."

He swept his hand in an arc down from the Dingle peninsula. "U-boats have a limited range, in the hundreds, not thousands, of miles. Our pincer at the Dover straits forces U-boats coming out of Zeebrugge to make the north-about passage around the Orkneys. By the time they reach the open sea, half their fuel is spent. Limited range is the U-boat's biggest problem, and till now it's been our salvation. But that could change. An Irish base would give the Germans absolute control over the North Atlantic sea lanes. Merchant shipping from America would be stopped cold. When America comes into the war—and it is delusion of the first order to think she won't, particularly because of concern for so-called Irish freedom—German submarines will be in a position to interdict every form of American supply. From Zeebrugge the U-boats now control the North Sea and they threaten the Channel. From Cork, Galway, Tralee, or Kilrush, or from a combination of those harbors, they would control access from the North Atlantic." Hamilton stopped, visibly affected by what he'd said. He returned to his chair and sat.

General Friend leaned toward Tyrrell. "The Germans are turning out three new U-boats a week, and our navy is not destroying them."

Gates cast a harsh look at Friend, but the army man ignored him.

Tyrrell sensed that they were waiting for him to speak, but he couldn't think of anything to say. The implication of Casement's perfidy stunned him. The two who had yet to speak were Price, the intelligence man, and Nathan.

Nathan was fifty-two years old. Long service in delicate positions with the Colonial Office—he'd served as governor both of Gold Coast and Hong Kong—as well as an association with Lloyd George, then chancellor of the exchequer, had prepared him for his recent appointment to Dublin. His job was to prepare Ireland for Home Rule while damping down the malcontents on both extremes who had reason to oppose it. Some of his colleagues who might have scorned him for being Jewish agreed he was the right man for the job; what better qualification for ruling the Irish than to have previously been the governor of black men and yellow?

Now he stroked his mustache and, aware of Tyrrell's eyes upon him, he said, "Obviously, Captain, given these prospects, there are various measures we must take."

"Yes, sir."

"These gentlemen are concerned with military measures. My concern is somewhat broader. We must counter, for example, any tendency among the Irish to sympathize with the German cause. Casement's behavior is despicable. Even Irish nationalists would find the effort to inspire sedition among your men reprehensible."

Tyrrell saw at last why they were telling him this. "You want me to testify publicly to Casement's treason. I would do so willingly."

Nathan shook his head. "We haven't come to that. It is a delicate matter. One doesn't wish to express alarm in public. We mustn't advertise the activities of insurrectionist groups and thereby lend them significance they lack apart from Berlin's manipulation. But we must prevent those activities from growing."

General Friend interrupted. "Here's what we must do at once," he said, pulling on his fingers. "Forbid the ownership of arms by Irishmen. Impose rigorous censorship on the native press, since Irishmen are more affected by what they read than other people. Outlaw political rallies and outlaw the Irish Volunteers. Send the Reserve Infantry Brigades to Ireland at once, and give me the Ulster Division to sweep the coastal counties, arresting disloyal persons. It would have to be the Ulster Division, because we can't trust Catholics, whether RIC or the other Irish regiments."

Tyrrell bristled. "I beg your pardon, sir, but it's Ulstermen who've sworn to oppose His Majesty on Home Rule, not men of the south."

"Good point, Captain." Friend peered at him. "The loyalty of every Irishman must be suspect now."

"I am an Irishman, General," Douglas said.

Kitchener put his hand up to silence Friend and he addressed himself to Douglas. "Indeed so, Captain. And your loyalty is beyond question. That's why you're here. Major Price is chief of intelligence for Dublin Castle. Perhaps he can explain a bit more."

Price stood and went to the map. He ran his forefinger

slowly along the jagged western coast of Ireland. "A dozen potential harbors," he said. "And in place, settlements where insurrectionist sympathies run strong. Frankly it will make little difference to the Germans what happens in Dublin, whether speeches are given or pamphlets circulated. What will matter to the success of a German invasion is the initial support of local people. The insurrectionists must organize them to be prepared with small vessels of every kind to off-load matériel and men from the German flotilla. It is the only way, given the limited facilities of all these harbors. The ships cannot come in close. They must have help in landing."

Friend put in, "Once landed, the German force could be difficult to deal with, but in that period of transfer from ship to shore, they will be absolutely vulnerable."

"The vulnerability, sir, occurs well before that." Price touched the map again, fingering Galway. "It is the prior organization of shore support that will tell us where the German landing is to take place." Price looked at Tyrrell. "It is a simple question of information, Captain. My sources are well placed in the cities of Ireland, but as you see, the cities are not relevant. It's my contacts in the remote west which are limited, to say the least. That's why we need you."

"Me?" Douglas looked at once to Kitchener. "My lord, I'm to return to my company in France."

Kitchener nodded. "If you choose to."

Tyrrell's statement had been automatic; his return to the Front was something he assumed. Whether to want to return or not simply hadn't occurred to him. His place was with his men. But now he felt something new. Not returning to the Front meant not dying; Tyrrell was not immune to the pull of that.

Price faced the map once more. "Your home is here." He placed his finger on the peninsula below Galway Bay. "Your father has long had ties with the Farm Cooperative movement, which has active groups here, here, here, here, and here." The spots he touched took him right down to Kerry. "In civil life you were a barrister with practice here. Ennis. You are a west-of-Ireland man, Captain. The region would open itself to you like a book."

Douglas stared at the map, at his home country, trying to untie the knot in his mind. It was impossible to imagine that his army service would bring him home. "I'm a west-of-Ireland man, sure enough, Major, but you're wrong if you think Connaught will open itself to a British army officer no matter where he's from. You mentioned my father. Even my father has reservations about my service."

"I didn't picture you going from pub to pub in your boots and Sam Browne, Captain."

"What, then?"

"Something more discreet, I'd say."

After a long silence in which the knot only tightened in him, Douglas said, "You're asking me to spy on my own people."

Kitchener coughed. "Not lightly, Captain. We do not ask it lightly."

"My lord, I cannot do it. I simply cannot do it. It would be breaking faith with my family. My family, Lord Kitchener, has maintained the most fragile balance of loyalties. Don't ask me to upset it. Serving against the Germans in defense of England is noble and I'm proud to be a part of it, but don't ask me to serve against the Irish. Don't ask me to return to my own country as a secret agent, with an eye on my neighbor or my father's foreman."

"Captain Tyrrell . . ." Kitchener looked down at his smooth hands. "I was born in Kerry. The west of Ireland owns my heart still, Captain. I know the balance of loyalties of which you speak. I would never put a man in this position if I had a choice." He looked up sharply. "But there simply is no choice. The war against Germany has now moved to your home country. You can do more there than a thousand men like you can do at the Front."

"I'm sorry, my lord, but—"

"Listen to me, Captain! We are talking about the defeat of England here! We are in danger of starving to death! Do you understand me? It is a question of food supply. The Germans have great fertile tracts of farmland in northern France and Poland. They have pressed two million Russian prisoners into slave labor growing corn. Their silos are overflowing. Grain from Rumania pours into Germany, while here in England we have barely more than one week's stock of wheat. Do you hear? One week's stock of wheat! If that stock is not replenished *every day* from the holds of merchant ships, then we starve. Never mind what happens at the Front or in Turkey. Never mind what the Russians do. Without merchant ships, England starves. England dies. And where do those merchant ships come from?" Kitchener swung around and pointed at the map. "Our fertile tracts of farmland are in New Zealand, Australia, and Canada. They are in America. All of those ships must come to us across the North Atlantic, passing within sight practically of your home, of your county, of your neighbors, and of your father's foreman. U-boats operating from Ireland will kill us in a matter of days." He whipped around. "Do you hear me, Captain? Days!" Kitchener fell back against his chair. *Kitchener wants you!* His outburst had alarmed everyone in the room, but at last, Ireland had England's full attention.

Douglas stared at the map. Who would have thought that remote Cragside would be the eye of such a storm? The war in France swirled about it. Nothing mattered, finally, but the war and winning it. Chastened, he said, "I understand, my lord. And of course I am prepared to do my part."

"Good." Kitchener looked over at Price, who remained by the map.

Major Price went on as if he hadn't been interrupted. "This is the book of your opera. You have returned from an ordeal in a brutal German prison camp, Captain. It is quite to be expected that you should be sent home on leave. Your health is broken. You've had, as they say, a bad war. It will take you weeks or months to recover. In addition, you have seen with your own eyes evidence of the despicable policy by which English officers invariably send Irish troops out of the trenches into No Man's Land before sending Englishmen—"

"The men grouse about that, Major, but it isn't true."

"Of course it isn't true. But it's what the Irish rabble-rousers say in their speeches against recruitment."

Kitchener interrupted. "The thought of lending credence to such slander is anathema to us, particularly in the present climate. But this situation justifies it."

Price nodded. "I'm telling you, Captain, what you will say to explain your disillusionment. You'll say the Germans broke your health, but the English broke your spirit. You're not prepared to support Germany, but you don't believe in England either. Rather than return to service when your leave is up, you will resign your commission. Word of your position will spread. You will be increasingly accepted. Seditionists will become known to you. You will make them known to us."

General Friend said, "At the appropriate time they will all be arrested under the Defense of the Realm Act and brought at once to England."

Douglas was unable to imagine that such events involved him. His mind seized upon a detail, took refuge in it. He said,

"But with conscription enacted, won't such men already be in the army in any case?"

Kitchener snorted. "Conscription will never apply to Ireland, Captain."

"But Carson—"

"Carson is a fool."

"But on this, there's a point. The army opens men to their basic feelings of loyalty to the King. I've seen it happen. Conscription would bind Ireland to the cause of England."

Nathan said simply, "Most Irishmen won't serve, Captain."

"That's not so, sir, with all respect. It isn't service they object to. It's the oath. The oath sticks in their throat. If you abolish the oath, they'd line up for you."

Nathan took off his glasses and peered at Tyrrell. "Abolish the oath when the issue is loyalty? Do use a little common sense, Captain. One might as well strike the *nots* from the Ten Commandments."

Douglas saw his mistake. Conscription wouldn't apply to Ireland not because Irish citizens would protest, but because they could not be trusted in the ranks.

He was at a loss for what to say. His mind reached for other details, as if details were logs in the rushing current. He grabbed at them to keep from drowning. "Major Price," he said.

Price crossed from the map to his chair and sat.

Douglas had to work to keep a stammer from his voice, as if he'd had too much to drink. "What you describe implies a period of time."

"That's right, Captain. You have several months in which to do this for us."

"But how can you be sure?"

Price said nothing.

Admiral Hamilton looked at Kitchener, who nodded.

Hamilton said, "The combined invasion and insurrection is set for the Friday before Easter, April twenty-first."

Douglas shook his head. "How could you possibly know that?"

Hamilton answered smoothly. "We know it from Berlin." What he didn't say was that the Admiralty was reading and breaking German radio traffic to Berlin. The date for the Rising had been settled on between Pearse, Devoy, and the German ambassador in Washington. It was the ambassador's signal to Berlin the British intercepted. No one in the Irish Citizen Army or the Irish Volunteers or anyone outside the secret military council of the IRB knew that date. But the British did.

Price said, "That gives you more than five months. Regrettably, we cannot count on learning the details of the invasion plan from Berlin. Nor can we secure the entire coast of Ireland. That's why we need you. We want to sweep the region you identify clear of seditionists the week before Easter."

"Say Wednesday." Nathan smiled. "What the Catholics call Spy Wednesday." He could have been describing a bizarre Ashanti custom.

Douglas nodded slowly, aware of what all of this would mean. "In honor of Judas."

It would have been the perfect last word, but they weren't finished.

"There are two other points to cover." Price opened the file in front of him and picked up another photograph. He tapped the table with it. "Bishop O'Dea of Galway . . ." He paused.

Nathan picked it up. "Bishop O'Dea is a nationalist, but he puts the Church first and Ireland second. He regards Ireland as the Pope's back garden. At His Majesty's behest, the Vatican has instructed him to oppose a German invasion and to forbid sympathy for it among members of his flock. He will cooperate with you, and his priests as well."

Douglas said nothing, but the idea seemed naïve to him. West-of-Ireland priests didn't take their cues from Bishop O'Dea when it came to hating England. In the silence his gaze drifted back to Price, who was still tapping the photograph on the table. Finally Douglas said, "And the second point, Major?"

Price simply slid the photo across the expanse of polished wood. Douglas reached for it. He knew the man in the picture at once. "Yes, that's him," he said.

"Who?" Price asked.

"The Irishman with Casement in Trier. He spoke to us after Casement did." Douglas stared at the bearded face, the ill-kempt hair. He felt a constriction in his chest, wire around his heart, pulling tighter. He was trying to remember something else. Focused as he was on the photograph, he did not see the mystified look that Price, Nathan, and Hamilton exchanged.

Price said, "That's not what I was going to say about him."

Douglas slowly raised his eyes. He felt like the victim of an interrogation in which even the questions were secret. Was it that, if he guessed the answer, they'd let him go and none of this would have happened? "It isn't?"

For once Price and the others seemed as confused as he himself felt. The map behind the board of officers shimmered, seemed to move toward him, the green land, the blue sea. Ireland, poor Ireland, adrift, lost. But then Douglas thought, Not Ireland, me. He had never been more perplexed in his life. Nothing made sense to him now, yet all that had gone before would seem as clear as Irish crystal, clear as the dawn after a night's wet fog, compared to what Price told him next.

"I was going to say, Captain, that he is a close associate of

Patrick Pearse and as such he could be of use to you. I didn't
know about Trier."

"But Trier is my only . . ." Douglas stopped and looked
from man to man. Each knew the answer already; then why
not simply say it? "Apart from Trier . . ." He looked down at
the photograph again. Something told him to imagine that face
without its beard, without the crop of hair. ". . . what has he
to do with me?"

He knew before Price said it. Hyde Park. How for that
first instant Jane had clung to the man's arm, an act of absolute dependency.

"His name is Curry," Price said flatly. "And he's your sister's
lover."

15

The servant girl who was packing Jane's trunks knew better than to address her. Ladies' maids spoke only when spoken to, and Jane knew that the girl would have preferred to be left alone to fold the clothing in her own way. The truth was she would gladly have packed her things herself, without help, but she felt unable to transgress the tacit rules of the household. For months now, Pamela's servants had made her feel like an interloper in the Chelsea house. This morning the girl made her feel that the simple dresses, skirts, and blouses which she had brought with her from Ireland were not even hers. Only now that she was actually doing it did Jane allow herself to feel what a relief it was to be going home.

"Auntie Jane?"

Jane looked across the large bedroom toward the snug window seat into which her niece had curled herself. Douglas's child had been watching the progress of the packing from that perch. Ordinarily a lively, talkative girl—she had a five-year-old's enthusiasm for her own expression—Anne had said nothing till now. Jane smiled at her. "What is it, my little hazelnut?"

"Auntie Jane, will you ever come back to visit us?"

"Of course I will. And better than that, before too long you and Timmy and your mother and father will come home to Ireland, and we'll all be together again."

"Nanna says this is our home."

Jane glanced at the servant, who seemed not to have heard. Letting the wool nightgown she'd been folding fall to the bed, she crossed to Anne. She sat on the cushioned window seat beside her. The window was firmly shut against the chill November drizzle. Even so, the wet wind from the nearby Thames jostled the panes. Jane said softly, "This is your home in London, darling. But you're so much more fortunate than other children because you have a home in Ireland too. And when your father is finished with the army, you'll be coming back to that home, and I'll be there to make you chocolate, just like always."

Giving her such a brazen look it startled Jane, the child said, "We don't like Ireland."

"Who doesn't?"

"Mama and Nanna and Timmy and me."

Jane put her arm around the girl. "Of course you like Ireland. You like your Grandpa Hugh, don't you?"

Anne nodded.

"And your baa-baa lambs and your rabbits and Chaser." Chaser was the Cragside collie Anne worshiped.

The child's eyes had filled. It wasn't brazenness at all that she felt, but a terrible confusion, and now with Jane's departure, a terrible loss. Jane felt both emotions too, and suddenly she saw that this child, her brother's daughter, would be cursed with the same divided soul that was throbbing at this moment inside her. Why shouldn't Anne's mother and grandmother dislike Ireland? They were English people, pure and simple. Disliking Ireland was the same as liking mutton pie. Jane held the girl close, and she admitted to herself for the first time that if Douglas hadn't returned from France alive, Pamela would never have brought the children back to Ireland. And for the first time Jane understood why. Jane had not before this grasped the importance of her sister-in-law's Englishness or the power of it. Pamela had a hold on her identity that was as clear and fierce as her own was muddied and tentative. In Ireland Jane felt English. In England she felt Irish. All she knew was that she never felt at home. As she hugged her niece, she thought, And who wouldn't seek to spare the child such loneliness?

Loneliness? That this word should have sprung to mind as the definition of her condition surprised Jane. But it was true. She'd longed for Douglas's safe return, as if that would assuage the pain she felt. And now Douglas was home, for which she felt a gratitude that surpassed in intensity any she'd ever felt before. But it was Pamela's loneliness, not Jane's, that his return had obliterated. Douglas's presence, in a cruel irony, made hers worse by underscoring the difference between a sister's love and a lover's passion. In the previous nights, in this very room, Jane had lain awake picturing Pamela in her brother's arms, relieved for their sakes, yes, but more aware than ever of the emptiness of her own arms. Her longing outran her happiness, in other words, and her brother's face, which once, with her father's, had occupied the very center of her affection, now served only to make her think of someone else's. It didn't matter that Dan Curry was gone, their love impossible. Her anguish, part loss and part confusion, kept him near. The alienation she felt in her brother's wife's family house made her want Dan Curry more than ever. It was to be rid of that pain—that desire—that she was leaving London now. Pamela had asked her to stay for the length of Douglas's home leave, and Douglas seemed to want it too, but Jane couldn't consider it. It was a twisted thought and she knew it: she was going back to Ireland, where Curry was—but to be free of Curry because back in Ireland she would be English again, and unlike him. In Ireland her loneliness, at least, would be familiar.

"Will you be going to live with Grandpa Hugh?" Anne pulled out of her arms and was staring up at her now.

"Yes." It was the first time she'd admitted this too, and she was surprised that going back to Cragside did not feel like more of a defeat. With what unspoken defiance had she left the place. But how could she return to the Abbey Theatre now, and if not the Abbey, how could she return to Dublin? Cragside was the only place left.

She twirled her finger in her niece's tawny locks. "I'll always be there for you to visit."

"Will you always be my Auntie Jane?"

Jane's impulse, of course, was to crush the child to her breast, saying, Yes, yes, my sweet hazelnut! But she couldn't, for she heard Anne's question as a question like Curry's: Will you be with me against those others? And she had not ever answered him. Jane felt the blade of events that had no business here slicing down between her and her niece, the way it had between her and Dan. And she simply would not let this happen, not with Anne, not with Timmy, not with Pamela or Douglas. Now she did press the child to her and she did say, "Of course I'll be your Auntie Jane. Of course I will." But neither took the consolation from her words and gesture that they would have if she had not hesitated. What's happening to us? Jane asked herself. And then, a slight correction: What's happening to me?

She'd forgotten the servant.

"Miss?" A silence. And then, less tentatively, the word repeated: "Miss?"

Jane looked around at her.

The girl stood in her lace cap and severe black dress, a pair of Jane's blouses over her arm. She said, "There's been a knock at the door, miss. Shall I answer it?"

Just then the knock was repeated, this time more loudly, an implicit demand. Not a servant's knock.

Jane forced a brightness into her voice and said, "Come in!"

The door opened at once and there stood Douglas in his gleaming boots and Sam Browne belt, his carefully tailored uniform, his sharp-eyed, bony face and perfect mustache, his riding crop swatting at his thigh. He was a war-years' woman's dream. Jane felt a rush of her old, instinctive awe. The thrill that he'd survived his nightmare and come back to them was what filled her now.

Anne leapt off the window seat and scurried across the room to him, and Jane felt like doing the same thing. She wanted to throw herself into his arms and have him hold her. Douglas was the only one in the whole world like her; only Douglas could make her feel all right again.

But he stood woodenly in the doorway, looking at her with something awful in his eyes, something she'd never seen before. Not even Anne, when she jumped up to his arms, forcing him to take her, broke the spell of his stare.

After a long moment he put his daughter down. He looked at the servant without seeing her and said, "Take the child to her mother."

The servant crossed to the doorway and took Anne by the hand. That she did not protest this dismissal was striking evidence that something was terribly wrong. Jane sat again on the window bench while Douglas closed the door. He walked toward her, never dropping his eyes, and it was as if an invisible wave of his fury preceded him, consuming all the oxygen, for suddenly Jane could not breathe. Her eyes fell to the riding crop, the short

whip, which he carried at an angle. For the first time in her life it
seemed to Jane that her brother was going to strike her. And that
expectation, as he drew closer, filled her, perversely, with relief.

He raised his free hand, but instead of hitting her he reached
into his tunic, pulled something out, and threw it at her. "What
the hell is this?"

A photograph.

It hit her arm and fell to the cushion beside her. A photograph, she saw at once, of Dan. Why should Douglas have a
picture of him—this was her strange thought—when she herself
didn't? Jane picked it up and instinctively cradled it, as if she
had to protect Dan's image from her brother's anger. She felt
the familiar pull of affection, and it rescued her from the fright
Douglas had given her. The sight of Dan, her old Dan, with
his great barbarossa beard and wild hair and gleaming eyes, was
like a welcome blast of the oxygen she'd been deprived of, and
she could breathe again.

Who was she? Her most basic feeling cut through all the
others. Why, she was the woman who loved Dan Curry.

"What the hell is it?" Douglas repeated.

When Jane looked up at him, he was like a shadow blocking the sun. Hadn't he always been that to her? "What do you
mean?" she asked calmly.

But her mind ran on with its new thought. Hadn't he always
made her feel like a child? Wasn't that the condition of their
relationship, that she should regard him forever from below,
with awe and worship? That she should see his great light from
her obscurity, that she should know his fulfillment from her
service to it? It made no difference to her at that moment that,
among Victorians, such was every female's relationship to the
males with whom she was raised. The insult of it hit her full
force, blasting open the shutter of her most cherished illusions.

"He's a traitor!"

"Not to me, he isn't."

"You knew! You knew! And you didn't tell me!"

"What should I have told you? That the world's a more complex place than you thought it was?"

He stared at her, struggling to control his rage. It seemed impossible that Jane should be its object. Suddenly he brought his knee up and cracked the stock of his whip across it, breaking it in two. Then he held the pieces in his fists in front of Jane's face. "The man invited us to break our oaths! The man colludes with the monsters who gassed our trenches! The man is in league with the murderers of my boys. *My* boys, do you hear me?"

Jane had an impulse to drop her eyes, but she didn't. She said quietly and firmly, "He is working for Ireland."

"Nonsense! That's utter nonsense, Jane. Can you justify anything in the name of Ireland? Exploiting poor, miserable, frightened beggars rotting in a German prison camp? *Irish* beggars? Trying to purchase their souls with a ration of German horsemeat and the promise of glory when Ireland becomes the latest German colony? Working for Ireland, shit! Working for Berlin is what your bedmate's been doing."

Jane stood, forcing him back a step. "My bedmate! Is that the issue? That I've dared to take up with a man, and without coming to you first for a by-your-leave?"

"That has nothing to do with it. You're not my wife. It's worse: you're my sister, and you've disgraced us."

"Yes, your sister! The permanent baby sister! My role in life has always been to be there for you, waiting for your return from school so that you could dazzle me with what you'd become. When you married, my role was to be your wife's boon companion and then your children's bonny aunt. My role was to take care of Father so that you wouldn't have to. And in return for duties faithfully done, I would be permitted to bask in your presence, awed. Oh, the bloody insult of it! In your presence I would never have become a woman. But I'm a woman now, by God, and I know it because of him!" She held out the photograph of Curry.

Douglas stared at her. "What you've done with him overshadows me and even Father. Who are the Tyrrells now? They are the famous family who, in the hour of Britain's greatest need, served up a whore for Britain's enemy."

Jane slapped his face, jolting him.

He took the blow. "Lord Kitchener himself gave me that photograph, Jane. They know all about you."

"So it's the family reputation that concerns you, is it? They know all about me and Dan? And now you do, I suppose? You *dare* to presume to know about me? If the War Office concerns itself with sexual gossip, no wonder we're losing the war. You might have checked your information with me, dear brother. They know all about us, do they? Did they tell you that those few moments in Hyde Park before you arrived were to be my last with Dan Curry because I refused to go with him? Did they tell you that when it came to choosing, not between England and Ireland, but between him and you, I chose you? Did they tell you that? I'd sent him on his way, that man who never, ever would have come at me like you have, never would have—"

"Jane, I—"

"No, listen to me! You call me a whore? I've disgraced the family? You crack your weapon in my face? You threaten me? Listen to yourself! Your boys? Your poor Irish boys! Perhaps you're the one who betrays them by leading the way into hell! And making it seem like God's work! You've forgotten who you are, Douglas. The honor of our family is not measured by the standards you learned at Oxford or the Inns of Court. Any more than the feelings I have for Dan Curry make me a whore. Your saying that makes me see for the first time that I needn't take my lessons from you. I am not a whore. I only wanted what you and Pamela already have. But Ireland intervened. And, come to think of it, Ireland intervening is an old story in our family. And if we let her do so, that's the blood we have, Douglas. You've disgraced it, not me."

"How?"

"By letting Lord Kitchener make you think your sister is a whore. You've taken your lessons from them."

Douglas looked away from her. She was wrong. He knew she was wrong. But then why did he feel ashamed?

Now it was Jane holding the photograph before him angrily. "And they told you this thinking, no doubt, What a splendid opportunity! The rebel's whore belongs, like a Dalton figurine, to this proven servant of the Crown, and all we must needs do is have him nip at her, like Chaser nips at the sheep at Cragside. After you humiliated me and broke me, after you made me renounce this first free act of my life, not imagining I might have renounced it on my own, so well nipped at have I been until now, you were going to send me after him again, weren't you? First your sheep, then your sheep dog. You were going to tell me to go to him again, weren't you? Weren't you?"

Douglas felt his face redden.

She whipped him with it, the truth in all its ugliness. "They told you to send me back to him, didn't they? To learn his secrets and pass them on to you. And you could all expect that I would do my duty as you explained it to me, not for the reason you do yours—to save England from the German monsters who gas your boys—but for the old reason, the smaller reason, the less noble reason, the woman's reason—that I do whatever you want. And what you want, Douglas, is for me to stop being

Dan Curry's whore and become England's." She had said all this without an intake of breath. She gasped for a moment, then said, "Deny it! Deny it!"

Jane wanted him to, and Douglas wanted to, but he could not. That he had not consciously admitted it to himself did not refute the fact that this was precisely Price's strategy, and Kitchener's. He raised his eyes to look at her. He'd had this feeling once before, only once. It was near the crest of that hill near Messines when he'd come upon that belt of wire. There was no way through the wire! That was the feeling. He wanted through, not for his boys' sake or for England's, but for his own. He did not want to die; that was the feeling.

This time, faced not with a hardened German gunner but with his sister, he had no cutters. No way through, none.

After a long moment that neither could have endured more than once, she walked past him. At the door she turned back. "Thank Lord Kitchener for me, Douglas. He's given me my life." And then she left the room, the house, Chelsea, and England, clutching her one photograph of Dan Curry and thinking of her home, of Ireland.

———

On her first morning back in Dublin, she went to the Abbey as early as she dared, hoping the players would know where to find him. She could not wait, partly out of simple anxiousness to be with him, but more because she was afraid that any delay would undermine her impulse, which was the most welcome one she'd ever had. Even as she approached the drab, gray stone building with its art nouveau canopy, Jane felt her heart swell. The Abbey had been an enchanted kingdom to her. She remembered the awe with which she'd first beheld it from that curb across the street nearly half a year before. Half a year? It seemed like decades. As she crossed toward the theater, she wondered what she had in common now with that frightened innocent who'd come here from Cragside as a way of growing up?

The billboard was bare, and that panicked her. If the theater was dark, would anyone be here? But the door opened when she pushed it, and she knew that meant someone was inside. The unlit foyer was so familiar that she had no trouble crossing it. The Jack Yeats portraits hanging on the walls registered dimly, and she thought of Coole Park with affection. What consolation just to be here. She went to the office behind the ticket windows, but Miss Cleary hadn't come in yet. She saw a stack of playbills, *The Deliverer*, dated for late November, two weeks away. She opened one, hoping to see Dan Curry's name, but some other actor was listed. Still it reassured her that a play was scheduled, particularly Lady Gregory's celebration of Parnell. Some things, at least, never changed.

Jane was conscious of the loud noise her footsteps made as she crossed back into the lobby, but when she entered the darkened theater proper, she heard another sound. A faint, irregular tapping, like a bird's pecking. Slowly she went down the aisle toward the curtained stage. The black emptiness was eerie and unsettling. She mounted the five steps to the lip of the stage and timidly drew the curtain back, but the stage was empty. The tapping was coming from behind stacked flats—no, from the floor below, from the greenroom. As she crossed the stage she remembered that first day when she'd stood there with Curry, reciting Deirdre's lines to his Naisi's. "I see the trees naked and bare, and the moon shining . . ." She saw Curry leaning toward her and she saw herself in the reflection of his green eyes. ". . . Little moon, little moon of Alban, it's lonesome you'll be this night . . . for . . . the two lovers who slept so sweetly with each other . . ."

A wave of sadness for which she was not prepared swept over her. Perhaps she would never find him. Hadn't they played out the prophecy of their bleak story on that very stage? She shook the memory off and crossed to the wing to take the stairs down to the greenroom.

The tapping sound was a typewriter.

A lone figure in the yellow circle of a small conical lamp was hunched over the machine, facing away from Jane. Cigarette smoke curled up above his bent head as he worked with no dexterity at punching the keys. Jane did not recognize him. "Hello," she said.

And the person jumped and whipped around to face her.

"Nora!" Jane cried, delighted. She had taken the short-haired, trousered figure of Nora Guinan for a man once before. Nora leapt out of her chair and went to Jane, throwing her arms around her with startling warmth. Jane had never allowed herself to believe that people at the Abbey had come to regard her with anything like the affection she felt for them. But they had.

"Let me look at you!" Nora cupped Jane's face in her hands. "Is your brother safe?"

Jane nodded. How in the world to explain? "He got away from the Germans. He's in London."

"How wonderful!" Nora reached back for her cigarette and puffed on it greedily. With her other hand she held on to Jane and drew her to the tattered sofa.

No sooner had they sat than Jane said, "Nora, I've come back to find Dan. Is he here?"

Nora shook her head. "No one sees Dan anymore, Jane."

"Do you know where he went?"

Nora stared at her through the smoke, clearly considering her words before speaking. "I heard he went to Switzerland."

"Oh Nora, I know about that. I know where he went in Europe. I mean *now*. Where is he now?"

Nora shook her head.

Jane looked away. After a long silence she asked, "What will I do, Nora?"

Nora pressed her hand. "Have breakfast with me, that's what." She stood and crossed to the table. She bent over the typewriter and struck the keys half a dozen times. *"Finis!"* she exclaimed, then snapped the page out of the typewriter and collected half a dozen others. "I have to take this to the printer. Then we could go to Switzers. What do you say?"

"I'd love it."

"Good. Hold these for me while I clean this place." Nora gave her the pages she'd typed and then set about straightening the greenroom, emptying the ash-tin of butts and putting the typewriter in its box.

Jane began absently to read them, expecting a playscript or notes for a program. Not that, in her time there, Nora Guinan had ever done the typing. But the title in large letters read, "An Application of the Catholic Principles of Just War to the Present Belligerence in France, Belgium, and Turkey. By Father Seamus Kavanaugh, Saint Colum's Parish, Dublin."

"What's this?"

Nora answered without stopping her work. "The text of a pamphlet some of us will be handing out at the recruitment rally tomorrow. The Brits have been pushing hard for army volunteers in Dublin because the lads have begun thinking twice before joining up. We want to help them think yet again."

Jane began to read the text proper. The first paragraph outlined the five traditional conditions necessary for a war to be considered just: declaration by proper authority, reasonable prospect of success, and so on. The second paragraph began with a discussion of the meaning of proportionality, but Jane wasn't focused enough to follow it. "What does it say?"

"That the carnage in France is disproportionate to the warmakers' stated aims. Do you have any idea how many combatants have died? Millions, Jane! Millions! And for what? Who can say what the fighting's for? Can you?"

The question—as a question—had never occurred to her before. She said nothing.

"There's no proportionality between means and ends. Therefore the war is unjust, and any Catholic who participates in it is guilty of the mortal sin of murder."

Jane stared at the pages, shocked. "It says that?"

Nora nodded. "Father Kavanaugh is a Moral Theologian."

"But that can't be the Catholic position. Half the nations fighting in the war are Catholic."

Nora shook her head. "Father Kavanaugh says the mechanization of the war has changed its nature. He says . . . Oh read it, Jane. What can I say? I'm the typist."

"I didn't know you were involved, Nora."

"More and more of us are involved now, Jane. Parliament has passed the conscription act. If they apply it to Ireland, every man we know will be in the trenches. Including Brian. I'll be damned if I'll let them take Brian. My husband isn't dying in France for England. We say, if there's dying to be done, let it be for Ireland."

"But you always argued with Dan when he spoke that way. You said the Abbey Theatre was act of patriotism enough."

"It's not enough now, Jane. Dublin is different. Brian says things are heating up. You can feel it. We all must do our part." She took the pages back from Jane and folded them into an envelope. "Even the priests are pitching in. I'm telling you, Jane, things are starting to boil."

"Boil?" Jane smiled. "I feel the same old chill."

Nora grabbed her coat. "Biscuits and white coffee will take

care of that. Let's go." She threw her arm around Jane, a manly gesture, and led her out. "First the printer, then Switzers."

Switzers was the large, multistoried emporium on Sackville Street. The restaurant was on the third floor, but on the first floor, where dry goods and housewares were sold, Nora stopped. They were about to enter the stairwell. "That man there," she said, pointing quickly. A dark-suited man had just come in from Sackville Street. He was standing inside the entrance, looking around. "He was at the printshop. Do you know him?"

"No."

The man saw them and immediately turned away, crossing to a table on which crockery was displayed.

Nora led Jane into the stairwell and up a flight. Then they paused, listening. They heard someone hurry onto the stairs and begin to come up quickly. Nora took Jane's hand and led her into the second floor, the department reserved for ladies' garments. A dozen women were scattered about, hard at their shopping. Nora led Jane directly to the shelves holding corsets, and they began to examine them earnestly.

The man entered.

He looked about helplessly. No other male in sight, and across the broad room, a quarter-acre of underwear, nightgowns, stockings, and petticoats, there was nothing for him to feign interest in. He walked tentatively down an aisle, then stopped and awkwardly lit a cigarette.

When Nora saw the stout, frumpishly garbed department head, she coughed loudly, catching her eye, then raised a brow toward the man. The department head walked majestically toward him and began berating him loudly. "This is not a public thoroughfare, my good man. Will you please return to sections of the store where your presence is not an annoyance!"

The man hastily retreated to the stairwell and disappeared.

Jane had caught on, so that when the department head approached them to apologize, she said, "We'd like to avoid him if we can. Is there a back stairway up to the restaurant?"

The woman gladly showed them the employees' way upstairs.

"But who could he have been?" Jane asked when they were seated, linen spread in their laps.

"Dublin Castle, no doubt about it." Nora grinned at the thought of the embarrassment they'd caused him.

Jane was awed. "But why would they be following you?"

Nora shook her head and reached for the bread. "Not me, love. You."

"Me?"

"You're the one they think will lead them to Dan Curry." Nora grinned again. "I told you it was different. See, now you're in it too."

———

Saint Colum's Church was soot-blackened and obscure, lacking any distinguishing spire or exterior ornament, not much more from the outside than a hall with frosted windows. It was lost in the dark tenements of the Liberties that lay between Saint Patrick's Cathedral and the south bank of the River Liffey.

Jane went there with Nora the next morning to give Father Kavanaugh a copy of his printed pamphlet. It was Sunday and the rectory housekeeper said they would find him in the sacristy. As they entered the church, along with worshipers arriving early for mass, Jane was struck by the dinginess of the place. For the first time in her life she realized what it must seem like to Catholics when they compared this awful church to the massive grandeur of nearby Saint Patrick's, the ancient cathedral that since Henry VIII had been Protestant. What Protestants always boasted of when they passed by the cathedral was that Jonathan Swift had been its dean in the eighteenth century. Catholics, on the other hand, were always pointing to Saint Patrick's, who after all was *their* patron, and saying that Oliver Cromwell stabled his horses in its sanctuary.

Jane was surprised that a church could seem so different just for being Catholic. The coated windows admitted hardly any light, so, though it was a bright morning, the church interior was dark. The flickering votive candles in front of various statues cast eerie shadows and filled the place with the thick odor of wax. There was hardly a space on the walls that wasn't hung with a plaster figure of Jesus carrying the cross, or a corner of the aisles that wasn't occupied by a life-sized statue of a monk, a nun, a lady in blue, a Christopher or Joseph, all with their eyes cast toward, if not heaven, the dim ceiling light fixtures, as if awed still, like some of the parishioners, by the miracle of electricity.

When Nora bent, touching her right knee to the floor, Jane imitated her, then raised her eyes as Nora did to the crucifix over the high altar. That the very corpse of Jesus hung on the cross revolted her, but she could not take her eyes from that bleeding, broken body, from its agony.

Nora had seen it all a thousand times before and did not linger. She cut across the center aisle toward the door beside the sanctuary. She knocked once, then went in.

Father Kavanaugh was not what Jane expected. His pamphlet, its irresistible syllogisms and thundering conclusions, the boldness and certitude with which it condemned the war that Jane had hardly heard questioned, had led her to picture a large fist of a priest, a book under his arm—not the Bible, but Thomas Aquinas. She expected a stern face and accusing eyes, a prophet from the Old Testament, a figure from a stained-glass window. But he was frail, old, no taller than she was herself, and when Nora went to him, he opened his arms and embraced her.

Then Nora looked at Jane. "Father, this is my friend."

Jane blushed. She was in no way prepared for the warmth with which he took her hand. "God bless you, darling."

Nora added, "Jane is a friend of Dan Curry's."

"Is that so?" His eyes held her. Jane felt that he was seeing inside her, and she was afraid suddenly that a priest would consider her love illicit. But he pressed her hand and said, "Dan Curry is one of the best men I know. He was a student of mine at Maynooth." The old priest smiled. "Sure, neither of us fit in well there."

"Here's your pamphlet, Father."

He took it and looked at it for a moment, then said, "I hope it helps, Nora. The fate of our own beloved Ireland is one thing, but what's happening on the Continent is something else. We must have nothing to do with it." He looked at Jane. "Forgive me." He put the pamphlet inside his soutane and faced Nora again. "Just be careful when you give them out, will you?"

Nora nodded.

Father Kavanaugh looked at Jane. "You too."

Jane had an impulse to say, But I'm not doing it. Instead she nodded.

"Now be off the both of you so I can finish my preparations." He indicated the papers spread on the vesting case. "The Pope has sent a special letter to his flock in Ireland condemning, as it happens, all forms of revolution. The state has its power from above." He rolled his eyes to heaven. "Even if the state oppresses the people, rebellion is immoral because it is always hopeless. A special message for the Catholics of wee Ireland." He smiled sadly. "His Holiness has been getting his advice from the Archbishop of Canterbury. We're required to read his letter at all

the masses, and I haven't finished my translation. So be off with
you, and as for this afternoon"—he took each of them by the
hand—"let me give you my blessing." Nora knelt at once, and
Jane followed suit. The priest prayed over their bowed heads.
Jane closed her eyes tightly. She understood nothing that she
heard, but when the priest put his hands on her head, she felt
his power coming into her. It made her shudder, but then she
felt relief. The sharp edge of a pain she had not quite acknowledged having was soothed.

Outside Saint Colum's Nora stopped. "I'm going to stay
for mass, Jane."

"Oh, well . . . I'll be off."

"You could stay with me. You wouldn't have to kneel or
anything."

"No, I couldn't." Jane looked away, confused. Things were
happening too fast.

"But were you coming to the rally?"

"How could I, Nora?"

Nora touched her sleeve. "Jane, many of us have people on
both sides of it. You're not the only one."

Jane's eyes filled. "I'm the only one I know."

Around them, the somber men and women of the Liberties were filing into the church. Their best clothes were tattered.

Nora kissed Jane's cheek, then turned and went back inside.

Jane walked through the bleak streets of the Catholic slum
to Saint Patrick's Cathedral. She went in. It was empty and dark,
and walking down the ancient stone of the center aisle, she
stared up at the naked wooden cross, mammoth above the altar.
Suddenly she realized it was wrong. All her life she had imagined
three neat crosses on the hill of Golgotha, a sloping pasture, but
never had she pictured actual human bodies on them. At Saint
Colum's, in her repugnance against that corpse—that *corpus*—it

had been the truth of the Crucifixion that had hit her in all its horror. Someone had hung a man, a particular man, from nails. They had murdered him. The fact of it hit her, as in reading Father Kavanaugh's pamphlet, the fact of the "noble" war in Europe had hit her. Thousands of corpses, rotting even now in the wet fields of Flanders. And what of the "facts" of Ireland? Jane realized that she had walked through them, so blindly, by walking through the desperate slums of the Liberties in coming to this cathedral. Dublin had people as poor and hungry and sick as any city in Europe, and when had she ever seen them? There are corpses everywhere, she thought, in the alleys of the Liberties and the fields of France; everywhere but the one place a corpse belongs. She stared up at the bare cross for a moment longer and realized that this place no longer had anything to give her.

———

When at last the doors of Saint Colum's opened, the people poured out. Jane wanted to make herself small, as if they all knew what she was and what she'd been raised to think of them.

Then Nora appeared, her head covered with a black mantilla. Framed in the doorway of the modest church she looked beautiful, a figure on the stage. At once her eyes fell on Jane and she broke into a triumphant grin. Folding away her lace head covering, she came down to her. "Oh, Jane," she said, "I prayed for you!"

That threw Jane. "I don't know, Nora. I just—"

"I'll take care of you, you'll see."

"Will Maud Gonne be there? I've met Maud Gonne." Jane remembered that afternoon at Coole Park when her new life had begun.

Nora shook her head. "It's Maud's organization, the

Daughters of Ireland. But she's in Paris. If she comes to Ireland now, the MacBrides will get custody of her son."

"But John MacBride's a drunk!"

"Yes, but Maud's the one who left the marriage. It kills her not to be here now, but never mind. Mrs. Pearse will be there, and Countess Markievicz. This is what we women can do, Jane. Make the men see that it isn't England who needs them, but Ireland."

It relieved Jane to think of Countess Markievicz, the aristocratic Protestant, born Constance Gore-Booth, a woman like Maud, like herself. The cause of Irish freedom was an Anglo-Irish cause too. She reminded herself that she didn't have to be a Catholic to have these feelings. But then she thought of Douglas. He would never forgive her. But Douglas—she saw this with her first real clarity—was wrong, simply wrong. "I'll come with you," she said. She looked around at the men who'd just left mass, men she'd never really seen before. And at once she pictured herself handing pamphlets to them, to these living men, these Irish men, these particular men. Don't become corpses, she would say, on England's cross.

Nora hugged her. "Brave girl." And then she grinned. "We must be wily as wolves, the Bible says, like Father Kavanaugh. Remember the Pope's letter condemning the idea of an Irish revolution?" She laughed hard. "Father read it to us, every line of it, as required. But he read it in Latin and no one understood a word!"

16

Douglas Tyrrell had never deceived his father before, and if he did so now it was only partly to spare him. The perfect measure of Sir Hugh's position in the middle of the Anglo-Irish conflict was the fact that both his children, each having embraced an opposite side, expected him to disapprove of what they'd chosen. Douglas knew that, while his father could accept his role as an Irish officer in the British army, even without enthusiasm for the war, he could never have supported his function as a British spy in Ireland.

It was for a different reason that he maintained the fiction of his position with Pamela. If he'd confided in her, she'd have had to abet his deception. He couldn't ask her to do that, particularly where Jane was concerned. Not that Jane was home. She'd refused to visit Cragside since Douglas's return, and now she was simply gone, her whereabouts a mystery. But her absence made Douglas's charade possible. To his father, to his wife, to the Cragside community, to their neighbors in the surrounding Clare and Galway countryside, he showed the same face.

It was a disturbing face, and no one who came into contact

with Douglas Tyrrell in those months was unaffected by it. He had been a local hero, a young lord, held in esteem and affection by farmers and townspeople alike. He had always seemed happy and full of spirit, the liveliest son, husband, father, neighbor, or friend anyone could want. And now, after the nightmare of trenches and prison camp, he had returned a shell of himself, deprived of his youth, elegance, physical gracefulness, warmth and vigor. The community felt sorry for him, but they didn't know the half of it.

At the very first, while they were still in London, Pamela had not noticed the difference in him—hadn't he seemed the perfect wartime woman's dream?—but she came to assume that that had been because of her happiness at having him back. When the army doctor had told her of his condition, her first reaction had been gratitude because it meant he wouldn't have to return to France. But once they'd come back to Cragside, his oddness began to affect her. He was listless and solitary, spending hours alone in the dusty Cragside library or, if it wasn't raining, walking the edge of the high ocean cliffs, watching birds through his binoculars. Sometimes he went off in the automobile for entire days. Christmas came and went without perking him up, and not even the children seemed to interest him. He was like a ghost. Everything that had set him apart was gone, and it was obvious to all who had known him why the army sent him home. Douglas became the meaning by which the people of Connaught measured that other new term the war had introduced—shell shock.

One day in late February, the week news came of the ferocious German assault at Verdun, Sir Hugh saw the distant figure of his son on the cliff's edge, withstanding the winter wind and the wet spray shooting a hundred feet up from the crashing sea below. The sight of his boy, bereft and alone in that stark

landscape, filled him with such sadness that he felt compelled
to go to him. He mounted his horse and slowly rode across the
sweeping pasture.

Douglas was watching the turmoil of wave upon rock, and
the subtler motion beyond of the vast ocean swells that had
traveled, building all the while, five hundred miles. The waves
hurled themselves against the rock of Ireland as if to move it.
But Ireland had always held her own against the western weather.
She would not be moved toward England. If Douglas could
once have taken consolation from that dogged stability, now it
meant to him only that Ireland should not be moved toward
Germany either.

He appeared to be staring at the sea vacantly, as if its rhythm
had hypnotized him, but he was not. He was staring at it, as
he had been now for weeks, as German navigators would. The
fierce weather of the Irish coast was their main problem, and
what Tyrrell understood was that the date for the Irish uprising had been set according to the weather's pattern. April was
when the winter broke and the seas flattened; it was the soonest an ad hoc landing of troops and supplies would be possible.
The Dublin Castle intelligence officer had sneered at the mindless piety of the Catholic rebels, presuming piety had moved
them to choose Good Friday for their rising. But there was
nothing mindless about Pearse or Connolly or Casement. And
Douglas, after poring over the old charts and tide tables in the
Cragside library, understood that Good Friday's significance
two days before Easter lay in the fact that the date of Easter is
tied to the moon. The thought had come to him while idling
through the pages of the Book of Common Prayer. "Easter Day,"
a random passage read, "is always the first Sunday after the Full
Moon which happens upon or next after the Twenty-first day
of March." And the full moon, of course, is when the tides are

highest. Along the west coast at the full moon in April, landing
ships would have for a brief time a rare depth of water, fifteen
feet of it at least, above the mean. Therefore, he told himself, the
landing will not come at one of the protected harbors—Killary,
Galway, Kilrush, Castlemaine, Kenmare, or Bantry—that lie
at the heads of the fjordlike bays, in which the German vessels
would be easily trapped by British patrols. Look instead to a
lightning landfall at high tide on a spit of sand jutting from the
headlands themselves, minimally protected and close to the open
sea, into which the unburdened ships could escape on the ebb.
Tyrrell felt confident that he knew what the enemy was going
to do, but the charts indicated there were not dozens of possible
sites for such a strategy, but hundreds of them along the thousand miles of curving shoreline. During his own forays up and
down the coast, he'd found populations that seemed genuinely
indifferent to the cause of Irish freedom, or were they simply
closed to him? He felt a growing despair that he could uncover
in time the coastal nests of revolutionaries who were planning
to receive the German landing. He knew what they were going
to do, he was sure, but he still didn't know where.

He sensed the rider's approach behind him, and he raised
his binoculars to watch a bird, a white, goose-sized sharp-angled
gannet, wheeling high in the air and then plunging a hundred
feet into the sea, violently upon its prey.

"An early comer," Sir Hugh said behind his son. Gannets,
like most seabirds, don't begin returning from their migration
until mid-March. Then the west coast of Ireland becomes an
ornithologist's paradise. Local men easily distinguish among the
dozens of species that pass through the region after meandering
the North Atlantic.

Douglas lowered his binoculars and faced his father. "We
should have taken lessons from them." He nodded toward the

sea. "Fishing, I mean. How is it that Ireland is an island with no relationship to the sea?"

"I don't understand what you mean, Douglas."

"We have no fishing tradition. For centuries our peasants have been starving while food-laden waters all around us go unharvested. Look!" Overhead a gannet soared, its razor beak stuffed with a large fish. It seemed a bizarre, unconnected statement, but the realization had been a central one for Douglas. Because Irishmen didn't fish, except singly or in pairs in small, primitive canoelike curraghs, there were no fleets of fishing craft or workboats of the sort needed to offload cargo and men from oceangoing ships. Only in Cork's harbor, Cobh, which the English had begun calling Queenstown after Victoria's visit, were there true seamen and real vessels. But Cork was on Ireland's southern shore and British patrols had it sealed off. The recognition that the remote western harbors lacked the boats and facilities to receive a true landing force supported the idea that the Germans would bypass them for a high-water beach.

Sir Hugh said, "No one's starving this year. London buys all the butter and cheese we can turn out. The Irish peasant has his first abundance because England is hungry for a change. There's the irony." Sir Hugh shook his head. "They think well of the war at the co-op."

Douglas turned away. It was an affectation of his, part of his charade, never to discuss the war. His father had brought it up, no doubt, because doctors had told him it would be beneficial for his son to talk about it.

Douglas raised his binoculars again. "Look, a fulmar!" The men watched a circling white bird.

"It's a common gull, Douglas."

"No. I'm certain of it; that's a fulmar. Thick neck, short,

hooked yellow bill. Its wings are stiff. Gulls fly more loosely. It's a fulmar, I tell you." Douglas gave the glasses to his father.

Sir Hugh followed the bird. Because they were considered a delicacy by coastal people and because their feathers supplied down for their beds, fulmars had been hunted nearly to extinction in the previous century. In Sir Hugh's youth local rocks and cliffs had provided thousands of colonies of fulmars with nesting places, but it had been years since they were known to nest away from the Skellig Island off Kerry nearly a hundred miles to the south. "You're right," he said. "He's a long way from Skellig."

They watched the lone bird until it disappeared.

"Have you been there?" Douglas asked.

"Where?"

"Skellig."

"Years ago."

"There's a ruined monastery, isn't there?"

"That's about all, and several million birds. Puffin and kittiwake, razorbills, shearwaters. They'll be coming back, beginning now."

Skellig was actually a trio of stark, pointed sea crags towering above the ocean. They marked the southern extreme of the western coast. "I'd like to go there."

"It would make a fine summer journey."

"I mean now."

"Now?" Sir Hugh swung down off his horse and began stroking its withers. "You couldn't get out there now, Douglas. Winter waves break over the lighthouse road. The lighthouse keeper doesn't come ashore until April."

Douglas looked forlornly out at the sea. The wind feathered his hair. "I'd like to see the birds coming back."

Sir Hugh put his hand on his son's shoulder. "They come back here."

"I've been watching them."

"I know." What were these birds to his son? Ghosts, perhaps, of the boys whom he'd seen die? His son's obsession frightened him.

"I'd like to see where they make their nests."

"They do that many places besides Skellig."

"Yes, up and down the coast. I think I'd like to see." Douglas faced his father. The concern he saw in his eyes stunned him. This was wrong, to so deceive the man and to so worry him. He had an impulse to tell his father everything. He checked it, but only partly. "I'm all right," he said in his own steady voice. "You mustn't think I'm not all right."

For a moment Douglas displayed a resolve that his father hadn't seen since before he'd left for France. But when it faded, as Douglas dropped his eyes like an adolescent, Sir Hugh was more confused than reassured.

To offer a rationale for his obsessive bird watching, Douglas said, "At Messines a lad in Signals carried pigeons in the charge up the hill. He died in my arms, watching the birds soaring off to H.Q. with the news that we had made it. 'Ireland did this for us!' It was in my mind that those birds cried out to all of England, 'Ireland did this for us!'" The seabirds overhead were steady in the wind streaming up off the cliffs. "'Ireland did this for us!' It became a dream of mine that England would finally see us for what we are—brave, noble people, worthy of freedom."

"You are brave and noble, Douglas. I'm proud of you."

"But you wouldn't do what I've done."

"In my own way I did. I was in Her Majesty's service for a long time."

"But you renounced it."

"Times were different when I was laying out my fields."

"England wasn't vulnerable before. In your time she seemed invincible. But now . . ." He gave his shoulders a hitch to convey the impossibility of this conversation. He restrained his impulse to confide in his father. No one can know what I am doing, he thought. Not even him.

Douglas knew that deceiving his father like this was a mortal breach. Once more, far more in relation to this man than to Ireland, he felt the naked horror of what he was doing. And he felt disgusted with himself. His sudden impulse was to throw himself on his father, to tell him everything, to ask for his forgiveness. That his violation was so secret made it even more dishonorable.

But even so, his resolve held. He had to think only of Verdun, where for two weeks now the Germans had been throwing a hurricane artillery bombardment at the French. It was unlike anything the world had ever seen before. Already the eastern pillar of French defenses had fallen. If the western one fell as well, France was out of the war. *Well, I'm not.* Tyrrell was more in the war now than he had been at the Front. Lying to his father, like killing people, was what the war required; it was that simple. He said, in the teeth of his guilt, like the birds flying into the teeth of the wind, "I'll be going off for a time, down to Kerry." He smiled thinly. "I want to find those nests."

His father stared at him. "You'll be going through Tralee, then."

"I suppose so. Yes. Why?"

When his father did not answer, Douglas realized that he had secrets too. He suspected at once what they were. His father looked away with uncharacteristic embarrassment, as if he'd uttered an indiscretion in company.

"What's in Tralee?" He remembered it from the charts: one of the typical small harbor towns at the head of a narrow bay. Tralee Bay was bordered on the south by the Dingle peninsula, which reached farther out into the Atlantic than any promontory in Europe, and on the north by Kerry Head, which formed the lower jaw of the mouth of the River Shannon.

Sir Hugh ignored the question and swung up onto his horse.

Seeing that his father was becoming ensnared in the rats' nest of subterfuge too, Douglas wanted to say, Oh, let's tell each other the truth! It's Jane, isn't it? You *have* heard from her! And she's made you promise not to tell me where she is. But without meaning to, you just did, because to you she's not an accomplice of Republican extremists, but first and still my sister, who could take care of me because I'm ill.

Sir Hugh said nothing, which confirmed it. Instead he looked down at his son, mystified and forlorn.

Douglas said nothing either. It did not occur to him to ignore what was clearly his father's unintended slip, nor did he question the propriety of taking advantage of it. He had the instincts now of a man whose damnation was sealed, if only to himself.

The older man clucked his horse and wheeled away, to gallop back toward the house, away from the cliffs that gave the place its name, away from Douglas, who remained there on the edge, but not away, for this was impossible, from the flooding tide of a conflict that had drowned him long ago. It was rising again—he grasped this viscerally without understanding how it could be so—upon his children.

Douglas was moved by the sight of the hurrying, bent rider. For the first time, his father seemed old to him. He had become accustomed to the deaths of young men. It surprised him to realize that this old man would die too. Would that he could die without knowing what I'm about to do.

When he had disappeared, Douglas turned to face the sea. The wind had come up even stronger. Plumes of spray rose off the crests of countless breakers, making the ocean seem like a

black field of white-maned galloping horses. He let his eyes
drift like a vane toward the center of the wind, southwest, and
he squinted to see what was out there. Naked Aran, where no
tree grows because the wind is so fierce, where islanders wear
the look of the rock to which they cling like a thin layer of soil.
The stone tower houses dotting the coast of Clare, with their
secret narrow stairs spiraling clockwise so that defenders, but
not attackers, would have room to use their right arms. The
Cliffs of Moher, where the sheer fall defies scale, the only place
in Ireland where the sea seems small. The storied Shannon, the
largest river in Britain, running down from Ulster, dividing
the island in half, more barrier than roadway, its banks pocked
with a litany of holy ruins. Then the enchanted mountains of
Kerry rising on the misshapen fingers of peninsulas formed by
the long sea inlets, fingers clawing on the charts toward the sea
route from America. How the Germans could make use of that
wondrous southwest coast, with its hundreds of deep-water
coves, its massive tidal caves, its offshore islets from which lights
flashed to show navigators the way. One of those islands was
fang-shaped Skellig, home only to seabirds and a lighthouse
man. An inadvertent mention of it had led to this opening, to
this new sense he had of where to go.

His resolve had held against his self-contempt. No decent
man would do this, but I am doing it. He shook off the inhibiting guilt like rain off his shoulders. He put the glasses to his eyes.
Irish Catholics had placed Skellig under the patronage of Saint
Michael because it was a mountaintop island, and such places
were considered by that religion as belonging to the archangel.
In Normandy a similar island was called Mont-Saint-Michel,
and in Cornwall a third was Saint Michael's Mount. For more
than a thousand years each had drawn its monks and saints.
It amused Douglas to think of himself as setting out now on

a pilgrimage—such holiness!—but the ruins to which he was going in the name of all that was, by his meager conscience, holy and good, were not of a monastery, but of his own family.

He lowered the glasses because the spray had blinded him. He saw nothing of what was out there.

But it was not Skellig Michael, anyway, that he had to see. Tralee. He was going to Tralee.

———

The uneasy relationship between England and Ireland dates to the year 1171, when an invading army under Henry II ended once and for all the Gaelic hegemony. The distinctions, of course, are not what they seem to be and make little sense according to present references. Henry, the King of England, for example, was a Frenchman, and the first English conquest of Ireland was in fact the Norman Conquest. That conqueror who was French was acting as an agent of a pope who was himself English. Adrian IV was the only Englishman ever to sit in the chair of Peter, and he considered Irish Catholics lax and heretical. That Norman invasion is remembered by Catholics as the source of Ireland's agony, yet it resulted in her first respite from tribal wars, her first centralized agriculture, the building of the great cathedrals, Ireland's first step toward democracy with the establishment of a parliament, and the first settling of true towns, one of which was Tralee.

In 1916 Tralee was the largest town in Kerry, with a population of twelve thousand, and though it was near the coast, it was oriented to the land, not the sea. Founded as a medieval market town, it had remained a place where farmers from the surrounding country brought their produce. Its largest industry was the butchering of pigs and the making of bacon. As had happened in all the agricultural centers of Ireland, the bloody war in Europe had brought a rare prosperity to Tralee. In such times there were good reasons to think well of a people who had brought juries and cathedrals to Ireland. Thus, most of Tralee's citizens found the traditional uneasiness with England softened now, both by true sympathy for her beleaguered army and by being well paid to help feed it. In Tralee the English army was well thought of, and that was why its representatives came there with its recruiting campaign.

In a heavy, dank mist that threatened to become an outright drizzle, a military band was playing in the square opposite the Great Western Hotel. The hotel was hung with bunting, and a mammoth banner above the entrance proclaimed, YOUR NATION'S HOUR OF NEED. The broad lobby of the hotel had been transformed into the recruiting office, and a line of young men stretched out to the street, each one waiting patiently for his chance to sign up. They were not necessarily patriots. Conscription may not have come into effect in Ireland yet, but young men were newly motivated to enlist by a recent government decree that did apply. It forbade employers to offer available jobs to males between the ages of sixteen and sixty-two. Loyalist employers cooperated with London by firing all but their most essential workers. Those sacked had little alternative but to join the army, and employers were rewarded by being able to pay lower wages to the women they were then "forced" to fill vacant positions with.

On the far side of the modest square, beyond the army band, was the Catholic church, an undistinguished drab structure whose tower had more the feel of a battlement than steeple. On the steps of the church a dozen women had gathered in stoic vigil. Half of them held hand-lettered signs aloft: IRELAND FIRST! ENGLAND'S WAR IS NOT OUR WAR! WOMEN WON'T BLACKLEG! The

women stared impassively across at the line of men. Between
them, in addition to the bedecked musicians, were knots of
police and groups of idling onlookers, men in butchers' aprons
or farmers' heavy boots, women with baskets under their arms
and hands on their children's shoulders. Others could be seen
peeking out from windows.

Despite the jaunty music, which alternated between "Ta-ra-
ra-boom-dee-ay" and "It's a long way to Tipperary, it's a long
way to go," an ominous air hung over the square, as if the townspeople were waiting for something to happen—for the music
to end, the police to move against the women on the church
steps, the priest to appear and tell everyone to go home. For a
long time none of these occurred. The band played on while
the line of recruits wound steadily into the hotel. The police
stayed on their corner. The butchers and tradesmen drifted in
and out of their pubs. Dairymen and pig farmers went off to
buy their feed, and then came back to watch again. For a time a
few children cavorted near the band until their mothers snared
them. The mist never became rain and the women with their
signs never budged from the steps of the church.

Finally, though, the band stopped playing through sheer
fatigue, and it was then that one of the women began calling
to the people to gather around.

"It's Maud Gonne!" someone murmured.

But it wasn't Maud Gonne. The woman who stepped into
the central position, flanked by other Daughters of Ireland and
framed by the sharp arch of the church's stone doorway, was
dressed in Donegal tweed. She wore a cape and black leather
gloves and a dark woolen bonnet. As she waited while the people
of Tralee pressed close around her, she conveyed a sense of the
self-possession and dignity that was associated with the legendary Maude Gonne. The women who had been active in her

group, which in Irish was called Inghinidhe na hEireann, and
the women who were causing it even then to evolve into the
more revolutionary Irish Women's Council, Cumann na mBan,
were not ordinary women. They did not work for a living, their
husbands were not unemployed or in the British army, and they
weren't up to their elbows in babies. If they were married, their
husbands were members of Pearse's wing of the Irish Volunteers. If they were not married, they were the daughters of men
whose prosperity made their unsalaried idealism possible. The
harried mothers and the hardworking clerks and factory girls,
the worried wives and even war widows regarded the elegant
ladies who publicly spoke out for Ireland not with envy or
disapproval or class resentment or even bitterness, but with awe.
Ordinary women did not share the politics of the Daughters
of Ireland, but they were not indifferent to the wonder it was
when a woman of whatever class or political position dared to
stand openly in a street in Ireland and protest against a world
that men had made.

It wasn't Maud Gonne, but to the mothers and workers
around the steps of the church, the young woman about to
speak was not less the miracle for that. To the men who were
more circumspect, though not less efficient, in giving her their
attention, she represented a force that threatened London, and
they liked it for that, even if they were certain that London
barely noticed. But they sensed too that these women threatened something of theirs, and so even as they assumed the air
of men enjoying the show, they watched it somewhat warily.

"My name," she said when everyone in the square had fallen
silent, "is Jane Tyrrell. Those of you who deal with co-ops may
know of my father, a Cope man and dairy farmer in County
Clare, Hugh Tyrrell. I am a west-of-Ireland woman, born,
raised, and educated on this magnificent coast, the truest part

of our country, and I consider it an honor to address you." Jane stretched to her full height to look beyond the fifty or so immediately in front of them toward the young men waiting to gain entrance to the Great Western Hotel. "And to you, our brothers, our sons, our fathers . . ." Her voice had gone up in pitch and volume, resounding across the square with a clarity that startled all who heard it. She raised her hand toward the recruits and waited until some looked at her. ". . . We the women of Ireland, your sisters and mothers and wives, we who love you, have come to ask for a moment only of your attention. Before you give your lives to them"—she pointed to the hotel—"give your ears to us." She waved at them to come closer, but they didn't move. "Draw nearer, please." But they ignored the request, and that seemed to fluster her. She hesitated and stood there mutely. The crowd in front of her shuffled in embarrassment.

A man's voice cried out, "Go back home where you belong!" Then someone else added, "Sure, if it's a husband you're after, take me!"

A look of desperation crossed Jane's face, and she turned slightly to find Nora Guinan on the steps below her. Nora was staring up at her with fists clenched at her mouth, not a hint of softness in her, no give and no sympathy. Nora had an actor's contempt for the public display of self-doubt. At that moment her focus was not on Jane's problem, but on Ireland's. The sight of her resolute friend made Jane remember why they were there. She looked across the square again, at the recruits. Those who'd found it possible to ignore her forceful opening had been drawn in by the awkward drama of her hesitation. They were the ones she sensed sympathy from now and they were the ones she felt it for.

"I know you," she said loudly. "My brother is one of you, a volunteer with the Connaught Rangers and a veteran of Ypres." Was it shameless of her to refer to Douglas? She didn't care. "And I want to say to you what I would say to him if I could." Was it deceptive to let them think he was still in France? Her speech came of its own momentum now, and the peripheral elements of the scene—the other Daughters, the church, the hotel, the throng before her—dropped away as the field of her concentration was taken over by the men staring back at her and by what she so desperately wanted to say to them. It was true; she wished desperately that she'd known what to say to Douglas when it might have influenced him. "You want only to do what is right for your people. You want to uphold the honor of your families. You want to respond to the call of your nation. And we admire you for your courage and your selflessness. But you are making a terrible mistake. Your people are the Irish people. Your families are Irish families. Your nation is the Irish nation. And the war to which England would send you has nothing to do with Ireland. It is an evil war, and going to it is no test of your courage. It is the result of the same moral blindness that has made us Irish into the invisible people of the British Empire. Does London see our farming people when their crops fail and by the hundreds of thousands they starve to death? Does London see our city dwellers living ten to a room, infecting one another with rats' plague and watching helplessly while more Irish infants die than in any nation in Europe? Does London see our most gifted boys and girls who for generations now have had no alternative but to turn their backs on their homeland in the genteel treason of emigration? No! London sees none of it, not because we're invisible, but because she is blind. Blind to everyone in Ireland except you! You stalwart sons of Erin! For you she sends officers and musicians. She puts up bonuses. She hangs banners on our hotels. And why? Because once her soldiers get to France, they become invisible again. They disappear. They are gone forever. In this war England had begun to treat her own sons as if they were Irish. And because all the English boys have disappeared, they've come for you! But you don't have to join the British army to be invisible. You are Irish! You are already invisible!"

Jane paused, staring across the square at them. Even from that distance they knew her eyes had filled with emotion. There was not a sound in the entire square. She said more softly, though still audibly, "But you are not invisible to us. We are your women and we have seen you since the first moment of your birth and we will see you even if you leave us. We see your faces and your bodies. We see your strong arms and your proud shoulders. And we see what a difference you could make not only to Ireland but to the world. Refuse this war because it is England's and because it is wrong!"

The police had begun drifting toward the church steps, but no order was given and they eyed each other nervously as they advanced. Jane ignored them.

"Then accept the cause of Ireland, which is the cause of our famine victims and our city dwellers and our dead infants and our relatives who've been forced to abandon us. We want to make England see us all and all the time. *Then* let her come to us for help, and let us consider whether or not to give it. But now, refuse them!" Jane's arm shot up and she gestured. "Refuse them by coming over here to us!"

The army band members took up their positions in the center of the square.

Jane repeated herself. "Come over here to us!"

One man left the recruiting line and began to cross the square. A policeman stepped in front of him, but he pushed him aside. Two other policemen quickly grabbed the man, and when he struggled, they clubbed him and dragged him away.

Jane pointed and cried, "We are not blind! We see what you are doing! We are not blind and we are not invisible! Leave that man be!"

Then other recruits left the line, a pair first, then five, then seven. Some tried to melt into the fringe of onlookers. A few walked, without bravado, toward Jane.

Jane pointed after the police who'd hauled the first man away. "Irishmen doing England's dirty work! But we *see!* We *see!* On England's crosses even the body of Christ is invisible!" Was it a lie now to make them think she wasn't Protestant? "But we see! We see whom they have crucified! This is what I'd say to my brother: Don't do England's dirty work!"

The band struck up, a ragged attack, but effective. "Ta-ra-ra-*boom*-dee-ay!" The recruits who had been hesitantly crossing the square stopped. The police began to herd them back toward the hotel. They did not cooperate, precisely, but neither did they resist. The few who moved promptly to retrace their steps found that the recruitment queue had disintegrated. An army sergeant was ushering the remnant inside the hotel.

It was pointless to continue trying to speak above the music, and Jane stopped. It wasn't clear to her what had happened. The crowd dispersed.

But then Nora embraced her and said, "You were wonderful!" The other women pressed close, congratulating her.

Jane was mystified. If her eyes had filled before, now in the backwash of her anger, they threatened to overflow, which horrified her. She didn't want to cry. "But they would have come over to us," she said, and her disappointment was palpable.

"We're not recruiting, dearie. They are, remember?" Nora smiled in triumph. "But not today, they're not. Look."

The recruitment line was completely gone. The sergeant and an officer in his Sam Browne stood side by side in the hotel entrance staring out at the people who were scattering as if the rain had come.

"Don't they look miffed?" Nora kissed Jane. "I tell you, you were wonderful. I feel like Lady Gregory."

Jane shook her head. It was a mystery to her how Nora and the others could take satisfaction in such an aborted rally. She hadn't considered yet that it was even more aborted for the English than it was for her.

When the women had folded their signs and had themselves begun to disperse, Jane stayed behind, promising to meet them later. After her friends, including Nora, had drifted away, she turned and went into the dark church to look at Christ on His cross, knowing that there at least she could find some solace.

———

Two men watched her go into the church, one from behind the curtain of the window of an upper room in the Great Western, and the other from an automobile parked across the square. Each had seen everything, but only one moved now to go after her.

17

If Lot's wife turned to salt, what happened to Lot? As Dan Curry mounted the stairs of the drab church, he felt like a man going back to what had been forbidden him. He wasn't thinking of Pearse, but of the time he and Jane had last been together. It was in Hyde Park. He had told her days were coming when she could not have a divided heart, and she had said he could not love her while hating her people.

Behind him the army band was packing away its instruments and the square was nearly deserted. Before making himself conspicuous like this, he had waited to be sure the police and army showed no interest either in following the young woman into the church or in waiting for her to come out.

His hat obscured his face, and so he didn't take it off until he'd closed the heavy church door behind him. He crossed the small vestibule and quietly pushed open the inner door. At once the flickering blue votive candles drew his eyes to Mary's statue in the sanctuary. The Mother of God was standing on a blue ball, and under her bare feet was the writhing form of the world's first snake.

As his eyes adjusted to the dark, Dan looked for her. He saw no one and panicked. Had he imagined the scene outside? Or had she simply disappeared, becoming, in her own stunning image, invisible? He squinted, moving his eyes from pew to pew, until finally they fell upon a form hunched over. She was on her knees, bent over the back of a pew halfway up the side aisle. For some moments, he simply stood looking at her. She was as still as a statue, and he thought there should be votive lights. Quietly, he made his way over to the aisle, then up it. Without genuflecting, he slipped into the pew behind her. Only when he coughed did she become aware of him, and at once she knelt upright, listening like an animal.

Churchgoers keep their distance from one another unless the press of attendance forces them close. When Jane realized that someone had taken a seat directly behind her, she knew at once his business was with her, not God. She waited, not moving.

Curry was content to sit there in her incredible presence. Was it possible that he'd forgotten this sensation, the pleasure of just being near her? With his eyes, he stroked her neck at the place below the brim of her hat where her hair swept up from her skin. Only that inch of skin was available to him, but it seemed enough, a piece of the flesh in which he knew her. He remembered that, in writing his letters to her, there had always been that moment when, after taking hold of his pen with one hand and placing the other on the paper, he had tried to manufacture in his mind just this experience—her simple, factual nearness. And he could never do it.

Now, if he had paper, what would he write to her? She was waiting, he knew, for him to make himself known, and it was cruel not to, but he had no wish to speak. He had finally, talker that he was, nothing to say.

"Jane? Hello, it's me."

He saw the spasm of her shoulders and took it for stiffening.

But he misunderstood. To Jane his voice was like a note struck, the beginning of music. That her physical surprise registered before her pleasure only made her pleasure more acute, made it into something else—relief or rescue or redemption. Dan Curry was elusive now to everyone, not just her. For months she'd been longing for the chance to see him, to tell him that, yes, she understood now and that, yes, she believed now. Slowly she turned to face him, and at once she had to smile. "You have your beard again," she said quietly.

He nodded. "The British didn't know me without it, but neither did I."

"My Barbarossa . . ." The sight of him as he'd been in the beginning made her relax. She would have touched the smooth hair of his face, what had seemed once like feathers on her skin, but the back of her pew separated them. She was kneeling still, only the upper half of her body twisted toward him.

"I heard you speak. I never heard it put so well."

"I was speaking, I think, to you." She raised her hand toward him, moving from the kneeler to the seat. They intended only to clasp hands, but the movement carried them past what they intended. Their faces came together and their arms entwined about their necks and they kissed passionately above the rigid wood of the pew that kept their bodies apart.

Then Curry laughed, pressing his cheek against Jane's. His eyes went to Saint Mary's statue, the Immaculate Conception. "Good God," he said. "In church! It's like doing this in front of Ma!"

"What would she say?"

He pulled back to point at the statue. "See that snake she has her foot on?"

Now Jane laughed. "I thought that was Cromwell or someone, some Protestant."

Dan shook his head. "It's anyone who has a carnal thought in church."

"Then I'm right, it *is* some Protestant. It's me!" Jane drew his face to hers again, kissing him with more feeling still. "Let's go someplace, Dan, where there isn't wood between us."

"You must tell me first what happened. The woman I left in Hyde Park, trembling between two nations, is not the woman I heard just now, speaking with the very voice of Ireland. You had those lads walking away from the army bonuses. I've never seen that before. Your words had real bite, Jane, as if you believed them."

"Because of you, I saw the truth of what's been happening."

"How we Irish have been invisible in our own country."

"*I* was invisible. You were the first person who ever saw me, *me*. I couldn't see myself before because Douglas—" The sound of his name was like a wrong note; it jarred her and she stopped.

"Because Douglas was at the Front. He was a prisoner. You couldn't ignore that."

She nodded. "Then he came home. And . . ." She wanted to explain what had happened, but she had yet to explain it to herself. ". . . things changed. I changed. I returned to Ireland. I looked for you. I couldn't find you . . ." She shrugged. ". . . I found something else. My faith, my country. I kept praying the way you told me. 'Help Thou my unbelief.' And He did." She caressed his cheek, stroking his silken red whiskers. "Once I asked what you loved more, me or Ireland."

Curry remembered having answered, You. But when Pearse later asked for his promise never to see her again, he had given it.

"It was wrong of me," Jane said, "to put such a choice to you. You will never have to choose between me and Ireland again."

Words he'd dreamed of hearing, but what of Pearse? What of

his promise? Pearse would say, Don't trust her. She has a divided heart still. Without wanting to she will betray you. Grace, yes, he thought, but danger also. He put his fingers inside the collar of her coat, to touch the skin at her throat.

She shivered and creased her forehead at him. Here?

He traced his fingers along her throat into the cup of flesh at the base of her neck, as if feeling for the flame of a vigil light or for the exact place where the wax is melting into water, then for the place where throat becomes bone and bone becomes breasts, as if her breasts were what he wanted.

He let out a little gasp of disappointment when his fingers found it, the cold, hard thing he'd felt obliged to search for. "Your locket," he said. "You still wear it."

He imagined Pearse saying, Fool! What did you expect?

He brought the locket out from inside her blouse and coat and held it before her.

Her eyes did not waver. "Of course I wear it, I'll always wear it."

He didn't have to open it to see the sharp image of that man whose face he carried, as if in the locket of his own brain. He imagined the hair dark and slick, the brow strong, the mustache perfect above the pleasant mouth. But oh, how those eyes hated him!

Still, he opened it, flicking his fingernail between the two edges.

And it was empty. The wings of gold were empty. He looked up at her. "But there's no one's picture," he said.

"That's because the picture I have of you is too large."

Curry stood and went around to her pew and, as he took her into his arms, she lay back and he followed her down onto the hard bench. He opened her coat and found the curves of her body. When he kissed her, her mouth was open and the taste of her tongue shocked him. Only whores had opened their mouths to him like that, but Jane Tyrrell was no whore. She was the best woman he would ever know, and for the first time it did not seem wrong to want her body.

Abruptly he pulled away and stood, drawing her up after him. "Let's go somewhere else," he said.

Jane knew they had to leave the church, but she teased, "I don't mind if God watches."

Curry smiled and nodded toward the statue of the woman on the snake. "It's not God I mind. It's His mother."

———

He pointed down to the beach. A lone fisherman dressed in black was hauling his tiny black curragh out of the water. When it was beyond the reach of the lapping waves, he flipped it over and at once, from that distance, the curragh assumed the exact appearance of a large beetle. "He flips it like that because the tide comes in quickly and if his boat is upside down it won't float away."

They were standing at the window of the cottage in which Curry lived. It was in the hills outside the village of Fenit, six miles from Tralee. Spread below was the widest part of Tralee Bay. The looming Dingle peninsula across the water was invisible, obscured by the rain that had finally begun to fall, but its presence could be felt in the calm of the water it protected from the prevailing weather. The thin beach they were looking at reached into the bay from Fenit, stretching out half a mile like a line trailing from a boat.

"It's beautiful," Jane said. "I can see why you love it."

"And me a Dublin lad." He put his arm around her. The feel of his own heavy sweater on her shoulder gave him an unexpected pleasure. It wasn't a proper robe—she was naked under it—but it was just long enough to cover her nicely and keep her warm. She'd left his bed to make tea. When he saw her standing at the window while waiting for the kettle, he'd thrown on his shirt and pants and joined her.

"In the mouth of the bay—you can just make them out in the mist there—are the Magharee Islands. The Seven Hogs, the locals call them. You'd want to keep your eye on them if you were a ship out there."

"You talk like a local. You've come to know the area well."

"I'm taken with the place."

The whistle on the kettle began to blow, musically at first, then shrilly. Jane went to it, her bare feet slapping the cold, stone floor.

Dan remained at the window to watch the fisherman trudge along the beach. The man limped. It was Peter Hunt. Dan knew him from the Fenit pub. In his first weeks, just when the weather had turned rough and men like Hunt had begun taking their curraghs out less and less, Curry had sat in the same chair at the pub for hours every day until they began to talk to him. The more they told him about Fenit—the bay, that particular strand, and how the tides played upon it—the more certain he became it was the place. It had remained for him to plot the relevant coastal hazards, like the Seven Hogs, which he'd done with the help of the lighthouse keeper at Kerry Head. He drew up as precise a table of local tides as the expertise of curragh men could give him.

The fruit of that first phase of his work had gone on to Pearse. In the second phase he had selected from among the Kerry Volunteers a contingent of twenty men to serve as the shore party for the German landing. It was such a small party because the German soldiers themselves would accomplish the transfer of weapons crates to lifeboats and thence to the beach, but also because—and this was the most disturbing discovery of Curry's time in the west—Pearse would not trust any more than that with knowledge of what they were doing. The men whom Curry recruited were the most reliable IRB men in the west, though not even they knew exactly what they were being drilled to accomplish. The importance of the sliver of beach below him was a secret Curry shared only with Pearse. And Pearse, through Devoy in Washington, had shared it only with the German navy.

More recently, with the coming of March, it had become time to begin the immediate preparations, the training of the larger force of Volunteers—a thousand each from Galway, Clare, and Kerry—to seize the important western towns from Kenmare to Listowel. They would serve as the initial mustering points from which the first of the German weapons would be distributed to the fully mobilized Volunteers. Casement had been promised two hundred thousand rifles and a thousand machine guns, enough to equip the army that would rally once Irishmen saw that their freedom was within reach. That army would hold off England forever.

But the initial strike was Curry's concern. Within a day of the landing, a two-pronged force of ten thousand newly armed Irishmen, led by a thousand battle-hardened Germans, would advance simultaneously against Limerick and Cork before the British had a chance to reinforce their token garrisons. Within two days the entire southwest, including Ireland's only true port city, would be free. On the third day the southwest army and the force moving out from Dublin would link up in the ancient cathedral town of Kilkenny, and all Ireland, save parts of Ulster, would be theirs!

The thought of it made Curry's heart race, though his eye remained outwardly steady on the narrow beach where it would all begin.

"You take it without lemon, as I recall." Jane appeared at his side, offering him the cup of tea. "Which is just as well, since there isn't any in the kitchen."

"Oh sorry. You *do* take lemon."

She raised her brow at him, a good-humored gesture. "And the cream is curdled. The place lacks a certain touch, Dan."

"It's where I keep my pillow, Jane. I'm often away."

A small silence fell between them.

Jane knew better than to ask the seemingly natural question: Doing what? She returned to the kitchen for her own tea. When she came back into the parlor, Curry had taken one of the two wooden-backed chairs in front of the smoldering turf fire, the only source of warmth. She sat in the other, curling her feet under her legs and pulling the sweater down to cover them. They sipped their tea in silence. When Curry lit a cigarette, Jane asked for one. His surprise showed, but he gave it to her and struck a match. When she bent over it to inhale the flame, her hair fell around her face, and for a moment it was all he could see of her, the downpour hiding her exquisite face the way his overstretched gray sweater hid the miracle of her body.

When she looked up at him, she said, "Thanks," then sat back. Her eyes went to the fire. The smoke of their tobacco mingled with the musty smoke of the turf, a pungent burnt aroma that overpowered, to his regret, the acrid smell of sex.

"Whose is this place?"

"A friend of Pádraic's. A Gaelic folktale man at the university in Dublin. He comes out here summers to listen to the Irish-speakers." Curry paused, then added, "He's a priest."

Only at those words did Jane notice the crucifix on the wall above the fireplace. At that moment the writhing figure of Christ seemed grotesque to her. She had to remind herself that the *corpus* had become her symbol of life's hard truth, of Ireland's agony. But Christ's nakedness called to mind Dan's, which she preferred. It wasn't torture she wanted, but consolation. She flicked her cigarette toward the fire and looked at Curry. His eyes had followed hers to the cross and remained on it. She said, "So no matter where we go, one of them is watching. God's mother, God's son; they're a family of voyeurs."

Dan bristled inwardly at her mild blasphemy, but he forced a laugh. "You said in Tralee you wanted to be seen."

"Not in a priest's bed."

"But you aren't with a priest."

But at last he seemed like a priest to her, in the purity of his devotion. Did it matter that it was devotion not to a religion but to a nation? The gay ebullience she'd loved in him in those first days at the Abbey had given way to a fierce, politically motivated asceticism. She was herself the great exception, she saw, to the rigor of his single-mindedness. She assumed that he felt sullied, the way a married man would after such sexual passion with a woman not his wife. Or more to the point, the way a priest would. Well, Jane didn't feel sullied, and if he had, for his own reason, to be guarded with her, she didn't have to be guarded with him. "You seem distressed, Dan. I wonder why."

He stared at the tip of his cigarette. "'Distressed'? I wouldn't think 'distressed.'"

"What, then?"

"It's common, isn't it, for lovers to feel a certain"—what was the word he'd heard applied to this?—"*tristesse?*" He looked up, but away from her.

"With me, Dan, the *tristesse* just stopped."

He couldn't bring himself to look at her. Instead he fixed his gaze rigidly upon the glowing bricks of turf.

"What makes us different, do you think?" She had refused to push against such awkward feelings all her life, but this time she was going to push through them.

"History."

"You think my history is unlike yours? I'd never been with a man before you."

"I didn't mean *personal* history, Jane."

She answered sharply, "Are you thinking of Wolfe Tone, Dan? Or Oliver Cromwell? William of Orange? Or is it dear old Henry the Eighth? There comes a point when *that* history can be made to mean too much. What else does my being here like this mean but that you and I have reached that point?"

"But this isn't a bubble of air, untouched by what surrounds us."

"Enemies surround us, is that it? Why are these feelings of yours the result of what we've done together? You came inside me and touched me where no one has ever touched me before. But for you, instead of physical communion, our intimacy is the revelation of all that separates us. When we scrape away the glow, we see that even I'm your enemy. Is that it? Is that what you are feeling?"

"What I'm feeling is closer to you than I've ever felt to anyone."

"Then what's wrong?"

"I can't put it into words."

"You must. You simply must."

Yes, he knew that. But the heavy silence had gripped him again, and for a long time he could not speak.

Jane never stopped looking at him. She would outlast his inhibition.

Finally he said, "I left Maynooth because I was terrified of being alone. To have been so at the mercy of such a fear fills me with shame. Everyone is alone. I know that now. At the Abbey Theatre I was surrounded with people who thought well of me, were even fond of me, but I felt more alone than ever. And what assuaged the pain of that, what took it away, really . . ."

He looked at her now. What he was going to say would hurt

her. ". . . was the feeling of being at one with my people. Don't you see, Jane, the Cause is more than the Cause to me. It's been my salvation. Communion, you said. Yes, that's the feeling, but communion with my people. It's what I was supposed to feel as a priest, but couldn't. I feel it now, working for their freedom."

Jane put her teacup on the floor and reached across to him, touching his arm. "But Dan, I told you. You don't have to choose between me and your people anymore. I am one of them."

"But you're not, Jane."

Now she did flinch. She withdrew her hand. "Because I'm a Protestant?"

"Yes." A simple declaration, his affirmation glistened with its own purity.

And Jane was stunned, but not at all in the way she'd have expected to be. She knew the obvious arguments, how Protestants had played, and were playing now, central roles in Ireland's great struggle—the litany of heroes ran from Tone to Parnell to her own father, to Maud Gonne and Constance Markievicz, to Casement himself. The important divisions were not religious—she could recite this line in her sleep—but economic. But Dan Curry knew all those arguments too. He'd been at the Abbey, after all, and knew Synge and Lady Gregory, Douglas Hyde and Oliver Gogarty. He was talking about something more fundamental, the bedrock reality that had yet to fully manifest itself but that would be clear to all in a short time. The oh-so-rational syllogisms—All Daughters of Ireland are Irish patriots. Some Protestants are Daughters of Ireland. Therefore some Protestants are Irish patriots—that should have made it seem absurd hadn't yet and never would. He was talking about Catholic Ireland, Ireland Catholic, a Catholic nation for a Catholic people. He was saying its moment had finally come. And what stunned Jane was her visceral recognition, after all this time, that he was right.

Perhaps what made her know it was her own new experience that intense religious faith—and wasn't this the secret that lay beyond the grasp of "reasonable" people who were indifferent to belief?—could make a crucial difference to one's life. "Reasonable" people would never grasp that religion could be Ireland's central problem because they could not imagine that religion could have first been Ireland's main solution.

She said, "What I tried to explain before, Dan, is that when I lost you I felt completely set adrift. I was in England, but I discovered I wasn't English. Not English in any way. My brother came home and I discovered that my ties with my family had somehow been cut. I went to Dublin looking for you, but you were gone, and I faced the truth that I was alone. Perhaps that's what you did on leaving Maynooth, facing that aloneness. But you were ahead of me. You already had something I lacked. You had your faith. Well, now I have mine. I believe in God, Dan." The statement was momentous to her, and having made it, she fell silent. The words reverberated in her.

Curry sensed that she'd stopped short, and he knew that her commitment—to him, to Ireland—required more. He said, "Will you become a Catholic, Jane?"

Not a demand or request. An invitation, rather, but also a test. She nodded. "Yes."

And Curry saw that, in her one word, her half of the pact was made. And what of his? He could make his commitment now only by telling her the truth. "Jane, I'm here to prepare for a German invasion on the beach below this cottage. It's coming, in barely more than a month, the weekend of Easter. Collusion with Germany is what siding with Ireland and with Catholics has come to require. It's terrible, but true."

She didn't flinch. "I know what's required, Dan. And I'm prepared to be a part of it."

He looked away from her, moved by her refusal to let barriers stand between them. The great obstacle that made their love impossible did not exist. Now the only obstacle was in him. He said quietly, "But you may not be prepared for everything. Being with me may involve something you'd rather keep your distance from."

"You mean the Rising? I'm in it, Dan. What must I do to declare myself? What must I do to convince you? Is it distance you think I want?" She sensed his reluctance, and suddenly doubt filled her. Was any of this true? Her wanting to be a Catholic? Her wanting to be Irish? Her wanting to help bring about a free Irish nation? Or was it only that she wanted him? And wouldn't that make her ridiculous now if what he wanted was all of that but her?

He said quietly, "No, I don't mean the Rising. I mean my fear." When he looked at her, she saw that his eyes were brimming. He said with bewilderment, "I'm afraid of you."

"Why?" Her voice was a whisper.

"Because I love you, and I see now . . ." He stopped.

". . . that I love you," she said.

He nodded, full of an emotion that had gripped him his whole life, since the earliest gloom of the crowded rooms on Henrietta Street, where he'd fought through the chaos of a dozen howling or morose siblings for the scraps of his mother's distracted fondness, then later for scraps only of bread. In those rooms he learned to be his defeated father's son. It was his father's emotion, this certainty that in the center of himself— where a woman's love collects and from which hope and faith radiate and in which the resolute sense of self-worth quickens— there was a core of nothing. Curry's pretense collapsed, and he saw the nothing, nothing, nothing from which, as a spoiled priest, posturing actor, and now solitary patriot, he had been in lifelong, headlong flight. He fell onto his knees before Jane and crushed his head into her lap. "I love you, Jane," he repeated desperately, "I love you."

She stroked his head, pressing him with what she had— *her* experience, *her* strength, and now, ironically, the faith she felt he'd given her. Believing in God, she understood, was how certain human beings believed in themselves. She was distressed at his pain, of course, but relieved too, for she understood that his reluctance had been reluctance to feel this anguish. Like the Irishman that he was, he had yielded to his emotion in courage and now was handing it over to her, his first gift. This was his virginity, she saw. How surprising that she should feel prepared to take it from him. That she welcomed his expression and could receive his fear made her feel as Irish as he was. She saw what she could do for him—make him see that if he was truly nothing, nothing, nothing, how could she love him so and why would she do anything now—whether for God or Ireland or not—for him?

When he came up, their faces were only inches apart. Jane tried to read his eyes for their hard, dark secrets. She had never before been so close to a man's anguish; of course it frightened her. With her forefinger she traced the tearstain on his cheekbone, down to where it disappeared into his whiskers. She lowered her face to his, to kiss him. She welcomed it, despite the cold, when his hands went under the sweater. She expected that he would push it up to expose her, so that he could touch his face to her breasts. But instead he leaned against the soft, beaten wool, his hands pressed together at the small of her back. Instinctively she began to rock slightly. The small movement brought to mind her mother.

She tried to imagine her mother rocking her father in this way, him half kneeling, half leaning on her. But she knew her parents had never been together like this. Her father had never exposed such need, had never felt it. She said, "Let's move to the bed, darling."

It was a narrow bed, meant for one person. Jane pulled the sweater over her head and dropped it. She sat on the edge of the bed, drawing Dan close. He remained standing, unbuttoning his shirt. Jane worked at his trousers. For the first time, all self-consciousness left her, and she realized that he was submitting to her initiative. When he was standing naked before her, she pulled him down onto the bed.

Her legs opened and he pushed into her. His passion outran him, and he was afraid that he would come too quickly again. But no. As if their emotional turmoil bound them in a new way—they *had* made their commitment—she stayed with him perfectly throughout that carnal flight, that brief ecstasy of rescue, from all life's grief.

───────

"So you want to be a Catholic, eh?" He was up on his elbow, smiling down on her. His meaning was clear enough: she'd have to learn a Catholic's distaste for sex. She had the heavy brown blanket pulled to her chin, but out of cold, not modesty.

"Blatantly," she said and laughed. "And I shall require you to be my sponsor."

He shook his head vigorously. "That's a canonical impediment."

"What?"

"You've a lot to learn, my love. A canonical impediment. If I was to be your baptismal sponsor, I wouldn't be permitted to marry you."

"Why?" Jane had to stifle a native repugnance. He was

making light of it, but she'd been taught to regard such legal-
ism as the surest sign of the religion's morbidity.

Curry shrugged. "Spiritual consanguinity."

"What rubbish."

"Get used to it, darling."

Curry's gloating seemed inappropriate to Jane. He should have
been embarrassed. "But what does that mean? Spiritual what?"

"Consanguinity. I'd be like your brother."

An unfortunate reference, it shocked them both. Jane faced
away. "I hope not."

"Where is he, anyway? Back at the Front?"

Jane shook her head. "He's at home."

"In London?"

"No, Cragside. With my father. Pamela and the children
are there as well."

"How can that be? He's an officer. It's been four months."
Curry felt a visceral alarm. It shocked him to realize that he
hadn't asked her this before, that she hadn't told him. "Why is
he at Cragside?"

"Apparently he's unwell, after what he went through."

Curry sat up, indifferent to the chill air on his naked torso.
"He was well enough in London. I saw him. He was *perfectly* well."

"I thought he was too, but . . ."

"But what? What haven't you told me?"

Jane had yet to admit this to herself. How could she have
admitted it to him? Her refusal to confront the fact shamed her
as much as the fact itself did. "I think he's after you."

"And when you learned that, you were . . . ?

"It's what changed me. It changed everything." Her mind
was full of that scene: Douglas, in his brilliant uniform, coming
at her with his riding crop. "He called me your whore."

Curry wanted to turn away from her, but how could he?

He sensed at once the danger Tyrrell represented to him and to the entire plan. He should have put aside everything else to consider it. But put aside Jane? Her devastation overwhelmed him. He put his hand on her shoulder. "The bastard," he said.

Jane turned her head aside, tears spilling onto the pillow. When Curry touched her face, turning it back to him, she said, "I'm not your whore, am I?"

"You're going to be my wife, if I have my way." When he embraced her, she clung to him. His consolation meant everything to her, as hers had to him. The circle of their need was now complete.

But Curry's mind returned to Tyrrell—Tyrrell in the west of Ireland, pretending to be unwell. He knew he should report this to Pearse; it was the very link Pearse had warned him of. But Pearse would make him obey his own vow never to see Jane again, as if *she* were the threat. Pearse, of course, would see the way in which she was. He would remove Curry and abandon his plan for the German landing, devising another. Dan Curry, the spoiled priest, would be a spoiled patriot.

No. He would do what Jane had done: squeeze his eyes shut against the uncertain power of Douglas Tyrrell. Jane had promised Dan he'd never have to choose again between her and Ireland, but she was wrong. As he held her, his face in her hair, he knew he'd blurted out the truth that first time. Ireland was nothing to him, compared to her.

———

It was raining when they left the cottage early the next morning. Jane was returning to Dublin. Even in the weather, Curry paused in front of his automobile to point in the direction of the finger-thin strand, the long peninsula poking into Tralee Bay. The landing at half tide; a brilliant plan and a perfect place for it.

Curry's cottage was on the narrow plateau along which the Fenit road ran. The plateau was halfway up the broad hill that sloped back from the bay. On top of the hill, huddled by a trinity of huge boulders that once might have marked a Druid holy place, Douglas Tyrrell followed through his field glasses the direction of Curry's arm. Tyrrell saw the beach. He surveyed the waters of the rain-shrouded bay, which even in that downpour, protected as it was by mammoth Dingle, was flat calm, as if ready, waiting like the bay between the legs of a willing lover.

He turned his binoculars on Jane just as she took Curry's hand to climb into the motorcar. He had hoped to read her face, but he never saw it. It was just as well.

Curry cranked the motor efficiently, then climbed in beside her. Tyrrell followed the car, as it headed off toward Fenit and Tralee, until it disappeared.

Then he stepped out from behind the boulders, applied his glasses once more to the broad bay, memorizing it through the filter of the blowing rain. When he lowered the binoculars, he stood there impassively, looking down at the cottage, the beach, Tralee Bay, the Dingle peninsula, the Magharee Islands, the bleakness of it, the despair.

The rain streaked his face. After a long time he said to himself, Right.

18

The crucial meeting was held in Sir Matthew Nathan's office in Dublin Castle. In addition to Nathan, General Friend and Major Price were present, as Douglas expected they would be. That Admiral Hamilton, the naval intelligence chief, had come over from London to hear his report underscored the Admiralty's continuing concern.

This time it was Douglas who stood at the map of Ireland, ruler in hand. Dressed in a dark suit and tie, he looked more like a barrister briefing clients than an army officer to his superiors. "The assumption that the German landing will take place at one or more existing harbors"—he pointed at Westport, Galway, and Kilrush—"is incorrect. There are no facilities to receive ocean-going vessels in those harbors, and what few boats that might off-load the ships at anchor are controlled by men who have no sympathy with a German-sponsored revolution."

General Friend interrupted. He and the other two military men were seated in stiff-back chairs flanking Nathan, who, by contrast, leaned casually back in the large leather seat behind his ornate desk. This was Nathan's turf, but Friend seemed to challenge it suddenly by challenging Tyrrell. "How do you know that, Captain?"

"I know it, General, because I've spent the last three months talking to them."

"All of them?"

"General, the west of Ireland is not the west of England. There are barely fifty motor-powered workboats from Kerry to Mayo."

"And you want me to believe their crews are all loyal?"

Douglas shrugged. "Loyalty is a relative matter. Corner boys in Dublin can spout slogans, even treasonous ones, but they never have to confront the reality of a German alliance. In the west such slogans have a specific meaning: an active collusion with England's enemy. However much they may squirm under London rule, men of the west are not throwing in with Berlin. That's why the leaders of the rebellion have kept their dealings secret not only from England, but from Ireland. Ireland won't support it."

Major Price sat forward. "That conviction of yours, Captain—"

"Not a conviction, Major. A conclusion."

Price waved the distinction off. "—is what justifies your refusal to identify by name the coastal insurrectionists?"

"The names I could give you are of the Irish Volunteers in Cork, Limerick, and Galway. You have those names. Those men are quite public. You'll find them on their parade grounds wearing their homemade uniforms, drilling with broomsticks, every Sunday. My point to you, sir, is that the Germans will not need a large shore party because they won't off-load their ships at anchor."

"Then there will be no German landing, is that what you're saying?" General Friend made a show of his impatience.

Douglas stared back at him. "No, sir. I'm saying the

opposite. The rebels are planning an elaborate landing, but not the one that you expect. The ships will *beach* themselves. They will off-load what cargo must be kept dry—weapons and ammunition—in their own lifeboats. The troops will go over the bows into shallow water. The only Irish-based support required will be a pilot boat to rendezvous with the ships offshore, to guide them in, and a handful of Irishmen to direct the invaders to their first bivouac. You said in our meeting in London, sir, that the period of transfer from ships to shore will be the period of absolute vulnerability. I'm telling you that period will last from midtide to high, a period of less than three hours. The transfer itself will cover not a half-mile of open water, but a few dozen yards of lapping surf."

"Ridiculous!" Friend snorted. "Ridiculous! The west coast of Ireland is all rocks. There's no such beach."

"There is." Douglas poked the map with the ruler. "It's here, at Fenit in the lee of Dingle, in the Bay of Tralee." Tralee. The name hung in his mind. Now Tralee meant Jane—the place where he had witnessed his sister's perfidy. And he hated himself now for thinking that she might even be there to welcome the bloody Germans.

General Friend was still snorting. "It's impossible!"

Douglas turned away from the general toward Admiral Hamilton. He sat, his hands pursed at his mouth, staring at the map. After a long silence, he asked, "What's the slope of the beach?"

"Gradual, sir. Twenty degrees, sloping out from low water three hundred yards."

"What is the range of tide?"

"Maximum of eleven feet between low and high water."

Hamilton let his gaze drift to Douglas; it conveyed the experience of his awakening. "And next month's maximum falls . . ."

"Right, sir. Easter weekend. In point of fact, Good Friday."

The date registered with all of them.

Hamilton looked at Friend. "Not impossible, General, not at all. Wooden-hulled ships beached themselves all the time. Iron is less resilient than wood. One doesn't want to take a metal vessel ashore like that every day, but for proper cause . . ." Hamilton shrugged. What was proper cause for the Germans if not the blow to England this landing would be? "Given the right slope, suitable weather, and perfect timing with the tides, it's not impossible at all. Of course, every naval operation requires perfect timing." He looked back at the map, and now his amazement showed itself. "I didn't think such a beach existed in the west of Ireland."

"Well, by God, we'll have it covered!" Friend turned to Sir Matthew. "Now will you get me proper reinforcements? I need real soldiers. Not Irishmen. I need Tommies!"

Nathan sat forward, his chair snapping under him. "You know what our job is, General. It's to handle this without asking London for troops. The German victory occurs in Ireland the moment we draw off forces from the Front to defend against it. We will not do that. There *are* no troops for Ireland."

"There must be troops! Give me the Ulster Division at least. Do we leave this to the RIC? They're Catholics!"

Tyrrell slapped his own hand with the wooden stick he held. "General, I must protest. The Royal Irish Constabulary has proved itself again and again. It serves no one's purpose to lump every Irish Catholic in with rebels but the rebels themselves."

"Captain Tyrrell, you've made your report, such as it is." Friend glared at him. "What we wanted from you were the names of the insurrectionists. Unless that's what you have to give us, further comment from you is unnecessary and shall be regarded as insubordinate." He faced Nathan. "I tell you, these Irish will welcome the Germans! They'll pull them ashore!"

Admiral Hamilton, with a supremely patronizing touch of General Friend's sleeve, said, "The Germans won't be pulled ashore by anyone, my dear General. They won't get as far as the surf. Now that we know where to await them, those ships will be intercepted"—he gestured at the map—"as they steer between Kerry Head and, what are those islands, Captain?"

"Magharee Islands, Sir Edward."

Hamilton nodded. "The British navy will stop them there."

"The British navy!" This was too much for Friend. "It's everything the navy can do to keep a supply line to the BEF open across the Channel. The British navy can't even protect the east coast of England from German attacks! The Germans shell Harwich and Ipswich! They cruise at will off Great Yarmouth! How the hell can you protect the west coast of Ireland?"

"Not the west coast, General." Hamilton nodded at Tyrrell. "Because of your army man here, the navy's task is simpler than that. Quite within our competence, believe me." His finger shot up toward the map. "What your man has brought us is worth far more than the names of rural malcontents. Tralee Bay! If nothing else in this trying season, Tralee Bay will be secure!"

Sir Matthew tapped his desk nervously. "Still, General Friend has a point. We must, of course, reinforce our garrisons in the southwest, even if it means leaving the country elsewhere undermanned. And we must preempt the rebels' initiative with Defense of the Realm arrests everywhere."

"Absolutely not!" Hamilton bellowed. "We must do nothing to alert the Germans to our foreknowledge. They would call the landing off. Don't you see, we *want* them to try it. They must fail, of course. But we want them to try it."

"Why, in God's name? If we can demonstrate ahead of time a level of readiness that deters them?"

"Because Ireland joins Belgium then as a small nation they

are trying to devour. A German attempt to invade Ireland for
whatever motive makes our point better than anything we can
say or do ourselves."

"Makes it to the Americans," Friend said.

"Of course, to the Americans, General. Imagine the effect of
it when our destroyers escort half a dozen German ships, flying
false flags and carrying weapons and gray-uniformed German
soldiers, into the harbor at Queenstown! We won't sink them,
we'll capture them. And then we'll turn the newspapermen
loose on them, like red ants. A German assault not only against
Ireland, but against the shipping lanes of the North Atlantic!
This event will bring America into the war, which, gentlemen,
I'm afraid to say, is our only hope of winning it."

Tyrrell said, "In which case, the Irish rebels will have saved
England."

Hamilton nodded, but said, "A debt we won't acknowledge."

The group fell silent.

Douglas alone remained standing. After a moment he
shifted his weight awkwardly.

General Friend said to Sir Matthew, as if no one else were
present, "I understand the Admiral's concern, but we simply
must have a force at standby in the region."

Hamilton began, "General, please indulge my—"

"I was addressing the secretary for Ireland!"

Nathan shook his head. "Sir Edward represents Lord Kitchener, General, and not merely the Admiralty. He has authority in
the matter." It was a concession made without animus. Nathan
had learned nothing in all his years of colonial service if not
when to step aside for London. And he knew better than to step
between military men who had their pistols cocked.

As if the secretary's announcement freed him to display his
authority, Hamilton stood up. "I had hoped not to make you

feel intruded upon, General. But you give me no choice." He crossed to the map as Douglas stepped aside. "The RIC has normal jurisdiction throughout this area. They are to maintain it. As the date approaches, we will bring the chief constable in and, with him, establish a special service unit that will move, simultaneously with the naval operation, though not before, against the rebel shore party."

"I'm telling you the RIC can't do it."

"Of course, there should be overall army authority, if that's your point. An army man in charge—your coachman on the box, so to speak. What rank would it require?"

"Major at least," Friend snapped. His eyes shot quickly toward Major Price.

Hamilton turned to Tyrrell. "I want you in charge." Then he looked stonily at Friend. "I'll rely on you to arrange Captain Tyrrell's promotion, General."

Good Friday dawned, as it often does in theological Ireland, chill and bleak. Douglas Tyrrell had posted a dozen mufti-clad RIC men each in Fenit, Spa, Derrymore, and Blennerville, the towns ringing the shores of Tralee Bay. He had taken up his own position at Church Hill, a promontory jutting out into the bay above Fenit. It wasn't far from the place, marked by three boulders, from which he'd first watched his sister leave Curry's cottage. From his new vantage he could see the whole of Tralee Bay out to Kerry Head and the sea beyond. He could still see the cottage, but he knew that Curry wasn't in it. Curry had spent the night on board the *Sea Lark*, a thirty-foot fishing boat that had been tied to the small wharf at Fenit. Now, in first light, Tyrrell watched through his binoculars as the boat headed out to sea with two men aboard, the helmsman and Curry. If he could keep the *Sea Lark* in his glasses, Tyrrell knew, he would see everything.

He scanned the open water beyond Kerry Head for signs
either of the German ships or the British force that was waiting for them—two heavily armed destroyers, HMS *Zinnia* and
HMS *Bluebell*, and two lightly armed but swift eighty-foot
motor launches, HMS *Sand Lance* and HMS *Minnow*.

He saw nothing. The gentle swells of the bay became choppy
water beyond the sheltering reach of Dingle, but the mists of
dawn made it impossible to see much farther than the mouth
of the bay. Not even the Magharees were visible.

He lowered his glasses and looked at his watch. It was shortly
after six, nearly an hour before low water. The Germans would
be planning to steam into the bay proper in three hours, hitting
the beach in four, getting off with the tide in seven. It consoled
Tyrrell to realize that everything would be over, one way or the
other—the nightmare of these six months would be over—by
early afternoon.

With his naked eyes he watched the *Sea Lark* steadily moving
away, growing smaller, yet pitching more severely as it left the
lee of Dingle. He pictured Curry holding on to a stanchion, his
bearded face in the wind. He tried to imagine Curry's feelings,
and realized they would be something like his own. Douglas
wondered suddenly what Curry had told Jane. But he ruthlessly
put his sister out of his mind. At least Jane had not reappeared in
Tralee. Douglas had not had to repeat the ignominy, for which
he still loathed himself, of turning his glasses on her.

Soon the *Sea Lark* disappeared in the distant fog. Time
passed. Again and again his thoughts drifted to Pamela. That
distraction he did not resist. He wanted the horror of these
events over for many reasons, but none more than to have done
with the awful deception of his wife. That was *his* perfidy. He
longed to tell her everything. Only Pamela would understand
what these months had cost him.

But even thoughts of Pamela were dangerous now. This was the time for alertness, not consolation; for will, not love. He shut his mind against her.

From where he waited, Douglas could see one of his detachments of RIC men huddled near a ruined stone oratory on the hill above Fenit. He looked over at them regularly, then would check his watch compulsively. He tugged at the leather strap of his Sam Browne, and he nervously fingered the snap on his holster. This was the first time he'd worn his uniform since coming home to Ireland. It contributed to the strange feeling of unreality that now threatened to override his calm. When had he had this feeling before? It haunted him, filled him with dread. Then he remembered that morning in the poisoned trenches at Messines, waiting for the order to go over. Then, at least, he'd had his lads nearby, so that by bolstering them he could bolster himself. Here, he was alone, watching like some divinity from his solitary ledge.

What kind of thought was that? Divinity indeed! He reined his anxiety and channeled it into the simple act of focusing his eyes, as if by an act of will he could increase the field of his vision. Over the next period of time that seemed to happen, as first the dawn hill mists evaporated and then the sea fog rolled back.

Nearly three hours had passed; the time had come. Just as he began to fear that nothing was going to happen, a black form appeared in his glasses, a ship. He watched it grow and waited for others to appear beside it. But none did, apart from the tiny vessel just ahead of it, which he took to be the *Sea Lark*. Without breathing, Tyrrell watched their progress. They were headed directly into the bay. Soon it was apparent that the ship was a freighter, therefore not one of the British warships. German therefore! A single ship only, but a German vessel! A German landing after all; a deadly cargo—troops and weapons! Tyrrell realized with shock that until now he had not really believed this could happen, as in Trier he had not believed he was really hearing Irishmen coax Irishmen toward treason. Was there a brigade of Irish traitors aboard this vessel? Were some recruited from the men he'd left behind? Suddenly he felt the power of the rage he'd first felt in the prison camp, that compatriots of his would truly do this, and he wanted to see this ship blown to smithereens as the Germans in those very waters had blown the *Lusitania*.

With a rush of panic, it occurred to him that this ship had somehow eluded the British destroyers and that it was actually going to succeed in coming fully into the bay. It was close enough now that he could see its flag, the flag of Norway—falsely flown, of course. He checked his watch once more. The ship would make it to the beach precisely on the tide and disgorge a force of hardened troops against whom Tyrrell's own constables would be no match.

Just as he began to think General Friend had been right, there appeared from beyond the jagged hill of Kerry Head the distinctive black bow of a destroyer. As it came fully into view, Tyrrell saw the three smokestacks and the telltale fore-to-aft sloping wedge of the hull. From inside the Magharees a smaller form shot out into the open water, a swift motor launch, converging, with the destroyer, on the freighter. The freighter showed its broadside suddenly, changing course—he could read its name, the *Aud*—and then a ball of smoke rolled off the destroyer. A second later Tyrrell heard the faint report of a heavy gun, a warning shot. The freighter seemed to stop. The two British vessels bore down on it.

The other warships were nowhere in sight. Tyrrell could only presume that they had intercepted the main body of German ships farther out to sea, perhaps near Skellig—that place which had first led him here to Tralee.

The *Sea Lark* meanwhile continued to power toward the head of the bay, the British vessels apparently ignoring it. That would have been fine with Douglas—This one's mine, he'd have said—but then he realized he was going to have to move now against Curry. It was a moment he'd somehow expected would never come.

He left his position, dashing toward the road where the Crossley and its RIC driver waited. He wanted to be at the Fenit wharf before the *Sea Lark* was. As he leapt aboard the mud-colored military vehicle, waving the driver toward Fenit, his eyes snagged on something in the open water on the opposite side of the Church Hill peninsula. A fast-moving curragh, he thought at first, because of its small, black beetlelike form. But it was moving far too fast for a curragh. He stared back at it as the Crossley jolted under him, headed in the opposite direction.

"Wait!" The armored car stopped abruptly and Tyrrell stood, balancing against the windscreen. In the distance the *Aud* and its two escorts were just disappearing behind the Magharees, while here, well into the bay, something new was happening.

He watched unbelieving as the sinister black form grew larger. "What the hell is that?" he asked no one in particular. Before it had surfaced fully—for that's what it was doing—he knew, though he'd never seen one before, that it was a submarine. A bloody submarine.

The sight staggered him. As the water streamed off the conning tower and hull, and as its cigar-form became fully visible—he read the stark bow number, 19—he felt the visceral repugnance one feels for the obscene. That Ireland's fate should have become entwined with that machine, as the place from which the Germans hoped to extend its range, seemed like a primitive Gaelic myth, the island devoured by a monster from the deep. The machine was all, Tyrrell realized, and for a moment so was his hatred. It cut both ways. Neither Germany nor England cared a whit for Ireland as Ireland. Their argument was over this fucking machine.

But it wasn't heading into the bay. Though why should it have? Would a U-boat have beached itself? It seemed to wallow, pitching and rolling unsteadily. With his glasses, Douglas scanned that part of the bay. The nearest land was the Banna Strand, a rough, rocky shore that took the full brunt of ocean swells in an impossibly heavy surf. With his binoculars fixed on the U-boat, Douglas waited. What in hell was happening? He tried to guess its dimensions, but, lacking a reference point, he couldn't. The thing might have been fifty feet long or four hundred, the tower five feet high or fifty. A heavy wave crashed over it, forcing the nose down, and for a moment Douglas feared the boat was going under again. But the water coursed free and the U-boat bobbed in its own wash.

Something moved on the deck, behind the conning tower, and Douglas adjusted the focus wheel on his glasses, trying to bring it up. A mistake: the boat blurred. In the seconds it took him to find focus again, a man had come out of a hatch and was now stooping down to it, hauling another man up after him. Then they stooped together and pulled an object—a crate?—up to the deck. Not a crate, he saw, as they righted it and began to slide it overboard, but a tiny boat, a dinghy.

The pair clambered into it and floated free. The craft nearly swamped at once in the swirl of water off the hull of the submarine, and Tyrrell thought it was going to sink. But it was the submarine that sank. More quickly than he'd have believed possible, the black hulk simply disappeared beneath the waves. The dinghy tossed wildly, then found its course as one of the men began pulling on the oars. They made at once for the nearest point of land, the rocky, surf-ridden Banna Strand. Never, he thought.

He scanned the bay again—not a sign of a ship anywhere. If not for the *Sea Lark* and the tiny skiff struggling landward in the rolling Atlantic swells, Tyrrell might have wondered if he'd imagined it all.

"Move!" he said to the driver. "Not to Fenit . . ." There was not time to summon the others. ". . . to Banna!" He pointed the way, and the driver wheeled the lumbering vehicle around. The road off Church Hill sank into an inland valley, and for a crucial ten minutes their view of the water was blocked. Tyrrell kept pressing the driver to go faster, but the road was dangerously rutted. At one point they had to stop to clear a fallen tree, which, in their hurry, they tossed aside as if it were brush.

Finally the road cut back toward the shore. The sea came into view and the road snaked down toward it. The dinghy was just then struggling into the far edge of the rough surf, where the whitecaps became breakers. The *Sea Lark* was bearing down on it from behind. Curry had seen the submarine too.

More than two hundred yards of steeply sloping headland—boulder-strewn and covered with thick briers—separated the road from the water's edge. Tyrrell halted the Crossley, ordered the driver to bring his rifle, and they plunged into it. If the dinghy did not capsize in the surf or get crushed against the rocks, it would hit the beach about the time Tyrrell and the RIC man would. What he could not calculate yet, crashing through the thorny undergrowth, was what role Curry would play in this.

The *Sea Lark* was still coming full-throttle toward shore. Tyrrell realized he'd made a mistake in bringing the Crossley into view.

Thirty or forty yards from shore, a fierce wave tossed the small rowboat into the air. An oar pinwheeled into the spray, and the men flailed as they were hurled into the water. The boat disappeared in the cascading foam.

Tyrrell and his man arrived at the beach.

The *Sea Lark* continued to gun for it at a distance now of less than a hundred yards.

The form of a man appeared in the surf, tossed helplessly about, flotsam. The water hurled him ashore, but just as quickly sucked him seaward again. Tyrrell started for him as the second man appeared farther out, equally helpless. "Go for that one!" he ordered. He and the RIC man separated.

The *Sea Lark*, breasting the waves, was aimed right between them, and it barreled into the surf.

Tyrrell ignored it. The man he'd gone after was in danger of being pulled back out to sea. He plunged into the water and grabbed him. The man was wearing drenched leather overalls, what submariners wore to protect against scalding pipes, and was hopelessly encumbered. Only with the greatest effort was Tyrrell able to hold him and then drag him ashore.

With a great futile roar of its engine as the propeller came out of the water, the *Sea Lark* hit the beach, then bounced back from it against a large rock. With half its hull exposed, it seemed huge.

Tyrrell dropped the half-drowned man onto the sand—the German C-in-C?—to reach instinctively for his pistol. Had the water made it useless?

A man appeared over the cockeyed rail of the *Sea Lark*. He too had a pistol drawn, and when he saw Tyrrell, he fired.

Tyrrell shot him dead.

The German at his feet grabbed Tyrrell's legs, crying, "No! No! No!"

The German?

Only when Tyrrell looked down at him—a haggard, bearded scarecrow lost in the oversized leather overalls—did he recognize Roger Casement, the bastard from Trier.

"Stand still, Major!" Dan Curry showed enough of himself from under the prow of the *Sea Lark* to make it clear to Tyrrell that he had him in the sights of his pistol, but not enough to make a decent target.

Instead of dropping his weapon, Tyrrell lowered it, pressing its snout against Casement's head and cocking it.

Curry came out from behind the wrecked boat, his gun level, but his indecision was apparent. Tyrrell did not waiver, while Curry, whose own resolve only moments before had brought the boat crashing onto the beach, did not know what to do.

It was Casement who broke the impasse, clutching at Tyrrell. But Tyrrell forced the pistol harder against his skull.

"I've come back to call it off," Casement said. "We can't do it! We can't do it!"

Despite himself, Curry demanded, "What?"

Casement looked toward him. "Call the Rising off! The Germans have reneged. They won't help us! We can't do it!"

Even Tyrrell looked down at Casement now. "What about the *Aud?* I saw the *Aud.*"

Casement shook his head. "It's nothing, a German nuisance gesture, scavenged rifles from the Russian front, a tenth of what we need. The *Aud* is all there is and it is nothing!"

"No brigade?" Curry asked in disbelief. "No German troops?"

"Nothing, I tell you!" Casement screamed at them. He seemed mad. "Nothing! They betrayed us!"

"But why?" Curry had convinced himself, as Pearse had, that the Germans would do anything for their North Atlantic U-boat base.

"Because the chancellor won out over the admirals. The Kaiser has called off the U-boat onslaught. They are afraid of bringing America into the war."

Tyrrell pushed the pistol harder against Casement's head. "Because you couldn't raise an Irish Brigade and they saw that they'd have to come to Ireland as conquerors. Isn't that it? They saw that the Irish people would never support you. Isn't that it?"

Casement slumped. "Yes." He reached an arm toward Curry. "So go to Pearse and MacNeill and call it off. Tell them it's hopeless. There's no help. There's no point. Our men will be slaughtered. Call it off."

Curry stared at him as at a ghost. He recognized the failures Casement described as the very failures he had himself predicted once. Why, then, had he ignored his own instinctive rejection of the German alliance? But he knew. He had ignored it because of Pearse. He felt doubly devastated by what Casement said. Casement had been the first to believe in the Rising and was now the first to abandon it. This was the truth Curry himself had seen in a flash at that prison camp in Trier; what fools they'd been to throw in with Germans. And now it was an obvious truth that the plan drawn to depend on Germany could not go forward; a Catholic people could not rise up in hopeless revolution. It would be suicide, and killing done in its name would be murder. But it had taken a Protestant to point it out. Curry took a step back from Tyrrell and Casement as the recognition crystallized of what he had to do.

But then he felt the blunt object in his back, and he heard the uncertain Irish voice behind him. "Don't move. I'll shoot you."

It was Tyrrell's driver. The man he'd pulled ashore after a great struggle in the sea was sprawled on the beach behind him. The driver was terrified that he was actually going to have to shoot Curry, so it came as a large, if mysterious, relief when Major Tyrrell said, "Let him go, Sergeant." The RIC man hesitated, then withdrew the point of his rifle from Curry's back.

Curry fled at once.

Tyrrell watched him running up to the road. He thanked God for the more than ample reason he'd been given to spare the man his sister loved.

Curry, for his part, felt an infinite desolation. It was nearly noon, the hour when the sky darkened and the temple veil was rent. All over Ireland, for the next three hours, there would be silence. But there was no silence inside Curry. The words reeled through his mind. He repeated them over and over as he ran, the words of Roger Casement: "Tell them it's hopeless. There's no help. There's no point. Our men will be slaughtered."

And the words of Jesus Christ on the cross: "*Eloi! Eloi! Lama sabactani?*" My God! My God! Why have You forsaken me?

————

It was early evening when the train from Limerick carried Curry into Knightsbridge Station in Dublin. By then more than ten thousand Volunteers had been on alert status at mustering points all over Ireland. Only a few insurgent leaders were privy to the broad outlines of strategy, but local groups everywhere had successfully met the first tests of timing and coordination. Now they were waiting for the order to go forward, and most of them were waiting for their rifles.

Any revolution requires an exquisite correlation of diverse efforts, and in those first hours the Irish revolution achieved it. The various factions had in the ultimate moments laid aside their disagreements. For example, once it seemed that the initiative Pearse, Casement, and Devoy had taken toward Berlin was going to bear extraordinary fruit, the others swallowed their misgivings and rallied to the plan. Only when the hours of Friday morning passed without word from Kerry, and then, in the early afternoon, when the word that came was an unconfirmed rumor of disaster, did the organizational disagreements begin to surface again. The message from Dan Curry—"Hold all operations! Casement captured! No arms! Await arrival Dublin!"—exacerbated those disagreements, but the leaders agreed there was nothing to do but wait for Curry and learn what had happened.

The streets outside the railroad station were deserted and, rather than wait for a cab, Curry began to run. Two blocks to the Liffey, the gray sunken wound of a river, which seemed to spawn the dank mist that choked the twilit city of all its color. Then up the Ormond Quay past the drab warehouses and sober shipping companies, trying to remember which building it was, thinking for once only of his duty, for this was duty, at last— calling off the Rising—in which he believed.

His footsteps echoed eerily behind him as he ran, as if the adjacent river water was a skin stretched tight to amplify sound. It carried across the Liffey into south Dublin, perhaps as far as Merrion Square, where Jane was. He would be with her tonight.

But now, now was running, finding the place, an innocuous narrow brick building that he knew, when he came upon it, by the cracked glass in the first-floor window. He hurled the door open, flew by the lone sentry, and took four flights of stairs without slowing. On the landing he stopped to recover his breath, but the door snapped open at once and Eoin MacNeill stood there. He was dressed in a formal black suit, as for a funeral, but his collar was open, his shirt disheveled. "Where the fuck have you been?"

Curry stared at MacNeill, gasping still. It hadn't occurred to him that the leaders would be in a state of barely reined rage or that they'd greet him with it. Curry knew that to them he was the messenger of disaster, but the disaster could be trimmed, and his job was to show them how. "I've been getting here, Commandant."

"Let the man in, Eoin!" someone ordered from within the room. When MacNeill stepped aside, Curry saw that it was Connolly. He had discarded his suit coat; his shirtsleeves were rolled past the elbows of his powerful arms. He looked ready for a fistfight.

Even from the way Connolly stood there in the center of the dingy room, Clarke and Plunkett on either side of him, like seconds, Pearse at a table by the window, bent over a pencil like a scorekeeper, it was apparent that Connolly was now the man with authority. A surprise, since MacNeill was the chief of staff of the Volunteers, who far outnumbered Connolly's Citizen Army. Curry grasped instinctively that Pearse, removed at his table, had been undercut more than the others by the day's events.

MacNeill closed the door behind him. "What the hell happened?" He glared at Curry.

Curry still wasn't breathing right, and he hesitated. MacNeill misunderstood, thought Curry was panicked, and he grabbed his shoulder. "Damn it, man, tell us . . . !"

But it was MacNeill on the brink of panic, not Curry. Curry calmly removed MacNeill's hand from his shoulder. "I've come to make my report, Commandant, not to be caned."

"Give him room, MacNeill," Connolly barked. "Jesus, man, give him room!"

Curry sensed their tension and imagined how they'd been bickering while they waited for him. He glanced at Pearse, his one friend, who had yet to greet him or even look at him. Pearse's collar was firmly closed, his necktie securely knotted, his schoolmaster's dark suit perfectly creased. But the stern impression he made was not a matter of his clothing. Pearse was cloaked in his despair. Curry thought of the defeated band of Jesus' disciples on that Friday night in a shuttered upper room. But enough of that! he told himself. This was not a pious tableau.

"What exactly did Casement say?" Connolly asked.

"He said, it's off. The Germans reneged. There can be no rising."

"There's not another landing planned?" Clarke asked. "We thought perhaps tomorrow or—"

"Nothing!" Curry was abrupt. He looked from Clarke to Connolly to Plunkett and MacNeill. They were all waiting for him to explain the new strategy. Curry realized that they'd have embraced any new arrangement he chose to describe for them—a flotilla of dirigibles landing on the Aran Islands? What they didn't want was all he had. "The Rising must be canceled," Curry said. "Casement risked his life to tell us as much."

"We expect to hear from Washington," Plunkett began.

Again Curry was abrupt. "Don't. Washington has nothing to do with it. The invasion was always nine parts Casement's dream. If Casement has abandoned it, then it's over. Forget it. We're alone."

The leaders stared at Curry. No one could refute him. He spoke with the absolute conviction of a man who'd seen already what other men, like them, could only vaguely conjure. Curry had seen the beginning and the end of the great revolution. He was the one among them with authority now.

There was a kind of communal sigh as the officers implicitly registered the finality of Curry's report.

It had happened, then. The worst rumors were true. There would be no new arrangement, no alternative strategy. Nothing.

For a moment they stood awkwardly, facing away from each other, ignoring Pearse still, unable to think what to do next.

Then Plunkett whined, "But how did the British know?"

"We've been betrayed, obviously," Connolly said. "Perhaps the Germans learned we'd been compromised and they pulled back."

MacNeill protested. "Don't justify what the Germans have

done. We were fools to trust them. They've destroyed our best chance."

But Tom Clarke banged the wall. "We can't call it off now! The British will round us up in any case, and if they prevail in Europe, they'll turn their massive army against us. England will occupy us forever! But now, now she's vulnerable! England will never be this vulnerable again!"

Curry stared at Clarke, disbelieving, and he waited for the others to dismiss his lunatic reaction. But instead Connolly agreed. "We have the men. Everyone's ready. When we declare ourselves, we've still the Americans. The Americans will weigh in with us."

MacNeill, who'd seemed unstable before, was the one who shook his head. "Not once it's known we threw in with Germans."

Connolly waved impatiently. "What Germans? We deny it."

Curry thought, They haven't heard me. They don't know what really happened. He waved his hands and spoke now as if his experience had made him their equal. "You're not paying attention, Commandant. How do you deny the *Aud?* The British have the German freighter. I saw the gunboats take it away."

But Curry was the one who hadn't heard. Connolly sneered at him. "The *Aud* sank in a hundred feet of water this afternoon off Cobh. The captain put his crew in lifeboats, then blew his vessel up. The Germans want to deny this thing too, as who wouldn't?"

MacNeill was still shaking his head. "None of this matters." He stood. "We can't send our boys out into the streets to be gunned down. Casement's right and so is his man here. The Rising's off." He started to leave.

"Eoin, wait!" Connolly grabbed his arm. Though the labor leader was a burly man and MacNeill was goose-necked and frail-looking—his collars were always loose—MacNeill shook himself free.

"I've opposed this from the beginning. I knew it would come to no good and it has. Now I am ordering the Volunteers to go home."

"You can't! I refuse to allow it."

"You issue an order, Connolly, and see who obeys it. Apart from your Socialist hooligans, no one will. My order will be obeyed by ten thousand men." MacNeill looked at them all. "You're the ones with grand strategies and desperate maneuvers and the willingness to shed blood to no purpose. I'm the one with the men." At that MacNeill left the room. The others listened as the loud clomping of his feet on the stairs faded.

At last Pádraic Pearse stood up. To Curry he seemed strangely detached, a man removed from his own emotions, as he said with eerie calm, "We have set our faces on Jerusalem. It is the will of our Father that we go up."

Curry waited for the others to protest, but they didn't. Pearse was like a ghost to Curry, and it shook him to be the one to have to challenge him. "Pádraic, without MacNeill, without the Volunteers . . ."

Pearse looked at Curry as if he were a mulish pupil. "We have Dublin. Our men can take Dublin. And when we do, the Irish nation will rally to us."

"Pádraic, the British have men in Dublin too. It's their one stronghold. They'd slaughter us." Curry stared at Pearse, completely lost. Once this man had seemed possessed by reason itself. This was the man who was going to replace the emotionalism of pub talk with a realistic operation calculated not to purge the ancient feelings, but to succeed. Only the cold logic of his strategies had convinced Curry before. But this was no strategy. This was the blind mysticism of his play. "One man can free a people," he'd written, "as one Man redeemed the world."

Curry shuddered as he grasped what they'd come to. These

men would free their people by leading them out to die. And then he understood that, despite the elaborate veneer of military planning, of strategic alliance, of practical preparation, the Irish rising was from the beginning fated to be a bloody spasm of mystical hope.

What a fool I've been, he thought. Actually to have believed that this date was chosen because of the calendar of the tides. *Dies irae, dies illa.* He wanted to turn and follow MacNeill from the room. But he was held fast by the burning eyes of Pádraic Pearse.

"Who arrested Casement, Dan?"

And Curry heard the question, as Pearse wanted him to, as, Who is it who has betrayed me? He stepped back as if he'd been hit. He saw it all now, how he'd been used by both sides, how he'd so lacked a will of his own on which to stand that he'd repeatedly embraced the will of whoever he was with. And with what horror did he feel himself now preparing to do it again.

Pearse, before he was a teacher, had been a barrister, and he was staring at Curry not with the schoolmaster's hauteur, but with the lawyer's stark accusation.

"Who arrested Casement?" he demanded again.

"It was Tyrrell," Curry answered miserably. Yes, Tyrrell. The bastard had beaten him and, through him, Ireland.

Pearse nodded. "The woman's brother."

"Yes." Jane, Douglas, and himself, Curry thought. The unholy Trinity.

"And he let you go?"

"Yes."

"Why?"

"To warn you. To tell you what Casement said."

"To convince us to call the Rising off."

"Yes, but—"

"And you, Dan, what are you going to do?" Pearse put the question to him gently. And you, Simon Peter, who do you say that I am?

Thou art the Christ.

There was only one way for Dan Curry to establish his innocence—not of the crime of ambivalence now, but of treason—establish it not only with Pearse and the others, but with himself. Not my will—how easily it came back to him—but Thine.

"I'm with you, Commandant," he said.

19

In the beginning was the Word . . ." The priest proclaimed these opening lines of Saint John's Gospel at every mass said in Ireland or anywhere. ". . . and the Word was with God, and the Word was God."

And in Ireland it was as if that theology of the Word took root in a unique way, for no other nation had so staked its destiny, finally, on the power of the Word itself. No other nation launched its revolution believing that language might be enough.

But that was precisely the position, however implicit, of the men and women who gathered on that glorious spring day in the shadow of the massive columned portico of the General Post Office on Sackville Street. But then, no other nation had ever launched its revolution under the leadership not of military men or of merchants, but of poets.

Pearse had composed the proclamation himself, although it would be signed by seven men. Thomas MacDonagh and Joseph Plunkett were professional poets, but the others—Sean Mac-Diarmada, Thomas Clarke, James Connolly, and Eamon

Ceannt—were ennobled too by the literary mysticism that held sway in Ireland then. Say it well, they believed, and it will come to pass because God is not merely *with* the Word, but God *is* the Word. Yeats knew this about his fellows, and he had enshrined their sensibility at the Abbey. First their Church, then their theater, then their revolution all depended on the theology of tongues. God is a new language, the Church proclaimed at Pentecost. The new language, Yeats and his poets replied, is God. "Speak but the Word," they prayed, priests and poets alike, "and our unworthy souls shall be healed."

It was what they always did, speaking but the words, the words, the words.

But what else, finally, did the Irish ever have?

Pearse stood at noon on the highest step of the GPO, his supporters clustered about him, numbering a few more than a hundred. Half of them, like him, wore the heather green uniforms of the Volunteers, while the others wore the dark green of Connolly's ICA. For every one of them, more than a thousand Irishmen were fighting at that moment in France, wearing the muddy brown of the BEF.

The great boulevard before Pearse was nearly deserted because of the holiday, but what strollers there were passed by indifferently. Far above them, on the classical balustrade of the huge municipal building, the stone statues of mythic Irish warriors stared out over the city mutely.

Pearse unhunched his shoulders to make himself as large as what he was about to say. And with a voice that faltered at first, perhaps because of the language, he began, "*Poblacht NA H Eireann!*"

Oh no, Curry thought. He was shoulder to shoulder with the Republican soldiers in front of Pearse, and he too was in uniform. Not in Gaelic!

But immediately Pearse went on in English. "The Provisional Government of the Irish Republic to the people of Ireland!"

Pearse looked out at the foot traffic, but no one had stopped to listen yet. He spoke more loudly. "Irishmen and Irishwomen! In the name of God and of the dead generations from which she receives her old tradition of nationhood, Ireland, through us, summons her children to her flag and strikes for her freedom."

Still, the bowler-hatted men and the soberly gowned women were going on their ways, unaware that the earnest man with the high forehead and pale skin was speaking to them. A few ill-clothed urchins from the slums of the Liberties or of nearby Henrietta Street watched curiously, but with apparent incomprehension.

Pearse went on, nevertheless, with increasing fervor, for the Word had soothed him and he was sure now it would be heard. "Having organized and trained her manhood through her secret revolutionary organization, the Irish Republican Brotherhood, and through her open military organizations, the Irish Volunteers and the Irish Citizen Army; having patiently perfected her discipline; having resolutely waited for the right moment to reveal itself, she now seizes that moment and, supported by her exiled children in America and by gallant allies in Europe, but relying in the first on her own strength, she strikes in full confidence of victory."

At that moment an ill-armed force of less than fifteen hundred men and women were occupying strategic buildings, fourteen in all, elsewhere in the city. As Pearse continued reading the proclamation, which announced the formation of a Provisional Government, sporadic gunfire could be heard. Most of the rebels carried ancient pistols, little ammunition; some were armed only with the mythic Irish weapon, the pike.

Still Pearse read his proclamation as if that were the act that would accomplish their purpose. When he finished, he turned to James Connolly and shook his hand, then led the band of his supporters into the GPO, while behind them one of the few passersby who'd stopped to listen indulged himself in a first act of Irish freedom. He shouted that if they had their own republic now, they could do any damn thing they pleased, and he urinated in the street for all to see.

A group stormed Dublin Castle. Because the British stronghold was defended with a token force—the British guard was down because they'd taken MacNeill's order canceling the Rising as definitive—the group could have captured it, making something real of their revolution. But when the guns they fired actually killed the lone guard at the gate, they fled in panic. The British had taken the German threat seriously, but never the rebels', and this, reflected Sir Matthew as he watched from his window while they scattered, was why.

It was heartbreaking, but the men who'd seized the various undefended buildings were too exhilarated to feel that yet. After seven hundred years the dream of Irish heroes had become the dumb show of clowns. The massive confusion resulting from the two sets of orders—MacNeill's canceling and Pearse's summoning—kept all but a few revolutionaries home. Those who dared to act were therefore hopelessly outnumbered even by the thin British garrison, and their strategy of locking themselves inside the GPO, the Four Courts, the Imperial Hotel, Jacob's Biscuit Factory, and other buildings made them volunteer prisoners whom the British could dispose of at will. The theory, of course, was that the Word would be heard and have its effect. The Word may have been with God or may even have *been* God, but John goes on to say, also, that the "people did not know Him."

After reading the proclamation and securing their occupation of the GPO, Pearse and his band piled the desks, chairs, couches, shelves, and cabinets from the various offices into the street outside, forming the mythic revolutionary barricade to which the oppressed population of Dublin, and then all of Ireland, were supposed to rally. Hadn't the words of the proclamation claimed "the right of the people of Ireland to the ownership of Ireland"?

Well, the Word *was* heard and the people, led by the Liberties urchins, did rally. But not in the way that Pearse expected.

While the rebels watched helplessly, the people of Dublin, once they learned what was happening, came to the barricade in droves, not to man it, but to dismantle it; not out of opposition to the rebel cause, but to get the furniture. They carted away the desks, cabinets, and couches, which thenceforth would be the proud centerpieces of their dingy rooms.

"Jesus Christ!" Dan Curry said from his place by the story-high window in the main hall. Behind him, with a boisterous animated din, the officers of the revolution were establishing in separate clusters the various centers from which operations would be coordinated. Curry watched as the furniture barricade, piece by bloody piece, disappeared. The sight alarmed him, but Pearse and the others seemed indifferent to it.

Curry fingered the trigger of the pistol he'd been holding since they'd entered the GPO, but he didn't need it. He was posted as a sentry to watch for the first sign of the British reaction. But Sackville Street was crowded now with ordinary citizens—not only looters, but idling spectators. They could be seen muttering to each other that at last the bush-hatted Irish tin soldiers had begun to move. They were waiting for the police to come, and it struck Curry that they were like the crowds who went to steeplechases not out of love of the sport but to see horses fall and watch riders get crushed.

Curry reined his disdain. It behooves not the revolutionary to feel contempt toward those in whose behalf he acts. Still,

He'd watched only moments before when the first man to come into the post office after it was seized marched up to James Connolly not to volunteer but to buy a stamp. When Connolly told the stranger that stamps were not for sale because a new republic had been proclaimed, the man asked, "What the hell kind of republic is it that doesn't sell penny stamps?"

The first sign that someone was coming from the direction of Dublin Castle was the commotion across the street as the spectators craned, pointed, and began to vie for a better position from which to watch. Curry braced himself, wiped his gun hand free of perspiration, and prepared to sound the alarm. But what came into view was not a Crossley Tender or a phalanx of troops, but a farmer's wagon pulled by a pair of horses and carrying eight women, one of whom held up a hand-lettered sign that read CUMANN NA MBAN.

More than ninety women would participate in the Rising by its end, most of them members of the Women's Auxiliary. They had not been consulted about the Rising and they hadn't been asked to be part of it, but they were patriots too. They knew what contribution they could make, even if the men didn't. They presented themselves at the various outposts; at some they were simply turned away, as for example by Eamon de Valera at Boland's Mill. But mostly their sheer determination carried them past the first objections, and they served effectively as nurses, cooks, and messengers, although a few like Countess Marki-evicz found themselves pressed by circumstances into service as combatants. Despite the rhetoric of sexual equality found in Pearse's proclamation, most rebels, including Pearse himself, considered it unthinkable that women would take part in military action as such. The men were the soldiers as they were the vision-aries, and if the glory was to be mainly theirs, so was the sacrifice.

Curry watched the women gathering up their skirts to leap

off the wagon and begin to unload it. They carried steaming vats, baskets, sacks, and tins up the stairs of the post office. As one by one they disappeared from his view behind the stout Ionic columns, he felt an unexpected shock when he recognized the figure of the last woman in the line. Her face was obscured by the bag of flour she'd hoisted on her shoulder, but he knew her anyway, as surely as he knew the Rising was doomed.

He began to rush toward the entrance to make her go away, to *demand* that she go away, but then he stopped. He couldn't leave the window, his post. Curry realized with a further shock that if he failed to take his small responsibility seriously, then he would be just another of the buffoons who'd lost this battle before it began. He retraced the dozen steps until he was in the bright warm light of the afternoon sunshine again, but instead of looking out the window he stared across the vast, bustling hall, watching for Jane.

Of course he feared for her and couldn't stomach the thought of her being in such danger, but her presence in the GPO would pose another problem too. It would deprive him of the satisfaction he felt as a man who'd finally handed himself over to what was, after all, only the ancient Irish fate. By reminding him, simply in being there, of the other future he'd wanted for himself, she would force him up against the absurdity of the future they'd made inevitable. She would cause the transformation of his multiple misgivings and criticisms into what he had so far staved off—infinite regret.

But then the circle of his concern came around again. If she was in the GPO when the British moved against it, she would die.

Without a further thought to his duty as a sentry, he crossed the hall to the entrance and reached it just as Jane, behind the other women, came through.

"Jane!" He took the sack from her shoulder. Before she even spoke, he said, "You can't stay here."

Jane wasn't going to let him see how hurt she felt, not for anything. She knew they were not enacting a mythic lovers' drama now, that the Rising was real and its prospects were bleak. But it had never occurred to her that he would snub her at the door.

She turned away from him and followed the other women into the center of the hall, where they proceeded to set up a food line.

Curry had no choice but to follow her, because he was carrying the flour.

"Lieutenant Curry!" It was Connolly who barked at him. "Why aren't you at the window?"

Jane spared him the humiliation of watching as he put the flour sack down and sheepishly returned to his post. She knew he was looking back at her as he went, and suddenly she had an impulse to call out to him, Dan, I'm sorry! But he'd have misunderstood. He'd have thought she meant she was sorry she'd come to the GPO, sorry she'd joined the Rising, when all she meant was she was sorry her coming had made his situation more difficult than it was.

————

Someone had to bring him his stew and bread. It might as well be me, she thought. This was nearly an hour later. Everyone had gone through the food line but the sentries.

"Here you are, Lieutenant."

When he faced her, she couldn't read him. He took his plate impassively.

"Dan," she began quietly, "how could you imagine the

Rising should at last take place and I not be part of it, after all
we've been through?"

He looked up at her sharply. "Jane, it's a disaster. You stay
here and you're going to get killed."

"And you?"

Curry shrugged. "I'm like the poor bastards on the Western
Front. I've no choice in the matter."

"That's not so, Dan."

"But it is. You were hoping, no doubt, to see the glory of
Irish defiance in me. But I'm not made for martyrdom. If I was,
I'd never have left Maynooth." He made a sweeping gesture
across the great hall. "These are the martyrs, Jane. The saints
and poets and heroes. I've tried and tried to be one of them.
I've tried and tried to believe in what we're doing, but my faith
depended on the conviction that there was at least *some* chance
we'd succeed. There isn't. If there was a way for me to be gone
from here without the marks of cowardice and treason on my
forehead, I'd be on the train, you can count on that."

"Treason? What mark of treason?"

"The British knew every move we made in Tralee. Your
brother was waiting for us and he arrested Casement. Someone helped him. Naturally, the flag of Pádraic's mind blows
toward me."

"Because of me?"

Curry looked away from her.

"Dan, you don't think—"

"I don't know what to think, Jane. But you see my situation." He smiled grimly and faced her. "The only way for me
to prove my loyalty is to be here when the English come for us.
That would be enough, perhaps, unless, of course, your brother
was at the head of the column. If he was, Pearse would order
me to shoot him, just to see if I would do it."

Jane leaned back against the wall, averting her face because she didn't want him to see what pain was in it.

He touched her sleeve, sensing her emotion. "And Jane," he said softly, "I wouldn't do it."

"I know."

"And that's why I'm not meant to be here. And why I wish you weren't. I'm the pale shadow of a proper rebel." Curry looked across the hall toward Pearse, Connolly, and Clarke. The leaders carried themselves with martial swagger, giving orders, sending off dispatches, receiving reports with sage nods—altogether an impressive display of confidence, as if they knew something Curry didn't. Though, of course, it was the other way around.

Jane was watching them too. "Perhaps it's not as hopeless as you think. All over the city Republicans have taken buildings."

"But they're just waiting now, like us. Without proper weapons and many more forces, we can take no initiative."

"The Germans could still help us, couldn't they?"

"The Germans betrayed us, Jane."

"Then why would the proclamation pay tribute to 'our gallant allies in Europe'?"

Curry shrugged. "The copies were already printed. '*Quod Scripsi scripsi.*' 'What I have written I have written.'" He laughed bitterly. "That's what Pearse said when someone asked him about that line. He thought he was quoting Jesus, but it was Pontius Pilate who said those words, and he was referring to what he'd written on top of the cross."

Jane said nothing.

Curry forced himself to brighten. "Anyway, by having to postpone things, we got out from under the weight of English omens."

"What do you mean?"

"How like the Irish to schedule a revolution for Easter Day, not thinking what else it might be. *This* Easter Day was the birthday of William Shakespeare *and* the tercentenary of the day he died *and* the feast of Saint George, their militant patron. How could they lose?"

Jane smiled. "So what's today?"

"No idea." He watched his fellows moving about the hall. "For the rest of time, in Ireland at least, it will be the day that we did this."

Then he turned and faced the window. "I've a job here." He put his untouched plate on the sill.

The onlookers across the street were growing bored. Some had drifted off. The earlier gunfire from elsewhere in the city was replaced now by an eerie silence.

Jane began, "I came here, Dan, to do my part—"

He interrupted her. "Then do it. Don't give a thought to me."

"—but I also came to be with you. My thought was to be at your side. But if you don't want me here, I'll leave. If you tell me to go, I'll go."

He took both her hands in his. "Then for God's sake, go, Jane! I'm only saying it because I love you."

No matter what the other women felt about the self-aggrandizing "chivalry" of the rebels who shooed them back to safety, Jane felt the power of Dan's love, and it filled her with gratitude and a love for him that matched it. "I wouldn't leave you, Dan, no matter what you said, but for one thing." She looked away from him suddenly, then said in a whisper, "I'm carrying your child."

For a moment nothing happened.

Jane looked at him anxiously. She was relieved to watch the surprise that filled his face give way to pleasure, and when he took her into his arms, she allowed herself to feel at last her own deep longing. She needed the reassurance with which, simply by holding her then, he showered her.

"You see, darling," she said, her mouth at his ear, "I *can't* be without you."

He pulled back to look in her eyes. "For now you can. But I promise you, Jane, when it's time for you to deliver that child, I'll be there with you. I'll do everything I can to . . . to be there." To stay alive, he meant. He smiled happily, but he couldn't keep his fear from showing. "As if I needed another reason; but you've given it to me. A child! Oh, Jane, it fills my heart, what you've said." He put his hand shyly on her stomach. "But Christ, you're still so small."

She turned so that no one could see him touching her, and she pressed his hand. "That's because our baby is. We'll both get bigger."

"To think a child has to work free of these slim hips." Wonders of her body had struck him before, but never this one. He cast his eyes around the hall. "It'll be easier for us to work free of this building."

"I hope so."

"I know it will, Jane." He circled her waist and pulled her to him. "Suddenly you've made me certain that something good will come of all this. Oh woman, you've given me back my hope."

At once, in Jane's eyes, he was transformed from the dispirited, reluctant revolutionary back into that largehearted stranger dancing blithely across the polished Abbey lobby, and she felt a vast relief.

Since then, she'd come to know him as she'd known no other person. She'd seen past his panache and through his air of command to the softness in him, which he regarded as his weakness but she knew as the soul of his strength.

When she looked at Pearse and Clarke and Connolly, they seemed hard to her. Pearse particularly had a mean look about him, and though Jane barely knew him, she'd felt the chill of his coldness. Nora Guinan said those men carried dolmen stones in their Druid hearts. But Jane wondered. Were they all like Dan? Men with no real stones to hide behind and no real stones to hurl at their enemies and no real stones on which to stand? There was a core of softness in the Rising itself, and if that was its military problem, it was also, to Jane, its appeal. Even Pearse, tough and charismatic in public, was, she sensed, trembling below the surface. They all were. These men had nothing with which to protect themselves now but what their people gave them.

Beginning, in Dan's case, Jane thought, with me. She held him more tightly than she ever had before, to press him with her abundant life. Life, even more than hope, was what he needed now, and wasn't that lucky? The child quick in her body had quickened her. She would leave this place, yes, but she would work night and day to rally support for those left. Only the people can save these good men—the child had so expanded her sense of herself that she could think this—and we will!

———

Everything came to a halt in the center of Dublin. By Tuesday British troops from all over Ireland had arrived, and by early Wednesday their number had been doubled by reinforcements that crossed from England without harassment from German U-boats. The rebels were outnumbered twenty-to-one.

But the British strategy did not depend on soldiers. They'd learned on the Western Front to depend on their machines. The Irish had no way of anticipating what impact the trench war in France would have on them, but these British, unlike others against whom Fenians had hurled themselves, had the reflexes of a people who were fighting for their very existence. They set up howitzers in Trinity College and at sites ringing the heart of Dublin. They brought the gunboat *Helga* into the River Liffey. None of their positions was threatened. Yet they commenced the bombardment of Dublin on Tuesday night, April 25, a date on which something previously unthinkable in warfare began to happen. Artillery shells were not aimed at particular targets but at whole sections of the city. The shells were modern ones, high-explosive and incendiary. Thus Dublin has the distinction of having been the first fire-bombed city. George Bernard Shaw said that what the Germans accomplished over two years in shelling Ypres and Arras was nothing compared to what the British did to Dublin in four days. Fires were allowed to burn out of control. Looting went unchecked. The rebels had occupied only 14 buildings, but 179 buildings were totally destroyed. Everything east of Sackville Street as far as North Earl Street was leveled, and Sackville Street itself, one of the great boulevards in Europe, was reduced to wrecked buildings, smoldering rubble, and piles of broken masonry. It was not that the British lobbed their explosives without regard for civilian casualties but that civilian casualties was their objective. In four days there were thousands of them. The British response to the Dublin rebellion, in sum, was not aimed at the rebels but at Dublin, which had refused to support them.

Pearse and the others may have been prepared to sacrifice themselves, but not their city. After fleeing the blazing post office on Friday, they surrendered on Saturday, and by Sunday, the seventh day, the remains of all the rebel positions were in British hands. Eighteen hundred men, including Dan Curry, were arrested, along with seventy women, including those who'd brought food to the GPO and stayed, but not including Jane Tyrrell, who'd left.

Jane's first impulse early in the week had been to talk to

people about the Rising—to strangers in the street, to friends of her father, to her father himself, who'd come from Cragside to make her leave Dublin when he'd heard what was happening. She'd refused to leave, however, and when the British bombardment began, it was apparent that talking was beside the point. With Lady Gregory's approval and her father's help—if his muleheaded daughter wasn't leaving Dublin, neither was Sir Hugh—she converted the Merrion Square house into a makeshift hospital. She spent the week nursing the wounded and watching people die. Time and again she saw Father Kavanaugh, the priest from Saint Colum's in the Liberties, apply thumbprints of sacred chrism to the foreheads of the severely wounded. At night she held the candle for him, and once, so that the terrified old woman whose lung had been punctured by a shard of flying glass could see it in her last moments, Jane held the wall-sized crucifix in front of her until her arms ached. Still, it wasn't until the eerie calm of the cease-fire descended on the city late on Saturday that the full horror of what had happened hit her.

She walked from Merrion Square toward the center of Dublin, retracing the route she'd followed so happily on that first morning of her time at the Abbey. Saint Stephen's Green, the most elegant park in Ireland, looked now like pictures she'd seen of battlefields in France: trees uprooted, lawns cratered, paths blocked by the smoking hulks of burned-out automobiles. The footbridge over the swan lake, the bridge on which she'd first encountered Dan Curry, was collapsed. Only hours before Jane passed through the green, Countess Markievicz, commanding a pitiful force of barricaded Irish boy scouts, had kissed her pistol before handing it over to a British officer who hesitated because he considered it impossible that a woman had the authority to surrender.

As Jane passed Trinity College, she saw the vacant faces of

hundreds of Tommies sitting by their tents, smoking cigarettes with the impassive, brutal air of men who would do anything they were told, no matter what, no matter to whom. But the repugnance she felt toward them paled when, coming around a last corner, she was in sight of the Carlisle Bridge and what had been Sackville Street. She stood stock-still, staring across the Liffey at the devastation of the north side of Dublin. Her eye, in a function of its own panic, flickered as it sought something familiar on which to rest: the graceful rotunda of the Four Courts, the stolid buildings of quayside merchants, the rococo of the Metropole Hotel, where she'd stayed as a girl with her father. But they were gone. All gone.

And from the devastated General Post Office, its jagged walls looming, isolated in the ruins of Sackville Street, smoke poured as the last of its fires consumed themselves.

It was the sight of the GPO that undid her. The composure that had carried her through the sight of emergency amputations and the sound of death wails collapsed. She felt an intense pain in her womb, and as she ran toward the Carlisle Bridge, crying "Dan! Dan!," she clutched at her belly.

The bridge was barricaded. A contingent of British soldiers stood guard behind an overturned dairy wagon and an improvised pile of debris. Jane began to claw her way up the pyramid of jagged concrete, to climb over it, while the soldiers shouted at her to go back. One of them grabbed her, and she began to strike him wildly, crying now, "You monsters! You monsters!"

The soldier suffered her blows, as if he agreed, but the officer in charge pulled her roughly away.

Douglas! At first Jane thought it was her brother, but it wasn't.

"Go home, miss." He said. He had a mustache like Douglas's. "There's a curfew on. It's not safe."

"Where have you taken them?"

"Go home, miss. Don't concern yourself with it."

"Where!"

Her fury shocked him. "Kilmainham Jail," he answered.

It was more than a mile up the River Liffey, beyond Christ Church Cathedral and the Royal Hospital, to which she'd traveled daily that week for bandages and supplies. Now she ran the entire distance, though the pain she felt worsened. When she approached the jail, a stern, high-walled granite compound that she had passed repeatedly but had not noticed in all its hard ugliness, she heard the din of a crowd jeering and booing. At the gates of the jail were hundreds of people. The people of Dublin, she thought, at last! They are doing what I did, expressing their contempt for the brutal English, who've made a new Carthage of our city.

But she was only partly right. They were the people of Dublin, yes, but when she joined them she saw that a phalanx of captured rebels was being marched through their midst into the jail. The people, instead of crying "Monsters!" at the English, who'd destroyed the heart of Dublin, were shaking their fists at the Irish Volunteers, blaming *them* for what had happened, shouting, "Shoot the traitors! Bayonet the bastards!"

———

Like a woman walking in her sleep, Jane crossed through block after block of south Dublin without knowing where she was. A cloud of ash hung over the city and, unknown to her, it was that that burned her eyes. She walked, staring at the pavement stones, not seeing them. The deserted streets were narrow, winding, dark, and unfamiliar, and only when one of them opened on an unexpected view of the great spires of Saint Patrick's Cathedral did she realize she'd been wandering through the Liberties.

Without thinking she turned back into the heart of the Catholic slum, making for Saint Colum's. She went directly to it, as if now the mean district was her own.

Inside the dark, empty church the heavy aroma of wax, once so unfamiliar, reassured her. She slipped into a pew to kneel. After burying her face in the black of her hands for a time, she looked up. Her eyes went automatically to the flickering red sanctuary lamp, the sign that Christ was present. Nothing was left to her now, it seemed, but her exhaustion. But in Saint Colum's, beneath the gaze of the ravaged Christ, it felt like peace.

"Jane?"

The voice startled her, and when she felt a hand on her shoulder, she nearly screamed.

But when she saw it was Father Kavanaugh who'd slid into the pew next to her, she threw herself on him. The frail priest held her. He had seen this woman stand strong all week. He'd been in awe of her. But now he sensed how little she saved for herself. He wanted to say something that would console her, revive her, rekindle her spirit. But he could think of nothing.

Jane was the one who knew what she needed. The moment had come.

She pulled back from the priest's embrace and said, "Father, I want to be a Catholic."

Father Kavanaugh was startled and at first said nothing.

Jane said, "Please, Father, would you baptize me?"

Whether she was a Catholic or not had nothing to do with what the priest had been feeling for her, but he sensed at once the importance of her request. He said, "Of course I will. We can meet to—"

"Now! I mean now!"

Baptism apart from canonical procedure—for an adult, proper instruction, the filing of forms, the testimony of

sponsors—was permitted only in emergency. Father Kavanaugh read the woman's eyes, the record of what they'd seen. If this
was not an emergency, what was? "We'd need a witness," he said.

Jane placed both her hands on her stomach. "I have one,
the child of Dan Curry." She announced her pregnancy without shame, as without triumph. This child had simply changed
the meaning of her existence. No previous notion of shame or
triumph any longer applied.

"Oh, darling," the priest said. When he put his hand gently
yet firmly on her shoulder, she understood how Catholics could
confess to such men and call them "Father."

20

The story of the Irish rising reads like a litany of blunders that ran from the rebels' naïve embrace of self-interested German allies, through the disastrous eleventh-hour argument over whether to go forward, to the harebrained static strategy of occupying indefensible municipal buildings. The Irish committed blunders of practice—they kept orders indefinite as a way of throwing informers off-balance, but therefore never understood each other—and blunders of theory—the Irish Volunteers had constitutional politics but a revolutionary mission. Some blunders were ludicrous—the driver of a rebel car looking for the rendezvous point with the German invasion force took a wrong turn and drove off a pier into the sea, drowning himself and two other Volunteers. Some blunders were potentially decisive—the failure to take Dublin Castle and thereby capture Sir Matthew Nathan.

But all of the Irish blunders, even these, pale when compared to the great mistake the British made in the Rising's aftermath. On May 3, four days after he surrendered, Pádraic Pearse was marched to the wall of Kilmainham Jail and shot dead.

Over the next few days all of the other proclamation signatories were executed, as well as several rebel commanders. Maud Gonne's husband, John MacBride, was among those killed, as was a famous pacifist named Sheehy Skeffington, though he'd refused to join with the Rising. In all, ninety-seven rebels were condemned to death, including Countess Markievicz and Eamon de Valera.

The general officer commanding-in-chief, Irish command, was now Sir John Maxwell, who'd replaced General Friend on April 28 with orders to use any means necessary to suppress the rebellion as quickly as possible. He ordered the digging of a pit that would hold a hundred corpses. On May 12, James Connolly, though crippled by a gunshot wound above his ankle, was hauled before the firing squad in a chair. Even the Tommies who had to shoot him winced, since decency has always required that a man be healthy before you kill him. Thus the execution of Connolly seemed too brutal even for the war-hardened, and a storm of protest that had been building in Ireland and in England too since the executions had begun, broke over the British government.

The executions accomplished an act of political transubstantiation, turning a string of desperate, incompetent men whom Ireland herself had at first reviled, into the greatest heroes of her history. Jack Yeats said that if England had simply let the Sinn Feiners rot in jail, "Ireland would have pitied and loved and smiled at these men, knowing them to be mad fools. In the end they would have come to see that fools are the worst criminals."

Instead the fools were invested with martyrdom, and the mystical, messianic hope of Pádraic Pearse was fulfilled. Irish people poured into the streets of every large city and clamored for an end to the executions. In England, led by George Bernard Shaw, great figures like Sidney and Beatrice Webb, Conan

Doyle, Arnold Bennett, John Masefield, G. K. Chesterton, John Galsworthy, and Ben Tillett denounced the shootings and petitioned for clemency. Bishop O'Dwyer of Limerick, breaking the lock-step silence of Vatican-domineered prelates, condemned General Maxwell as wantonly cruel and declared that the executions had "outraged the conscience of the country." The British would simply have weathered all of this, however; they would have shrugged it off. What were the protests of Irish mobs, English bohemians, and trembling priests compared to the barrage of German shells they'd withstood now—behind a barrier of their sons' bodies—for nearly two years? But there was another reaction to the executions they could not ignore. Their ambassador, Sir Cecil Spring-Rice, reported from Washington that the Irish in America "have blood in their eyes when they look our way." Woodrow Wilson, who had no sympathy with the Irish, nevertheless secretly warned his cousin, a senior British official named Sir Henry Wilson, that the massive American intervention against Germany on which Britain was already counting would never take place, whatever else happened, if British justice was seen by Americans as a mere exercise in vengeance. The executions had to stop.

At that point in the war with Germany, no one in the upper circles of the British government doubted that the Entente was failing. The French losses by then at Verdun alone were counted in the hundreds of thousands. And the war of attrition had gone steadily on in the English sector, if less dramatically. The English knew they had to move decisively on the Western Front and soon, if a French defeat—and separate peace—was to be averted. Yet within a few weeks the Germans would stun England by defeating its grand fleet in the war's first, long-awaited full-scale sea battle off Jutland Bank, and immediately after that, on June 5, Field Marshal Lord Kitchener himself would die when his ship, the HMS *Hampshire*, was sunk.

So when faced with the prospect of American hostility because of Ireland—a matter of relative inconsequence if ever there was one—the government had no choice but to check its vindictive reaction. It was forced to suspend the executions—Connolly was the last of the rebels to be summarily shot—to commute the death sentences of other leaders, to replace the controversial Irish Executive members, though not General Maxwell, and even to order the freeing of the hundreds of Irish prisoners against whom legal cases were weak. Once more, as they had been doing now for seven hundred years, the British took a crucial set of decisions for Ireland with reference not to Ireland, but to events and reactions elsewhere. Their eyes were not on Dublin, much less on Galway or Cork, but on sections of the Bronx, on a stretch of water off Denmark, on fortresses along the River Meuse. To British perceptions Ireland was no better than a pesty insect one slaps down viciously or brushes off gently, depending on whether one's children are watching.

———

Douglas Tyrrell had accompanied the prisoner Casement to London, and he'd remained there since the beginning of May without posting. He had been reporting daily to the War Office, as required by his status as an officer held available, but he never received his orders. Each afternoon he returned from Whitehall to the house in Chelsea, where not even Pamela and the children could lift the deepening gloom he felt. Every able man in England was now engaged in the war effort. Douglas had a better sense than most of its horrors, but that did not free him from feeling wrongly spared. He had an officer's sense of exile because he was not with his men.

And as for Ireland, it frustrated him unspeakably to hear

reports of Maxwell's harsh measures and then of their quite predictable consequences. He shared the universal revulsion, and he knew what a mammoth miscalculation the executions had been. As an Irishman in the army, the brutal response to the half-baked Dublin revolution shamed him, but equally, as a veteran of the permanent panic of the Front, it did not surprise him. Both efforts, in Ireland and in France, seemed doomed, but all he wanted was a chance, nevertheless, to play a part in either one.

And the day after the shocking news of Lord Kitchener's death swept London, he got it.

At the War Office that morning the dispatching officer handed him his orders envelope. He opened it at once, aware of the tremble in his hands as he did so. Nothing in all the awful events of the war until then had seemed so ominous to him as Kitchener's death. He thought he was prepared for anything, but when he read his orders, he could not believe it. He was to report at once, neither to the Front nor to Dublin, but to the attorney general's chambers, a twenty-minute walk away.

The Law Courts had been at the center of his world for three years, but he rarely had occasion to go near there now. As Douglas walked up the Strand from Trafalgar Square, he tried to imagine what the attorney general could want with him. F. E. Smith, the son of a provincial lawyer, was a staunch Unionist who had been forced on Asquith by the Tories. He was the rare politician who'd made his first reputation at the bar, where he had made his mark as an extremely aggressive cross-examiner. Now he was the most flamboyant member of the Cabinet, often described as brilliant, but his opponents doubted the depth of his intelligence. His brains, they said, went to his head.

The Royal Courts had still been considered new in Douglas's day. Queen Victoria dedicated the building in 1882. But

it was a masterpiece of High Gothic architecture, and as soon
as one entered the Great Hall—with its soaring vaulted ceiling, the high pointed arches at the tops of stone pillars, the
huge leaded windows—it seemed like a fresh, airy version of
the Middle Ages. The Great Hall, its size, its architecture, its
stone floor, which amplified each footstep, its huge portraits
of red-robed Right Honorables, its bustling barristers in their
wigs, gowns, collars, and bands—it could all intimidate a man
and was intended to. But as Douglas crossed it, he reminded
himself that he and other students at the Inns had snuck into
the place at night to play eerie games of candle-lit badminton.

When he presented himself to the clerk in the outer room
of the attorney general's chambers, he was shown in at once.

Smith was at his desk, bent over a brief—Douglas saw the
purple ribbon lying beside the pile of papers—and he made no
move to greet Douglas. He felt the blast of the man's cold supe-
riority. Smith wasn't going to acknowledge Tyrrell until he read
through the paragraph, nor did he make a move to introduce
the man who was seated on the leather couch to Douglas's left.
But when Douglas glanced across, he recognized him at once.
It was his father's old enemy.

Carson.

Douglas drew himself up to stop in front of Smith's desk
and stared out the narrow Gothic window behind him. He
stifled his resentment against Smith, but he was at the mercy
of the repugnance he felt for Carson, sitting there impassively,
smugly. Such negative feelings might have begun as an inher-
itance from his father, but they were now very much his own.
The Unionists, by making the effective repeal of Home Rule the
price of their support for the war, had demeaned every soldier
killed in it. They had made the revolution of Irish nationalists
inevitable. He remembered Carson's glib, heartless words from

the conscription debate in Parliament—"The necessary supply of heroes . . ."—and started to hate him even more.

"Thank you for coming, Major," Smith said absently, still reading. He spoke with the nasal artifice of a man who has acquired even the mode of his articulation.

After a further moment, he looked up and indicated Carson with a wave of his hand. "You know Sir Edward Carson, I believe."

"No, sir. We've never met."

But now Carson stood and offered Tyrrell his hand. He was as large a man as Smith and as well tailored, although he was considerably older. A pair of pseudo-bluebloods, Douglas thought, in flight from their backwater roots.

"Major Tyrrell, how do you do?" Carson's grip was strong, and he had a politician's eye, not a prosecutor's. It was direct and, when he wanted it to be, friendly. Douglas was surprised at the apparent sincerity with which he then said, "Your father and I were good friends." For an instant Carson paused, as if to give Douglas an opportunity to rebut the claim.

Douglas recalled how Carson, as a young Irish M.P. from Dublin, had stunned Parliament by turning against Parnell. When nearly everyone else in the House of Commons embraced the notion of Home Rule for Ireland, and when even Gladstone made it a priority for his party, Carson swore he would stop at nothing to oppose it, and he did. It was even said that Carson had been the one to prompt Kitty O'Shea's weak-kneed husband to sue her for divorce and cite Parnell in the proceedings. When that flame flared, Carson fanned it. He was a known philanderer—Jennie Churchill was just one of his conquests—yet he gave a speech worthy of any priest, denouncing Parnell's immorality. At that, Sir Hugh Tyrrell had made a powerful rebuttal, famous for its irony, in which he praised the Tories for their newfound chastity. He turned Carson's anti-Home Rule slogan back on them by allowing that now, with their refreshed moral sensitivity, they could find a home in Rome after all. The real irony, of course, was that Carson and the priests he hated with such vehemence did, in that instance, collaborate. Their movement carried when Gladstone abandoned Parnell. Douglas had understood, even as a seven-year-old boy, when his family moved back from London to Cragside, that his father had been defeated by a powerful enemy. And here was that enemy now, claiming to have been his friend.

"How is your father?"

"Well, Sir Edward. Thank you."

"Pray, give him my warm regards, would you?"

"Certainly, sir."

Carson sat on the couch again, but made no move to invite Douglas to join him. Smith snapped a finger, and a man whom Douglas had failed to notice appeared from a corner behind him carrying a stiff-backed chair. He placed it for Douglas. Then the man brought forward a chair of his own to the far edge of Smith's broad desk, where he sat, opened a portfolio, and prepared to record the minutes.

Finally, Smith said, "Major Tyrrell, I'm told you were a barrister in civil life."

"Yes, sir."

"And you read law at . . . ?"

"Here, sir. Lincoln's Inn."

"Ah, yet . . ." Smith reached for a folder that lay beside the scattered pages of the legal brief he'd been reading. He opened it and eyed the topmost page—Tyrrell's dossier, obviously. "You applied to the Irish bar, not English."

"I knew my practice would be in Ireland, sir."

Douglas watched Smith carefully. Only a paranoid Unionist

would have snagged a thread on such a detail. Those men were
always looking for signs of disloyalty in their compatriots.
Having completed a course of legal initiation in Britain's most
prestigious chambers, was it a sign of Tyrrell's insolence that
he'd returned to the remotest province in Ireland? Or was it,
perversely, ambition? Such provinces still sent members to Parliament. It amused Douglas, watching the man worry the small
bone of a legal career that hadn't gotten off the ground. How
could he have explained to the pinch-faced attorney general
that he'd read the law in London instead of Dublin in order
to be near a girl with whom he'd fallen in love? A girl—Douglas looked at Carson—whom he'd married and to whom he'd
never been unfaithful.

Smith said at last, "Well, London or Dublin, it's neither
here nor there. The court's subpoena carries the same weight
in either place."

"Subpoena, sir?"

"You are aware of the binding force of subpoena?"

"Certainly." On entering the room Douglas had felt mystified; now he felt alarmed.

Smith put his dossier aside, exposing a formal-looking folded
document that was closed with a waxen seal. Smith picked it up.

Carson raised a hand toward his colleague. "A moment, Mr.
Smith." He may have been seated to the side, but it was clear
suddenly that Carson's authority needed no desk to bolster it,
and no minister's portfolio either. When Asquith had refused to
appoint Carson himself to the office of attorney general on the
grounds that the laws of the realm could not be administered by
a man sworn to oppose the Home Rule Act—a measure already
passed—Carson had simply put forward Smith. Now he went
on smoothly, as if he was in charge of these proceedings, and his
protégé did not object. "No compulsion necessary here. Major

Tyrrell is an honorable man and does his duty when it's shown to him. Not so, Major?"

Douglas imagined Carson, obsequious and ingratiating, making such a statement to Kitty O'Shea's husband. He said nothing, but he was aware of the pulsing in his veins. He was alert, like prey that hears the hunter before seeing him.

Carson seemed unfazed by Tyrrell's silence. "Let me explain. You know better than anyone what a disaster for our nation has unfolded in Ireland. As Irishmen you and I feel acutely the shame of what has happened."

Douglas was surprised to hear Carson describe such a feeling, but as he went on it was clear that he was referring not to the shame of the brutal English reaction, but the prior shame of the Irish rebellion.

"And as members of His Majesty's forces, you in your noble capacity, me in my humble one, we understand what a dastardly blow has been struck, a knife in the back of every man who serves our cause on the Western Front."

Carson paused dramatically. Douglas realized that the man had spent his whole adult life giving speeches, and he was giving one now.

"And in the last month, owing to rank incompetence and a pitiful failure of nerve"—that would be Asquith's suspension of the executions, Douglas surmised—"the world has failed utterly to grasp the meaning of what happened in Ireland. The government has failed utterly to make apparent for all to see that the heinous crimes enacted in the most hallowed buildings of my own Dublin were, before they were crimes of the Sinn Fein, crimes of the Hun. It's acknowledged even in their notorious proclamation: '. . . supported,' it said, '. . . by gallant allies in Europe'! Whom do Americans think that refers to, gypsies? Why are the 'Sin Feigners' seen now as Irish patriots when they were merely instruments of

a foul German plot to invade our shores? And to turn the poor,
unthinking peasantry against their Crown, which has always been
their best defender! You know this better than anyone—Germans
inspired the tragic events of Easter past, not Irishmen. Therefore,
anyone who thinks well of these events is thinking well of the
oppressor of small nations and the user of poison gas."

"*We* use poison gas, Sir Edward." Douglas spoke firmly.

But Carson seemed not to hear his statement. "And that is
why we have brought you here." Abruptly he stopped talking
and looked across at the attorney general.

Smith's voice, in comparison to Carson's, was lacking in resonance and vigor, but its undertone of resolve was still striking.
"It behooves the government to draw attention to the facts of
German involvement in the rebellion. In America, owing to the
hysteria of Hibernian politicians, that man Pearse is regarded
now as having sprung whole from the heart of Daniel O'Con-
nell, and his rebellion is already revered as belonging to the
tradition of ancient Gaelic self-assertion when it is nothing of
the sort. We must publicize the provenance of this movement.
We must expose its tracks back to Berlin, where it began."

Carson fidgeted in his corner of the couch. "It would have
been easier if we'd prevented the scuttling of the German arms
ship. The *Aud* should have been boarded at once and her captain
shackled."

Douglas was amazed, as if one act of political transubstantiation—turning fools into heroes by martyring them—required
another—turning a revolution, for which Americans, who had a
Wolfe Tone of their own in Thomas Jefferson, felt innate sympathy, into a new reason they should come to Britain's aid. But he
realized at once that Carson and Smith, however much they were
motivated by partisan concerns, were right. The German spon-
sorship of the Irish insurrection had prevented Tyrrell himself

from feeling any sympathy for it whatsoever, and he was no Unionist. And if Americans could be made to understand that the German objective had been an Irish U-boat base poised to strike across the reaches of the North Atlantic, then even the Sons of Erin among them might disavow the Rising too.

Still, this was the politicians' problem. What had it to do with him?

Smith soon began to explain. "His Majesty's government proposes forthwith to bring to trial at the Old Bailey the German agents responsible for this gross sedition. You"—he pushed the folded, sealed document across the table to Tyrrell—"will be called to give evidence."

Douglas stood, stepped to the desk, picked up the document, cracked the seal and read it.

Then Smith pushed a second paper toward him, unfolded and unsealed, a copy of the bill of indictment. Douglas read it without picking it up. The page was crowded with cramped printing, but toward the bottom, standing out in bold Gothic letters, were the words "High Treason Without The Realm of England." Below those, in similar script, were two names: Roger Casement and Daniel Curry.

"Why Curry?" Douglas asked.

Smith fingered the dossier and said coldly, "Because you identified him in your report as being Casement's accomplice at the internment camp in Trier."

"Not in my report, sir. I did not know his name at that point." Douglas's mind was working carefully now. He had put nothing in writing linking Curry to Casement. He looked briefly at the clerk at the end of the table, who was busy making notes. He thought at once of his old Lincoln's Inn pupil master, Engleman. He would know how to handle this. But Douglas remembered that even he was at the Front, or dead.

Carson said, "Curry is the less notorious, of course. Casement has betrayed his class, his service, the honors done him, his native Ulster, *and* his king. But he is an eccentric man and not typical of those who took part in the rebellion. He was not formally associated with Sinn Fein or any of the other seditionist groups. Irishmen will say he didn't represent them, indeed that as a knighted Protestant, former servant of the Crown, his treason was his alone." Carson sneered. "If it comes out that he is a homosexual, as he is, they will say that proves it. This man Curry, on the other hand, comes right from the midst of these people, a Dublin slum dweller, a Catholic who studied at Maynooth, an actor in the Abbey Theatre, a man intimate not only with revolutionists like Pearse but with all stripes of nationalists from Lady Gregory to—"

"—the daughter of Sir Hugh Tyrrell." Douglas had to suppress his anger. Curry, as they all knew, was no homosexual.

Carson stared at him bluntly. "That is not our concern with Curry, Major, and it shouldn't be yours. The point is, the man accompanied Casement. Is that not so? He was present at the attempted rendezvous with Casement on the Bay of Tralee. Is *that* not so?"

"I made no report about his presence in Tralee."

Smith slid a page to his clerk, who passed it along to Carson. Carson glanced at it and said, "We have testimony of a sergeant of the Royal Irish Constabulary placing Curry at the scene of your arrest of Casement in Tralee. Do you deny it?"

"No, sir."

"You affirm it, then?"

Douglas said nothing, but he felt the stiff parchment of the subpoena in his hands as something hot suddenly, something to be rid of. If not Engleman, he thought, who?

Carson stood and crossed to Smith's desk, casually leaning

against it. "Major, I understand your trouble here. You have personal reasons for feeling a certain reluctance. We can all sympathize with personal reasons. But Curry is the link between Casement and Pearse. Curry is the link between German intrigue and Irish sedition. He may not have been an instigator either in Berlin or Dublin, but he was at the center of the cabal that bound them together. Surely you see that. Surely you appreciate the importance of making a case against him."

"What about Bailey, the man who was put ashore with Casement from the German U-boat? He's an Irish Catholic. He's a Sinn Feiner. He'd been in Germany with Casement since Curry returned. Why not bring him to trial?" Instead of Curry, was Tyrrell's meaning.

Carson looked quickly at Smith, but didn't answer. Then Douglas understood: Bailey would be giving evidence to the attorney general's prosecutors. That was an acceptable form of treason, of course. From England's point of view it was Ireland's great virtue, how willing her sons so often were to betray each other. Douglas said, "So you have Bailey's testimony against Casement. You need mine only against Curry." He laughed. "But I would testify gladly against Casement. He dishonored my men. There's no question of his treason."

"And is there, in your mind, Major, of Daniel Curry's?"

Now when Douglas did not answer, the old principle of law applied. He could hear Engleman declaiming it: silence means assent. Of course Curry was guilty, and of course using him to link Pearse with Casement was essential, and of course the combined effect of British jurisprudence and British propaganda—from his time on the home front Douglas had learned that the publicists alone won campaigns in this war—would be to make crucial American support more likely instead of less. And how could Douglas refuse to be part of that? It did not matter that he hated the scheme and the men behind it, and that he loved the one person his testimony would destroy. He looked at the subpoena again but knew that, however he might justify it, he had no choice but to obey.

"I will expect you to prepare your testimony in consultation with my prosecutors." Smith stared at him blankly.

"When does the trial begin?" Douglas asked.

"June 26, less than three weeks."

Douglas faced Carson, but Carson looked away, as if it embarrassed him to have done this, as once it must have embarrassed him to throw open the door of another man's bedroom. He said, "I will arrange with your superiors to have you permanently assigned to duties in the War Office."

Was this to be his reward? He would not have to return to the Front? What had been O'Shea's reward? he wondered. Despite himself, though, he felt relieved at that, and if he had rewards coming, he wanted one more. "I should like to apply for a short home leave. It would be better for my family . . ." How could he possibly explain this to Jane or to his father? But how could he not? Could he let them read of it in the tabloids? ". . . if I prepared them myself for what will happen."

Carson looked at Smith, who nodded. Carson said, "I'll arrange it. Report to the attorney general in one week."

"Yes, Sir Edward," he said and saluted. But once through the door, he couldn't help but feel that he had damned himself.

———

At the station in Gort he hired a phaeton, and as they set out into the green Burren of his childhood, he was moved by the beauty of the glorious June day, by the feel of the reins in his hand, and by Pamela's presence at his side. It hadn't been his notion that she should accompany him to Cragside, but she'd insisted. He had not discussed the interview with her, but he knew she sensed that painful business was bringing him home.

They came to the road that would have taken them to Coole Park, and Douglas stopped the carriage. He and Pamela sat in silence, looking off toward the place where they had met a full decade before. He laughed. "I thought you were Irish when I first saw you, remember? An Irish beauty, I thought, displayed like a faerie queen against the Connemara hills." They laughed together then, hard. How her naked ankles had smitten him!

He leaned to kiss her, and he said, suddenly serious, "I've come here to tell my father and Jane something terrible. I should begin by telling you."

"What?"

"Carson and Smith are bringing Dan Curry to trial for treason—"

"I thought the rebels were to be released—"

He pressed her arm. "Don't interrupt me, Pamela. They're bringing him to trial and they expect me to testify against him."

"You! But how could they ask you to do that? Don't they know—"

"Of course they know. My relationship through Jane to Curry is the talk of Whitehall." He laughed bitterly. "What they don't dare do to Ireland, they want to do to my sister's man. She'll hate me for it, Pamela." Douglas put his hand in her hair. His surge of love for his wife was an instructive feeling at that moment. "My only hope is that what she feels for Curry is less than I feel for you, that someday she will meet someone else whose love will let her forget, let her forgive me for sending the man to his death."

"Carson's the one doing that, Douglas, not you."

He shook his head. "Without my testimony they have nothing.

An RIC sergeant puts him on Banna Strand, but doing no worse than the thousand prisoners they've already determined to set free. On the contrary, he could have shot me, but didn't. A paucity of evidence wouldn't stop them, of course, except the Americans will be watching, which is the point. The Americans must be convinced. Without my testimony they would have to let him go."

Pamela stared at him, unable to speak. Had she no voice of her own, finally? Horror upon horror until this. She saw perfectly what Douglas had to do and, because she knew what it would mean, she could not say it.

He looked away. "I don't know whom I dread seeing more, my father or Jane."

Pamela, by the fiercest will of her life, said, "It will destroy them, Douglas. You're right. But first, if you do this, it will destroy you."

He faced her, a stony look in his eyes. "Why do you say 'if'? Do you think I've a choice in the matter?"

"Of course you do."

"And?"

Pamela wanted to drop her eyes, to flee what she saw so plainly in his—the fear, the pain, and how he loathed himself. She held his gaze, however, and said simply, "You should choose Jane over Carson."

"But what of England? Don't you see, it's larger now than my family. Of course I hate Carson, but he's right. Curry is a traitor! And his trial with Casement can bring America into the war for us and we—"

"Oh, Douglas, stop! Stop! All I know is what it will do to you if you refuse to stand for Jane."

He was amazed at his wife and showed it. "But this runs counter to everything you've said. You *hate* the Irish, Pamela."

"How can you say that when I so love you? It's you I'm here

for, Douglas. No one else." She embraced him and felt him release the hold he had on himself.

He said, "Then you're with me no matter what I do?"

"Of course, darling. Of course." She held him in silence then, moved that at last he was the one receiving.

The horses grew impatient and their skittishness broke the spell. Douglas sat upright and, without looking at Pamela again, he snapped the reins. The carriage jolted off, leaving behind the road to Coole Park.

At Cragside Douglas pulled the pair of horses up in front of the great house. For a moment he simply sat there looking at the place, enthralled with the simple grandeur of the Palladian design, the balance of hard rectangular lines and gentle curves by which the rough gray stone had been made to seem almost alive. The house was the perfect expression of his family's love of order and of its self-respect. As such, it suddenly seemed the opposite of what he'd become. The house had never seemed more beautiful, but also never less his.

He turned away from it, and as he leapt free from the carriage his eyes went automatically to the distant sea, a deep rich blue against which he saw the small figure of a woman standing alone by the cliff's edge. He had no capacity to postpone facing her.

As he took Pamela's hand to help her down, he said, "Greet my father, would you? I'll be back shortly."

He crossed the broad field, taking the wind full in the face and remembering how, as a boy of ten, he'd played there with his infant sister. In those days the gentle slope had been a well-maintained green carpet, not a pasture dotted with wild flowers. He remembered rolling over and over like a runaway log, with the baby girl protected in the shell of his arms. He had felt responsible for her. She had squealed with pleasure, trusting him absolutely. It was then, in relation to her, that he had understood that he was made to care for another person. What joy that knowledge filled him with, and how it had shaped him ever since. The man he was as a husband to his wife, as a father to his children, as an officer to his men, was the fulfillment of the brother he'd been to his sister.

She was facing away and did not see him coming. A light knitted shawl was wrapped loosely around her shoulders, and it covered her to below her waist. The wind tugged at it, swept her dress up from her ankles, feathered her hair, and carried the scent of her cologne back to him.

Why, he wondered suddenly, wasn't she in Dublin agitating with the other women for the quick release of their men? Did she know that Curry had been secretly taken from Kilmainham Jail to Pentonville Prison in London, where Casement was? Wouldn't she have gone to London herself?

"Jane!"

She faced him.

And he saw that she was pregnant.

As if nothing had come between that moment and the moment more than twenty years before when she had rolled inside his safe embrace across the lawn that sloped to the sea, he went to her and took her into the shell of his arms. She fell against him at once and wept.

When at last he spoke, it was to declare himself. "I've come to tell you, Jane, that I will do everything I can to make them set him free."

———

Two days later Douglas returned to the attorney general's chambers, but without having announced himself. This time Pamela insisted on coming. She alone knew the measure of his dilemma. But how could he stand before Carson and Smith now in the company of his wife? That would do, perhaps, if he had an Irish Catholic's taste for martyrdom, but he was hoping to avoid an act of open defiance. He'd been subpoenaed, after all. His purpose was to press the case for an altered course, a barrister's case. Pamela would wait for him where barristers' wives waited, in the gardens of the Inns of Court.

Smith kept him waiting in turn. Douglas guessed that he'd have become alarmed and sent for Carson, and he was right. What surprised him when the clerk finally showed him into the attorney general's chambers was the presence of a third man, a stocky, hollow-eyed, weary-looking general officer. It was Maxwell. He was sitting at Smith's side at the broad desk. As before, Carson was on the couch, since his position, of course, was purely unofficial.

General Maxwell had been summoned from Dublin to London by Asquith to make his case before the American ambassador for the brutality of his response to the Rising. Obviously, that case depended on proving the German link. No one could object to the use of extreme measures against a German-sponsored adventure in Dublin, given what measures were taken for granted by then in France.

When Tyrrell saluted, Maxwell returned it, but Carson and Smith only stared at him. The attorney general had his portfolio in front of him again, squared with the edge of the desk as before, as if he hadn't moved it in four days.

"Thank you for seeing me," Douglas began. "I regret troubling you in this way, but I was afraid my question would not wait."

"Your question, Major?" Smith tilted his head slightly, like a dog.

"My lord, I think it's a mistake to bring Curry to trial.

Casement's another matter, but Curry can't be guilty of treason. Whatever he did, he acted out of loyalty to his own nation.
He is not bound as Casement is by an oath of allegiance. No
English court will deny the primacy of his Irish citizenship. If
his attorneys define the Easter events as an act of war between
one nation and another, as I'm sure they will, then Curry can
hardly be guilty of treason. Guilty of other crimes, no doubt,
but not treason. Even if we establish his collusion with German
agents, that may prove to be in the jury's mind equivalent
to England's collusion with Russia—nothing to boast of, but
necessary in the effort against a common enemy. The much
stronger case against Casement is jeopardized by joining it
with Curry's."

Smith said nothing. He glanced at Carson, who cleared his
throat dramatically to say, "I take it, Major, that you saw your
sister. Or was it your father?"

"I'm making a point of law, sir."

Carson made a show of looking back at the attorney general.

Smith said, "We will note the point of law, Major."

And then there was silence. Maxwell looked from man to
man, bewildered. He was unaccustomed to proceeding so indi-
rectly. These men spoke in curves, not straight lines.

Douglas was afraid that the meeting would end, that he
would have been so easily turned aside. He said, "Before you
make the indictments public, you should take into account,
gentlemen, that I am not prepared to offer testimony in the
case of Daniel Curry."

Smith leaned forward. "You are prepared to defy the court's
order?"

"By no means, sir. But I have never satisfied a qualm of
conscience as to the identity of the man I saw with Casement
in Trier. The conditions under which we were being held by the

Germans did not make for the most lucid state of mind, if you receive my meaning, sir."

"You are prepared to assert this qualm under oath?"

"It is because of my oath, sir, that I feel I must assert it." Douglas had never felt so calm before in his life. So this was what it was to speak a naked lie. "And I knew my testimony was central to the Crown's case against Curry, and that is why I felt obliged to come before you now."

Smith looked first at Carson, then at Maxwell. He nodded to the general, a tacit handing over of jurisdiction. General Maxwell cleared his throat. "On another matter, Major, it is my duty to inform you that I have received from the judge advocate general a recommendation that you be brought before His Majesty's court-martial on the charge of lending aid and comfort to the enemy in the course of armed engagement."

"A charge of . . . ?" It was a blow from a blind side, and it staggered Douglas. He'd been prepared to deal with accusations of insubordination or contempt of court. ". . . But that's treason!"

"Indeed so," Smith said. He opened his portfolio and slid a single piece of paper toward Douglas.

It was a formal affidavit, sealed and signed by Sergeant Michael Costello, his driver at Tralee. "But this says I released an enemy prisoner and ordered subordinates who could have killed or apprehended him to allow him to escape."

"That's correct."

"Who?"

"Curry, of course."

"But I wasn't *releasing* him! He was going back to Dublin with Casement's message, to call the Rising off."

"And was it called off?"

"No, but—"

"Enough!" Carson's authority was absolute. It was possible to imagine that everything Irish nationlists said of him was true. He faced Maxwell. "What is the penalty if a man is found guilty of such charges?"

"Death by firing squad."

Carson looked at Douglas. "And your qualm now, Major?"

Douglas was staring at the commanding general for Ireland, the man who'd reduced the heart of Dublin to rubble and who'd proposed to solve the Irish problem with a mass grave. Douglas said, "No one in the British army has qualms, Sir Edward." He faced Carson. "Now I realize that I was wrong about Casement too. I cannot testify against either of them."

21

Pamela waited at the Middle Temple Garden, where she'd waited for him as a girl. Women had not been and were still not allowed through the cloistered archways of the Inns, not even as clerks, and the only way they gained admittance to the High Court was as defendants.

Nothing had changed. Victoria Embankment on the Thames and the ancient brick buildings of Crown-Office Row and King's Bench Walk, each with its *bas relief* pediment, formed the far boundaries of the living island in which she strolled. The paths were rigidly edged. The grass was shaved smooth as a man's chin, like a bowling green. In the center of the garden and surrounding it were hedges of rampant rosebushes. In front of a large trellis over which roses crawled profusely was a weathered brass plaque mounted on a waist-high pedestal. Pamela stopped to read it as she had a decade before, and as others had, perhaps, for centuries. "According to Wm Shakespeare," it read, "the War of the Roses began with the plucking of the Red and White roses in this garden in 1430."

A war of roses? Why hadn't the absurdity of such a notion

struck her when she'd stood there before, or when she'd first heard of the war as a schoolgirl? Weren't roses the opposite of war? Wasn't that the point of the compulsive, endless ordering a gardener does? She let her eye drift to the flowers themselves. The red, she thought, and the white. The flowers were equally beautiful to her. Without knowing it, had she chosen between them? Is that what they wanted Douglas to do? But these were questions she could not answer. The War of the Roses was a series of bloody, sectarian struggles. Why, then, was it remembered in the romance of history as noble, grand, an English triumph, like Shakespeare?

She turned away from the plaque and its trellis, and strolled the paths of the garden. Eventually she sat on one of the prim benches.

During the lunch hour, for the rare sun, barristers diverted through the garden in earnest conversation. Some of them carried bundles of lawbooks, belted in white straps, over their shoulders. They ignored Pamela and the few other wives who waited there.

It had been nearly three hours. It might have embarrassed her. Handsomely coiffed, well dressed, physically self-possessed women like her were never kept waiting for such a length of time. They were never seen to occupy a bench seat, alone for hours. Yet embarrassment wasn't what she felt, not at all.

The red and white, she thought. How absurd to fight a war for roses. Yet what was the present war in Europe for? And now the war in Ireland? It amazed her, now that the recognition swept over her, that she understood neither. She hadn't a clue as to why all those men were dying. Yet her husband was across the Strand now, having to declare himself.

Why? And where was he? She looked about constantly, hoping to see him coming at her, grinning like a law student, his own books on a strap across his shoulder, running to go off with her to The Lyons Corner House for tea.

What she felt was panic. She couldn't remain where she was, yet how could she intrude upon the men? Douglas had allowed her to come this far only because she'd insisted. And why had she insisted if not out of some instinctive foreknowledge that he would need her?

But she had not expected, really, to be faced with this decision. Should she remain where she was until, say, the settlement-house workers came for her? Should she return to Chelsea and tell her mother, as she always did, that everything was fine? Or should she leave this garden, cross through Christopher Wren's famous arch, and enter the forbidden—literally "barred"—sanctuary of the Royal Courts from which men, and men only, had been administering justice—as down the road they'd been fighting their wars—for centuries?

Pamela Tyrrell stood up. She was a woman in her prime—intelligent, well bred, an exemplary daughter, wife, and mother. She was devoted to all that was associated with the best of her kind. Yet she had and could expect to have no relationship whatever to the central events not only of her time, but of her personal life. The brutal public sphere now tyrannized the private. As one of the still unenfranchised, she hadn't even a vote in the process that managed events in the larger world. As a civilian in London at the mercy of a censored press, she had no vantage from which to view them. Yet those events, whatever they had done to the nations of Europe, had already drowned her father. They threatened now—this was the fear that overwhelmed at last her inbred inhibition—to take her husband.

She left the garden, crossing into the narrow, cobbled passage of Middle Temple Lane, cutting through the warren of Inns and Courts, of Pump Court, Essex, Brick, Elm, and Mitre, passing the Cloisters, and finally crossing the Strand to the Royal Courts themselves. But as she did, she felt nothing but the dull ache of her worry. Certainly, she felt no exhilaration to be crossing a border, any more than any of the war-emancipated women did. What pleasure is there to be had in the destruction of such barriers when, previously, they were hardly regarded as such, and when their destruction is the result of the prior destruction of nearly everything one values? Such events caused a homefront version of shell shock, a kind of, yes, amnesia. Pamela Tyrrell was a woman who had, as the Tories were always saying about the suffragettes, forgotten her place. Her place was in the garden where the War of the Roses had begun.

Remarkably, no one stopped her as she entered the building. The vast Gothic hall seemed at once like a church to her, with its arched windows and towering vaulted ceiling. But instead of worshipers sitting quietly, men crossed it impatiently, carrying their books, wearing their wigs, their gowns flaring behind them. Some eyed her openly, but perhaps because she matched their officious airs with one of her own, no one addressed her. She walked the length of the Great Hall, past the huge portraits of the former chief justices and attorneys general, and she continued right up the stairs at its far end. If this had been a church, these would have been the stairs to the inner sanctum to which no lay person, much less a woman, would be admitted. Yet still no one stopped her.

The sign said CROWN OFFICES, and she pushed through the door as if she did so every day. She followed the corridors far enough into the massive building to be sure she could not be easily shown outside again, and only then stopped a short clerk who was carrying a wire basket full of purple-ribboned folders.

"I'm looking for the attorney general's chambers," she said briskly, and he, stuttering slightly, directed her to them.

She presented herself to Smith's chief clerk, the man who'd sat at the corner of Smith's desk taking notes. Now he was at his own desk in the outer office, a paneled room off a main corridor. It was furnished with, in addition to the clerk's desk, cabinets, bookshelves, and a black leather settee.

The clerk looked up at her with surprise.

"I am Mrs. Douglas Tyrrell. I'd like to see my husband, please."

"I beg your pardon, madam?"

"Major Tyrrell, where is he?"

The clerk gaped at her for a moment, then said, "If you leave your card, madam, I will see that a message is brought round to you."

"I'm not leaving my card. I'm not leaving. I demand to see my husband."

The clerk stared at her for a moment, then sighed dramatically, rose from his desk, and crossed to the door to Smith's office. He rapped once, then went in.

Moments later he came out and closed the door behind him. He sat down and began to write, while saying, "Major Tyrrell has been taken to the Wellington Barracks. You may present this to the commanding officer to whose authority your husband has been committed." He blotted the paper and handed it to her. "Whether you will be permitted to see him or not I cannot say."

"What are you telling me?"

"Your husband is under arrest."

"For what?"

"It is not my place to say."

Pamela threw the paper onto his desk. "Then get me someone whose place it is." She turned and crossed to the leather couch and sat. She met the clerk's stony gaze with one of her own. "You can tell the attorney general that I'm not leaving until I know what is happening to my husband."

Smith's door opened, but instead of Smith, it was Sir Edward Carson who stood there. The attorney general hovered behind him. "Mrs. Tyrrell," Carson said smoothly, "your husband is in army custody. You should direct your inquiries to the War Office."

Carson stepped toward her, smiling sympathetically, to ingratiate himself, but she cut him before he said a word. "He came at your summons. I want an explanation from you."

He stopped abruptly and shrugged: since you give me no choice. "Major Tyrrell faces court-martial."

"For what?"

He raised his eyebrows: how to put it delicately. "For certain conduct which raises questions having to do with loyalty."

Her shock was absolute. "My husband is a hero."

"In France he was, but this has to do with Ireland."

Pamela saw at once she was no match for this. Ireland? Damned Ireland? It has to do with Ireland? She felt herself sinking. Who *was* a match for it? Who could help her?

And then she knew.

Sir Hugh had come to London only twice in more than two decades: for the wedding of his son and at the report that he was missing at Ypres.

And now. If over those years the city had represented the locus of his own disillusionment, after the fall of Parnell it had never threatened him personally and he had imagined that it never could. But like all parents, who are eternally powerless to protect their children from what they themselves fear most, Sir Hugh had not foreseen how his son's jeopardy was merely an extension of his own. All he knew as he crossed the width of Ireland and the swells of the Irish Sea was that, whatever England had done to Ireland, and whatever Carson had done to Parnell, they were not going to do it again to his child.

His train arrived in London less than twenty-four hours after Pamela had left the Royal Courts. She met him and told him everything that had happened. Then, instead of sending her home as she expected, he said, "Shall we do this together?"

Instead of going back to the High Court, they went directly to Westminster, to Parliament. Sir Hugh led the way to Carson's office. These were corridors he knew as well as he knew the gulleys that crossed his land. When Carson's startled private secretary looked up to see that formidable man bearing down on him, he blanched.

Sir Hugh said politely, "We'd like to see the party leader, please."

The private secretary shook his head. "Sir Edward isn't here. He's lunching."

"Where?"

"His club, sir."

"Which club?"

"I'm not at liberty to tell you that. Surely you understand."

"Of course," Sir Hugh said, and he led Pamela away.

Outside she protested. "But we can't just—"

He silenced her with a finger to his lips, then raised that hand toward their driver. "The Griffen Club," he said. "It's in Mayfair."

The Griffen was an exclusive club whose members were politically eminent, but also socially well connected. It wasn't the Athenaeum, but it certainly belonged on any list of the better clubs. It was one of Carson's achievements that he was elected to it as a young man. Lord Randolph Churchill, whom he would later cuckold, was his sponsor.

As the motorcar pulled up in front of the granite-faced mansion, Sir Hugh opened the door, and even before it had quite stopped, he stepped to the pavement. He went up the four stone stairs without waiting for Pamela, but she followed.

The lobby gleamed with brass and marble, and in its center at a small desk sat a stone-faced young functionary. Sir Hugh ignored him and made as if to pass, heading for the elaborate curving staircase at the far end. The man stood up and blocked Sir Hugh's way. "I beg your pardon?"

"I'm going to the dining room."

"This is a private club, sir."

"Yes"—Sir Hugh stared down at the man—"and I have been a member since before you were born."

The man blushed, but managed to ask, "Your name, sir?"

From the doorway of a small office beside the cloakroom came the voice of another man, the old stoop-shouldered club steward. "Sir Hugh Tyrrell," he said, and he stepped toward him.

"Hello, Manson," Sir Hugh said.

"It's been a long time, sir." The steward bowed. He had ruled the Griffen, servant though he was, with the scepter of his courtesy for decades. "The club has missed you."

To his surprise, the steward's simple statement touched the small place in Sir Hugh where he felt the same thing. "I've missed the club."

Manson graciously bowed to Pamela. "Perhaps Madam would care to wait in the Reading Room." He indicated an adjacent doorway. In two centuries no woman had mounted the stairs of the Griffen Club except to clean it.

Pamela's eyes went to Sir Hugh. He nodded, then turned and continued toward the staircase and up it alone.

The dining room was adazzle with light streaming in from four enormous windows that stretched the full height from floor to ceiling, a space equivalent to two stories. The wall opposite the windows was hung with a silk-thread Belgian tapestry that glowed magically as if its scene of some medieval *fête champêtre* enchanted the very air. A narrow balcony overhung the room on a third side, throwing a shadow over the long buffet on which, now, pies and cakes, cheeses and fruits were spread. Arranged in the center of the room were perhaps twenty tables, sparkling with silver, cobalt glass, and gilt-edged china. Each one was occupied by a pair or quartet of perfectly tailored men imbued with a *gravitas* that took them toward each other's ears.

Then he saw him. Carson sat in a far corner at a large table, but with only one other man, a mustachioed army officer. Carson looked remarkably the same, and Sir Hugh recognized at once the marks of his extraordinary energy. He held utensils aggressively in each hand as he always had, for his method in eating, as in all things, was to attack. He was leaning toward his companion, gesturing with his knife, speaking urgently even while chewing a mouthful of food. The sight of the man disgusted Sir Hugh, but he reined his feelings. He was glad that Carson's self-absorption was still absolute, because now it meant that he could cross the entire dining room while his old adversary continued to jabber.

"Hello, Carson," he said.

Carson's jaw froze when he looked up, and a piece of meat protruded from between his lips. He dropped his fork and knife and put his napkin to his mouth, staring at Tyrrell. He coughed the unchewed meat into the linen. Then he pushed his chair back, half stood, then sat again. "My dear Tyrrell," he said miserably. He seemed to shrivel in the chill of his enemy's stare.

"You seem surprised. Don't you know when you land a blow on an old wound, it opens up? Did you think you wouldn't have to face me?"

Carson's silence grew brutish, obstinate.

Tyrrell leaned toward him across the table, placing his hands on the linen cloth, bringing his face close to Carson's, which was a violation already of the rules that hold sway in such places.

"You must know that if you bring charges against my son, you will have to defend them before all of Britain."

"All of Britain hardly cares about one more retrograde Irishman."

"Oh? Is that who is he?" Sir Hugh clipped each word, a staccato, like a policeman banging his stick against a fugitive's door. "The hero of Messines? The man who escaped Trier? Lord Kitchener's agent in Ireland? Lord Kitchener himself nominated my son for the Military Cross."

"Lord Kitchener is dead."

"Yes, otherwise you would not have been allowed near him. If I have to print the papers myself, England will know what you are doing to an officer who has proved himself. The King will know what you are doing to the grandson of the Fourth Viscount Turlough."

Carson sneered at Tyrrell. "You renounced that title."

"But not the blood."

"Nevertheless, that you did so may suggest a certain familial ambivalence, shall we say?"

"Are you going to charge me with treason too?"

Carson shrugged, but a line of perspiration had broken out on his lip.

"You'd better." Tyrrell drew even closer. "You'd better find a way to jail me too because otherwise I am going to destroy you. If I have to do it from Speakers' Corner in Hyde Park, I am going to rail and shriek and curse until everyone knows what you are doing, until even your fellow roundhead Unionists are embarrassed by your abuse of one of the King's good and true officers, one of the *few* Irishmen whose loyalty is beyond question. You want to be prime minister. You will walk over the rubble of Ireland and over the corpses of England's sons, but not my son's. You will not climb to the top of your obscene pile on my boy's body. When I finish—I swear this by my last breath, Carson!—you will have lost not only your position in the party, but your seat in Parliament." Tyrrell swung aburptly toward Carson's companion. "And you, Maxwell," he said scornfully. "You are willing to try to salvage your reputation, which you squandered in brutalizing guilty men, by brutalizing now an innocent one. You have an RIC lackey who will testify against my son? I'll find a dozen who were there who will testify for him. I will call General Friend and Major Price and Admiral Hamilton and ask them whether my son was loyal or not, and whether he played a part in foiling the German invasion of Ireland. I'll call Casement himself and ask him to describe his own arrest. Imagine what the army will think of a general who hands over for destruction one of its best officers to a politician whose only purpose is to advance himself. The Irish already hate you, General. When I'm finished, your mother will!"

Tyrrell straightened abruptly and turned to go. A hush had fallen throughout the dining room. Nearby diners could not hear what he had said, but his fury had carried across the entire room.

Maxwell said, "Wait!"

Tyrrell stopped without turning back.

"Sit with us."

He turned and came close again. It was not in his interest to be overheard—yet. "We have nothing to say to each other. I want my son released and I want the charges dropped."

Maxwell said quietly to Carson, "The man isn't going to testify for us anyway. That's established. It serves no point—"

Carson made an impatient gesture with his hand, but said nothing. His face had become as red as the unicorn's blood in the tapestry above him.

General Maxwell touched a napkin to his mouth and said

behind it, "I haven't signed the charge. I was hoping he would change his mind."

"He won't," Tyrrell said. He is my son.

"It was all a mistake. I'll see that he is released."

"Do it now."

Maxwell looked at Carson, but Carson was riveted on Tyrrell.

Tyrrell said to him, "You are a damned man, Edward."

Carson nodded, conceding the point. "You've accomplished your purpose, Hugh. Now your son will be free"—his face broke into a sinister grin—"to go back to France."

To Carson at that moment the trenches were just another trump to be played against this man and against Ireland.

Sir Hugh wheeled about and, leading Maxwell, walked out of the room.

———

Within weeks the final preparations for Casement's trial were complete, and it began on June 26. On the basis of evidence that included counterfeit documents and the testimony of his friend, Bailey, he would be convicted of treason.

During precisely the same period, preparations for the great British offensive on the Western Front were completed, and at the end of June it began. The plan was not only to take the pressure off the French, but finally to achieve the long-awaited breakthrough that would force the Germans back. The battle would involve more men on both sides than any in history, it would last nearly five months, and would make the carnage of Verdun pale. The battle would be called simply, for the river that meanders through the territory, the Somme.

Not even Douglas Tyrrell could have guessed what he was

going to. The War Train at Victoria was taking him from London once more. It was June 28, the day on which, originally, he was to testify in court. But now his orders were to join the remnant of the Connaught Rangers, which had been lumped in—because to the English command wasn't one Irishman, finally, like another?—with the Ulster Division. It was billeted near a small village called Thiepval. He was grateful to be going back to his own regiment, but otherwise everything would be different. Already, on the train platform across which stunned men walked as if in their sleep, not greeting each other, not yelling or laughing, the difference was apparent. No one carried cakes. The Tommies wore tin helmets where before they'd worn soft peaked hats. The war, wearing on, had ground the life out of those it hadn't killed yet. Only one thing was as it had been before to Tyrrell—his rank. Upon his release from custody he'd been reduced to captain.

"Why?" Pamela had asked that night. His rank had been far from important to her. Just having him back had made her happy, and she'd resolved to keep her dread at bay by asking nothing. But then, as she hung his tunic in the wardrobe, she fingered the place on its sleeve from which the major's crown had been removed.

Douglas shrugged. "I was promoted to major for the special assignment in Ireland, to give me seniority over the RIC. It was temporary."

She looked across the bedroom at him. He knew his answer had not satisfied her, but how could he tell her that he'd been demoted because majors don't lead men over the top into No Man's Land.

She had put the question aside because she knew that it opened onto the entire field of what she simply could not think about. It was too absurd that after surviving the chaos of events in Ireland, Douglas should now be returning to the trenches. They simply could not speak of it to each other.

How could she ask the larger question, for example: In impugning his loyalty, hadn't England somehow undermined it? All she knew was that events had undermined hers, or rather defined it. Her only loyalty now was to him. She crossed the bedroom that night, after hanging his uniform, lit a pair of candles, extinguished the ceiling light, and in the flickering glow of the flames which danced in the breeze that blew in from the Thames, she made love to him as if she wouldn't again.

Now, in Victoria Station, Douglas held her. The endless flow of soldiers swirled past, forming a current on either side of them; they were like a stanchion in white water. He did not hear the din, the hissing of engines, the blare of announcements, the clunking of cargo wagons. Nor did he see the dull-eyed resignation in the faces of the Tommies or the soot cloud hanging in the iron girders of the enormous station canopy. Every corner of his mind was taken up with Pamela.

"It isn't only that I love you . . ." He stopped. "You've been . . ." But he could not betray the solemn moment of their last farewell—each knew it for that—by speaking of the past *as* past. Because this *was* farewell, he could not say it. He took her into his arms once more, and they depended, each of them, as they always had, on their mere bodies to convey the harsh truth of their bond.

His father appeared from out of the crowd, and in his arms he carried Douglas's children. It startled Douglas to see them, because they'd deliberately said their good-byes in Chelsea. Why would he have come here? Douglas watched them approach, still in Pamela's embrace, his mouth by her ear, his cheek brushing against her soft hair, its sweet aroma filling his nostrils. He felt the ache of his love for Timmy and Anne, and then the sharp pain of regret that they would not remember him.

Then he saw why his father had come, for trailing him, pushing through the surging crowd in Sir Hugh's wake, was his sister, Jane. Douglas had not seen her since the day weeks before when he'd gone to Cragside. It surprised him that she'd come to London, in violation of her confinement. The sight of her body, which loomed under her dark cloak, startled him. One never saw expectant women in public, and certainly not in such a harsh, male-dominated setting as Victoria. The men whom she brushed by stared after her, but Jane was oblivious. All she saw was Douglas.

He left Pamela to go to her. When she went into his arms, she clutched at him and said, "It's because of me—"

"Don't be silly."

"—that they're sending you back."

"Nonsense, Jane." But of course it was true. If it wasn't for her, he'd have testified against Curry. He'd have had a safe rank and a London slot for the rest of the war. And he'd have hated himself.

He held her at arm's length to look at her. "How are you?"

She nodded.

"When will the baby come?"

"Before Christmas."

"You and the Blessed Virgin." She had to smile at that, and when she did, he grinned and teased, "A pair of unmarried mothers."

Jane lowered her eyes.

Douglas thought he'd embarrassed her, and he regretted it. He hooked a finger around her chin to lift her face. "I'm sorry. I didn't mean to make light of it."

She shook her head. "I'm not unmarried, Douglas. They

let Dan out of prison this week. We were married yesterday. You gave me back my life." At that Jane collapsed against him, shaking with sobs.

———

Curry had been brought back to Kilmainham Jail and then released along with more than two hundred other prisoners. Now the citizens of Dublin who had cried "Bayonet the bastards!" greeted them like heroes, lining the streets to cheer them. His mates welcomed that reception, felt they deserved it, and forgot, if they had noticed, how the people had rejected them at the first. The people's fickleness only intensified Curry's feeling of disgust. He left Dublin at once, reversing his Good Friday flight across the country. His thoughts now were all of Jane.

He had never been to Cragside, but he knew where it was. From the train at Gort, he flagged rides with farmers and cartmen to Kinvara and then Ballyvaughn. Between rides he kept up his pace. He was incapable of not moving toward her.

It was just coming on dark—at that time of year light lasts in Ireland until nearly eleven o'clock—when he finally ran the half-mile in from the road to the looming dark house. As he crossed the yellow apron of gravel toward the elaborate front door, a man's voice from the shadows of the side building said sharply, "Stop right there, mister, or it's a bellyful of shot you've given yourself!"

"I'm Dan Curry. I've come to see Jane."

Jane? Con O'Brien had never referred to Miss Tyrell by her given name. Nor had he ever heard a man with what he knew at once as a Catholic's accent do it either. "If you've business with anyone in this house, mister, come back tomorrow at a proper hour."

Curry began to cross toward O'Brien. "Tell Sir Hugh I'm here. He knows me. Tell him Curry is here."

O'Brien said nothing, which told Curry Sir Hugh was away. Curry slowed but continued to move cautiously toward the man. "Look, friend, if you're in charge, I understand your hesitations. But it's important. You must let me in to see Miss Tyrrell."

"Stop where you are!"

But Curry continued to close on him. When he too had entered the shadow, he could see the man's eyes, and he held them. He was aware of the leveled shotgun, but it was the man's face he watched as he went closer. "I'm a friend, I tell you."

"Stop or I'll shoot."

But Curry kept coming, and his decisiveness was what cowed O'Brien. If Curry had hesitated, he'd have fired. Instead he let Curry take the weapon away from him. Curry cracked it and dropped the shells. "If Miss Tyrrell doesn't want to see me, believe me, I'll be on my way before you can get it loaded again. Come along."

Curry handed the gun back and led the way across the yard to the door.

O'Brien rapped once quietly and the door promptly opened. A serving girl. "Tell Miss there's a Dan Curry here. We'll wait." The girl closed the door as promptly as she'd opened it.

And moments later it was flung wide, and there, without a sound from her gaping mouth, was His Honor's poor daughter. She threw herself on the man Con O'Brien had nearly shot. He watched them for a moment, then slipped away thinking, Good for Missy. She has herself a man there.

Jane led him to the parlor. They sat, holding each other. Finally Dan put his hand on her belly and said, "At last I know what I was put on this earth for."

"For me."

"Yes. Will you marry me, Jane?"

She laughed. "Haven't I done that yet?"

But Curry could not treat it lightly. "It means leaving every-thing you have and everything you know. *Everything*." He cast his eyes about the room, then looked at her again.

She was shaking her head. "All I have and know is you, Dan. And the child you've given me. Of course I'll marry you."

Two days later they stood before Father Kavanaugh in Saint Colum's. Nora and Brian Guinan were there as witnesses. The priest put the ancient questions to them each in turn. Jane answered softly, for she was beginning something wholly new and losing something she still loved. Curry, though, felt that his life of false starts was over now. At last, in becoming her husband, he was becoming the man he'd forever longed to be. His voice rang when he said, "I will."

———

Douglas stroked his sister and whispered, "That makes me very happy, Jane. I know what it is to love someone like that. It's how I love Pamela."

When he looked up, his eyes went directly to those of Dan Curry, who was standing a dozen yards away, jostled by soldiers. His tattered dark coat and open shirt, his brilliant red hair and beard set him apart from everyone around him. Douglas remem-bered him from Banna Strand and from the camp at Trier, the desperate impulse that took him up to the platform after Case-ment, crying, "Brothers!" to the roomful of Irishmen who had their backs to him. "You have to do what you think is right, but so do we." In the simple eloquence of his appeal, he had laid bare the problem, though Douglas had not seen it at the time. There were two justices in conflict with each other. God's and man's. England's and Ireland's. Curry's and Tyrrell's. Wasn't it Tyrrell's problem that, even until now, he had been trying to serve them both?

Curry approached him slowly. Jane sensed his presence behind her and pulled back. Now their circle was complete. Douglas indicated each of them and said, "So we're the family now." He offered his hand to Curry. Curry hesitated. Years before he'd felt unworthy in the presence of certain priests, but that was hubris compared to what he felt now. He took Douglas's hand and shook it.

Douglas indicated Jane's pregnancy. "And the family keeps growing."

Curry refused to be deflected even into affection for his new wife. "I have to thank you."

"That I wouldn't denounce you as a traitor? You're no more a traitor than I am. And neither is Casement. I see that now."

"You are . . ." What could Curry say to such a man? You are a hero? A patriot? A man of honor? The word that the needle of his mind settled on was the old Catholic one, the word men used at Maynooth, though never of the living. You are a saint.

He could not say that, of course. How could he give voice to what he felt, that once he'd objected that Jane should carry her brother's picture in her locket, but now, if men wore lockets, he would have. He said simply, "You are good."

Tyrrell shrugged. "I'm your child's uncle." He stepped to his father to take Timmy. The boy was wide-eyed. Douglas nuzzled him, then turned him toward Curry. "This is your Uncle Dan." Then, to Curry, "Make sure my children get to know their cousin, will you?"

Curry looked quickly at Jane, and on that cue, so did the others. She said, "We're not going back to Ireland."

Sir Hugh put Anne down, though she continued to cling to

his leg. "What do you mean?" How could Curry stay in England, much less Jane? What did her conversion to the Roman Church mean, if not that she would be forever Irish?

She said, "We're going to America."

There was a stunned silence.

Finally Curry said, "If I return to Ireland, either I'll be drawn once more into an Irish movement I've no stomach for or conscripted by the British for a war I have no part in. The men of Easter may be heroes now, but to me they were something else." To me, he might have said, they were self-canonized suicides like the martyrs of Maynooth, like the legion of Marys I've been running from my whole life.

Douglas's thought was, If it's a movement you oppose, then oppose it, while his father's was, If you Irish Catholics love your nation so, why do you find her so easy to abandon?

It was to his daughter, not Curry, that Sir Hugh said, simply, "America?"

She had to look away.

He channeled his emotion into a characteristic practicality. He asked of Curry, "What will you do?"

Curry put his arm around Jane and grinned. "Go to Minnesota or someplace and start a little theater." He knew what a solemn, sad moment this was for these people, but he could not restrain his happiness.

Jane touched her father's sleeve, a gesture of remorse. But her hand shook, a hint of the panic she felt suddenly to be going so utterly away.

Sir Hugh covered her trembling hand. "We have to see Douglas off."

Jane realized what an intrusion her announcement was. She hadn't intended to bring it up at all. She'd come only to say farewell to Douglas. She looked at Pamela, who was staring at her husband. Pamela didn't care what Jane did, and she was right. Jane said to Douglas, "I'll pray for you."

The Anglo-Irish never verbalized such sentiments, and it was a mark of Jane's distance from them already that she'd said it. Nevertheless, Douglas was moved. Events had changed them all. He could hear Bernard Keefe saying such a thing; indeed, if it would console his boys before he sent them over, he could imagine saying it himself. But what, he wondered, would it mean? Would God be kinder to him now that Jane was going to ask Him to? What exactly would God's kindness look like on the Western Front?

Dan Curry took half a step toward Douglas, carried by an obvious, sudden impulse. He said, "Come with us!"

And Douglas knew that was the answer to his question: God's kindness on the Western Front would only be—not being there. Because he didn't dismiss it at once, Jane picked up on Curry's notion. "Yes! Yes! Come with us! Leave now!" She looked around at the throng of tin-hatted Tommies. No one was forcing Douglas on board the train. He was not in custody now. "You don't belong in France," she said. "It isn't our war any more than the war in Ireland is. These wars are wrong. They have no right to take you! Come with us!" Jane looked at Pamela. "Tell him."

Pamela dropped her eyes. She would have given anything to keep Douglas from the trenches. She didn't care whether the war was right or wrong, or where they had to go to avoid it. America? Borneo? This war was as absurd as the War of the Roses. She knew only one thing—she wanted him alive. But she was not going to add to his burden by suggesting such a thing, because she knew he could not do it. Salvation to her—desertion to him. She leaned against him, clinging to his arm in silence.

Douglas could not have explained why it was unthinkable that he should not board that train. He was responding to orders, yes. To a sense of being bound by a certain fate, no matter how unfair it felt, or how insane. Douglas simply felt a bond, still, with the men of his generation, and despite what he'd been through, he accepted the structures by which they measured the meaning of their lives. He was an officer and he had a duty to the men who would be entrusted to his authority. *They* were his nation now. Whether in fulfilling that duty he lived or died was secondary. Death was not the worst thing that could happen to him. To lose his fragile grasp on meaning would be. And that was certain to happen if he went now to America.

It had nothing to do—and this was what the Rising and its aftermath had taught him—with defending the Crown and defeating the Hun, as if it mattered which empire held sway in the world. Two armies fighting to possess Europe destroy Europe in the process, as two armies fighting over Dublin destroy Dublin. No ideal vision or patriotic urge was left him, in other words; but neither had ever been the source of his commitment. Like all the men who continued to respond in that era long after events had revealed the rhetoric for lies, Douglas felt an implicit brotherhood with his fellows on the line. Ironically, the more hopeless, the more absurd, the more obscene their situation became, the more their bond with each other intensified. He loved his family as much as any man could, but the owners of his heart were the anonymous, dull-eyed Tommies, Jocks, and Micks all around them.

Nothing more was said about his going to America.

The train whistle blew shrilly, and the pace of men heading for it picked up.

Jane kissed Douglas. Curry stood with his hand on his wife's back, as if through her he could transmit his feeling. When Douglas looked at him, Curry nodded and said, "Good luck."

Douglas turned to his father; they stared at each other for

a moment, then embraced roughly. Sir Hugh, for the first time since his Anita died, fought back tears.

Then Douglas stooped to take his children in his arms. He said to Anne, "Take care of your mother and your brother until I come back."

What Timmy saw in his father's face made him burst into tears, and he clung to his mother. Sir Hugh coaxed him away, then scooped up both children once more. He led Jane and Curry off, leaving Pamela alone with Douglas.

They looked at each other dry-eyed. No tears now.

Pamela said, "The last time you left, I chased your train halfway to France."

Douglas nodded. "None of the men believed it could be my wife." He laughed. "No one could know how we love each other."

She nodded.

The train whistle sounded again. The platform was empty.

Douglas had an impulse to say, I'll be back, but either he would or he wouldn't, and mere words couldn't change that.

They kissed.

He walked to the train and boarded it.

Pamela waved once, but as the train began to move, she remained where she was, immobile, not wincing, though the fox inside her shirt was feasting.

———

When Douglas could no longer see Pamela, he walked through the cars of the train, looking at the men. A burly Irish sergeant made him think again of Lieutenant Keefe. It will be good to see Bernard once more, he thought, as if he weren't dead.

22

In the way that July 4 takes its meaning for Americans from the year 1776, July 1 had always taken its meaning for Irishmen, both green and orange, from the year 1690. But that changed in 1916, when July 1 became something else.

Before 1916 that date was observed, either in celebration or grief, depending on religion, as the anniversary of the Battle of the Boyne. The Boyne was the meandering Ulster river at which James II, the last Catholic King of England, was vanquished by William of Orange. From then on, the Protestant stranglehold on the north of Ireland was secure, and it was beginning then that the infamous Penal Laws were enacted against Irish Catholics everywhere in the country. James II's defeated army went into exile in France—"the flight of the wild geese"—never to help Ireland again.

Hence the irony that France should have been the scene of the transformation of the meaning of the first of July, and that it should have taken place at another meandering river, at another epic battle in which descendants of the "wild geese," Irish soldiers at war in exile, were the first to fall. But they were so far from the last to fall as to make that stalemate battle the central emblem of the entire war. In sheer disproportion between gains and casualties, it was the worst battle in British history, and the worst day of it was the first.

The Somme wound in loops through a wide valley dotted by small villages surrounded by apple orchards and by squared fields. The river was lined with rushes and low willows and fed by slow-moving tributaries, each of which had cut its own shallow valley, and so the country was crisscrossed by plateaux and ridges that gave the advantage to defenders, whose positions rose in tiers up which attackers had to crawl. Unlike the drenched earth of Flanders, the chalky soil here lent itself to elaborate dugouts, and in the low hills there were caves and grottoes and ancient passageways between the medieval châteaux and abbeys. These underground labyrinths were linked by fresh tunnels on both sides of the trench line, but the Germans especially had spent their time digging. They were ready for it when the attack came, even though the numbers the British hurled at them along a twenty-five-mile front were staggering.

The British thought July 1 was going to be the date of the great breakthrough, and for that reason Tommies, Jocks, and Micks up and down the line wore flowers in their helmets. Behind the line masses of cavalry waited to pursue the advantage once the German front cracked open. The main reason for their optimism was that for a solid week, commencing on the day that Roger Casement's trial began, British artillery had been pounding the German positions with the greatest concentration of shellfire in history. But the howitzer was, relative to what it would become, a primitive weapon in 1916; it could not be aimed with real precision, and the greater part of its destructive force was squandered above the ground with great showers of smoke, dust, and debris, the sight of which cheered

British observers. But those dramatic explosions hardly dented the forty-foot dugouts in which the Germans waited. The bombardment failed even to smash the vicious belts of barbed wire that in some places were now thirty yards thick. When they were hit, the coils of wire simply bounced. So much, in other words and once again, for gunnery. Unfortunately for the soldiers who would have to assault it, the machine gun, unlike the heavy weapons of artillery, had already achieved the zenith of its destructive power, and where the British had tied their hopes to the one, the Germans had tied theirs to the other.

At dawn a cloud of mist hung over the region, but by 0730, when the platoon officers' whistles began to blow all along the British line, the sun blazed in the sky. As the trenches emptied, the first waves of a force numbering over a hundred thousand advanced into No Man's Land in broad view, shoulder to shoulder, each man staggering under the burden of enormous packs. And at once German machine guns opened fire and began to sweep the approaching Tommies, Jocks, and Micks away like leaves. British commanders understood the killing potential of the German weapon, even after two years' running up against it, as little as they understood the limits of their own. Instead of ordering a halt to the advance, they redoubled it, thinking that what artillery had failed to do, the sheer hurling mass of an army's bodies could do. The thought, if there was one, must have been to overwhelm the machine gunner, if not his gun, by sending an infinity of targets at him.

So throughout the day, line after line of British soldiers went over the top, and those who fell back were ordered out again. Crossing into the bomb-cratered zone of No Man's Land, for those sent out in the afternoon, became the daylight nightmare of walking on ground made mushy by the corpses of the morning. And through all that horror the machine guns never faltered.

They were something wholly new—the Industrial Revolution come to war, mechanized killing—and with their depersonalized, unthinking crews, who could as easily have been tending lathes in a monotonous factory, they could have gone on forever. By the end of the day the British had suffered the highest proportion of losses of any battle in their history. Sixty percent of the officers fell and forty-five percent of the men, more than sixty thousand in all. But what remains truly remarkable is the fact that the response of the British Command to the disaster of July 1 was frantically to prolong it.

Between the first assault and the last, five months later on November 18, nearly two million men would fall and the British line would have been advanced exactly six miles across the useless field of mud. While the battle lasted and the casualties mounted, many men snapped. If they were officers, they were sent home as victims of shell shock. If they were of the other ranks, they were shot at once for cowardice. One British soldier would be executed on the Somme every five days for attempting to desert, but many more, knowing that desertion in such circumstances was impossible—there was nowhere to flee but into No Man's Land—and unable to bear the terror of their situation, would simply commit suicide. In official reports those men were always posted as killed in action, an implicit acknowledgment that at the Somme the usual definitions did not apply. Suicides were listed as dying nobly, while the heroes who mustered the will, out of patriotism or out of fear of their own superiors, to obey the order to mount the parapet and advance might as well have been throwing themselves in front of a runaway locomotive.

Douglas Tyrrell, like everyone on the line that first day, had no idea what was happening up and down the twenty-five-mile front. Division, brigade, and battalion commanders had their Morse shutters, carrier pigeons, semaphore flags, and, where

the wires weren't cut, telephone and telegraph, but communications ended at the edge of No Man's Land, and that's where the
company commanders went. Douglas's world was compressed
into the chaos of what he could see, and all that his eyes told
him as he led his boys out of the trenches was that they began
falling around him damn soon. His memory of the action at
Messines was bad, but this was different.

The first surprise after his return to Regiment from England
was that the Connaught Rangers were now made up of men
he'd never seen before. It came as a great shock to realize that
all of the officers and many of the other ranks were now in fact
Englishmen. The pristine Irish character of the regiment, which
had been so valued by its members, had completely disappeared.
That was the kind of year it had been on the Western Front.
During the time since his capture, the original members had
been lost, as had a full generation of their replacements. The
Rangers had changed utterly, but it wasn't only events in France
that accounted for it. Events in Ireland had had their impact
too, for once it was clear to authorities that a true nationalist
rising was in the offing, Irish recruits had been dispersed in
other regiments, and the Irish regiments had been replenished
with Englishmen.

This watering-down of the national character of the Rangers
explained why it was possible, in the great regrouping before the
Somme offensive, to assign what had been a mainly Catholic
Redmondite regiment to the Thirty-sixth Division, which was
dominated by the fiercely Unionist, anti-Catholic Ulster Volunteers. On the dawn of that July 1, while other British units had
prepared themselves at worship services—even the notoriously
agnostic private soldiers took communion—or in somber, silent
reflection, the Orangemen of the Ulster Division had prepared
themselves by banging their ancient Lambeg drum, which for

generations on that date had struck terror in the hearts of Catholic children in Derry and Belfast. Why shouldn't it frighten Fritz as well? Never mind that the Orangeman's fabled Billy was a Dutchman, more German than not, or that the Apprentice Boys' victory over the Papist King was the result of the failure of the King's artillery—that again—to breach the wall of Derry. Douglas had watched with bitter distaste as the Ulstermen, with their officers' encouragement, snake-danced in nearby trenches under their banner, ULSTER WILL FIGHT AND ULSTER WILL BE RIGHT! It didn't help him think well of their tribal battle antics that their slogan had been coined not against their German enemy but, in resisting the Home Rule his father had fought for, against their Irish one.

But what the hell, once the whistles blew, the Ulster lads were as likely as any to wet themselves while scaling the parapets, and once in the desperate cratered moonscape of No Man's Land, they fell under the withering fire of the German machine guns the same as Catholic boys from Galway did. If anything, one had to wonder if the British brass hadn't lumped the Irish, orange and green, in the frontmost lines to have done once and for all with both of them.

Douglas had no idea how or why he survived that day. By the time the sun was setting, he had been out into No Man's Land and back from it four times with the natural flux of a line that knows only falling or falling back. Each time he and the ever-diminishing number of Rangers collapsed back into the forwardmost trench, he had roused them, despite his disbelief, when the runners came up from the rear with the mad order to advance once more. Four times he led men out into the zone of disaster, and four times, like them, in terrified flight before the walls of bullets, he retreated. But with each futile effort his company, which had numbered three hundred at dawn, was reduced by half, until by dusk there were three dozen left. All of his platoon leaders had disappeared.

With darkness came silence. The assaults ceased and the German guns stopped for the first time in twelve hours. Douglas assembled his men at the bulge in their section of the trench, in front of the dugout that served as the orderly room. When they'd counted off and they realized how few had survived, including only two junior officers and three NCOs, one man began to shriek hysterically. Douglas cut him off with the order, forming them into six stretcher parties, to go back out through the night in shifts, searching the mile-wide stretch of No Man's Land for the wounded. Normal procedure would have left such work to the medical corps, but not with these numbers. The effort of all the survivors would be required. It was a question of rescuing not only the men who'd been hit, but also those who'd been spared. Only the purposeful work now of pulling to safety those who were still alive out there would keep them all from the hysteria their situation quite justified. When they did not protest his order, though it meant leaving the womb of the trench again, Douglas felt an overwhelming admiration; what these men would do for each other!

For a moment, faced with such willingness, he felt he was looking down from a mountain into the goodness of the earth itself, a strange thought on such a day and an uncharacteristically religious one for him. As he dismissed them, preparing to lead the first party out himself, Douglas realized that each man had plumbed the well of his own selflessness because he'd asked him to. And then his thought was, What they do for their officers!

But nothing could prepare him for the experience of criss-crossing No Man's Land that night. The feel of human flesh underfoot, the ungodly groaning of men who'd lost limbs, the gasping of the dying who clutched at his tunic when he knelt to them. Instinctively adopting an implicit policy of triage, he went from one to the other, determined to at least touch each one who was still living, to console him somehow, if moving him was pointless. When he lifted one Mick who was quite conscious, lucid even, the man's shirt flopped open and his intestines, the color of worms from under rocks, fell into Douglas's lap. The Mick grinned awkwardly to have his secret so exposed, then said, "Sorry, Captain" before expiring. Douglas put the man down gently—"That's all right, old man"—then turned aside and vomited.

He had intended only to serve out his shift as a stretcher-bearer, like the others, but the sheer numbers of victims overwhelmed him. Going from one to the other, he lost all sense of time and, in the end, it was after midnight when one of the NCOs approached him.

"Captain, you're wanted for order group."

Douglas stared at the man uncomprehendingly.

"Battalion sent a runner up, sir. You're the only company commander left alive and the C.O. wants you."

Douglas's mind refused to settle on what the man was saying. "The C.O.? Colonel MacIntyre?"

"No, sir." The sergeant stepped closer to Tyrrell. In the darkness he couldn't read his face. "Colonel Hall."

"Colonel Hall?" An Englishman, the C.O. of Connaught? "Yes, sir."

"Colonal Hall should be out here helping us." Douglas looked at his watch. "We have to get these poor men back to our line by dawn."

"Yes, Captain, I know, but . . ." He stopped talking at the sound of an otherworldly groan that ended as abruptly as it began. ". . . order group is going on now. It began at midnight."

Suddenly the thought of neatly tailored officers sitting

at a long gleaming table in the gilded dining room of whatever château served as headquarters filled Douglas with anger.
"Order group?" he bellowed suddenly. "Don't they know
what's happened out here? Why aren't they helping us to get
the wounded?"

"I don't know, sir." The NCO looked forlornly about, a dull
expression on his face which suggested, ludicrously, that he'd
seen such things before.

Then Douglas understood. "They *don't* know, do they?"
When he looked about, it was not forlornly, but wildly, for
the first time not in despair, but in rage. "They couldn't know
unless they'd been out here! And they haven't been and they
never will be!"

"Perhaps you should go and tell them then, sir."

———

Battalion Headquarters was no château but a small stone farm-
house on the bank of the River Ancre, one of the Somme's
tributaries. The officers who had gathered there, not around a
gleaming table but in a room with no furniture, lined the four
walls. On the floor in the center of the room was a large map
on two corners of which stood oil lamps, the only illumina-
tion. Lit from below like that, their faces were like the faces
of ghouls. Douglas burst in on them unannounced. Colonel
Hall, crouched at the map on one knee, stopped talking. His
half-dozen staff officers, the chaplain, and three lieutenants,
formerly adjutants but now commanders, all stared at him.
Douglas had no idea how blood had disfigured him, and they
had no way of knowing it wasn't his own.

Irrationally, it was the chaplain on whom Douglas turned.
"Sir, you should be out there with the men. They need you."

Colonel Hall did not appreciate the interruption. "Captain, take a place from which you can see the map, please."

When Douglas only stared at him, the brusque Englishman said, "My information was that you are fit. Is that not so?"

"I'm fit, sir."

"Then take your place, please."

"But Colonel, two-thirds of my company are left in No Man's Land—"

"Yes, Captain, with half of my battalion."

"It was that bad in our entire sector?"

Colonel Hall glared at him. "It was that bad along the entire front."

Tyrrell could not grasp it. He'd seen what had happened on a stretch of the line perhaps three hundred yards long, and he was now to believe the same horror had occurred everywhere on the twenty-five-mile ribbon of Britain's greatest army?

"You are not a common stretcher-bearer, Captain. Your place was here when I summoned you."

"But Colonel, after what happened today—"

"Our concern is not with today, but tomorrow."

Again Douglas fell over the thought. Tomorrow? Of what possible relevance could tomorrow be? He felt his skin go cold.

Colonel Hall turned to his map to resume. He poked it. "Captain Tyrrell, your C Company will now incorporate D Company and Mr. Dozer here will serve as your adjutant. C Company will move tonight to this position, facing Hamel. Because of the shape of terrain here, between the Ancre and, in the distance, the slopes of Thiepval on which the Germans have taken positions, No Man's Land reaches a breadth of more than four miles. In the middle of it are systems of trenches and bunkers which the Germans abandoned during the barrage. Today men of the Fifth North Staffords took refuge in those trenches instead of pressing on to the German line. That will not happen tomorrow. We will have no such cowardice from men of the Fourth Connaught." Colonel Hall looked up sharply at one of his staff. "I want Battle Police posted along that line of abandoned trench-work. If any man refuses to leap over it or tries to hide in it, I want him shot. Is that clear?"

"Yes, sir."

"And I want the Battle Police selected from among Englishmen."

Douglas watched the others for their reaction to this, but there was none. He was the only Irishman in the room, but he guessed they didn't know it.

He interrupted Hall again, but before he knew what his question was. He stammered, "C Company, Colonel?"

Hall looked at him.

"Are we to link up . . . ?" What his mind refused to grasp was that this was talk about yet another assault. They were telling him to take his lads out there again. "I mean, sir, does the plan call for . . . ?" Plan? What possible plan could there be?

He stopped. Staring into Colonel Hall's shadowy eyes was like staring down over the rail of a great ship into the sea. He saw the thing clearly, the deep, blue truth of it. In a wholly different voice, he said, "Surely, Colonel, you're not under orders to resume the assault?"

The other officers glanced at each other uneasily.

"In point of fact, Captain, those are exactly the orders I'm under. And you are under them too. General Haig himself—"

"General Haig wasn't out there today! Neither was Rawlinson and neither were you! It's impossible! You must go back and tell them: it's impossible, Colonel!"

Hall shook his head slowly. "It seems impossible, I know that. But the Germans will never expect us to follow up—"

"No, of course they won't, because they are military men, not butchers!"

The C.O. stood up abruptly. "Military men do what they are told! You've said quite enough, Captain."

But Douglas realized he had said nothing, nothing of what there was to say. All up and down the Front, this scene was being repeated at Battalion and Brigade and Division and Corps, but who was telling them the truth of what happened? And of what would certainly happen again? He fell not so much silent as mute, but his eyes continued to accuse the colonel.

Hall was not unaffected by this blood-covered apparition, this mythic fury. He looked at the others for support. They were men in whom the discipline held, but no one spoke. He said awkwardly, "Casualties are heavy, but Command knew they would be. And Command alone knows now what the entire situation is. The Germans have been battered. Another blow of the hammer could finish them."

When Tyrrell said nothing to indicate his obeisance, the colonel said, "So the proper thing to do, Captain, would be to relieve you of your command?" What was one more shattered officer sent to the rear? What was another evacuee, another basket case?

The words cut through Douglas, and the image of what they implied. At once he shook his head. "No, sir." My men, he thought. And also, I'm not breaking; you misunderstand if you think I'm breaking. "No, sir," he repeated with a certain abject note of acquiescence—the note, he knew, that Colonel Hall was listening for.

"Then take your place, please."

Tyrrell stepped back against the wall between a young lieutenant, Dozer, and a major, a member of regimental staff. Tyrrell looked at each of them in turn. The major wore a vacant expression, exhaustion posing as indifference. The lieutenant's jaw was clenched and his cheeks were streaked with the dried tracks of tears that he had not bothered to wipe or had not known to.

————

The idea was to advance coolly, steadily, behind a moving barrage of artillery shells, a protective curtain always twenty-five yards ahead. Of course, the artillery never advanced steadily, and after several rounds of fits and starts that brought the men into the heat of their army's own fire, the Rangers stopped trusting it and began to move at the pace of their own instincts. All artillery at that point, whether German or British, threatened equally. It was then, when they began to run through the shrapnel bursts, hoping only to stay on their feet for the next ten or twenty paces, that infantrymen understood that the gunners a mile behind the lines knew as little about their jobs as they, the infantry-men, knew about their own. Nobody knew enough about this situation, but even the private soldiers sensed that they knew more than the generals.

For once, Douglas Tyrrell had not led the front rank of his company out into No Man's Land. Instead, he left the charge to the platoon leaders mustered by Dozer. Not that he was content to let them go, but that, for the first time, he could not encourage his men to advance. They were going to die, and die to no purpose.

He marveled at the spirit of self-sacrifice that propelled the men forward in response to the simple shrill sound of their lieutenant's whistle, but now instead of edifying him, their will-ingness shamed him. He turned the distinction over in his mind like a coin, like a corpse; was it patriotic suicide or suicidal patriotism? But he knew it was a sophist's question, for their act was neither. They leapt the parapet because they trusted their officers, that was all. They trusted them not to squander their lives. Yet that was what their Captain Tyrrell—*their* General Haig—was doing.

He followed them.

Because No Man's Land was farther across here, enemy fire was longer in coming, and that set up a false hope in the men, who'd felt the heat the minute they'd left the trenches the day before. He sensed it when their pace picked up and they began to think, By God, we're going to make it this time.

But then, just as they hit their stride and as even the grimmest fatalist began to hope, they came within range of the machine guns.

Just beyond that point were the first of the abandoned German trenches—the perfect cover, the perfect holes in which to hide. Instinctively, to get out of the breast-high tattoo of bullets, the men in front of Douglas dove headfirst into the earthworks as if they were tidal pools off Dunkirk from which they could swim home.

Right, Douglas thought, and he was going to dive too.

But by the time he reached the trenches, he saw the regimental Battle Police, Tommies with white rags tied to their sleeves, looming over the pit of terrified men. There were four B.P.s, and they began to fire their rifles, not at the Germans, but at the Rangers cowering in the mud of what, as it now turned out, was their open grave.

"Stop!" Tyrrell ordered.

But the police ignored him.

"Stop!" he shrieked.

They didn't even see him. They pumped away at the unresisting figures, a mass of them, in the trenches at their feet.

German gunfire whizzed around them. This was madness. It was obscene: British soldiers shooting their fellows for taking cover. And then, even in the din, Douglas heard one of the Battle Policemen crying, "Fucking Irish bastards!"

He was the one Douglas shot first. He didn't know he'd even drawn his pistol. Quickly, systematically, before they could react, he pressed off shots at the other three. And like that, Captain Douglas Tyrrell had killed four BEF Battle Policemen, four—he was acutely aware of this—Englishmen whose last thoughts were that primordial English thought: These fucking Irish bastards. To which Tyrrell said out loud, at last, "Yes, aren't we?"

And then he jumped down into the forbidden trench with his men.

Every member of the BEF had bandages and antiseptic sewn into his tunic. Working with their kits, he dressed the wounds of the men who were still alive.

When he stood and looked up and down the length of the trench, he was amazed to see it crowded with men. They were hunched against the dirt walls and sandbagged parapets, but their eyes were on him: Don't make us go back out there, Captain.

At that moment the sound drifted over them with an eerie unreality, the Battalion Pipers, who were playing as they advanced, and the tune was "God Save the King." Instinctively the men who were crouching struggled to their feet, and others came to attention. But near Tyrrell a short, bony soldier with the red face of a drinker—he smelled of rum—cried in a sharp Cockney accent, "Never mind the bloody King! He's safe enough! God save us!"

The man winced when Tyrrell faced him, expecting a rebuke. But Tyrrell put a hand on the man's shoulder. "Well said, Private."

The anthem bagpipes stopped abruptly as the musicians marched into the range of the German gunners.

Tyrrell raised his voice for everyone to hear. "All right, lads, stay low, hold your places. Anyone else wants to come in, let him come." They stared at each other for a moment, those desperate men and their captain, each knowing they'd crossed a line together. Tyrrell's impulse was to say, You know I cannot give permission for this. But what was the point? Of course they knew it. He turned and began to walk along the trench, to see where it took him.

It was half collapsed, and every twenty or thirty feet the parapet had been cratered by artillery shells, but since the trench had been built by Germans it was still better than what they'd left, with duckboard underfoot, square traverses, and saps extending off to the right. At one point he had to step over an undefined mass of bloody pulp—he smelled it before he saw it—and it was with great relief that he realized the thing was the corpse of a cow.

The trench led down to a deep, sandbagged dugout, an orderly room, from which such a stench came that Tyrrell had to cover his face to enter it. Inside all was darkness. He struck a match with one hand while closing his nostrils with the other. The flickering light revealed an underground communications center with wires, tables holding telegraph keys and field telephones. Pinned under a huge fallen beam were the moldering corpses of two Germans.

Beyond the dugout, the trench line divided and divided again, following the contour of the uneven terrain. Instead of one zigzagging cut in the earth, it became a network of craters, tunnels, chalk caves, sandbagged gulleys, and underground rooms, all abandoned. He came upon the main tunnel connecting this system with the German rear lines; it was collapsed and completely closed off. Fritz had blown it when he withdrew to the next line on higher ground.

Douglas realized that for as long as the battle stalemated—each side keeping the other at bay—these holes in the ground, covering acres midway between British and German positions, would be his. But how long would that be?

He returned to the trench where his men waited. By now there were fifty of them. He led them back the way he'd come, down into the tunnels and caves. He took them underground.

So began what came to be known up and down the lines of both armies as the "warren of the wild deserters." Their numbers grew—first those few Rangers, Irish and English both, but then Ulstermen from the Thirty-sixth and Canadians and Newfoundlanders from the colonial regiments joined them: men who might have killed themselves before began slipping into No Man's Land at night.

Days passed. While one futile British charge after another crossed the ground above them, their casualities mounting ever higher, Tyrrell's men hid in their caves. At last the capacity of war machines—including, for the first time ever, tanks—was proving to be limited only by the number of potential victims. At night, when the guns fell silent and the moans of the men who'd been hit filled the air, he sent parties out into No Man's Land to find them, to bandage their wounds or try to comfort them as they died. Like ghouls, Tyrrell's men had to loot the corpses of the dead for rations and blankets, for their prized cigarettes, but they chased away rats and carrion birds, their fellow scavengers, and tried to leave the bodies in repose. When the wounded asked them who they were, they answered with a phrase from McCrae's famous poem: "We are the dead," they said.

And so in their caves, where they waited out daylight hours, they recited the lines to each other. "We are the dead. Short days ago / We lived, felt dawn, saw sunset glow / Loved and were loved, and now we lie / In Flanders fields." Anyone who wanted to join them could. Within weeks their numbers had grown to more than two hundred.

One night while Tyrrell stood in an open trench peering up at the stars, the ungodly sounds of suffering all around him, he picked out another, fainter sound, the muffled scuttling of a man crawling toward him. But it was coming from the German side of No Man's Land. He turned, but in the darkness saw nothing. The distant hill loomed black. He peered and peered, as if what was coming were his own awakening, which would end this strange sleep, this dream. Only the simple acts of meeting the needs of his men sustained him now, those and the memory into which he drifted repeatedly, a dream truly, of his first day with Pamela at Coole Park, her loveliness framed against the Connemara hills, how she'd teased him by pretending to be Irish.

"Who goes?" he called out.

And at once a voice came back. "*Bitte! Bitte! Ich bin ein Freund! Ich bin ein Freund!*"

Tyrrell still saw nothing and could not believe that he'd heard the voice, let alone that he'd understood it.

A face emerged from the dark at the level of his own eye—ground-level, since the man was crawling. He wore the distinctive German helmet, and as he came closer, Tyrrell made out the gray of his uniform. His face was streaked with mud—a boy's face, a child's. He couldn't have been more than fifteen. "*Sind die Geiste?*"

Douglas shrugged. "*Ich versteh nicht.*"

"*Die Englische Geiste?*" The English ghost?

"Ah, the ghost." He smiled. "Yes, the ghost. We are the ghosts here."

"*Ich auch!*" Me also! "*Bitte!*"

"*Ja!*," Douglas said automatically, and he pulled him into the trench. They collapsed against the sandbags together. Douglas offered him a cigarette and said, "*Willkommen!*" The boy was the first German to join them, but the Tommies had already begun to understand that Germans were in flight from a nightmare too.

On August 3, Sir Roger Casement was hanged in London. By then the group of deserters was the size Douglas's company had been at the beginning of the battle—three hundred men, mostly Irish, Scots, and English, but now including Frenchmen and more than thirty Germans. The massacre raged on above them, artillery shaking the earth, gunfire zipping endlessly, countless ranks of men hurling themselves laboriously up those sodden, battered slopes. But below ground the deserters slept, curled in their holes like burrowing animals, for their reality of time had reversed itself and they lived now at night. They were so relieved to be out of the killing that they gave themselves over without complaint to the rigorous routine Tyrrell organized. In addition now to forays out onto the battleground to forage among the dead, or to try to relieve the pain of the wounded, there were work parties to shore up the walls of the dugouts, to reinforce the tunnel timbers, or to extend the caves deeper into the earth. They were divided into platoons and they elected their own leaders, but everyone, no matter his nationality, deferred to Tyrrell. He was the one who made each man feel that what he'd done instinctively—though now he lived like an animal—was the act of a human being. Tyrrell's poise, intelligence, patent self-respect, and his respect for them underwrote his authority. And his authority, they all knew, was what drew the best out of them—their tenderness toward each other, the courage required to crawl into the black horror of No Man's Land each night—in a situation that should have brought out their worst. No one put any of this into words, of course, and certainly no one expressed what they all came to feel for Tyrrell, that love. Instead, the virtue—from the Latin word for "men"—of their bond with each other filled the air above them, an aura that drew others, for every night a few more men from both sides found the way to their warren.

And that was what made their situation dangerous. If their number had not grown and if their existence in the middle ground had not become an object of fascination, endless speculation, and elaborate rumor everywhere on the Western Front, the commanders could have ignored them. Though in fact they occupied a stretch of trenches only a few hundred yards long in the widest part of No Man's Land, there were reports of their activity all along the twenty-five-mile front of the Battle of the Somme. And though they numbered at most less than four hundred, reports had them the size, several times that, of an entire battalion. The attitude of the men in the ranks toward them was profoundly conflicted. Because the deserters lived in an underworld and looted the dead, they were thought to be devils. But because of their nightly treatment of the wounded, they were regarded as friendly apparitions, as angels, even, and by some as the spirits returned of the men who'd fallen first. But the commanders, German and British alike, felt no conflict, for the men in the middle made the act of desertion thinkable for every man in both armies, and their refusal to treat each other like enemies undercut the supreme nationalism that was essential if the soldiers were to continue to fight each other. The men in the middle embodied the idea that there was an alternative to orders. If that idea spread, then the war was over. But it couldn't be. Peace was what had become unthinkable.

These were the considerations, then, that led to that rarest event of the Great War or any war. It took place on August 19, two years, nearly to the day, after the war began. The event was

this: for a moment—an entire morning—hostilities between
the Central Powers and the Entente were suspended along a
limited but brutally contested sector of the Front. In that place
Germany and Britain became allies in another war, a very short
one, a war against an idea.

Led by guidons bearing white flags, units from both sides
crossed into No Man's Land, making for the same objective, a
section of abandoned trench work between the by now shattered villages of Hamel and Thiepval. And these units, German
and British side by side, similarly armed with rifles adapted for
grenade launching and their faces similarly covered—as if *they*
were the outlaws—by grotesque black masks, combed those
trenches, holes, dugouts, tunnels, and caves, the warren of the
wild deserters, firing into them canisters full of chlorine gas.

23

Pamela brought his body back to Cragside and there, with only a few intimates of the Tyrrells in attendance, they buried Douglas in the family grave. The sun shone brilliantly. The minister read the Psalms but attempted no eulogy. No one wept but Anne, though at one point, moved by his sister's inconsolability, Timmy imitated her.

Pamela channeled her grief into the focus of her gaze, looking beyond the fenced-in cemetery to the classic Palladian house in the distance, its wings reaching to embrace the farther sea. She was trying to picture Douglas as he had been in that place—a child, a boy, a young man. She could so easily see him running through those fields, his shoes soaked from the dew, paying no heed to them in his hurry to arrive. Arrive, such was Pamela's fantasy, in her own arms. She could see only Douglas as he had been with her.

Afterward she stood alone in the house in the high-ceilinged formal parlor, looking out through the great window at those same fields sloping toward the cliff above the tame Atlantic. Now her two children were chasing each other through the late summer wild flowers. And Pamela was thinking that not even they could assuage this loss.

"I used to stand here . . ." Sir Hugh's voice behind her startled Pamela. She looked at him, but his eyes upon her children drew her back to them. He went on quietly, ". . . looking out at my own boy and girl."

The sight was too dazzling for what had just happened, the blues of the sky and ocean too brilliant.

"They love it here," Pamela said. "In Chelsea they never run like that."

Sir Hugh stared in silence, as if he were alone and twenty years had not happened. This grief must be for Anita.

Pamela faced him. "He will not have a regimental tombstone."

Tyrrell looked at her uncomprehendingly.

"I didn't tell you until now because . . ." She put her knuckle in her mouth, biting.

"Tell me what?" He touched her arm.

"'Interred without honors,' the War Office said. I didn't tell you what happened when I claimed his body. His uniform had been stripped of badges and buttons. His rank insignia and shoulder title had been torn off. They wouldn't tell me why. Something happened, but they wouldn't tell me what. They made it seem . . ." Again she stopped.

"That he died dishonorably?"

"Yes."

"But we know he didn't, don't we?" The calm certainty with which his father said that relieved her distress absolutely, all at once.

"Yes, we do," she said. "That's why I was so angry. The injustice of it, Douglas of all men."

"The times don't favor men like him, no more in his dying

than in his living. I'm angry too, but I don't know who to be angry at anymore." He laughed suddenly. "What a terrible thing, Pamela. In Ireland everyone knows who his enemy is."

"That was Douglas's problem: he never did."

Sir Hugh shrugged. "It's who he was; a man in the middle of this madness, a man for both sides. Ireland needed him."

For the first time she saw how much of Douglas had sprung from the blood of his father. Suddenly concern for Sir Hugh welled in her. "You'll be alone now." She took his hand. "Come live with us."

"In England?" He laughed, but then with sharp solemnity, looking out across the field, the children playing, the sea gently furrowing itself, he said, "Men like me are leaving Ireland for England as quickly as they can. Coole Park is closed. Even Willie Yeats is gone. The Anglo-Irish who come of the best blood of the opposing sides are of the worst too, because they're afraid to stay and claim the place. Soon nothing will be left to this country but the bullyboys on one side and the ruffians on the other. I can't leave. Any more than Douglas could have. Forgive me if it seems self-important, but Ireland needs me, not for something grand, mind you, but just to be here, to live out my days as what I and my people have always been. We hold the center. The others can leave." He paused, thinking of Jane. "I can't."

When she didn't reply, he laughed to lighten the mood. "Ireland will prove Darwin wrong, for here the fittest don't survive. They move to Boston, goddamn Boston. We hate the English, but its our beloved America that's bleeding us to death." When he fell silent, it was to think of Jane. How he missed her. He looked out at the sea, as if the ghosts of all those exiles who had crossed it would wave back at him. No, not all those exiles, but only Jane. Oh, Jane.

"But then, when you . . ."

He nodded. "When I die . . ." He gestured around himself, at Cragside. And he said, not with fatalism, not resignation precisely, but acceptance, ". . . this dies."

She pressed his arm. "But what if we came here too?" An unpremeditated proposal, yet having made it, it seemed inevitable.

Her words jolted him. The weight of all his years fell upon him like a wall; he felt old. Quickly he looked away, ashamed of his emotion, of his need.

Waves of summer light trembled above the grass. Soon it would be time for the autumn mowing. His eyes teased on the sight of Timmy, tumbling there, disappearing in the green, then reappearing, hopping like a puppy. Anne twirled to let her dress fly.

"We are part of this," she said. Pamela knew that he'd always sensed how she held herself back from Cragside. But it was Ireland she'd resisted, the pinched, troubled island, so dreary with self-hatred, so stingy with hope. Until now, though, she had not seen that the remorseless shadow across Ireland fell from that other island, from her own. England had dishonored itself by dishonoring the best man she knew. In cutting the crown from the lapels of the tunic in which he died, England had cut it, with a dull knife, from her heart. "We want to be Tyrrells." This was not mere sentiment, a gesture to console an old man or assuage her own loss. This was their truth now, and she saw it. "We *are* Tyrrells."

She sensed how she'd stunned him.

She followed his gaze out to the children. After a moment she said quietly, "They would grow up knowing the importance of their place in this nation, their father's place. The past would make them strong. And they'd give Cragside back its future."

"But think of yourself, Pamela."

"I am, father." She had never called him that before. "This is my place too."

He took her, unexpected, into his arms. "Then, welcome! Welcome!" A thousand welcomes, was the feeling. "Welcome!"